THE BILLIONAIRES AND BABIES COLLECTION

The men in this special 2-in-1 collection rule their worlds with authority and determination. They're comfortable commanding those around them and aren't afraid to be ruthless if necessary. Independent and self-reliant, they are content with their money and lack of commitment.

Then the babies enter their lives and, before they know it, these powerful men are wrapped around their babies' little fingers!

With the babies comes the awareness of what else might be missing. Seems the perfect time for these billionaires to find the women who will love them forever.

Join us for two passionate, provocative stories where billionaires encounter the women— and babies—who will make them complete!

If you love these two classic stories, be sure to look for more Billionaires and Babies books from Harlequin Desire.

D0727831

Olivia Gates has always pursued creative passions such as singing and handicrafts. She still does, but only one of her passions grew gratifying enough, consuming enough, to become an ongoing career—writing.

She is most fulfilled when she is creating worlds and conflicts for her characters, then exploring and untangling them bit by bit, sharing her protagonists' every heart-wrenching heartache and hope, their every heart-pounding doubt and trial, until she leads them to a gloriously satisfying happy ending.

When she's not writing, Olivia is a doctor, a wife to her own alpha male and a mother to one brilliant girl and one demanding Angora cat. Visit Olivia at oliviagates.com.

USA TODAY Bestselling Author

Olivia Gates

and

USA TODAY Bestselling Author

Heidi Betts

CLAIMING HIS OWN
&
HER LITTLE SECRET, HIS HIDDEN HEIR

H HARLEQUIN® BILLIONAIRES AND BABIES

Recycling programs
for this product may
not exist in your area.

ISBN-13: 978-0-373-60148-6

Claiming His Own & Her Little Secret, His Hidden Heir

Printed in U.S.A.

CONTENTS

CLAIMING HIS OWN

Olivia Gates

To my brother. Thanks for being you.
Everyone who's ever known you
will understand just what I mean.

Prologue

Eightleen months ago

Caliope Sarantos stared at the strip in her hand.

It was the third one so far. The two pink lines had appeared in each, glaring and undeniable.

She was pregnant.

Even though she'd been meticulous about birth control, she just…was.

A dozen conflicting emotions frothed over again, colliding inside her chest. Whatever she did about this, it would turn her world upside down, would probably shatter the perfection she'd forged with Maksim. If *she* didn't know what to feel about this, what would he…

Suddenly her heart fired so hard, she almost keeled over.

He was here.

As always, she felt Maksim before she heard him. Her whole being surged with worry this time rather than welcome. Once she told him, nothing would remain the same.

He walked into the bedroom where he'd first taught her what passion was, where he continued to show her there was no limit to the intimacies and pleasures they could share.

His wolf's eyes sizzled with passion as he strode toward her, throwing away his tie and attacking his shirt as if it burned him. He was starving for her, as usual. But what she'd tell him was bound to extinguish his urgency. An unplanned pregnancy was the last thing he expected.

This might end everything between them.

This could be her last time with him.

She couldn't tell him. Not before she had him.

Desperate desire erupted, consuming her sanity as she met his urgency with her own, pulling him down to the bed on top of her, trembling with the enormity of having him in her arms. His lips fused to hers, his rumble of voracity and enjoyment pouring into her, spiking her arousal. Before she wrapped herself around him, he yanked her up, bent her over one arm, had her breasts jutting in an erotic offering. Pouring litanies of craving all over her, he kneaded her breasts, pulling her nipples into the moist heat of his mouth, sucking with such perfect force that each pull had her screams of pleasure rising. Then he glided a hand over her abdomen until he squeezed her trim mound.

Just as she screamed again, he slid two fingers between the slickness of her folds, growling again as her arousal perfumed the air.

With only a few strokes, he had her senses overloading and release scorching through her body in waves, from his fondling fingers outwards. He completed her climax with rough encouragements before he slid down her body, coming between her shaking legs, spreading them over his shoulders, exploiting her every inch with hands, lips and teeth until she was thrashing again.

"Please, enough," she moaned. "I need you...."

He subdued her with a hand flat on her abdomen, his face set in imperious lines. "Let me have my fill of your pleasure. Open for me, Caliope."

His command had her legs falling apart, surrendering everything to him. He latched on to her core, drank her flowing essence and arousal until she felt her body would unravel with the need for release. As if he knew the exact moment when she couldn't take any more, he tongued her, and she cried herself hoarse on a chain reaction of convulsions.

Before her rioting breath had a chance to subside, he slid up her sweat-slick body, flattening her to the bed. Her breath hitched and her dropping heat shot up again as soon as his tongue filled her, feeding her his taste mingled with that of her pleasure. It was unbelievable how he ignited her with only a touch.

He fused their lips for feverish seconds before he reared up, his eyes searching hers, his erection seeking her entrance. Finding both her eyes and her core molten, he growled his surrender and sank into her.

She cried out at the first inevitable shock of his invasion, that craved expansion of her flesh as it yielded to his daunting potency and poured more readiness to welcome him.

He groaned his own agonized pleasure as he rose to his knees between her splayed thighs, cupped her hips and thrust himself to the hilt inside her, hitting that trigger inside her that always made her go wild beneath him.

Knowing just what to do to wreak havoc on her senses, he withdrew, plunged again and again until her breath became fevered snatches and she writhed against him, demanding that he end his exquisite torment. Only then did he give her his full ferocity, in ram after jarring ram, in the exact force and cadence she was dying for.

He escalated to a jackhammering tempo inside her until she shrieked, arched in a spastic bow, crushed herself to him as pleasure detonated her, undoing her to her very cells.

Through the delirium she heard him roar, felt his great body shuddering, his seed splashing against her intimate flesh, dousing the inferno that threatened to turn her to ashes. She held on to awareness, to him, until he collapsed on top of her, filling her trembling arms, before she spiraled into an abyss of satiation, hitting bottom bonelessly, consciousness dissipating....

She came back into her body with a gasp as, still fused to her, he rose above her, his breathing as labored as hers, his eyes crackling with satisfaction, melting with indulgence, his lips flushed and swollen with the savagery of their coupling. He looked heartbreakingly virile and vital, and he was...hers.

She'd never allowed herself to think of him this way... but he was.

Since she'd met him, Maksim Volkov had been hers alone.

Though she'd long known of him, the Russian steel tycoon who was on par with her eldest brother, Aristedes, as one of the world's richest and most powerful men, it had taken that first face-to-face glance across the room at that charity gala a year ago for a certainty to come to her fully formed. That he'd turn her life upside down. If she let him.

And she'd let him, and then some.

She still remembered with acute intensity how she'd breathlessly allowed him to kiss her within minutes of meeting, how he'd claimed her lips, thrust his tongue inside her gasping mouth, fed her the ambrosia of his taste, turned her into a mass of mindlessness. She'd never imagined she could feel anything so suffocating in intensity, so transporting in headiness. She'd never imagined she could need a man to take her over, to dominate her.

And within an hour, she'd let him sweep her to his presidential hotel suite, knowing that she'd allow him every intimacy there. It had only been on the way there in his ultimate luxury Mercedes that she'd regained enough presence of mind to tell him that she was a virgin, even when she'd been dreading that the revelation would end their magical encounter prematurely.

She'd never forgotten his reaction.

The banked fire in his eyes had flared again as he took her lips again in a kiss that was possession itself, a sealing of her surrender.

As he'd released her and before he'd set the car in motion, he'd pledged, "It's my unparalleled privilege to be your first, Caliope. And I'm going to make it your unimaginable pleasure."

And how he'd fulfilled his pledge. It had been so overwhelming between them, they'd both known that a one-night stand was out of the question. But because of the disastrous example of her own parents, then the disappointing track records of almost everyone she knew, she believed commitment was just a setup for anything from mind-numbing mediocrity to soul-destroying disappointment. She'd never felt the least temptation to risk either.

But wanting more of Maksim had gone beyond temptation into compulsion. The very intensity of her need had made it imperative she make sure their liaison didn't take a turn in the wrong direction.

To ensure that, she'd demanded rules, upfront and unswerving, to govern whatever time they had together. They'd be together whenever their schedules allowed. For as long as they shared the same level of passion and pleasure, felt the same eagerness for each other. But once the fire was gone, they'd say goodbye amicably and move on.

He had agreed to her terms but had added his own nonnegotiable one. Exclusivity.

Stunned that he'd propose or want that, with his reputation as a notorious playboy, it had only made her plunge harder, deeper, until she'd lost herself in what raged between them. But all the time she'd wondered how long it could possibly last. Not even in her wildest dreams had she hoped it would burn that brightly for long, let alone indefinitely.

But it was now a year later and it kept growing more powerful between them, blazing ever hotter.

And she couldn't lose him. She *couldn't*.

But she had to tell him…

"I'm pregnant."

Her heart hammered painfully as even she was taken aback at her own raggedly blurted out declaration. Then more as silence exploded in its wake.

It was as if he'd turned to stone. Nothing remained animate in him except his eyes. And the expression that crashed into them was enough.

Any unformed hope she might have held—that the pregnancy might lead to something more for them—died an abrupt and agonizing death.

Suddenly, she felt she'd suffocate under his weight.

Sensing her distress, he lurched off her. She groaned with the pain of separation as he left her body for what was probably the last time.

She sat up unsteadily, groping for the covers. "You don't need to concern yourself with this. Being pregnant is my business, as it is my business that I decided to have the baby. I only thought it was your right to know. Just as it is your right to feel and act as you wish concerning the fact."

His grimness was absolute as he, too, sat up, as if rising from under rubble. "You don't want me near your baby."

Did her words make him think that she didn't?

She forced out a whispered qualification through her closing throat. "It is your baby, too. I welcome your role in its life, whatever you want it to be."

"I mean you *don't* want me near your baby. Or you as a new mother. I'm not a man to be trusted in such situations. I *will* give the baby my name, make it my heir. But I will never take part in its upbringing." Before she could gasp out her confusion over his contradicting statements, he carried on, "But I want to remain your lover. For as long as you'll have me. When you no longer want me, I'll stay away. You will both have my limitless support always, but I cannot be involved in your daily lives."

He reached for her, his eyes piercing her with their vehemence. "This is all I can offer. This is what I am, Caliope. And I can't change."

She stared up into his fierce gaze, knowing one thing. That the sane thing to do was to refuse his offer. The self-preserving thing was to cut him off from her life now, not later.

But she couldn't even contemplate doing that. Whatever damage it caused in the future, she couldn't sacrifice what she could have of him in the present to avoid it.

And she succumbed to his new terms.

But as the weeks passed, she kept bating her breath wondering if she'd been wrong to succumb. And right in believing the pregnancy would shatter their perfection.

She did sense his withdrawal in everything he said and did. But he confused her even more when he always came back hungrier than ever.

Then just as she entered her seventh month, and was more confused than ever about where they stood, her world stopped turning completely when Maksim just… disappeared.

One

Present

"And he never came back?"

Cali stared at Kassandra Stavros's gorgeous face. It took several disconcerted moments before she reminded herself her new friend couldn't possibly be talking about Maksim.

After all, Kassandra didn't even know about him. No one did.

Cali had kept their...liaison a secret from her family and friends. Even when declaring her pregnancy had become unavoidable, with Maksim still in her life, she'd refused to tell anyone who the father was. Even when she'd clung to the hope that he'd remain part of her life after her baby was born, their situation had been too... irregular, and she'd had no wish to explain it to anyone. Certainly not to her traditional Greek family.

The only one she knew who wouldn't have judged was Aristedes. Her, that was. He would have probably wanted to take Maksim apart. Literally. When he'd been in a similar situation, her brother had gone to extreme lengths to stake a claim on his lover, Selene, and their son, Alex. He'd consider any man doing anything less a criminal. His outrage would have been a thousand fold with her and his nephew on the other end of the equation. Aristedes would have probably exacted a drastic punishment on Maksim for shirking his responsibilities. Knowing Maksim, it would have developed into a war.

Not that she would have tolerated being considered Maksim's "responsibility," or would have let Aristedes fight her battle. Not when it hadn't been one to start with. She'd told Maksim he'd owed her nothing. And she'd meant it. As for Aristedes and her family, she'd been independent far too long to want their blessings or need their support. She wouldn't have let anyone have an opinion, let alone a say, in how she'd conducted her life, or the…arrangement she'd had with Maksim.

Then he'd disappeared, making the whole thing redundant. All they knew was that Leo's father had been "nothing serious."

Kassandra was now talking about another man in Cali's life who'd been a living example of "nothing serious." Someone who should also hold some record for Most Callous User.

Her father.

The only good thing he'd ever done, in her opinion, had been leaving her mother and his brood of kids before Cali had been born. Her other siblings, especially Aristedes and Andreas, had lifelong scars to account for their exposure to his negligence and exploitation. She'd at least escaped that.

She finally answered her friend, sighing, "No. He was gone one day and was never heard from again. We have no idea if he's still alive. Though he must be long dead or he would have surfaced as soon as Aristedes made his first ten thousand dollars."

Her friend's mouth dropped open. "You think he would have come back asking for money? From the son he'd abandoned?"

"Can't imagine that type of malignant nonparent, huh?"

Kassandra shrugged. "Guess I can't. My father and uncles may be controlling Greek pains, but it's because they're really hopeless mother hens."

Cali smiled, seeing how any male in the family of the incredibly beautiful Kassandra would be protective of her. "According to Selene, they believe you give them just cause for their Greek overprotectiveness to go into hyperdrive."

A chuckle burst on Kassandra's lips. "Selene told you about them, huh?"

Selene, Aristedes's wife and Kassandra's best friend, had told her the broad lines about Kassandra before introducing them to each other, confident they'd work spectacularly well together. Which they did. But they'd only started being more than business associates in the past two months, gradually becoming close personal friends. Which Cali welcomed very much. She did need a woman to talk to, one of her own age, temperament and interests, and Kassandra fulfilled all those criteria. Although Selene certainly fit the bill, too, ever since Cali had given birth to Leo, being around family, which Selene was now, had become too…uncomfortable.

So Kassandra had been heaven-sent. And though they'd been delving deeper in private waters every time they met, it was the first time they'd swerved into the familial zone.

Glad to steer the conversation away from herself, she grinned at her new confidante. "Selene only told me the basics, said she'd leave it up to you to supply the hilarious details."

Kassandra slid lower on the couch, her incredible hair fanning out against the cushions in a glossy sun-streaked mass, her Mediterranean-green eyes twinkling in amusement. "Yeah, I flaunted their strict values, their conservative expectations and traditional hopes for me. I wasted one huge opportunity after another of acquiring a socially enviable, deep-pocketed 'sponsor' to procreate with, to provide them with more perfect, preferably male progenies to shove onto the path of greatness, following my brothers' and cousins' shiningly ruthless example, and to perpetuate the romantic, if misleading, stereotype of those almighty Greek tycoons."

Cali chuckled, Kassandra's dry wit tickling her almost atrophied sense of humor. "They must have had collective strokes when you left home at eighteen and worked your way through college in minimum-wage jobs and then added mortification to worry by becoming a model."

Kassandra grinned. "They do attribute their blood-pressure and sugar-level abnormalities to my scandalous behavior. You'd think they would have settled down now that I've hit thirty and left my lingerie-modeling days behind to become a struggling designer."

Kassandra was joking here since at thirty she was far more beautiful than she'd been at twenty. She'd just become so famous she preferred to model only for causes now. And she was well on her way to becoming just as famous as a designer. Cali felt privileged to be a major part of establishing her as a household name through an innovative series of online ad campaigns.

Kassandra's generous lips twisted. "But no. They're

still recycling the same nightmares about the dangers I must be facing, fending off the perverts and predators they imagine populate my chosen profession. And they're lamenting my single status louder by the day, and getting more frantic as they count down my fast-fading attractions and fertility. Thirty to Greeks seems to be the equivalent of fifty in other cultures."

Cali snorted. "Next time they wail, point them my way. They'd thank you instead for not detonating their social standing completely by bearing an out-of-wedlock child."

A wicked gleam deepened the emerald of Kassandra's eyes. "Maybe I should. It doesn't seem I'll ever find a man who'll mess with my mind enough that I'd actually be willing to put up with the calamity of the marriage institution either for real, or for the cause of perpetuating the Stavros species. Not to mention that your and Selene's phenomenal tykes are making my biological clock clang."

Cali's heart twitched. Whenever Kassandra lumped her with Selene, it brought their clashing realities into painful focus. Selene, having two babies with the love of her life. And her, having Leo…alone.

"Being a single parent isn't something to be considered lightly," she murmured.

Contrition filled Kassandra's eyes. "Which you are in the best position to know. I remember how Selene struggled before Aristedes came back. As successful as she is, being a single mother was such a big burden to bear alone. Before her experience, I had this conviction that fathers were peripheral at best in the first few years of a child's life. But then I saw the night-and-day difference Aristedes made in Selene and Alex's lives…." She huffed a laugh. "Though he's no example. We all know there's only one of him on planet earth."

Just as Cali had thought there was only one of Maksim. If not because of any human traits...

But Aristedes had once appeared to be just as inhuman. In his case, appearances had been the opposite of reality.

Cali sighed again. "You don't know how flabbergasted I still am sometimes to see how amazing Aristedes is as a husband and father. We used to believe he was the phenomenally successful version of our heartless, loser father."

It had been one specific night in particular that she'd become convinced of that. The night Leonidas—their brother—had died.

As she and her sisters had clung together, reeling from the horrific loss, Aristedes had swooped in and taken complete charge of the situation. All business, he'd dealt with the police and the burial and arranged the wake, but had offered them no solace, hadn't stayed an hour after the funeral.

That had still been far better than Andreas, who hadn't returned at all, or even acknowledged Leonidas's death then or since. But it had convinced her that Aristedes, too, had no emotions...just like their father.

She'd since realized that he was the opposite of their father, felt *too* much, but had been so unversed in demonstrating his emotions, he'd expressed them instead in the support he'd lavished on her and all his siblings since they'd been born. But after Selene had *claimed him,* as he said, something fundamental had changed in him. He was still ruthless in business, but on a personal level, he'd opened up with his family and friends. And when it came to Selene and their kids, he was a huge rattle toy.

"So your father was that bad, huh?" Kassandra asked.

Cali took a sip of tea, loath to discuss her father. She'd always been glib about him. But it was suddenly hitting her how close to her own situation it all was.

She exhaled her rising unease. "His total lack of morals and concern for anything beyond his own petty interests were legend. He got my mother pregnant with Aristedes when she was only seventeen. He was four years older, a charmer who never held down a job and who only married her because his father threatened to cut him off financially if he didn't. He used her and the kids he kept impregnating her with to squeeze his father for bigger allowances, which he spent on himself. After his father died, he took his inheritance and left."

Cali paused for a moment to regulate her agitated breathing before resuming. "He came back when he'd squandered it, knowing full well that Mother would feed him and take care of him with what little money she earned or got from those who remained of her own family, those who'd stopped helping out when they realized their hard-earned money was going to that user. He drifted in and out of her and my siblings' lives, each time coming back to add another child to his brood and another burden on my mother's shoulders before disappearing again. He always came back swearing his love, of course, offering sob stories about how hard life was on him."

Chagrin filled Kassandra's eyes more with every word. "And your mother just took him back?"

Cali nodded, more uncomfortable by the second at the associations this conversation was raising.

"Aristedes said she didn't know it was possible for her not to. He understood it all, having been forced to mature very early, but could do nothing about it except help his mother. He was only seven when he was already doing everything that no-good father should have been doing while mother took care of the younger kids. By twelve he had left school and was working four jobs to barely make ends meet. Then when he was fifteen, said nonfather disappeared for the final time when I was still a work in progress.

"Aristedes went on to work his way up from the docks in Crete to become one of the biggest shipping magnates in the world. Regretfully, our mother was around only to see the beginnings of his success, as she died when I was only six. He then brought us all over here to New York, got us American citizenships and provided us with the best care and education money could buy.

"But he didn't stick around, didn't even become American himself, except after he married Selene. But his success and all that we have now was in spite of what that man who fathered us did to destroy our lives, as he managed to destroy our mother. All in all, I am only thankful I didn't have the curse of having him poison my life as he did Aristedes's and the rest of my siblings'."

Kassandra blinked, as if unable to take in that level of unfeeling, premeditated exploitation. "It's mind-boggling. How someone can be so…evil with those he's supposed to care for. He did one thing right, though, even if inadvertently. He had you and your siblings. You guys are great."

Cali refrained from telling her that she'd always thought only Leonidas had been deserving of that accolade. Now she knew Aristedes was, too, but she felt her three sisters, though she loved them dearly, had been infected with a degree or another of their mother's passivity and willingness to be downtrodden. Andreas, sibling number five out of seven, was just…an enigma. From his lifelong loath interactions with them, she was inclined to think that he was far worse than anything she'd ever thought Aristedes to be.

But while she'd thought she'd escaped her mother's infection, perhaps she hadn't after all.

Apart from the different details, Cali had basically done with Maksim what her mother had done with her father. She'd gotten involved with someone she'd known she shouldn't have. Then, when it had been in her best interest to walk away, she'd been too weak to do so, until he'd been the one who'd left her.

But her mother had had an excuse. An underprivileged woman living in Crete isolated from opportunity or hope of anything different, a woman who didn't know how to aspire to better.

Cali was a twenty-first-century, highly educated, totally independent American woman. How could she defend her actions and decisions?

"Look at the time!" Kassandra jumped to her feet. "Next time, just kick me out and don't let little ol' kidless me keep you from stocking up on sleep for those early mornings with Leo."

Rising, Cali protested, "I'd rather have you here all night yammering about anything than sleep. I've been starving for adult company…particularly of the female variety, outside of discussing baby stuff with Leo's nanny."

Kassandra hugged her, chuckling as she rushed to

the door. "You can use me any time to ward off your starvation."

After setting up a meeting to discuss the next phase in their campaign and to go over Cali's progress reports, Kassandra rushed off, and Cali found herself staring at the closed oak door of her suddenly silent apartment.

That all-too-familiar feeling of dejection, which always assailed her when she didn't have a distraction, settled over her like a shroud.

She could no longer placate herself that this was lingering postpartum depression. She hated to admit it, but everything she'd been suffering for the past year had only one cause.

Maksim.

She walked back through her place, seeing none of its exquisiteness or the upgrades she'd installed to make it suitable for a baby. Her feet, as usual, took her without conscious volition to Leo's room.

She tiptoed inside, though she knew she wouldn't wake him. After the first six sleepless months, he'd thankfully switched to all-night-sleeping mode. She believed taking away the night-light and having him sleep in darkness had helped. She now only had the corridor light to guide her, though she'd know her way to his bed blindfolded.

As her vision adjusted, his beloved shape materialized out of the darkness, and emotion twisted in her throat as it always did whenever she beheld him. It regularly blindsided her, the power of her feelings for him.

He was so achingly beautiful, so frightfully perfect, she lived in dread of anything happening to him. She wondered if all mothers invented nightmares about the catastrophic potential of everything their children did or came in contact with or if she was the one who'd been a closet neurotic, and having Leo had only uncovered her condition.

Even though she was unable to see him clearly in the dark, his every pore and eyelash were engraved in her mind. If anyone had suspected she'd been with Maksim, they would have realized at once that Leo was his son. He was his replica after all. Just like Alex was Aristedes's. When she'd first set eyes on Alex, she *had* exclaimed that cloning had been achieved. Now their daughter Sofia was the spitting image of Selene.

Every day made Leo the baby version of his impossibly beautiful father. His hair had the same unique shade of glossy mahogany, with the same widow's peak, and would no doubt develop the same relaxed wave and luxury. His chin had the same cleft, his left cheek the same dimple. In Maksim's case, since he'd appeared to be incapable of smiling, that dimple had winked at her only in grimaces of agonized pleasure at the height of passion.

The only difference between father and son was the eyes. Though Leo's had the same wolfish slant, it was as if he'd mixed her blue eyes and Maksim's golden ones together in the most amazing shade of translucent olive green.

Feeling her heart expanding with gratitude for this perfect miracle, she bent and touched her lips to Leo's plump downy cheek. He gurgled contentedly and then flounced to his side, stretching noisily before settling into an even sounder sleep. She planted one more kiss over his averted face before finally straightening and walking out.

Closing the door behind her, she leaned against it. But instead of the familiar depression, something new crept in to close its freezing fingers around her heart. Rage. At herself.

Why had she given Maksim the opportunity to be the one to walk out on her? How had she been that weak?

She *had* felt his withdrawal. So why had she clung to him instead of doing what she herself had stipulated from the very beginning? That if the fire weakened or went out, they'd end it, without attempts to prolong its dying throes?

But in her defense, he'd confused her, giving her hope her doubts and observations of his distance had all been in her mind, when after each withdrawal he'd come back hungrier.

Still, that *had* been erratic, and it should have convinced her to put a stop to it.

But she'd snatched at his offer to be there for her, even in that impersonal and peripheral way of his, had clung to him even through the dizzying fluctuation of his behavior. She'd given him the chance to deal her the blow of his abrupt desertion. Which she now had to face she hadn't gotten over, and might never recover from.

Rage swerved inside her like a stream of lava to pour over him, burning him, too, in the vehemence of her contempt.

Why had he offered what he'd had no intention of honoring? When she'd assured him she hadn't considered it his obligation? But he'd done worse than renege on his promise. Once he'd had enough of her, he'd begrudged her even the consideration of a goodbye.

Not that she'd understood, *or* believed that he had actually deserted her at the time.

Believing there must be another explanation, she'd

started attempting to contact him just a day after his disappearance.

The number he'd assigned her had been disconnected. His other numbers had rung without going to voice mail. Her emails had gone unanswered. None of his associates had known anything about him. Apart from his acquisitions and takeovers, there'd been no other evidence of his continued existence. It had all pointed to the simple, irrefutable truth: he'd gone to serious lengths to hide his high profile, to make it impossible for her to contact him.

Yet for months she hadn't been able to sanction that verdict. She'd grown frantic with every failure, even when logic had said nothing serious could happen to him without the whole world knowing. But, self-deluding fool that she was, she'd been convinced something terrible had happened to him, that he wouldn't have abandoned then ignored her like that.

When she'd finally been forced to admit he'd done just that, it had sent her mad wondering...why?

She'd previously rationalized that his episodic withdrawal was due to the fact that her progressing pregnancy was making it too real for him, probably interfering with his pleasure, or even turning him off her.

Her suspicions had faltered when those instances had been interrupted by even-wilder-than-before encounters. But his evasion of her attempts to reach him had forced her to sanction those suspicions as the only explanation. Then, to make things worse, the deepening misery of her pregnancy's last stages had forced another admission on her.

It hadn't been anguish, or addiction, or needing closure.

She'd fallen in love with Maksim.

When she'd faced that fact, she'd finally known why he'd left. He must have sensed the change in her before she'd become conscious of it, had considered it the breaking point. Because *he'd* never change.

But if she'd thought the last months of her pregnancy had been hellish, they'd been nothing compared to what had followed Leo's birth. To everyone else, she'd functioned perfectly. Inside, no matter what she'd told herself—that she had a perfect baby, a great career, good health, a loving family and financial stability—she'd known true desolation.

It hadn't been the overwhelming responsibility for a helpless being who depended on her every single second of the day. It had been that soul-gnawing longing to have Maksim there with her, to turn to him for counsel, for moral support. She'd needed to *share* Leo with him, the little things more than the big stuff. She'd needed to exclaim to him over Leo's every little wonder, to ramble on about his latest words or actions or a hundred other expected or unique developments. Sharing that with anyone who wasn't Maksim had intensified her yearning for him.

Her condition had worsened until she'd started feeling as if he was near, as if she'd turn to find him looking at her with that uncontainable passion in his eyes. Many times she'd even thought she'd caught glimpses of him, her imagination playing havoc with her mind. And each time this mirage had dissolved, it had been as if he'd walked out on her all over again. Those phantom sensations, that need that wouldn't subside, had only made her more bereft.

Now all that only poured fuel on her newfound fury. But anger felt far better than despondence. It made her feel alive. She hadn't felt anywhere near that since he'd left.

She was done feeling numb inside. She'd no longer pretend to be alive. She'd live again for real, and to hell with everything she…

The bell rang.

Her heart blipped as her eyes flew to the wall clock. 10 p.m. She couldn't imagine who it could be at this hour. Besides, anyone who came to see her would have buzzed her on the intercom, or, at the very least, her concierge would have called ahead to check with her first. So how could someone just arrive unannounced at her door?

The only answer was Kassandra. Maybe she'd left something behind. Probably her phone, since she hadn't called ahead.

She rushed to the door, opened it without checking the peephole…and everything screeched to a halt.

Her breath. Her heart. The whole world.

In the subdued lights of the spacious corridor he loomed, dark and huge, his face eclipsed by the door's shadow, his eyes glowing gold in the gloom.

Maksim.

Inside the cessation, a maelstrom churned, scrambling her senses. Heartbeats boomed in her chest. Air clogged in her lungs. Had she been thinking of him so obsessively she'd conjured him up? As she'd done so many times before?

Her vision distorted over the face that was omnipresent in her memory. It was the same, yet almost unrecognizable. She couldn't begin to tell why. Her consciousness was wavering and only one thing kept her erect. The intensity of his gaze.

Then something hit her even harder. The way he

sagged against the door frame, as if he, too, was unable to stand straight, as enervated at her sight as she was at his. His eyes roamed feverishly over her face, down her body, making her feel he'd scraped all her nerve endings raw.

Then his painstakingly sculpted lips twitched, as if in…pain. Next second it was her who almost fell to the ground in a heap.

The dark, evocative melody that emanated from his lips swamped her. But it was his ragged words that hit her hardest, deepened her paralysis, her muteness.

"Ya ocheen skoocha po tebyeh, moya dorogoya."

She'd been learning Russian avidly since the day she'd met him. She hadn't even stopped after he'd left, had only taken a break when Leo was born. She'd resumed her lessons in the past three months. Why exactly she'd been so committed, she hadn't been able to rationalize. It was just one more thing that was beyond her.

But…maybe she'd been learning for this moment. So she'd understand what he'd just said.

I missed you so terribly, my darling.

Two

That was it. Her mind had snapped.

She was not only seeing Maksim, she was hearing him say the words that had echoed in her head so many times, waking up from a dream where he'd said just that. Then, to complete the hallucination, he reached for her and pulled her into his arms as he'd always done in those tormenting visions.

But he didn't surround her in that sure flow of her dreams, or the steady purpose of the past. He staggered as he groped for her. His uncharacteristic incoordination, the desperation in his vibe, in every inch that impacted her quivering flesh, sent her ever-simmering desire roaring.

Then she was mingled with him, sharing his breath, sinking in his taste, as he reclaimed her from the void he'd plunged her in, wrenching her back into his possession.

Maksim. He was back like she'd dreamed every night for one bleak, interminable year. He was back...*for real*.

But he couldn't be. He'd never been with her for real. It had never become real to him. She'd accepted that in the past.

She wouldn't accept that anymore. Couldn't bear it.

No matter how she'd fantasized about taking him back a thousand times, that would remain an impossible yearning. Too much had changed. She had. And he'd told her he never would.

The fugue of drugging pleasure, of drowning reprieve, slowly lifted. Instead of a resurrection, the feel of him around her became suffocation, until she was struggling for breath.

He let her go at once, stumbled back across her threshold. "*Izvinityeh*... Forgive me.... I didn't mean to..."

His apology choked as he ran both hands through hair that had grown down to the base of his neck. One of the changes that hadn't registered at first that now cascaded into her awareness like dominos, each one knocking a memorized nuance of him, replacing it with his reality now.

He looked...haggard, a shadow of the formidably vital man he'd once been. And, if possible, she found him even more breathtaking for it. That harsh edge of... depletion made her want to crush against him until she assimilated him into her being....

God... Was she turning into her mother for real? Is this the pattern she'd establish now? He'd leave without a word, stay away through her most trying times then come back, and without a word of explanation, say he'd missed her and one soul-stealing kiss later, she'd breathlessly offer him said soul if only he'd take it?

No way. He'd submerged her mind because he'd taken her by surprise, just when he'd been dominating her thoughts. But this lapse wouldn't be repeated.

Maksim was part of her past. And that was where she'd keep him.

Yet even with this resolution, she could only stare up

at him as he brooded at her from his prodigious height, what was amplified now by his weight loss.

"Won't you invite me in?"

His rough whisper lashed through her, made her breath leave her in a hiss. "No. And before you leave, I want to know how you made it up here in the first place. Did you con a tenant to let you in, or did you intimidate my concierge?"

He winced. No doubt at the shrill edge in her voice. "I won't say these things are beyond me if I wanted something bad enough. And I certainly would have resorted to whatever would have gotten me up here. But in this case, I didn't have to con or coerce anyone to get my way. I entered with your pass code."

How did he know that?

She'd once thought it remarkable a man of his stature walked around without bodyguards and let her into his inner sanctum without any safeguards. She'd thought he'd trusted her that much.

But what if she'd been wrong about that, too? Had he just seemed trusting because his security measures were of such a caliber they'd been invisible to her senses?

It made sense his security machine dissected anyone with whom he came in contact, especially women with whom he became sexually intimate. Come to think of it, they probably collected evidence on his conquests to be used if they stepped out of line. He probably had a dossier on her every private detail down to the brand of deodorant she used. What if he...

"I once came here with you."

His subdued statement aborted her feverish projections.

She stared up at him, unable to fathom the correlation.

"You inputted your pass code at the entrance."

If anything, that explanation left her more stunned. "You mean you watched me as I entered it, and not only figured out the twelve-digit code, but memorized it? Till now?"

He nodded, impatient to leave this behind. "I remember everything about you. Everything, Caliope."

With this emphasis, his gaze dropped to her lips, as if he was holding back from ravishing them with a resolve that was fast dwindling.

Her lips throbbed in response, her insides twitched…

He took a tight step, still not crossing the threshold. Which really surprised her. The Maksim she knew would have just overridden her, secure that he'd melt any resistance. Not that he'd ever met with that, or even the slightest hint of reluctance, from her. But that had been in another life.

"Invite me in, Caliope. I need to talk to you."

"And I don't want to talk to you," she shot back, struggling not to let that…vulnerability in his demand affect her. "You're a year too late. The time for talking was before you decided to leave without a word. I got over any need or willingness to talk to you nine months ago."

His nod was difficult. "When Leonid was born."

So he knew Leo's name, though he used the Russian version of Leonidas. He probably also knew Leo's weight and how many baby teeth he had. All part of that security dossier he must have on her.

"Your deduction is redundant. As is your presence here."

His hands bunched and released, as if they itched. "I won't say I deserve that you hear me out. But for months you did want to hear my explanation of my sudden departure. You wanted to so badly, you left me dozens of messages and as many emails."

So he had ignored her, let her go mad worrying, as she'd surmised. "Since you remember everything, you must remember why I kept calling and emailing."

"You wanted to know if I was okay."

"And since I can see that you are…" She paused, looked him up and down in his long, dark coat. "Though maybe I can't call what you are now *okay*. You look like a starving vampire who is trying to hypnotize his victim into letting him in so he can suck her dry. Or for a more mundane metaphor, you look as if you've developed a cocaine habit."

She knew she was being cruel. But she couldn't help it. He'd sprung back into her life after bitterness had swept away despondence and anger had cracked its floodgates. Feeling herself about to throw all her anguish to the wind and just drag him in after one kiss had brought the dam of resentment crashing down.

"I've been…ill."

The reluctant way he said that, the way his eyes lowered and those thick, thick lashes touched his even more razor-sharp cheekbones made her heart overturn again in her chest.

What if he'd been ill all this time…?

No. She wasn't doing what her mother had done with her father—making excuses for him until he destroyed her.

He raised his gaze to her. "Aren't you even curious to know why I left? Why I'm back?"

Curious? Speculating on why he'd left had permanently eroded her sanity. Her brain was now expanding inside her head with the pressure of needing to know why he was back.

Out loud she said, "No, I'm not. I made a deal with you from day one, demanding only two things from you. Honesty and respect. But you weren't honest about having had enough of me, and you would have shown someone you'd picked off the street more respect."

He flinched as if she'd struck him but didn't make any attempt to interrupt her.

It only brought back more memories of her anguish, injected more harshness into her words. "You evaded me as you would a stalker, when you knew that if you'd only confirmed that you were okay, I would have stopped calling. I did stop when your news made the confirmation for you, forcing me to believe the depth of your mistreatment. You've forfeited any right to my consideration. I don't care why you left, why you ignored me, and I don't have the least desire to know why you're back."

His bleakness deepened with her every word. When he was sure her barrage was over, he exhaled raggedly. "None of what you just said has any basis in truth. And while you might never sanction my true reasons for behaving as I did, they were…overwhelming to me at the time. It's a long story." Before she could blurt out that she wasn't interested in hearing it, he added, almost inaudibly, "Then I was…in an accident."

That silenced her. Outwardly. Inside, a cacophony of questions, anxiety and remorse exploded.

When? How? What happened? Was he injured? How badly?

Her eyes darted over him, feverishly inspecting him for damage. She saw nothing on his face, but maybe she was missing scars in the dimness. What about his body? That dark shroud might not obscure that he'd lost a lot of his previous bulk, but what if it was covering up something far more horrific?

Unable to bear the questions, she grabbed his forearm and dragged him across the threshold, where the better lighting of her foyer made it possible for her to check him closely.

Her heart squeezed painfully. God... He'd lost so much weight, looked so...unwell, gaunt, almost...frail.

Suddenly he groaned and dropped down. Before fright could register, he rose again, scooping her up in his arms.

It was a testament to his strength that, even in his diminished state, he could do so with seeming effortlessness, making her feel as he always had whenever he'd carried her: weightless, taken, coveted, cosseted. The blow of longing, the sense of homecoming when she'd despaired of ever seeing him again, was so overpowering it had her sagging in his hold, all tension and resistance gone.

Her head rolled over his shoulder, her hands trembled in a cold tangle over his chest as all the times he'd had her in his arms like this flooded her memory. He'd always carried her, had told her he loved the feel of her filling his arms, relinquishing her weight and will to him, so he'd contain her, take her, wherever and however he would.

He stopped at her family room. If she could have found her voice, she would have told him to keep going to her room, to not stop until they were flesh to flesh, ending the need for words, letting her lose herself in his possession, and even more, reassure herself about his every inch, check it out against what she remembered in obsessive detail, yearned for in perpetual craving.

But he was setting her down on the couch, kneeling on the ground beside her, looking down at her as she lay back, unable to muster enough power to sit up. And that was before she saw something…enormous roiling in his eyes.

Then he articulated it. "Can I see Leonid?"

Everything in her, body and spirit, stiffened with shock.

All she could say was, "Why?"

She was asking in earnest. He'd told her he wouldn't take any personal interest or part in Leo's life. She could find no reason why he would want to see him now.

His answer put into words what she'd just thought. "I know I said I wouldn't have anything to do with him personally. But it wasn't because I didn't want to. It was because I thought I couldn't and mustn't."

The memory of those excruciating moments, when she'd accepted that he'd never be part of the radical change that would forever alter her life's course, assailed her again with the immediacy of a fresh injury.

"You said you're not 'a man to be trusted in such situations.'"

A spasm seized his face. "You remember."

Instead of saying she remembered everything about him, as he claimed to about her, she exhaled. "That was kind of impossible to forget."

"I only said that because I believed it was in your and his best interest not to have me in your lives."

"Is the reason you believed that part of the…long story?"

"The reason *is* the story. But before I go into it, will you please let me see Leonid?"

God… He'd asked again. This was really happening. He was here and he wanted to see Leo. But if she let him, nothing would ever be the same again. She just knew it wouldn't.

She groped for any excuse to stop this from spiraling any further. "He's asleep…."

His eclipsed eyes darkened even more. "I promise I will just look at him, won't disturb his sleep."

She tried again. "You won't see much in the dark. And I can't turn the lights on. It's the only thing that wakes him up."

"Even if I can't see him well, I will…feel him. I already know what he looks like."

Her heart lurched. Had she been right about this security report? "How do you know? Are you having us followed?"

He stared at her for a moment as if he didn't understand. "Why would you even think that?"

Regarding him warily, she told him all her suspicions.

His frown deepened with every word. "You have every right to believe the worst of me. But I never invaded your privacy. If I ever were to have you followed, it would be for your protection, not mine. And I had no reason to fear for your safety before, since associating with me would have been the only source of danger to you, and I kept our relationship a firm secret."

"So how do you know what Leo looks like?"

"Because *I* followed you."

Her mouth dropped open. "You did? When?"

He bit his lip, words seeming to hurt as he forced

them out. "On and off. Mostly on for the past three months."

So she hadn't been imagining it or going insane! All the times she'd felt him, he had been there!

Questions and confusions deluged her. Why had he done that? Why had he slipped away the moment she'd felt him? Why hadn't he approached her? And why had he decided to finally do so now? Why, why, *why?*

She wanted to bombard him with every why and how could you, to have answers *now,* not a second later.

But those answers would take time. And though she might be her mother's daughter after all, she couldn't press him for them now. She couldn't deny him access to his son. Even without explanations, the beseeching in his eyes told her enough. He'd waited too long already.

She nodded, tried to sit up and pressed into him when he didn't move. His hands shot out to support her when she almost collapsed back, his eyes glazing as that electricity that always flowed between them zapped them both.

As if he were unable to stop, his hand cupped her cheek, slid around her nape, tilting her face up to his. He groaned her name as if in pain, as if warning her he'd kiss her if she didn't say no. She didn't. She couldn't.

As if she'd removed a barbed leash from his neck, relief rumbled from his depths as he lowered his head, took her lips in a compulsive kiss.

She knew she shouldn't let this happen again, that nothing had been resolved and never would be. But at the glide of his tongue against hers, the mingling of his breath with hers, she was, as always, lost.

She surrendered to his hunger as his lips and teeth plucked at her trembling flesh, as his tongue plunged into her mouth, plundering her response. Her body melted, readied itself for him, remembering his invasion, his dominance, his pleasures, weeping for it all. He pressed her back on the couch and bore down on her, restlessly moving against her, rubbing her swollen breasts and aching nipples with the hardness of his chest... Then, without warning, he suddenly wrenched his lips from hers, shot up on his knees, his eyes wide in alarm.

It took her hard-breathing moments to realize the whimper she'd heard hadn't come from her. *Leo*.

It took a few more gurgles for her to remember the baby monitor. She had a unit in every room.

This time when she struggled up, Maksim helped her. She didn't know if his hands were shaking or if hers were, or both.

He rose to his feet, helped her to hers then stood aside so she'd lead the way.

The unreality of the situation swamped her again as she approached Leo's room, feeling Maksim's presence flooding her apartment. The last thing she'd imagined when she'd last made that same trip was that in an hour's time, Maksim would be here and she'd be taking him for his first contact with her... With his... With *their* son.

She felt his tension increase with every step until she opened the door, and it almost knocked her off her feet.

She turned to him. "Relax, okay? Leo is very sensitive to moods." It was why he'd given her a hellish first six months. He'd been responding to her misery. She'd managed to siphon it into a grueling exercise and work schedule, and to compartmentalize her emotions so she didn't expose him to their negative side. "If he wakes, you don't want him seeing you for the first time with this intensity coming off you."

She almost groaned. She'd said "the first time" as if she thought this encounter would be the first of many. When Maksim probably only wanted to see him once because… She had no idea why.

Unaware of her turmoil, grappling with his, he squeezed his eyes shut before opening them again and nodding. "I'm ready."

Nerves jangling, she tiptoed into the room with him soundlessly following her. She hoped Leo had settled down. She really preferred this first, and probably last, sighting to happen while he was asleep. The next moment, tension drained as she found Leo snoring gently again.

Before she could sigh in relief, everything disappeared from her awareness, even Leo, as Maksim came to stand beside her. Adapting to the dark room, she stared at his profile, her heart rattling inside her chest like a coin in a box. She'd never imagined he would… would… God.

His expression, the searing emotion that emanated from him as he looked down at Leo… It stormed through her, brought tears surging from her depths to fill eyes she'd thought had dried forever.

His face was a mask of stunned, sublime…suffering, as if he were gazing down at a heart that had spilled out of his chest and taken human form. As if he were beholding a miracle.

Which Leo was. Against all odds, he'd come into being. And with all she'd suffered since she'd seen the evidence of his existence, she would never have it any other way.

"Can—can I touch him?"

The reverent whisper almost felled her.

He swung his gaze to her and she nearly cried out. His eyes! Glittering in the faint light…with tears.

Tears? Maksim? How was that even possible?

Feeling her heart in her throat, she could only nod.

After hard-breathing moments when he seemed to be bracing himself, he reached a trembling hand down to Leo's face.

The moment his fingertips touched Leo's averted cheek, his inhalation was so sharp, it was as if he'd been punched in the gut. It was how she felt, too, as if her lungs had emptied and wouldn't fill again. And that was before Leo pressed his cheek into Maksim's large hand, like a cat demanding a firmer petting.

Swaying visibly now, or maybe it was her world that was, Maksim complied, cupping Leo's plump, downy cheek, caressing it with his thumb, over and over, his breathing erratic and audible now, as if he'd just sprinted a mile.

"Are all children this amazing?"

His ragged words were so thick, so low, and not only on account of not wanting to disturb Leo. It seemed he could barely speak. And his words weren't an exclamation of wonder or a rhetorical question. He was asking for real. He truly had no idea. It was as if it was the first time he'd seen a child, at least the first time he'd realized how incredible it was for a human being to be so tiny yet so compact and complete, so precious and perfect. So fragile and dependent, yet so overpowering.

She considered not answering him. The lump in her throat was about to dissolve into fractured sobs at any moment. But she couldn't ignore his question, not when his gleaming eyes beseeched her answers.

Mustering all she had so she wouldn't break down, she whispered, "All children are. But it seems we are equipped with this affinity to our own, this bond that makes us appreciate them more than anything else in the world, that amplifies their assets, downplays their disadvantages and makes us withstand their trials and tribulations with an endurance that's virtually unending and unreasoning."

His expression was rapt as he listened to her, as if every word was a revelation to him. But suddenly his face shut down. The change was jarring, and that was before his rumble repeated her last word, reverberating inside her, fierce, almost scary.

"Unreasoning..."

Before she could say or think anything, he looked down at Leo for one last moment, withdrew his hand and stalked out of the room.

She followed, slowly, her mind in an uproar.

What was up with this confounding, maddening man?

What did he mean by all that? Coming here, the unprecedented show of emotions for her, that soul-shaking reaction at seeing Leo up close...and then suddenly this switch to predator-with-a-thorn-in-his-paw mode?

Was this what he'd meant when he'd said he wasn't a man to be trusted "in such situations"? Did he suffer from some bipolar disorder that made him blow hot and cold without rhyme or reason? Did that explain his fluctuations in their last months together? His unexplained desertion and sudden return?

She caught up with him in the living room. He stood waiting for her, his face dark and remote.

She faced him, anger sizzling to the surface again. "I don't know what your problem is, and I don't want to know. You came here uninvited, blindsided me into a couple of kisses and wheedled your way into seeing Leo. And now you're done. I want you to leave and I don't want you to ever come back or I..."

"I come from a family of abusers."

To say his out-of-the-blue statement flabbergasted her would be like saying that Mount Everest was a molehill.

Her mind emptied. There was just nothing possible to think—or to say—to what he'd just stated.

He went on, in that same inanimate voice. "It probably goes back to the beginnings of my lineage, but I only know for a fact that my great-grandfather was one, and that the disorder got worse with every generation, reaching its most violent level with my father. I believed it ran in my blood, that once I manifested it, I would be the worst of them all. That was why I never considered having any relationship. Until you."

She could only stare at him, quakes starting in her very essence, spreading outward. She'd lived for a year going crazy for an explanation. Now she no longer wanted to know. Not if the explanation was worse than his seeming desertion itself.

But she couldn't find her voice to tell him to stop. Not that he would have stopped. He seemed set on getting this out in the open once and for all.

"From that first moment," he said, his voice a throb of melancholy, "I wanted you with a ferocity that terrified me, so when you stipulated the finite, uninvolved nature of our liaison, I was relieved. I believed it would be safe as long as our involvement was temporary, remained superficial. But things didn't go as expected, and my worry intensified along with my hunger for you. I lived in fear of my reaction if you wanted to walk away when I wasn't ready to let go. But instead, you became pregnant."

She continued to stare helplessly at him, legs starting to quiver, feeling he hadn't told her the worst of it yet.

He proved her right. "As you blossomed with Leonid, I was more certain every day I'd been right to tell you I'd withdraw from your life eventually and never enter his. I found myself inventing anxieties every second you were out of my sight, had to constantly struggle to curb my impulses so I wouldn't smother you. I even tried to stay away from you as much as I could bear it. But I only returned even hungrier, feared it would only be a matter of time before all these unprecedented emotions snapped my control and manifested in aggression. That was why I forced myself to leave you before you had Leo. Before I ended up doing what my father did after my sister was born."

He had a sister?

His next words provided a horrific answer to her unvoiced surprise. "He'd been getting progressively more volatile. There were no longer days when he didn't hit my mother or me or both of us. Then one night, when Ana was about six months old, he went berserk. He put us all in the emergency room that night. It took my mother and I months to get over our injuries. Ana struggled for a week before she…succumbed."

Three

Maksim's words fell on Cali like an avalanche of rocks.

She stood gaping at him, buried under their enormity.

His father had killed his sister. His baby sister.

He feared he suffered from the same brutal affliction.

Was that what had overcome him back there in Leo's room? This "unreasoning" aggression toward the helpless?

Sudden terror grabbed her by the throat.

What if he lost control now? What if— What if…

As suddenly as dread had towered, it crashed, deflated.

This man standing across her living room, looking at her with eyes that bled with despondence she recognized only too well, having suffered it for far too long, wasn't in the grips of uncontrollable violence. But of overwhelming anguish.

He feared himself and what he considered to be his legacy. That fear seemed to have ruled his whole life. He'd just finished telling her it had dictated his every action and decision in his interactions with her. The limits he'd agreed to, the severance he'd imposed on them, had been prodded by nothing else. He'd thought he was protecting her, and Leo, from his destructive potential.

And she heard herself asking, "Did you ever hurt anyone?"

"I did."

The bitten-off admission should have resurrected her fears. It didn't. And not because she was seeing good where there was none, as her mother had done with her father. As his own mother must have done with his father, to remain with an abusive husband.

She only couldn't ignore her gut feeling. It had guided her all her life, had never led her astray.

The one time she'd thought she'd made a fundamental mistake had been with him. But his explanations had reinstated the validity of her inner instincts about him.

From the first moment she'd laid eyes on Maksim, she'd felt she'd be safe with him. More. Protected, defended. At any cost to him. That nobility, that stability, that perfect control she'd felt from him—even at the height of passion—had led her to trust him without reservation from that first night onward. It all contradicted what he feared about himself.

She started walking toward him and he tensed. It was clear he didn't welcome her nearness now, after he'd confessed his shame and dread to her. What must it be like for him to doubt himself on such a basic level? What had it been like for him believing he had a time bomb ticking inside him?

She had to let him know what she'd always sensed of his steadiness and trustworthiness. That it had been why it had hit her so hard when he'd left. She hadn't been able to reconcile what she'd felt on her most essential levels with his seemingly callous actions. Thinking she'd been so wrong about him had agonized her as much as longing for him had.

But she'd been right about him. As misguided as his reasons had been, he'd only meant to protect her and Leo.

He took a couple of steps back as she approached, his eyes imploring her not to come any closer, not just yet. "Let me say this. It's been weighing on me since I met you. But if you come near me, I'll forget everything."

In answer, she stopped, sank down on the couch where he'd ravished her with pleasure so recently and patted the space next to her. He reluctantly complied.

"Those you hurt were never weaker than you are." It was a statement, not a question.

His hooded eyes simmered. "No."

"They were equals…" her gaze darted over the daunting breadth of his shoulders "…or superior numbers." His nod was terse, confirming her deduction. "And you never instigated violence."

"But I didn't only ward off attacks or defend the attacked. I was only appeased when I damaged the attackers."

"Were those times so frequent?"

He nodded. "My father left another legacy. A tangled mess in our home city. In the motherland, some areas are far from the jurisdiction of law, or the law leaves certain disputes to be resolved by people among themselves. The use of force is the most accepted resolution. I became an expert at it."

"So those times you hurt others, you were not only defending yourself but others. You did what had to be done."

"I was too violent. And I relished it."

She persisted. "Did you lose control?"

"No. I knew exactly what I was doing."

"A lot of men are like you…. Soldiers, protectors—capable of stunning violence, of even killing, for a cause, to defend others against aggressors. But those same men are usually the gentlest men with those who depend on them for protection."

His eyes grew more turbid. "I understood that mentally, that I had good cause. But with my family history, I feared it meant I had it in me…this potential for unprovoked violence. My passion for you was intensifying by the hour…but my fear of myself came to a head one specific night. It happened when I was waiting for you in bed and you were walking toward me in a sheer turquoise negligee."

Her throat closed. She remembered that night. Only too well. Their last night together.

She'd woken up replete from his tender, tempestuous lovemaking to find him gone.

"I'd never seen you more beautiful. You were ripe and glowing—your belly was rounding more by the day, and you were stroking it lovingly as you approached me. What I felt at that moment, it was so ferocious, I was scared out of my wits. I'd put bullies twice your size in traction…or worse. I couldn't risk having my passions swerve into a different direction."

Needles pricked behind her eyes, threatening to dissolve down her cheeks at any moment. "You hid it well."

His eyes widened in dismay. "I didn't have to hide anything. I never felt anything anywhere near aggressive around you. But the mere possibility of losing control of my passion carried a price that was impossible to contemplate."

He never said emotion. Did he use passion interchangeably, or was everything he felt rooted in the physical?

"You have to believe me. You don't have to look back and feel sick thinking you'd been in danger and oblivious of it."

She shook her head, needing to arrest his alarm. "I meant you hid that increasing passion. I never sensed that you felt a different level from what you had always showed me."

His nod was heavy. "*That* I hid. And the more I tried not to show you what I felt, the more it...roiled inside me. And if I felt like this when you were still carrying my child, I couldn't risk testing how I'd feel after you had him."

He must have been living a nightmare, worrying he'd relive what had happened with his father, reenact it.

A vice clamped her throat. "Abusers don't fear for their victims' well-being, Maksim. They blame them for provoking them, make themselves out to be the wronged ones, the ones pushed beyond their endurance. They certainly don't live in dread of what they might do. You're nothing like your father."

The pain gripping his face twisted her vitals. "I couldn't be certain, couldn't risk a margin of error."

"Tell me about him."

He inhaled sharply, as if he hadn't expected that request, as if he loathed talking about his father.

He still nodded, complied. "He was possessive of my mother to madness, insanely jealous of the air she breathed, suspicious of her every move. He begrudged her each moment alone or with anyone else. It got so bad he went into rages at the attention she bestowed on his children. Then came the day he convinced himself she was neglecting him on our account, because we weren't his."

"And that was when he...he..."

He nodded. "After he beat us to a pulp, he rushed us to emergency. On the day he was told my sister was dead, he walked out onto the street and let himself be run over by a truck."

God, the sheer horror and sickness, the magnitude of damage was...unimaginable. How had his mother survived, first sustaining the brunt of her husband's violence then suffering such an incalculable loss because of it? Had she survived? At least emotionally, psychologically? How could she have?

She finally whispered, "How—how old were you then?"

"Nine."

Old enough to understand fully, to be scarred permanently. And to have suffered intensely for far too long.

"And you've since been afraid you'd turn into him."

His eyes loathed the very thought that he might be so horrifically infected. She stopped herself from reaching a soothing hand to his cheek. Not yet. It wouldn't stop at a touch this time. And he needed to get this off his chest.

"Your mother didn't realize he was unstable before she married him?"

The loathing turned on the father who'd blighted his existence. "She admitted she'd seen signs of it while he was courting her. But she was young and poor and he was a larger-than-life entity whose pursuit swept her off her feet. She did realize he was disturbed the first time he knocked her down. But he was always so distraught, so loving afterward, that she kept sinking deeper into the trap of his diseased passion. It was a mess, a never-ending circle of fear and abuse. Then came Ana's unforeseen pregnancy."

Like hers, with Leo. Yet another parallel that must have poured fuel on his untenable projections.

"She thought of aborting her, terrified her pregnancy would trigger a new level of instability, as it did. The best thing he ever did was step in front of that truck, ridding her of his existence. But after all the harm he'd inflicted, it was too little, too late."

It was unthinkable what his father had cost them.

But… "Stepping in front of that truck might have rid her of his physical danger, but that he seemingly forfeited his life to atone for his sins must have robbed her of the closure that hating him unequivocally could have brought her."

His eyes widened as if she'd slapped him awake. "I thought I dissected this subject, and him, to death a million times already. But this is a perspective I never considered. You could be right. *Bozhe moy*...you probably are. That bastard. Even dying, he still managed to torture her."

There was no doubt Maksim loved his mother, felt ferociously protective of her. Would defend her to the death without a second thought. And this, to her, was more proof that he'd always been wrong to fear himself.

"But why did you even think you'd one day develop into another version of him? When you hate what he was so profoundly?"

"Because I thought hating something didn't necessarily mean I wouldn't become it. And the evidence of three generations of Volkov men was just too horrifically compelling. I learned about them later on, so they had no impact on shaping my life. I made my decision never to become involved with anyone that night Ana died. I didn't question my resolve for the next thirty years, never felt the need to be close to anyone. Then came you."

The way he kept saying this. *Until you. Then came you.* As if she'd changed his life. As if…he loved her?

No. He was being totally honest, and if this was how he felt, he would have confessed it.

"I left, determined to never come back, even when all I wanted was to stay with you…to be the first to hold Leonid, to be there every single second from then on for you and him. But I couldn't abide by the sentence I imposed on myself. I started following you, like an addict would the only thing that could quench his addiction. I had to see that you and Leonid were all right, to be near enough to step in if you ever needed me."

We needed you—I needed you every second of the past year.

But she couldn't say this. Not yet.

For now, he'd answered the questions that had been burning in her mind and soul. All that remained was one.

"What made you show yourself now, after you slipped away for months whenever I noticed you?"

This seemed to shock him. "You did? I thought I made sure you wouldn't."

"I still did. I…felt you."

The bleakness of dwelling on the tragic past evaporated in a blast of passion. She'd barely absorbed this radical switch when he singed her hands in the heat of his hands and lips.

Before she threw herself in his arms, come what may, he captured her face in his hands, the tremor in them transmitting to her whole body like a quake.

"That deal we made our first night," he groaned

against her trembling flesh, "and the one I made when you told me you were pregnant with Leonid…"

A thunderclap went off in her chest. He wanted to reinstate them?

"I want to strike new deals. I want to be Leonid's father for real, in every way—and your husband."

Maksim watched stupefaction spread like wildfire over Caliope's exquisite face.

*Bozhe moy…*how he'd missed that face. The face sculpted from the shape of his every taste and desire, every angle and dimple the very embodiment of elegance, harmony and intelligence. How he'd longed for every lash and fleck of those bluer-than-heaven eyes, every strand of this dipped-in-gold caramel hair, how he'd yearned for every inch of that sun-infused skin and that made-for-passion body. And then came every spark of her being—every glance, every breath, her scent, her feel, her hunger.

His gaze and senses devoured it all, his starvation only intensifying the more he took in. It wasn't only because he'd been deprived of her, or was maddened by the taste he'd just gotten of her ecstasy. He'd felt constantly famished even when he'd been gorging himself on all that she was.

It was why he'd distrusted himself so much, feared the intensity of his need. But everything had changed. He had.

As if coming out of a trance, Caliope blinked, then opened her lips. Nothing came.

His proposal had shocked her that much. Though her reaction was the only one he'd expected, it still twisted the knife he'd embedded in his own guts when he'd walked away from her.

She tried again, produced a wavering whisper. "You want to marry…" She stopped as if she couldn't say *marry me*. "You want to get married?"

He nodded, his heart crowding with too much.

Her throat worked, as if this was too big a lump for her to swallow. "Sorry if I can't process this, especially after what you just told me. What could have changed your mind so diametrically?" Suddenly those azure eyes that he saw in his every waking and sleeping moment widened. "Is this because of the accident you had? Has it changed your perspective?"

He could only nod again.

"Will you tell me what happened? Or will it take years before you're ready to talk about it, too?"

Unable to sit beside her anymore without taking her into his arms, he heaved himself up to his feet. He knew he had to tell her what she had a right to know. She stared up at him, a hundred dizzying emotions fast-forwarding on her face.

He braced himself against the temptation to sink back over her, convince her to forget everything now, just let him give them the assuagement they were both dying for.

He balled itching hands, smothering the need to fill them with her. "I'm here to offer you full disclosure."

She sagged back against the couch, as if she felt she'd be unable to take the rest of his confessions unsupported.

He wanted to start, but found no way to put the emptiness and loss inside him into words.

"Don't look for a way to tell me. Just…tell me."

Her quiet words surprised him so much his heart faltered.

Despite their tempestuous passion, he'd never felt they'd shared anything…emotional, psychological, let alone spiritual. He'd wondered if it had been because of their pact of noninvolvement, or if there was simply nothing between them beyond that addicting, unstoppable chemistry.

But she'd felt his inability to contain his ordeal into expression, his struggle to find a way that would be less traumatic than what it had been in truth.

Had she always possessed this ability to read him, but hadn't employed it—or at least shown it— because it had been against their agreement? Or had he hidden his feelings too well, as she'd said, and succeeding in blocking her? Had she ever wished to come closer? If she had, why hadn't she demanded a change in the terms of their involvement? Or was she only now reaching out to him on a human, not intimate, level?

This last possibility made the most sense. She *had* shown him understanding he hadn't felt entitled to wish for, had argued his case against his own self-condemnation with reason and conviction. When all he'd hoped for was to make a full confession, to beg for her forgiveness, to ask for any measure of closeness to her and to Leonid that she'd grant.

Not that he'd abided by the humble limitations of his hopes. One glimpse of her and his greed had roared to the forefront. He'd wanted all of her, everything with her.

But now that she hadn't turned him down out of hand, he could dare to hope that an acceptance of his proposal wasn't impossible. But he couldn't press for one. Not now. Not before he told her everything.

He inhaled. "You remember Mikhail?"

She blinked at the superfluous question. For she knew

Mikhail well. His only friend, the only one who'd known about him and Caliope.

Whenever they'd gone out with him, he'd felt she'd connected with Mikhail on a level she'd never done with him. He'd felt a twinge of dismay at the…ease they shared. Not jealousy, just disappointment that, in spite of their intense intimacy, this simple connection, this comfortable bond would always be denied them.

But he'd known there'd been no element of attraction. At least on her side. On Mikhail's— What man would not feel a tug in his blood at her overpowering femininity? But being his friend, and more, hers, had been Mikhail's only priority. And though Maksim had felt left out when those two had laughed together, he'd been glad she could share this with his friend when he couldn't offer her the same level of spontaneity.

Caliope's eyes grew wary. "How can I forget him? Though he disappeared from my life the same time you did, I like to think he became my friend, too."

"He did. He was." She lurched at the word *was,* horror flooding her eyes. He forced the agony into words that shredded him on their way out. "He died in the accident."

Her face convulsed as if she'd been stabbed. Then before his burning eyes, the anguish of finality gradually filled hers, overflowing in pale tracks down suddenly flushed cheeks.

He'd once delighted in the sight of her tears. When he'd tormented her with too long anticipation, then devastated her with too much pleasure. Her tears were ones of sorrow now, and those gutted him.

Suddenly confusion invaded her eyes, diluting the shock and grief. "You mean you weren't involved? But you said…"

He gritted his teeth. "I was involved. I survived."

Eyes almost black, she extended her hand to him.

She was reaching out to him, literally, showing him the consideration she'd said she didn't owe him. His chest burned with what felt like melting shards of glass.

Taking her trembling hand made the intimacies he'd taken tonight pale in comparison to that simple voluntary touch. With a ragged exhalation, he sagged down beside her again.

Then he began. "Mikhail was involved in extreme sports." She nodded. She'd known that…and had worried. "When I couldn't dissuade him to stop, I joined him."

Mikhail had left it up to him to tell her he shared his pursuits. He hadn't. The realization of yet another major omission on his part filled her eyes. Another thing he had to answer for.

He forced himself to go on. "I felt better about his stunts sharing them, so I'd be there if something went wrong. For years it seemed nothing could. He was meticulous in his safety measures, and I admit, everything he came up with was freeing and exhilarating. It also intensified our bond when I experienced firsthand what constituted a fundamental part of what made him the man he was. Then one day, during a record-setting skydive, my parachute didn't open."

The sharpness of her inhalation felt as if it had sheared through his own lungs.

Was she unable to bear imagining his peril, or would she have reacted the same to that of anyone?

It was at this moment that he realized. This woman he wanted with every fiber of his being, who had borne his only son… He didn't know her.

Not what affected her emotionally or appealed to her mentally, not what provoked her anger, what inspired her happiness, what commanded her respect.

Right now, her eyes were explicit, overflowing with dread, awaiting the rest of the account of what had changed his life forever…and had written the end of Mikhail's.

He exhaled. "Mikhail swerved to help me. We couldn't both use his parachute like in a tandem dive, as this was a record dive and our parachutes didn't have the necessary clips. We were fast approaching the point where it would be too late to open parachutes, and I kept shouting for him to open his own and I'd manage on my own. He wouldn't comply, forcing me to shove him away. But he dove at me again, grabbed me and opened his parachute."

Her hand convulsed over his. His other hand caressed her, shaking with remembered horror. "The force of the opening chute yanked him away. He miraculously clung to me with his legs, then managed to secure me. But our combined weight made us drop too fast, and we'd strayed far from our intended landing spot over a forest. I knew we'd both die, if not from the drop, then from being shredded falling through those trees. So I struggled away, praying that losing my weight would slow his descent and make him able to maneuver away. I struggled with my parachute one last time and it suddenly opened. It felt as if it was the very next second that I crashed into the top of the trees. Then I knew nothing more."

He stopped, the combined agony of what had come after and her reaction to his account so far an inexorable fist squeezing his throat. Her tears had stopped, but her eyes were horrified, her breath fractured.

He'd thought she'd only felt desire for him. Then when she'd become pregnant, he'd thought an extra dimension had been added to her feelings, what any woman would feel toward the man with whom she shared the elemental bond of a child.

But had she felt…more? Did her reaction mean she still did? How could she, after what he'd done?

The plausible explanation was that she'd react this way to anyone else's ordeal. He shouldn't be reading more into this. And he had to get this torture over with.

"It was dark when I came to. I was disoriented, not to mention in agony. Both my legs were broken—compound fractures, as I learned later—and I was bleeding from injuries all over my body. It took me a while to put together what had happened, and to realize I was stuck high up in a tree. It was so painful to move, I wanted to give up, stay there until I died of exposure. The only thing that kept me trying to climb down was needing to know that Mikhail had made it down safely."

Twin tears escaped from eyes growing more wary, as if she sensed there was much more to this account than just the catastrophic ending he'd told her about upfront.

"My phone was damaged, so I couldn't even hope anyone would follow its GPS signal. I could only hope Mikhail's was working, that he was okay or at least in much better shape than I was. I kept fading in and out of consciousness, and it took me all night to climb half the way down. Then it was light enough…and I saw him in a small clearing dozens of feet away, half covered in his parachute, twisted in such a position it was clear…"

The memory tore into his mind, blasted apart his soul

all over again. His throat sealed on the molten lead of agony. And that was before Caliope sobbed and reached for him, hugging him with all her strength.

He surrendered to her solicitude, grateful for it as he felt the tears he hadn't known except when Ana then Mikhail had died, surge to his eyes. He hugged her back, absorbed her shudders into his, feeling her warmth flood his stone-cold being. She didn't prod him to continue, wanted to spare him reliving the details of those harrowing times.

But he wanted to tell her. He couldn't hold any detail or secret from her. Not anymore. He needed her to make a decision based on full disclosure this time.

"I finally made it to his side, but there was nothing I could do for him except keep him warm, keep promising I'd get him through this. But he knew only one of us could walk out of this alive. I'm still enraged that it was me." He inhaled raggedly as she tightened her arms around him. "He confessed he'd directed his parachute toward me, afraid he'd lose me in the forest. He reached me as I hit the trees and twisted us in midfall to take the brunt. He killed himself saving me."

A whimper spilled from her lips as she buried her face in his chest, her tears seeping through his clothes to singe him down to his essence.

"But he didn't die quickly. It was a full day before he…slipped through my fingers. I lay there with him dead in my arms as night fell and day came over and over, praying I'd die, too. I kept losing consciousness, every time thinking the end had finally come, only to suffer the disappointment of waking up again, finding him in my arms—and feeling as if he'd just died again. It was four more days before his GPS signal was tracked down." Another wrenching sob tore out of her, shaking her whole body. He pressed her head harder into his chest, as if to siphon her agitation into his booming heart. "I reached the hospital half-dead, and they spent months putting me back together. The moment I was on my feet again, I came here."

She raised tear-soaked eyes to him. "And followed me and Leo around." He could only nod. She bit her trembling lip. "How—how long ago was the accident?"

"Less than a month after I left."

The hand resting on his biceps squeezed it convulsively. "I knew it. I felt something had happened to you. It was what drove me insane when you didn't answer me. But when I heard you were closing deals, I thought it was only self-delusions."

"My deputies were responsible for the deals, under the tightest secrecy about my condition to guard against wide-spread panic in my companies or with my shareholders. Though you know now the accident wasn't why I didn't answer you. I intended to never respond, but I kept waiting for your calls, rereading your messages incessantly, compulsively. And the day you stopped…"

His arms tightened around her. He'd been counting the days till her due date, and when she stopped calling, he'd known she'd given birth. Knowing that she and Leonid were fine had been the only thing that had kept his mind in one piece. He'd kept hoping she'd start calling again after a while, at the same time hoping she never would. And she never had. She'd given up on him as he'd prayed she would. Yet it had still destroyed him.

"You kept saying, 'Just let me know if you're okay.' But what could I have told you? 'I'm not? Not physically and not psychologically? And would never be?'"

Her tears stopped as she pulled back to look earnestly into his eyes. "It isn't inevitable the abused became abusers, Maksim. And heredity is not any more certain. You've displayed none of your menfolk's instability, certainly not with me. Why should you believe you'd turn into a monster when the record of your own behavior doesn't support this fear in any way?"

"I couldn't risk it then. But everything has changed."

Contemplation invaded her incredible gemlike eyes. "Because you faced death, and lost your only friend to it? Did that change what you believe about yourself?"

He shook his head. "It wasn't facing my mortality that did it. It was that last day with Mikhail. He told me he didn't risk his life for me only because of what he felt for me as his best friend, but also because I was the one among the two of us who had others who needed me... you and Leonid, and my mother. He made me promise I wouldn't waste any of the life he'd sacrificed himself to save, to live for him, as well as myself. The more I thought of what he said as I recuperated, the more the hatred toward my father, and by extension myself, dissipated. I finally faced that my paralyzing fear wasn't a good enough reason to not reach out to you, the one woman I ever wanted, to the child you've blessed me with. And here I am. But I'll make sure you'll both be safe, from me...and from everything else in the world."

She pulled back in the circle of his arms, eyes stunned.

And he asked again. "Will you take me as your husband and father of your child, *moya dorogoya?* I want to give you and Leonid all of me, everything that I am and have to offer."

Her eyes... *Bozhe moy...* He'd never hoped he'd see

such…emotion in them. Was all that for him, or was it maybe relief at the possibility of not being a single parent anymore?

Whatever it was, he hadn't told her everything yet.

He had to. It was the least he owed her.

He caught the hand that trembled up to his cheek, pressed his lips into its palm, feeling he was about to jump out of that plane again, without a parachute at all this time.

Then he did. "There's one last thing you need to know. I had a skull fracture that resulted in a traumatic aneurysm. No surgeon would come near it—as there's an almost hundred percent risk of crippling or killing me if they do—and no one can predict its fate. I can live with it and die of old age, or it can rupture and cost me my life at any moment."

Four

Maksim stared into Caliope's eyes and felt his marrow freeze. It was as if all life had been snuffed inside her.

He captured the hand frozen at his cheek. "I only told you so you'd know everything. But you don't need to be alarmed..."

She snatched her hand out of his hold, pushed out of his arms and heaved unsteadily to her feet, taking steps away, putting distance between them.

Without turning to face him, she talked, her voice an almost inaudible rasp. "You come seeking absolution and the sanctuary of a ready-made family, just because your crisis has changed your perspective and priorities. And you expect me to what? Agree to give you what you need?"

He opened his mouth, but her raised hand stopped his response, his thoughts.

She turned then, her voice as inanimate as her face. "Based on your own fears, you made the unilateral decision to cut me from your life without a word of explanation when I needed you most. And now you're back because you feel your life might end at any moment, and you want to grab at whatever you can while you can? How selfish can you be?"

When I needed you most.

That was what hit him hardest in all she'd said.

Had he been right just now, when he'd hoped she'd once felt more than desire?

He rose, approached her slowly, as if afraid she'd bolt away. "I never thought you needed me. You made it clear you didn't, only enjoyed me. It was one of the reasons I feared myself, since I started needing more from you than what you appeared to need from me. Had I known…"

"What would you have done? What would have changed? Would you have disregarded the 'overwhelming reasons' you had for leaving?"

He stabbed his hands in his hair. "I don't know. Maybe I would have told you what I just told you now and left it up to you to decide what to do. Maybe I would have stayed and taken any measures to ensure your safety."

"What measures could you have possibly taken against turning into the monster you feared you were bound to become?"

"I would have found a way. Probably some of the measures I intend to install now. Like telling Aristedes of my fears so he'll keep an eye on me. And having someone there all the time to intervene if I ever cross the line." He took her gently by the shoulders, expecting her to shake him off again. She didn't. She just stared up at him with those expressionless eyes that disturbed him more than any reaction from her so far. "I knew you had no use for the material things I offered, and I thought you didn't need anything else from me. Feeling of no use to you, then being unable to be with you, made me feel my existence was pointless. It wasn't conscious, but maybe I suggested that record-setting stunt to Mikhail wishing I'd self-destruct."

"Instead, you caused Mikhail's death. And ended up with a ticking time bomb in your head. A literal one, on top of the psychological one you feared would detonate at any time."

He hadn't expected cruelty. Not after she'd shown him such compassion. But her words were only cruel for being true.

His hands fell off her shoulders, hung at his sides. "Everything you say is right. But I am not after absolution, just redemption. I pledge I will do anything to achieve it, to earn your forgiveness, for the rest of my life."

"The life that can end at any moment."

Her bluntness mutilated him. Yet it was what he deserved. "As could any other's. The only difference between me and everyone else is that I'm aware of my danger, while others are oblivious to what's most likely to cause their death."

"But you're not only aware of a 'danger,' you're manifesting its symptoms quite clearly."

She must mean how much he'd deteriorated. He'd somehow thought this wouldn't be the point where she'd show no mercy.

"The aneurysm is a silent, symptomless danger. I'm far from back to normal because I didn't make any effort to get over the effects of my injuries and surgeries. But now I…"

"No."

The word hit him like a bullet. So harsh. So final.

But he couldn't let her end it without giving him a real chance. "Caliope…"

She cut him off again, harsher this time. "No, Maksim. I refuse your new deal."

"It's a proposal, Caliope."

She took a step back, then another, making him feel as if she were receding forever out of reach. "Whatever you want to call it, my answer is still no. And it's a final no. You had no right to think you can seek redemption at my expense."

"The redemption I'm seeking is *for* you. I'm offering you everything I can, what you just admitted you need."

"I only said you left at a time when I most needed you, not that I need you still. Which I don't. If you were thinking of me as you claim, the considerate thing to do was to stay away. The *last* thing Leo and I need is the introduction of your unstable influence in our lives. You had no right to force these revelations on me, to make those demands of me. And I'm now asking that you consider this meeting as having never happened, and continue staying away from me and Leo."

Every word fell on him like a lash, their pain accumulating until he was numb. But how could he have hoped for anything different?

In truth, he hadn't. He'd come here not daring to make any projections. Still, her coldness…shocked him. After baring his soul to her, he'd thought she'd at least let him down easy. Not for him, but because of who she was. He hadn't thought she had it in her to be so…ruthless. And for her to be so when he'd divulged his physical frailty—something beyond his control—was even more distressing.

It *had* been when he'd confided his medical prognosis that all the sympathy she'd been showing him had evaporated. And he had to know if his observations were correct. He hoped they weren't.

"Are you turning me down because you can't forgive me? Or because you don't want me anymore? Or…are you simply put off by my unstable physical condition?"

"I don't need to give you a reason for my refusal, just like you gave me none for your disappearance."

"I had to tell you the full truth, so you'd make an informed decision…."

"Thanks for that, and I have made such a decision. I expect you to abide by it."

He tried one last time. "If you're refusing because of my condition, I assure you it will never impact you or Leonid. If you let me be your husband and father for Leonid, you will never have anything to worry about in my life…or death."

"*Stop it.* I said no. I have nothing more to say to you."

He stared into those eyes. They smoldered with cold fire. Whatever compassion she'd shown him *had* been impersonal. Maybe only an expression of her anguish over Mikhail's loss, and she'd been sharing it with the one other person on earth who truly understood. Whatever she'd felt for him in the past he'd managed to kill, and in his current damaged state, everything he offered her now wasn't only deficient, but abhorrent to her.

And he couldn't blame her. It was his fault that he'd dared hope for what he'd never deserve.

He watched her turn stiffly on her heel, heading to the door. She was showing him out.

Following her, every step to that door felt as if it was taking him closer to the end. Depriving him of the will to go on. Like when he'd walked away from her before. But this felt even worse.

She held the door open, looking away from him as he passed her to step out of her domain, an outcast now.

He turned before she closed the door behind him, his palm a deterrent against her urgency to get rid of him.

Her gaze collided with his in something akin to… panic?

The next moment, what he'd thought he'd seen was gone, and she flayed him with stony displeasure at his delaying tactics.

But he had to ask one last thing.

"I'm not surprised at your rejection," he said, his voice alien in his own ears, a despondent rasp. "I deserve nothing else. But will you at least, on any terms you see fit, let me see Leonid?"

Cali collapsed in bed like a demolished building.

She'd held it together until she'd closed the door behind Maksim, then she'd fallen apart. She'd barely reached the bathroom before she'd emptied her stomach.

But that hadn't purged her upheaval. A fit of retching, the likes of which she'd only suffered once before, had wrung her dry until she felt it would tear her insides up, until she'd almost passed out on the bathroom floor.

She'd dragged herself to the shower after the storm of anguish had depleted her, to dissolve in punishingly hot water what felt like even hotter tears.

She'd told Maksim no. A harsh, final no.

Now her every muscle twitched, her stomach still lurched.

The blows had been more than she could withstand. From the moment she'd found him standing on her doorstep to the moment he'd told her that he…he…

Her mind stalled again, to ward off that mutilating

knowledge, swerved again to the lesser shocks. His unexpected return, the reason he'd left…then his proposal.

The first time he'd made it, her only reaction had been numb disbelief. It had been something she'd never visualized, not in her most extravagant fantasies of his return.

But by the time he'd told her everything and proposed again, her response had progressed from incredulity to delight. Acceptance wouldn't have been far behind.

Then he'd told her. Of his aneurysm. That he could be gone in a second. At any second.

And memories had detonated, with all the brutality of remembered devastation. Of what it had been like to love someone so much, to find out he had a death sentence hanging over his head then to lose him in unbearable abruptness.

Just the thought of repeating the ordeal had panic sinking its dark, bloody talons in her brain…and wrenching the life out of her.

Terror had manifested as fury. At him, for what he'd done to himself, and at fate, for taking Mikhail's life and blighting his with this sentence. And she'd lashed out at him.

Her harshness had only intensified at his disappointment.

Had he expected she'd be insane enough to say yes? Did he have no idea what it would do to her? Or how she felt at all?

She'd thought he'd felt her deepening emotions, and that had been why he'd left. But as it turned out, he'd been totally oblivious to her feelings, had just been focused on *his* needs and fears.

But she'd loved him when he'd been her noncommittal

lover. How much more profoundly would she love him if he became her committed husband? She'd barely survived losing him to his seeming desertion. Losing him for real wouldn't be survivable.

Out of pure self-preservation, she'd told him no.

But she'd said yes to something else. To his seeing Leo.

She couldn't deny him his child. Especially now.

But now that she'd defused his need for redemption, without the influence of honor-bound obligation, he'd probably see Leo, awake this time, and realize that having a child in his life, even peripherally, was every bit as repugnant as he'd originally thought. Then it would just be a matter of time before he disappeared again.

This time she'd be thankful for his desertion.

Soon was all she could hope for. For no matter how brief his passage through her life would be this time, she had no hope it would be painless.

The next day, at 1:00 p.m., she'd just finished feeding Leo lunch when the bell rang. She almost jumped out of her skin and her heart stumbled into total arrhythmia.

Maksim. Arriving at the exact minute she'd asked him to. Though she'd been counting down the moments since he'd left last night, his actual arrival still jarred her.

She plucked Leo from his high chair, hooked him on her hip and smiled at him indulgently as he yammered in his usual gibberish, enthusiastically pointing out things all the way to the door.

Though she walked very slowly, feeling if she went any faster she'd fall flat on her face, Maksim didn't ring the bell again. She could imagine him, patiently waiting for her to answer the door. Maybe even expecting her not to. And with every step the temptation rose. To renege on her word, to ignore him until he went away for good.

But she couldn't do it. She only hoped he'd quench his curiosity, or whatever it was that made him want to see Leo. In a worst-case scenario, if he asked for a role in Leo's life, what he'd discarded before Leo was born, she'd be willing to negotiate. She really hoped he'd end up wishing not to be involved.

Drawing a breath, she smiled down at Leo once more, holding him tighter as if to prepare him for this meeting that she feared would change his life forever.

Then she opened the door.

Maksim towered across the threshold, his sheer physical presence and size overwhelming her as it always did. He looked as if he'd had as sleepless a night as hers, haggardness making him even more hard-hitting to her senses. He was wearing light clothes for the first time ever, light beiges and cream, and it only made his gorgeousness overpowering.

She felt his agitation, but not because he was exhibiting it. He was containing it superbly, emanating equanimity, to observe Leo's acute response to moods. His eyes met hers briefly. Resignation at her rejection tinged their gold, along with the intensity that always made her every nerve burn. Then his eyes moved to Leo. And what came into them…

If she'd thought he'd looked moved when he'd beheld the sleeping Leo, now that he met his son's eyes for the first time, what stormed across his face, radiated from him was…indescribable. It was as if his whole being were focused on Leo, every fiber of him opening up to absorb his every nuance.

And Leo was looking back. As rapt, as riveted.

He wasn't used to other people, seeing even her family infrequently. With strangers, he usually buried his head in her bosom, watching them like a wary kitten from the security of her embrace. Leo had been his most uncertain around Aristedes, the most intimidating person he'd ever seen, until he'd gotten used to him. He should have reacted most unfavorably to Maksim, as he was even more daunting than Aristedes.

But it was just the opposite. His fascination with that huge, formidable, unknown being who was looking at him as if nothing but him existed in the world was absolute. It was the first time he'd reacted this openly, this fearlessly to anyone. It was as if he felt Maksim was different from everyone else. To him. She could almost *taste* their blood tie. It emanated from each of them, its influence instant and inextricable.

Suddenly, Maksim moved closer, intensity crackling from his eyes, making her instinctively press against the wall. When this squeezed a high-pitched gurgle from Leo, she rubbed her son's back soothingly and opened her mouth to tell Maksim not to test Leo's uncharacteristic acceptance.

Next second Leo squeaked again, but it was an unmistakable sound of delight this time. Then his six-toothed smile broke out.

Her nerves fired in surprised, agitated relief. But that was nothing to that smile's impact on Maksim. He looked as if a breath would blow him off his feet as he looked down at Leo's rosy-cheeked grin.

Then, as if touching priceless gossamer, he reached a hand that visibly shook to feather a caress down Leo's expectant face. Though he'd touched him before, it had been while Leo had been unaware. Now that same gesture, with Leo's sanction, became momentous. She watched it as it was given, received, felt as if a bond was being forged right before her eyes, felt caught in its cross fire, in the density of its weave, tangled in its midst.

"*Bozhe moy,* Caliope, how did I never notice how astounding children are? Or is it really because he's our son that I think him such a miracle?"

Her heart quivered at the ragged wonder in his voice, the agonized delight gripping his face. The hushed reverence in which he'd said "our son."

She had no words to answer his question, which wasn't one really, just this spontaneous venting of wonder she'd so many times longed to share with him. He was doing it with her now.

"Can I hold him?"

The rough, tentative whisper had tears squeezing out from her very essence.

It was as if he was asking for something so huge, he had little hope he was truly worthy of it. Yet he still braved asking, even as he looked as if he feared it was tantamount to asking her to relinquish a vital organ to him.

She shook her head as he turned his eyes to her. "It's not up to me. If he allows it, you can."

Maksim nodded as his reddened eyes tore from her face to Leo's, asking his baby for the privilege of his trust.

"Can I hold you, *moy malo* Leonid?"

My little Leonid. He talked to him as if he'd understand, at least the gentleness in his entreaty.

Next second, Maksim's sharp inhalation synchronized with hers. Leo held out his arms, hands opening and closing, demanding him to hurry and do what he'd asked for.

Maksim looked down on his hands, as if not sure what to do with them, before he swallowed audibly, raised his eyes to Leo and reached out to him.

A shudder shook through Maksim's great body as Leo pitched himself into his arms, as he received the little resilient body with such hesitancy and agitation.

A whimper escaped her. Leo hadn't hesitated, hadn't needed her encouragement before he threw himself at Maksim. Leo *had* recognized him. There was no other explanation.

Then she saw what snapped her control. Tears filling Maksim's wolf's eyes, accompanying a smile she'd never thought to see trembling on his lips, one of heart-breaking awe and tenderness. Her tears wouldn't be held back anymore.

They arrowed down her cheeks as she leaned against the wall so she wouldn't collapse, watching this meeting unfold between the two people who made up her world. Both father and son were so alike, so absorbed in their first exposure to each other, she felt her heart would shatter with the poignancy of it all.

Maksim held Leo with one arm, his other hand skimming in wonder over him. Leo allowed it all, busy exploring his father in utmost interest, groping his face, examining his hair and clothes. Maksim surrendered to his pawing, looking more moved with every touch than she had thought possible.

In the past, she'd never imagined this meeting would come to pass, so had never had any visualization of it. Even when she'd promised to let Maksim see Leo last night, she'd refused to anticipate his reaction, let alone

Leo's. Any projection would have created dread or expectation, and she hadn't been able to deal with either. But this surpassed anything she could have come up with, couldn't be as transient as she'd hoped. It certainly wouldn't end here, at her door.

So she whispered, "Come in, Maksim."

Caliope had given Rosa, Leo's nanny, the day off in anticipation of Maksim's visit. Not that she'd thought he'd stay more than an hour or two. He'd again defied all her expectations.

In those two hours, he'd lost his inhibitions around Leo, made himself at home in her private domain and slotted effortlessly into her routine with her baby. The rest of the day flowed in a way she couldn't have dreamed of, in increasing ease and enjoyment.

There *were* many moments of tension throughout the day, seething with suppressed sensuality, but Leo's presence relieved those, his avid delight in Maksim drawing both of them back to the unit they formed around him.

Every now and then, Cali realized she was bating her breath. Expecting something to go wrong, to fracture the harmony that reigned over their company. But nothing did.

Maksim was at first uncertain what to do except let Leo do whatever he pleased with him. She soon had to warn him that he should firmly yet gently stop Leo if he went too far or demanded too much. Her son was still testing his boundaries, and he must be taught the lines he should never cross. Even with Maksim passing through their lives, she wouldn't have him upset the balance she'd gone to so much effort to establish, even if he didn't mean to.

Expecting Maksim to argue, he surprised her by bowing eagerly to her directive and doing everything to implement it.

She found herself looking at him so many times during the day, wondering how he could have ever feared himself. She couldn't imagine him being anything but that stable, indulgent, endlessly patient entity. Had his father ever possessed any of those qualities, and then lost them?

She couldn't believe that. Someone so volatile could never feign or experience such stability even for limited times. With every moment that passed, she became certain of one thing: whatever else he was, Maksim was not his father's son.

Leo on the other hand, was that and then some. She began to see even more similarities than those that had tormented her during the past year. Facial expressions, head tilts, glances, even grins— Now she saw actual ones from Maksim.

And Maksim was something else, too. An incredibly quick study. In doing anything for Leo, he obeyed her instructions to the letter and carried them out meticulously. Then came diaper-changing time.

He insisted on accompanying her for the unpleasant chore, stood aside watching her intently. A few hours later when that chore had to be repeated, he insisted on relieving her of it. Believing he'd balk at the…reality of Leo's diaper, she was again stunned as she watched that force of nature changing it without as much as a grimace of distaste, and with the earnestness and keenness that she'd seen him employ in negotiating multibillion-dollar business deals.

In between, he'd jumped into the fray to do everything for Leo. Even when she started doing something for Leo by force of habit, it was Leo who stopped her, demanded that his new adult slave do it instead.

She more than once began to tell Maksim to temper his enthusiasm, that he'd soon burn out at this rate. But every time she had to remind herself that it wouldn't hurt to let him indulge the novelty. Which wouldn't last long…

After feeding Leo the dinner she'd taught him how to prepare, he sat down on the ground with his son and let him crawl all over him, like a lion would let his cub.

Soon, Leo started to lose steam until he climbed on top of Maksim and promptly fell asleep on his chest.

Maksim lay there unmoving, unable to even turn his eyes toward her as she sat on the couch inches away from him.

Her lips twitching, even as her throat closed yet again, she took pity on him. "You can move. Nothing could wake him up now." When he didn't answer, she talked in an exaggeratedly loud whisper, "You *can* talk, you know?"

His whisper was barely audible. "Are you sure?"

"Certain. After six months of sleeping in fifteen-minute increments, until I thought I was destined for the insane asylum, he started sleeping like a log through the night."

He still whispered, "You mean I can rise and take him to bed and he still wouldn't wake up?"

"You can juggle him in the air and he wouldn't wake up."

It was still a while before he risked moving, and he still did it with the same caution he would employ defusing a bomb. It was so funny—especially since it seemed beyond him to do anything else—it had her dissolving in laughter.

He at last did rise, but still walked in slow motion all the way to Leo's cot, with her giggling in his wake.

But with the click of the door of Leo's room, she was dragged back to the terrible reality. That Maksim was here temporarily, that she had refused anything more with him for the best of reasons. And that she was on fire for him…and he clearly felt the same. She could feel his eyes boring into her back, his hunger no longer kept in check by Leo's presence.

And she had to deny them both.

He followed her in silence to the door, not even saying good-night as he exited her apartment.

She shook with relief and disappointment as she started to close the door, but he turned, his eyes the color of cognac as they brooded down at her.

"Can I have another day, Caliope?"

Her heart jumped with eagerness. But she couldn't heed it. She had to say no. It was the sane thing to do.

Today had come at a bigger price than she'd expected, the day's perfection the worst thing that could have happened to her. Another day together would definitely compound the damages.

But this man, who stood imploring her for another day with his child, had already lost so much—and continued to live with such pain and uncertainty. She'd always known Maksim could be trusted with her, and he'd proved that he could be trusted with Leo. She'd already told him a final no to anything between them. But Leo was his child, and he hadn't abandoned him as she'd believed.

Anyway, the perfection was bound to falter. Leo was

a handful, was bound to wear him out. Maybe not in another day, but soon. And when Maksim pulled back to the position he'd originally wanted to occupy in his life, Leo would be too young to remember his transient closeness for long.

She'd be the one wrestling with need and dread. But how she felt wasn't reason enough to deny him his child, for as long as he needed to be close to him.

Fisting her aching hands against the need to reach out and drag him back in, she nodded in consent.

He still waited, needing a verbal affirmation.

Knowing she was going to pay for this in heartache but unable to do anything else, she whispered, "Yes."

Five

Cali had given Maksim the day he'd asked for.

But there had been one problem. He'd asked for another.

She'd granted him that, too, promising herself it would be the last. But she'd ended *that* day by agreeing, breathlessly, to let him be with them yet another day. Then another. And another.

Now it was ten weeks later. And Maksim had become a constant and all-encompassing presence in her and Leo's lives.

And with every passing minute she'd known she was causing them all irreparable damage by letting this continue. But she hadn't been able to put a stop to it, to go back to her status quo before Maksim's return.

She hadn't been happy, but she'd been coping well. But with Maksim sharing in Leo's day-to-day life with her, shouldering everything she allowed him to and offering more than she'd ever dreamed possible, she realized how much she'd been missing out on. She feared that his...completion was already indispensable.

She knew she'd always have the strength to go it alone if need be. But she no longer wanted to be alone, couldn't bear to think how it had felt when she had been, or to imagine how it would be again if she lost Maksim.

And she had to face it. She was insane. For letting him invade and occupy her being and life again. And now that of Leo, who woke up every day expecting to see Maksim, and more often than not going to sleep in his arms. She kept placating herself that no matter how dependent on his presence Leo had become, he was far too young to be affected in any permanent way if Maksim was no longer there for any reason.

But where *she* was concerned, it was already too late.

Even if Maksim was gone tomorrow, she had dealt herself an indelible injury with these ten weeks in his company.

Though she hungered for him with a ferocity that had her in a state of perpetual arousal, without the delirium of their sexual involvement, she was levelheaded enough to appreciate so much more about him than ever before. She constantly discovered things about him that resonated with her mentally, commanded her respect for the man and human being, when previously she'd only had esteem for the businessman. He'd told her he was discovering those things about himself right along with her.

He, too, hadn't imagined he could possibly be with her without touching her, that he could be satisfied with just talking to her, discussing everything under the sun, agreeing on every major front. Even when they argued, it was stimulating and exhilarating, and he never tried to browbeat her into adopting his views or attempted to belittle hers. He listened more than he talked, seemed to like everything she had to say and admired all her choices and practices, whether in business or with Leo.

And she regularly found herself wishing he didn't,

wishing he antagonized her or exasperated her in any way. How could she break free when he was being this all-around wonderful? She'd rather he started overstepping his limits and infringing on her comfort zones. It would be so much better if he became obnoxious or entitled. Or just anything that gave her reason to fear his existence in her life or to instigate a confrontation where she could cut him off.

But damn him… He didn't.

Worse still, it was no longer only her and Leo who'd been snared in his orbit. Her family and friends had entered the unsolvable equation, too.

Yeah, she'd told them. She'd had to. There'd been no hiding his presence in her life this time.

When pressed for details, she'd only said that they'd had an affair, he'd been involved in a serious accident and the moment he was back on his feet he'd come to see Leo.

Even with this dry account, their reactions to unmasking Maksim as Leo's father had been varied and extreme.

The women were stunned, delighted—not a little envious—and confused. They considered Maksim *the* catch of the millennium and couldn't imagine how she wasn't catching him, when he seemed to be shoving himself in her grasp.

The men thought she was plain bonkers that she wasn't already Mrs. Volkov, or at least putting the Volkov tag on Leo.

Selene, who had her own millennial catch and a similar history with him, thought it was only a matter of time before Maksim and Cali reached their own happy ending. It was Kassandra who had the most astute reading

of the situation, convinced that there was so much more
to the situation than her friend was letting on.

On the other end of the spectrum was Aristedes's reaction. After systematically interrogating her and finding out that Maksim had known about Leo from the start
and had still left, nothing else had made an impression
on him. Not that Maksim was back, or that he was offering her and Leo full access to his assets, name and time.
That year she'd struggled alone had been unforgivable
in his book. And no matter what Maksim was doing to
rectify his desertion now, it would never wipe the slate
clean. It was only after threatening to cut him out of her
and Leo's lives that she was able to obtain a promise that
Aristedes wouldn't act on his outrage.

"Did Maksim tell you he came to see me yesterday?"

The deep voice roused her from her reverie with a
start.

Aristedes. He was standing right before her.

She hadn't even noticed he'd walked into his expansive living room, where she'd come to take a call then
stolen a few moments alone before dinner got under-
way. She replayed what he'd said and her heart clenched
with dismay.

Maksim *hadn't* told her.

Throat suddenly parched, she could only shake her
head in negation. What had Maksim done now?

Aristedes sat down beside her. "He wanted to 'chat'
before we met for the first time in a family setting."

Aristedes and Selene were hosting one of their now-
frequent family dinners, and her sister-in-law had insisted Cali invite Maksim. Cali had at first turned down
the invitation. It was one thing for them to see him in

passing with her. But to have a whole evening to investigate him up close?

When Selene wouldn't take no for an answer, Cali had been forced to tell her that Maksim would eventually exit her and Leo's life, and she preferred that he didn't become even more involved in it, making that departure even more difficult and unpleasant. Selene had only argued that if Cali indeed wanted Maksim's withdrawal, what better way to help her achieve that goal than by exposing him to her meddling Greek family? One evening of them encroaching on him would be the best way to convince him to make a hasty exit.

Just because she'd known Selene would persist until she got her way, Cali had grudgingly accepted. Not that she had any hope whatsoever that Selene's scenario would come to pass. From the evidence of the past ten weeks, she was convinced Maksim would endure mad dogs shredding him apart to be with her and Leo. What was some obnoxious intrusion compared to that?

Maybe she *should* sic Aristedes on him after all.

Though she doubted even the retribution of her almighty Greek brother would do the trick. Not only was Maksim powerful enough to weather any damage Aristedes might inflict on him, she had a feeling he'd relish submitting to his vengeance. He'd probably consider it a tribute to her and to Leo, a penance for the time he hadn't been there for them.

"Aren't you going to ask what he said?"

She glowered at Aristedes. "I'm sure you'll inflict the details on me. Or else you wouldn't be sitting here beside me. You do nothing arbitrarily."

"My opinion of you is confirmed with each passing day." Though his tone was light, there was a world of emotion in his steel-hued eyes. Fury at the man they were discussing, protectiveness of her, amusement at her glibness and shrewdness as he scanned her soul for the truth he knew she was hiding. "You remain the most open-faced, inscrutable entity I've ever known. When you want to hide something, there's just no guessing it. I've known you had a secret for over two years, but even when I investigated, I came up empty-handed. How you hid something the size of Maksim, I'll never know."

"You investigated me?"

At her incredulous indignation, his nod was wry and unrepentant. "You think I'd leave my kid sister guarding a secret that implacably without worrying?"

"You mean without interfering." She scowled at him. "So what were your theories? That I was involved in some criminal activity or a victim to some terrible addiction?"

"Would that have been far from the truth? Weren't you involved with a dangerous scoundrel and, from the uncharacteristic behavior and length of your involvement, seriously addicted to him?"

Aristedes was one astute and blunt pain in the ass.

But she couldn't let one thing pass. "Maksim was never a dangerous scoundrel. As for my so-called uncharacteristic behavior with him, just ask any woman and she'd tell you that *not* being involved with him when I had the chance would have been incomprehensible, not the other way around."

Aristedes pursed his lips, clearly not relishing hearing her extol Maksim's attractions to women, starting with her.

"However irresistible you thought he was at the time, Maksim Volkov is certainly the last man I would have hoped you'd get involved with. He's not happily-ever-after material."

She snorted. "Isn't it fortunate then that I'm not, either?"

"And you still had a child with him."

"Something that I certainly didn't plan, and never considered pretext for a happy ending."

He lifted one formidable black brow. "So how do you define your situation right now? Where do you see this going?"

"Does it have to go anywhere? I would have expected you of all people to have the broadmindedness not to squeeze everything into the frame of reference of social mores. People can share a child without anything more between them."

"But that's not what Maksim thinks. Or wants."

God, what *had* Maksim told him?

Suddenly, it hit her. Aristedes, that gargantuan rat, was herding her with his elusive comments and taunts to goad her into asking what Maksim had said to him.

She skewered him with a glare that said she was onto him.

His storm-colored eyes sparked with that ruthless humor of someone who knew he always got his way.

"So…does your man like seafood?"

She blinked at the abrupt change in subject, at his calling Maksim "her man."

Then she slapped him on his heavily muscled arm. "I'm starting to think I liked you better when you were a humorless iceberg. Even when you developed a sense of humor, you wield it as a weapon."

"You mean he doesn't like seafood?"

The blatant mock-innocent pout earned him another whack.

He huffed a chuckle. "Just this time, I'll take pity on you, because I'm big that way…" She raised her hand threateningly, and he backed away, hands raised in mock defense. "…and because your deceptively delicate hand has the sting of a jellyfish." Her heart quivered as he paused. Then he exhaled dramatically. "*Nothing*. He told me a big, fat load of nada. You coached him well."

Her heartbeats frittered with the deflation of tension, with lingering uncertainty. Aristedes could be pulling her leg to make her spill info. She wouldn't put anything past him in his quest to get to the bottom of her situation with Maksim.

"He came offering his own version of what you told us," he added. "Nothing more. He said he wouldn't make any excuses for leaving, that if I saw fit to punish him for it, he would 'submit'—*his words*—to any measures I exacted." He smiled sardonically, looking as if he relished the thought of taking Maksim up on his offer of a good, old-fashioned duel. "Then he went into great detail about how committed he was to Leo, and that if you agreed, he wanted to give him his name—but even if you didn't, the two of you have every right to all his assets, in life and death."

Her heart felt it had squeezed to the size of crumpled-up wrapper. "That's plenty more than what I told you."

Aristedes shrugged, looking annoyed, evidently disagreeing. "He didn't give me one drop of info on what happened between you in the past, no comment on what's going on in the present and zero projections for the future."

"What do you find so hard to line up in your head

in an acceptable row? We had a…liaison, it resulted in a pregnancy then it ended. Now he's back because he wants to own up to his responsibilities toward his child, and he wants to be on good terms with the mother of his son."

Aristedes twisted his lips, his eyes wry. "He wants to be on the most intimate of terms with said mother. And don't even bother denying that. I'm a man who knows all the symptoms of wanting a woman so much it's a constant physical ache. I see my symptoms in him." He exhaled his displeasure with her. "Alas, I'm not as good a reader of women, and of you, I'm hopeless. That said, I still feel your answering attraction. So what's the problem? Is it your anti-marriage-or-long-term-commitment philosophy?"

She wanted to grab and kiss him for that way out. "Yes."

"Liar."

At his ready rebuttal, she shrugged. "You can think whatever you like, Aristedes. Bottom line is, I'm an adult, contrary to your inability to see me as one, and the way things stand between me and Maksim right now is the way I want them to be. When it's over…"

"Is this why you're so averse to letting him close?" he pounced, eyes crackling with danger. "You think he'll walk out on you again? Like our father? If he does that, I promise you, I'll skin him alive."

"Why, thanks for the lovely mental image, Aristedes. But no thanks. If he walks away, it's his right. Those were the terms of our liaison from the start. And then if he decides it's better for him not to be around us anymore, it certainly would be better for us not to have him around. So…give it a rest, will you? Let me conduct my life the way I see fit, and don't make me sorry I invited him here, or that I told you he's Leo's father in the first place."

"You didn't tell me. One glimpse of him all over you, with Leo all over him—his spitting image—outed you. It would have taken an imbecile not to put two and two together."

"You'll be one if you interfere, as I'll brain you."

"Any new reason you're threatening my husband with lobotomy?" Selene chuckled, striding toward them. "Just asking, since I happen to be very fond of his brain just the way it is."

Suddenly, terrible images cascaded in her mind's eye. Of Maksim, with his head cut open, surgeons exposing his brain…

"So what did he do now?"

Cali blinked as the overwhelming whoosh receded enough to let her hear the last snippet of Selene's question.

Exhaling her agitation, she grabbed the other woman's hand. "Your husband's doing the same thing you're doing. You both want to observe me and Maksim together—to judge the extent of our relationship and to try to influence its direction. And both of you will stop it right here, or I'll take Leo and leave and you can examine and probe Maksim on his own all you like. Then you won't see me again until you promise to behave."

Selene's other hand covered hers soothingly. "Hey, relax. We won't do a thing."

Selene turned gently warning eyes to Aristedes, asking his corroboration. As always, he immediately relented, this vast…adoration setting his steely gaze on tender fire. It was amazing to see this unstoppable force submitting, out of absolute love and trust, to his beloved's lead like this.

Maksim had been giving her the same reverent treatment.

And here he was now, entering the huge room, flooding it with his indomitable vibe and setting her perpetually racing heartbeat hammering. To compound his impact, he wasn't only laughing with his companions—her closest family and friends—he was holding Leo to his side, as if he was enfolding the heart that existed outside his body.

Seeing them together was, as always, the most exquisite form of torture.

Though Leo was his miniature replica, on closer inspection, she was in there, too. Maksim had pondered just yesterday that Leo made them look like each other. Her first reaction had been that this was preposterous, as they were as physically different as could be, but after catching a glimpse of all of them in a shop window, she'd had to admit he was right. Leo was the personification of everything they both were, as if the fates had mixed them up into a whole new being made of both. He did somehow make them look alike.

Maksim was preceded by his now-biggest fan, Leo's nanny. In the past ten weeks, Rosa had come to believe, right along with Leo, that the sun rose and set with Maksim and at his command.

When Cali had whimsically commented that Rosa had been struck by an acute case of hero worship, she'd looked at her disbelievingly and only said, "And you wonder why?"

Cali watched Maksim murmuring earnestly to Leo, as if agreeing on something confidential. She knew he

was convincing their son to let Rosa take him, as he had
something to do where no babies were allowed, then he'd
be right back with him.

She didn't know who was more reluctant to leave the
other: Leo, as he rubbed his eyes and grudgingly went
into Rosa's arms, lips drooping petulantly, or Maksim,
who looked as if he was relinquishing his heart to her.
Rosa swept Leo away as all the nannies were taking the
kids to Alex and Sofia's domain while the adult guests
converged in the dining room.

Maksim turned and snared her in his focus across the
distance. It was a good thing she was still sitting or his
devouring smile would have knocked her down.

He prowled toward her like the magnificent golden-
eyed wolf that he was, coming to escort her to dinner.
She gave him a cold, clammy hand and rose shakily to
her legs. He was glowing…for lack of another more accurate description. With vitality and virility.

In the past ten weeks he'd bounced back from his
wraithlike state by the day, as if being with her and Leo
had reignited his will to live, as if it infused him with
limitless energy and was a direct line to a bottomless
source of joie de vivre. He'd transformed back under her
aching eyes to a state that even surpassed his previous
beauty and vigor.

As he pulled the chair back for her at the table, she
could feel the combined scrutiny of everyone present on
her, almost forcing her down under its weight.

As soon as they all settled into their respective seats,
Selene beckoned to the caterer to start serving dinner. There was absolute silence as the first course was
served, everyone's eyes busy studying both Cali and
Maksim. Cali pretended to stir the creamy seafood soup,

while acutely aware of Maksim as he sat beside her, taking everyone's examination in total serenity.

Praying that they'd all start eating or talking—or doing anything other than counting her and Maksim's breaths—she heaved a sigh of relief when Melina, sister number one, her second-oldest sibling after Aristedes, finally broke the silence.

"So Maksim…" Melina was looking at him in awe and perplexity, no doubt wondering how her little sister had such a man in her life at all, let alone have him willing to jump through hoops for her and his son. "You're a steel magnate."

Maksim put down his spoon respectfully, inclined his head at Melina. "I work in steel, yes."

"How's *that* for understatement?" That was Melina's husband, Christos. He was…crass, mostly with Melina, and that was what Cali called him, instead of Chris. "Volkov Iron and Steel Industries is among the world's top-five steel producers and is the leader in the Russian steel sector."

Maksim turned tranquil eyes to Christos. "Your information is up to date."

Christos looked very pleased with himself at Maksim's approval. "Yeah, I've been reading up on you. I'm very impressed with the dynamic growth you've achieved through the past decade that stemmed from continuing modernization of your production assets and adoption of state-of-the-art technology, not to mention integration into the global economy. And with the economic and marketplace difficulties in Russia, that's even more remarkable."

"And that means you're a multimillionaire, right?" That was Phaidra, sister number two.

Christos snorted. "Multi*billionaire,* Phai, like our Aristedes here. Maybe even a bigger one, too."

"You mean you don't know our exact net worth already, Christos, to decide who's…bigger?" Aristedes mocked.

Christos grinned at him, clearly still flabbergasted that he was in the presence of such men as his brother-in-law, and now his sister-in-law's "man," as Aristedes had called Maksim. "It's hard to tell when you two megatycoons keep exchanging your places on the list."

"But we're talking an obscene amount of money in either of your cases." That was Thea, sister number three, the youngest of her older sisters. "But all talk of mind-boggling wealth aside, are you going to give Leo your name?"

And Cali found her voice at last. "Oh, shut up, all of you. Can't you control your meddling Greek genes and try to keep your noses out of other people's business, at least to their faces?"

"You mean it's okay if we gossip about you behind your backs?" Thea grinned at her.

Cali rolled her eyes. "As long as I don't hear about it, knock yourselves out."

"If only you gave us straight answers," Phaidra said, "we wouldn't have to resort to any of this."

Melina nodded. "Yeah, do yourselves a favor and just surrender the info we want and you can go in peace."

Cali let her spoon clang into her bowl. "Okay, enough. I didn't invite Maksim here so you can dissect him and…"

"I don't mind."

His calm assertion aborted her tirade and had her mouth dropping open as she turned to him.

"What are you *doing?*" she whispered. "Don't encourage them or they'll have you for dinner instead."

"It's all right, Cali. Let them satisfy their...appetite. I'm used to this. Russian people aren't any less outspoken or passionate in their curiosity to find out the minute details of everyone around them, whether relatives or strangers. I feel quite at home."

"You mean they're as meddlesome and obnoxious? God, what kind of genes have we passed down to Leo?"

Aristedes cleared his throat, his baritone soaked in amusement. "Just letting you know that we can hear this failed attempt at a private aside. And that the soup is congealing."

Cali relinquished Maksim's maddeningly tranquil eyes and turned to her equally vexing brother. "Oh, shut up, Aristedes." Then, she rounded on the rest of them. "And all of you. Just eat. Or I swear..." She stopped, finding no suitable retribution to threaten them with.

"Or what, Cali?" Thea wiggled her eyebrows at her. "You're going to pull one of your stunts?"

Phaidra turned to Maksim. "Did she ever tell you what she used to do when she was a child when we didn't give in to her demands as the spoiled baby of the family?"

Maksim sat forward, all earnest attention. "No. Tell me."

From then on, as her siblings competed to tell Maksim the most "hilarious," aka *mortifying,* anecdote about her early years, the conversation became progressively livelier. Maksim was soon drawing guffaws of his own with his dry-as-tinder wit, until everyone was talking over each other and laughing rambunctiously. Even Aristedes got caught up in the unexpectedly unbridled gaiety of the gathering. Even she did.

It was past 1:00 a.m. when everyone got up to leave, hugging Maksim as if he were a new brother. Then Cali waited with Aristedes and Selene as Maksim went to fetch Rosa and Leo. He came back carrying everything, to Rosa's continued objections, with a sleepy Leo curled contentedly in his embrace.

As thanks and goodbyes were exchanged, she watched the two towering male forces shake hands and almost laughed, sobbed and stomped her foot all at the same time.

Aristedes's glance promised Maksim that live skinning if he didn't walk the straight and narrow, and Maksim's answering nod pledged he'd submit to whatever Aristedes would inflict if for any reason he didn't. The pact they silently made was so blatant to her senses, as it must be to Selene's, that it was at once funny, moving and infuriating.

She barely held back from knocking their magnificent, self-important, terminally chivalrous heads together.

They left, and after dropping Rosa off, Maksim drove back to Cali's apartment. In her building's garage, he enacted the ritual of taking her and Leo up, shouldering all the heavy lifting, and accompanying her to put Leo in his crib. Then without attempting to prolong his stay, he walked back to the door.

Before he opened it, he turned to her, his eyes molten gold in the subdued lighting. "Thank you for this evening with your family, Caliope. I really enjoyed their company."

She could only nod. Against all expectations, she'd

truly enjoyed the whole thing, too. And it just added another layer of dismay and foreboding to their situation.

"They all love you very much."

She loved them, too, couldn't imagine life without them.

She sighed. "They're just interfering pains with it."

"It's a blessing to have siblings who have your best interests at heart, even if you have to put up with what you perceive as infringements." Maksim sighed deeply. "I always wished I had siblings."

Her heart contracted so hard around the jagged rock she felt forever embedded inside it.

Did he mean what…?

Before the thought became complete, forming yet another heartache to live with, he swept her bangs away, his gaze searing her as it roamed her face.

She thought he'd pull her into his arms and relieve her from her struggle, end her torment, give her what she was aching for.

He didn't. He only looked at her with eyes that told her how much craving he was holding back. And that he wouldn't act on it, except with her explicit invitation.

Then he said, "Will you come to Russia with me, Caliope?"

Six

Maksim saw the shock of his request ripple across Caliope's face. This had come out of the blue for her.

It had for him, too.

He could feel an equally spontaneous rejection building inside her, but he couldn't let her vocalize it.

Her lips were already moving when he preempted her. "My mother lives there. It would mean the world to her if she could see her grandson."

At the mention of his mother, the refusal she'd undoubtedly been about to utter seemed to stick in her throat.

She swallowed, the perfection of her honeyed skin staining with a hectic peach. "But...Russia!" He waited until the idea sank in a bit further. Then she added, "And you're proposing...we go right away?"

Relieved that he'd stopped her outright refusal in its tracks and that they were already into the zone of negotiation, he pressed his advantage. "It would be fantastic for her to attend her grandson's first birthday."

It took a moment before the significance and timing of that milestone hit her with their implications.

And she exclaimed, "But that's two weeks away."

"A trip to Russia shouldn't be for less than that."

"But if it's for Leo's birthday, we can leave a day or two beforehand."

He bunched his hands into fists, or he would have reached for her, crushed her against him, kissed her senseless until she said yes to anything he asked.

He held back, as he now lived to do. "I know she would appreciate as much time with Leo as possible, and I'm sure she'd love to prepare his birthday celebration and host it in her home."

That made her eyes widen. "Her home? Not yours, too?"

"I don't live with her, no."

That seemed to derail her meandering train of thought, bringing that gentle, curious contemplation he was getting used to to the forefront. "Then where *do* you live? I never got around to asking. When you're not traveling on business and staying in hotels?"

"If you're asking if I have a home, the answer is no."

He almost added he'd only ever wished for a home with her. The only home he wanted now was with her and Leo.

He didn't. She'd already told him she wouldn't be his home. And she had every right to refuse to be. Her first and last duty was to protect herself and Leo from his potential for instability and premature expiration. He should be thankful—he *was* thankful she was allowing him that much with her, and with Leo. He shouldn't be asking for more.

Not that what he should feel and what he *did* feel held any resemblance. He went around pretending tranquility and sanity when he was going insane with wanting more.

Considering his answer about having no home a subject ender, she resumed her unease about the original

one. "This is…so sudden, Maksim…and I'm not prepared. I have work…."

"Most of your work is on the computer, and you can
work anywhere. And I'll make sure you regularly have
the peace and quiet you need to."

"But Leo…"

"He'll be with me while you work, and with my
mother. And she has a *lot* of help. And we'll take Rosa,
too."

The peach heat across her sculpted cheekbones deepened. "Seems you have this all figured out."

It was all coming to him on the fly. But it didn't make
it any less ferocious, the need that was now hammering at him to whisk her away, to rush her and Leo to his
mother's side, to connect them before he…

Exhaling the morbid and futile thought, he shrugged,
hoping to look calm and flexible about the whole thing,
so he wouldn't scare her off. "Not really. I only thought
of it right now."

Her gaze became skeptical. "You mean you didn't
plan to eventually take Leo to see his grandmother before?"

The strangest thing was that he hadn't. Now, as she
confronted him with the question, the truth suddenly
dawned on him. "No, I didn't. I no longer plan anything ahead."

Her pupils expanded, plunging her incandescent
heaven-hued eyes into darkness. No doubt remembering why he didn't.

He hadn't brought up his condition since he'd admitted it to her. But as Caliope's and Leonid's closeness infused him with boundless energy and supercharged his
life force, he'd almost forgotten all about it. He felt so

invincible now that most times he couldn't believe there
was anything wrong with him. But he *had* been told it
was a silent danger.

Now her unspoken turmoil was more unbearable than
sensing that ticking time bomb she'd said he had inside
his head. He had to take her thoughts away from this
darkness.

The only way he knew how was to give her back the
control that his condition, something so out of anyone's
control, deprived her of. "Or I still make plans, but only
in work. With you and Leo I can't, since it's not up to
me to make any plans."

As he'd hoped, the terrible gloom that had dimmed
her vibe lifted, as her thoughts steered away from the
futility.

She lowered her eyes while she considered her verdict, and that fan of lashes eclipsed her gaze and hid
her thoughts. His lips tingled, needing to press to their
silken thickness, closing those luminous eyes before
melting down those sculpted cheeks, that elegant nose,
to her petal-soft lips. Just looking at those lips made his
go numb with aching to crush them beneath his, with
clamoring to tangle his tongue with hers, to drain her
taste, to fill her needs. For he could feel them, and they
were as fierce as his. But he knew she wouldn't succumb
to them. The price was too high for her, when she had
Leo to think about.

He understood that, accepted it. He could barely func-
tion with suffering it, but he'd known that if he pushed
through the boundaries she needed to maintain, she'd
slam the door in his face. And he would put up with
anything to have whatever she would allow him of herself, of Leonid.

But now that the idea had taken root, it was no longer about him. It was about his mother. And he decided to use this as a point of persuasion, since it was true.

A finger below Caliope's chin brought her now-turbid gaze up to his. "I didn't feel I had the right to ask this before, when I thought my admission into your lives would be short-lived. I couldn't risk letting my mother know of Leonid only to lose him again when I lost my unofficial visitation rights. If you feel you're not going to end those, or that even if you do you wouldn't cut my mother off from Leonid's life by association, let me take you to meet her."

"Maksim…don't…"

At her wavering objection, he pressed on with his best argument. "I always thought nothing could possibly make up for what she'd lost and suffered. But if there's one thing that can heal her and make it all up to her, it's Leonid."

She hadn't been able to say no.

How could she have when Maksim had invoked his mother?

She actually felt ashamed he'd had to, that she hadn't been the one to consider the woman and her right to know Leo, her only grandson. She'd known Tatjana Volkova was alive, but she'd shied away from knowing anything more about her. What Maksim had told her of his mother had been so traumatic she'd avoided thinking of her so she wouldn't have to dwell on what the woman had gone through. It had to have been so much worse than what her own mother had suffered, though *that* much less abusive experience had undeniably altered her own attitude toward life and intimacy. She had too much to deal with what with her situation with Maksim, and she couldn't add to her turmoil by introducing more of Tatjana's sufferings into her psyche.

But not only was Leo Tatjana's only grandchild, she was the only grandparent he had. He had a right to know her, just as Tatjana had more right to him as his grandmother than any of Cali's own family.

There had been no saying no to Maksim in this. Nor could she have played for more time. The timing was very significant. A first birthday was a milestone she couldn't let his mother miss. And she'd also bought his argument of going there ahead of time and letting Leo's grandmother share the joy of preparing that event.

This meant that she didn't have time to breathe as she threw together a couple of suitcases for the two weeks Maksim had said they'd stay. And the very next morning, she found herself, along with Leo and Rosa, being swept halfway across the world, heading to a place she'd never been or ever thought she'd be: Maksim's motherland.

The flight on his private jet had been an unprecedented experience. She was used to high-end luxuries, from her own financial success, and Aristedes's in-a-class-of-its-own wealth. But it was Maksim's pampering that went beyond anything she could have imagined. She squirmed at how much care he kept bestowing on them. Though he remained firm when needed with Leo, seamlessly keeping him in check with the perfect blend of loving indulgence and uncompromising discipline.

So she couldn't use spoiling Leo as a reason to demand he dial down his coddling, and he insisted that since she and Rosa were responsible adults, his efforts wouldn't spoil *them* and they should just sit back and enjoy it.

She couldn't speak for Rosa, but he was definitely wrong in her case. He was spoiling her beyond retrieval, taking her beyond the point where being without him would be impossible.

And self-destructive fool that she was, she'd only put up a token resistance, as halfhearted as all those other instances over the past ten weeks, before finally surrendering to his cosseting and reveling in his attention and nearness.

And now here she was. In Russia.

They'd landed in a private airport an hour ago. They were now in the limo that had been awaiting them at the jet's stairs, heading toward his mother's home. Rosa and Leo were in the limo's second row, while she and Maksim sat in the back.

And to top it all off? The city in Northern European Russia that they were now driving through was called Arkhangel'sk. *Archangel*.

How appropriate was that? For it to be the hometown of the archangel who was sitting beside her and acting the perfect guide?

"The city lies on the sides of the Dvina River near its exit into the White Sea…" he pointed at the river they were driving along "…and spreads for over twenty-five miles along its banks and in its delta's islands. When Peter the Great ordered the creation of a state shipyard here, it became the chief seaport of medieval Russia. But in the early eighteenth century, the tsar decreed that all international marine trade be shifted to St. Petersburg, leading to the deterioration of Arkhangel'sk. The decree was cancelled forty years later, but the damage was done and Baltic trade became more relied on."

Her gaze swept the expansive stone sidewalk running

by the river, trying to imagine how the city had looked all those centuries ago when Russia was an empire. She had a feeling it hadn't changed much. It had an authentic old-world vibe to it, echoes of long enduring history in every tree and stone and brick forming the scene.

"So did Arkhangel'sk's economy revive at all before *you* put it back on the map?"

Clearly gratified with her interest on his account, he nodded. "It did somewhat, at the end of the nineteenth century when a railway to Moscow was completed and timber became a major export. And until fifteen years ago, the city was primarily a center for the timber and fishing industries."

Her gaze melted down his face as she marveled yet again at his beauty, at the power and nobility stamped on his every feature. "Until you came along and turned it into the base for Russia's largest iron and steel works."

His lips twisted. "That implies that I switched its historical focus from timber and fishing to steel, when I only added that industry to the existing ones."

"And revived and advanced the other two beyond recognition." His dismissive shrug was another example of how he never took any opening to blow his own horn. She persisted. "I've been reading up on your contributions here. People no longer say this city is named after the archangel Michael, who'd been designated as the city's protector centuries ago, but after your nickname here as its current and far more effective benefactor."

His eyes glowed. Not with pride at his gargantuan accomplishments, which he treated with a pragmatic, almost indifferent matter-of-factness. His gratification seemed to be on account of her investigating said accomplishments and finding them—and him—worthy of admiration. It seemed to be her own opinion that counted to him, far more than what he believed of his actual worth.

This explicit reaction, whenever she lauded his actions or complimented his character in any way, always left her with a knot in her throat and a spasm in her heart.

To realize he needed her validation was at once delightful and heartbreaking. She'd lost so many opportunities to show him her appreciation during their year together, when she'd been so busy hiding the extent of her emotional involvement that she hadn't given him his due in fear he'd suspect it and it would change everything. Now that she had stopped pretending that she didn't see his merits and freely expressed her esteem, they were in this impossible situation....

She turned her eyes to the scenery rushing by her window, of that resplendent subarctic city draped in a thin layer of early November's pristine snow, and saw almost none of it as she wrestled with another surge of regret and heartache.

After an interval of silence, Maksim resumed his narration, continuing to captivate her with anecdotes of the city and region.

Then they turned onto a one-way road flanked by trees, their dense, bare branches entwining overhead in a canopy.

"We're here."

Her heart kicked into a higher gallop at his deep announcement.

This was really happening. She was going to meet Maksim's mother, and spiral further into the depths of his domain.

Swallowing the spike of agitation, she peered out of the window as they passed through thirty-foot-high, wrought-iron gates adorned with golden accents into a lushly landscaped park. She'd been to stunning palaces that had parks of this magnitude before, but those had been tourist attractions. She'd never seen anything like this that was privately owned.

The park seemed endless, nature weaved into the most delicate tapestry. Cut-stone passages wound through parterres of flowers and trimmed hedges, meeting at right or diagonal angles, with marble statues situated at each intersection, and lined with myrtle trees formed into spheres or cones and huge mosaic vases before converging on a circular pavilion.

"This is the French 'stage' of the park," Maksim said. "Then in the late eighteenth century, the Russian nobility's taste changed, explaining the zone we'll pass through next."

As soon as the limo left the pavilion behind, Cali saw what Maksim meant. There was a dramatic change in the park to something even more to her liking than the perfect geometry she'd just seen. An English landscape garden, an idealized version of nature, with winding paths, tunnels of greenery, picturesque groves of trees, lawns and pavilions, all with that dusting of snow, turning it into a winter wonderland.

She turned her eyes to him, awed. "This place is… breathtaking. Did you buy it for your mother when you started your steel business here?"

"No, this is where I grew up."

Her mouth dropped open at that revelation. "This is your family estate?"

That tight shrug again, which she by now knew indicated a subject he was loath to discuss. "It's a long story." His tone suddenly gentled. "The estate is called *Skazka,* by the way."

She repeated the word slowly. "*Skazka.* Fairy tale. How appropriate. This does look like the setting of one."

"Maybe a horror tale. At least in the past." A shadow crossed his face as he referred to the time when his father had been alive. "Now it's just the place my mother considers home." His eyes brightened. "But you never told me you knew any Russian. *Skazka* isn't a common word, which can only mean you know more than the basics."

She'd kept it to herself so far, had just savored understanding his spontaneous exclamations and endearments.

Feeling it was time to come clean, she attempted a grin. "I started learning it when we first…" she cleared her throat awkwardly "…started seeing each other."

His gaze lengthened, heated, as if he was seeing a new facet to her and it sent his appetites flaring.

She expected him to try to draw a confession that she had learned Russian for him. But, as always, she couldn't predict him.

One finger feathered her cheek in a trail of fire, his eyes also burning as they mimicked its action. "So you understood everything I've been saying to you." She nodded, and an enigmatic expression entered his eyes. Then he broke contact and gestured straight ahead. "And here's the mansion."

She tore her gaze to the place that had been the setting for the life-altering ordeal that had put him on a path of self-destruction, causing that chain reaction that might *still* succeed in detonating their lives.

The massive building was imposing, majestic. Built in the architecture of a summer country house in the neoclassical style with Grecian influences, it was so huge she thought it must house dozens of rooms. Plastered planks painted in soft beiges and cream comprised the exterior facade. The columned portico had a wide ramp leading to the front door, for cars now, but it must have been for carriages with horses back in the time it had been built. She could almost see a scene from that era as a carriage arrived, with servants rushing out the front doors to hold the horses while guests descended.

As soon as the limo stopped at the front door, Maksim stepped out, and she waited as she'd learned to for him to come around and open her door for her. He covered the fast-asleep Leo securely, then carried him out in his car seat.

In a few minutes, they were walking from the biting cold into the mansion, where it was perfectly warm. Drinking in her surroundings, Cali stared up into a vestibule with a thirty-foot ceiling with walls painted to resemble marble and columns to reflect the porticos.

Without stopping, Maksim led them to a reception room with an ornate fireplace and an oven decorated in colored tiles, with the rest of the decor and furnishings displaying the artistic traditions in Russia at the time the mansion had been built. Everything looked as if it had been just finished, which could only mean Maksim had had this place restored to its original condition.

And she again wondered how and why he had, when this place held nothing but horrific memories.

She shook away the speculations as Maksim led them in silence to another reception room, decorated with tapestries depicting the scenes from the parks. Between the tapestries, tall windows looked out onto the lake and gardens. And at one of those windows, with her back to them, clearly unaware of their silent entry, there she stood.

Maksim's mother.

The woman in her late sixties was very tall, which meant she'd been even taller as a young woman, much taller than Cali. This must be where Maksim had inherited his prodigious height. Or maybe he had from both parents. Tatjana Volkova looked like a duchess from the time of the tsars, with her thick dark hair held up in a sleek, deceptively simple chignon, and her statuesque figure swathed in a flowing, cream-colored pantsuit, with exquisite lace accents at the collar and cuffs.

"Mamochka."

Cali jumped at the word, the most loving form of mother in Russian, murmured with such fathomless tenderness in Maksim's magnificent voice.

It had the same effect on his mother, who suddenly lurched and swung around at the same time and stood facing them for a moment of paralysis that echoed Cali's. Then she exploded in motion.

Cali stood beside Maksim, unable to breathe as the woman streaked toward them, marveling at the fact that she was looking at the older, female version of Maksim.

Then she was in her arms, being hugged with the fervor of a mother who at last had her long-lost daughter in her arms.

Cali surrendered to the older woman's need to express her emotions physically. She felt her hugs were fueled by a long-held belief she'd never have more than Maksim in the world, and Cali was the reason she now had more—a grandson.

When Tatjana finally withdrew, she still held her by the shoulders, her hazel eyes, a slightly darker hue of

Maksim's, shining with tears. "Caliope, my dear, thank you so much for coming to see me. I can't tell you how much I appreciate it. I'm so sorry to drag you all the way here. I wanted to fly to you as soon as Maksim told me of you and Leonid, but my son insisted you'd be the ones who came to me."

"You fear flying, *Mamochka*," Maksim said. "And there was no reason to put you through that, even in my company."

Cali nodded. "You mustn't do anything you're uncomfortable doing. Leo can handle flying, and it's my pleasure to come to you."

Tatjana only grabbed her and kissed her again, and her eyes filled more as she drew away. Then she transferred her gaze to Maksim, or more specifically, to what he was carrying: Leo.

"*Bozhe moy,* Maksim… *On vam, kogda vy byli yego vozrasta.*"

My God, Maksim… He is you, when you were his age.

Cali swallowed the ball of thorns lodged in her throat, tears sprouting in her eyes. The anguished joy that gripped Tatjana's face was shearing in intensity, just like Maksim's had been, hitting her again with the power of that same instant connection to Leo.

She knew Leo had people who loved him, all her family. But Maksim and Tatjana were the only two who would love him more than life itself, just like she did.

She touched Tatjana, running a soothing hand down her slim arm, her voice not as steady as she hoped. "Wake him up."

"I can't…. He looks so peaceful…like an angel."

Cali's lips trembled on a smile. "And he'll be a devil if he sleeps any more. He's been asleep most of the trip and in the car, and if he doesn't wake up now, he won't sleep tonight. And between you and me, I'd really rather not have his rhythm thrown out of whack. So go ahead, wake him up."

Tatjana wiped away her tears. "Will you do it? I don't want him to get startled, finding a stranger rousing him."

Cali decided to heed Tatjana's worry. She wanted this first meeting to go perfectly, so why risk initial discomfort?

But she had a better idea, something Tatjana would appreciate seeing far more: Maksim waking his son up.

She looked at Maksim, her request explicit in her eyes. The flare of thankfulness in his almost blinded her.

Then he put the chair on the ground, crouched to his haunches beside Leo, kissed his forehead and cheeks, then crooned to him in the most loving, soul-stirring voice, *"Prosypat'sya, moy lyubimaya...* Wake up, my beloved Leonid."

Tears burned at the magnitude of love that poured from Maksim. She knew Leo basked in it, awake and asleep, thrived with it more daily, becoming progressively happier...stronger. She also loved how Maksim always talked to him in both English and Russian, making sure Leo would grow up speaking both fluently. He also urged her to speak in Greek to Leo, so their son would be raised with every facet of his heritage. Though Greek didn't come naturally to her, since she'd lived only six years on Crete before Aristedes took them to America, she did what he asked. And Leo was already trying out words in all three languages.

Leo stirred, stretched noisily as he blinked up sleepily at his father. Maksim's heart was in his smile as he gently caressed his son's downy head, delight radiating out of him as Leo reached out and clung around his neck, burying his face into his chest.

She heard a sharp sob, thought it was her own. It never ceased to overwhelm her, the depth of the bond both man and son had developed in the past weeks.

But it was Tatjana who was now crying uncontrollably. Anxiety crept up Cali's spine that Leo would see his grandmother for the first time like this, and might react to Tatjana's tears like he had to hers when she'd once let him see them.

But Maksim didn't seem worried as he scooped up an immediately alert Leo and approached his mother, talking to him in this soft, confidential way he reserved only for him. "I want you to meet someone who loves you as much as I do."

She could swear Leo understood, even nodded his consent; then he transferred his attention to the weeping woman.

Cali bated her breath, her nerves tightening in expectation of Leo's reaction. For long moments as Maksim brought him within arm's length of Tatjana, Leo just gazed at her as her sobs increased and her tears poured thicker, his watchful eyes gleaming with curiosity, his rosebud mouth a wondrous O.

Then she whispered, *"Ya mogu derzhat' vas, moy dragotsennyye serdtsa?"*

Can I hold you, my precious heart?

Leo looked at her extended arms, a considering look coming over his face. Then he swung his gaze to Maksim, then back to Tatjana, as if noticing the resemblance and realizing who Tatjana was. Then his smile broke out.

Next moment, he pitched himself from Maksim's

arms and into Tatjana's. With a loud gasp, the older woman received him in trembling arms, hugging him fiercely, her sobs shaking him and her whole frame. But Leo only squealed in delight and hugged her back.

He'd apparently recognized that her tears weren't ones of misery but of joy, and reacted accordingly, with the pleasure of being the center of attention and the pride of being the source of such overpowering emotions.

Cali found her tears flowing freely, too, then found herself where she yearned to be every second of every day…in Maksim's arms, ensconced against his heart.

She looked up at him, to catch his reaction, and found him looking down at her, his eyes full.

He held her tighter to his side. "*Spasiba, moya dorogoya.* Thank you, for Leo…for everything."

Her tears poured faster as she sank into his embrace, having no words to express her own gratitude—for him, for this, the family she and Leo suddenly had. And mingling with all that joy was the dread that this would only be temporary. His eyes told her no words were needed, that he understood her upheaval. Then hugging her more securely, he turned his loving gaze to his mother and child, clearly savoring those poignant moments.

She leaned against his formidable shoulder and wondered how this would end.

And when it did end, since nothing this good could possibly last, would she survive it?

Seven

Maksim sighed as he gazed out his bedroom window.

Not that it was really his, just the suite he occupied when he stayed here. The one he'd had as a child he'd turned into part of a living area his mother used for her weekly gatherings with her various public-work committees. His mother had given Caliope and Leonid the suite across from him.

He'd almost moved out when she had.

Being in constant proximity to Caliope during the day was something he could relish…and withstand. During the nights, to feel her so close, to visualize her going about her nightly routines was sheer torture.

That first night, he'd lain in bed imagining he could hear her showering, feel the steam rising to shroud her lush body, the lather sliding tantalizingly over her every swell and into her every dip, the water sluicing over her curves, washing suds away. Then he'd seen her drying her hair until it cascaded around her smooth shoulders in a glossy mass, applying lotion to her velvet flesh, slipping into a silky nightgown, sinking into bed between the covers with a sigh of pleasure. All those things he'd so many times done for her as she'd surrendered to his ministrations, as he'd pampered her, indulged her, possessed her all through that magical year. Exquisite pleasures he'd never have the privilege of having again.

He'd woken up aching, wrecked, intending to hole up somewhere on the far side of the mansion. But she'd exited her bedroom suite at that same moment, a smile of pure joy flashing at the sight of him, and he'd known. He'd put up with any level of frustration and agony for the possibility of a moment like this.

The last time he'd stayed here had been six months ago, when he'd finally succumbed to his mother's fretting and had come to visit her. He'd tried everything to put off that visit, hating to let her see him in his condition back then.

She'd been horrified when she'd laid eyes on him, but she'd thought he was just desolate over Mikhail's death. He'd let her think that. It had given her hope he'd eventually climb out of the abyss of despair and regain his health. He hadn't even thought of telling her the truth.

Then a miracle had happened. He'd reached out to Caliope, and though she'd refused to let him back into her own life, to bestow her intimacy on him again, she'd let him into her precious family unit with Leo. Beyond all expectations, she had given him a closeness he'd never thought possible to have with her, or with anyone else after Mikhail.

She'd become his friend, his ally, when before she'd only been his lover. Every minute with her made him realize how much he'd been missing—with her, in life. He couldn't help but keep envisioning how much deeper it could all be if she let him cross that final barrier into passion once more.

But he would never ask for it. What she continued to give him was enough, more than enough. The past ten weeks had been a heaven he'd never dared dream existed, or that he would ever be worthy of having anyway. He still couldn't believe it was really happening.

But it was. He was beholding it in the gardens his suite overlooked. They were talking, laughing and reveling in being together. Caliope. Leonid. And his mother. Everything that made his heart beat, that formed his world and shaped his being.

For the past two weeks, he'd often found himself overwhelmed with so much emotion, so much gratitude, he had to force himself to breathe. Both Leonid and Caliope had taken to his mother as he could have only hoped they would. Leonid's instant attachment had been the far less surprising one. That sensitive, brilliant baby had recognized his mother for what she was to him, and as an extension of the father he had accepted and claimed from the very first instant. But it was Caliope's delight in his mother that sometimes threatened to crush his heart under its significance.

During one of their intimate fireside chats, she'd confided that she'd never really had a mother. Her own had been a shadow by the time Caliope was born, and had died when she'd been not yet six. Now it felt to Maksim as if in his own mother she'd found that maternal presence and influence she'd never known she'd missed, let alone craved. While it also felt his mother had found the daughter she'd lost in Caliope.

To crown the perfection, tomorrow was Leonid's first birthday. He'd had only the last three months of that first precious year, and he ached for every minute he'd wasted, lost, not been there for Caliope and his son. But he would be there for them both from now on. Till his dying day.

Although he lived every second with them as if it would be his last, he prayed that day wouldn't come anytime soon. Nevertheless, he'd put everything in order for all of them, just in case. And now that he had the peace of mind that Cali and Leo's future was secure, he could focus on making plans as if he'd live forever. He now had every reason to hope he would live as long as humanly possible. He'd never felt more alive or robust. His energy levels were skyrocketing, and he continued to grow more vigorous with each passing day, as if his will to live had come into existence. Before Caliope and Leonid, he'd only had a will to survive, to decimate obstacles and reach the next level, then the next. But all that hadn't amounted to living. Not without them filling his heart and making it all worthwhile.

He sighed again at the sight of them, let it permeate his soul with its sheer beauty and magic.

How he loved them all.

He didn't know how long he remained standing there, hoarding yet more priceless memories, before he roused himself. He had plans for today and he'd better get going so he'd have time to see them all through.

He rushed down to the gardens, and as he approached the trio, they turned to him, eager to see him. And he wondered again how he could possibly deserve all that.

But if he never had before, he would now. And he'd revel in every single second of their blessings and give them back a thousandfold, until he'd given them all that he was.

His gaze went first to his mother. In spite of all the ordeals she'd suffered, she'd always remained strong, stable, even, most of the time, amazingly sunny. But now… Now she radiated *joy*. And it was all thanks to Leonid. And Caliope.

His gaze moved next to Leonid. That little miracle that always had his insides melting with a million emotions, half of them sublime and the other half distraught. He wondered again how parents survived loving their children and worrying about them this much. But he was learning how, with Caliope's constant support and guidance. This again led him to wonder how his father had been able to hurt him. He'd rather have his arms hacked off before he even upset Leonid.

Yes, he was now certain. He had none of his father's sickness. And not because his ordeal had reconfigured him. He just didn't have it in him. All his dread now was from external sources. Life had so many dangers, it suffocated him at times to think of Leonid being exposed to any of them.

But even with the constant fears that had become part of his consciousness, he wouldn't change a thing. He wanted nothing but to be Leonid's father, to give him the safest, happiest, most adjusted and accomplished life.

He'd left looking at the center of his universe, the spark of his existence, for last. For she was where his gaze would stay, where his heart would lie down to rest. Caliope.

How was it possible that she was more beautiful every time he beheld her?

Her radiant smile rivaled that of the bright Russian autumn sun. Her naturally sun-kissed complexion glowed with vitality in the cold, her caramel-gold hair gleamed and undulated in the tranquil breeze and her azure eyes were incandescent with warmth and welcome. Her lips, flushed and dewy, spread to reveal those exquisitely uneven white teeth in that smile that splintered his heart with its beauty. He hardened all over, as he always did when he even thought of her, which was almost constantly. Now, with her so close in the flesh, warding off the blow of longing was nearly impossible.

Then Leonid threw himself at his legs, looking up at him, demanding his full attention.

He swooped to pick him up, groaning as Leonid's total trust and dependence inundated his heart. He almost succumbed and followed the pattern they'd established, the daily activities that included their quartet—or quintet, with Rosa.

But today would be Caliope's. She'd been here two weeks and had barely seen anything beyond the estate's boundaries. He wanted her to explore his motherland, experience it with him, share a part of him that she hadn't so far. And when she did, she'd make this land a true home for him. Up till now he'd only considered it his birthplace and base of operations.

He looked up from kissing Leonid to find her and his mother gazing at them with their hearts in their eyes, savoring the picture they made together, father and son.

He kissed the top of Leonid's head again. "*Moy dorogoy,* I have to take your *mamochka* on a sightseeing tour that you won't appreciate just yet, so you have to remain here with your *babushka,* Tatjana, and *nyanya,* Rosa, until we come back. But I promise you, tomorrow is all yours, birthday boy."

Caliope's smile faltered. "He can come. I'm sure he'll like it. He likes everything we do together…."

Khorosho. Good. He'd feared she'd say a point-blank no to the tour. But she only didn't want to leave Leonid behind.

Caliope turned to his mother, and to his hyper senses, there was a hectic tint to her smile. "We can all go. It would a lot of fun with all of us together. I'll go get Rosa."

Ne tak khorosho. Not so good. This was even worse than saying no. She was trying to get out of being alone with him.

Before he could think how to say he wasn't trying to get her alone in front of his mother, said mother intervened.

"I need Rosa while I see to last-minute details of tomorrow's celebration. And you two *will* leave me something to do on my own. And *you,* Caliope, need to see something outside the boundaries of my retreat. Leonid would get bored to tears in tourist attractions and he'd turn your outing into a struggle for all of you." She snapped Leonid out of his arms and almost ran away before Caliope could react, calling across her shoulder over Leonid's gleeful shriek, "Off you go. Shoo."

Caliope gaped after his mother's retreating back for a moment before she turned on him, eyebrow raised.

"You planned this, didn't you?"

His lips spread at her half accusing, half amused expression. "With my mother? No. She's just quick on the uptake. So quick it seems she's been impatiently waiting for me to act your proper host for longer than she could bear."

Her eyes twinkled turquoise with teasing. "If she has been, why didn't she give you a nudge?"

"She's the most progressive mother on the planet and would never interfere in my life. Not that I make it easy for her to be so restrained. My only drawback in her idolizing eyes is my lack of social skills."

She sighed as she fell in step with him. "I used to think so, too. But turns out you're not so bad."

He sighed, too. "I'm trying to recover from a lifelong atrophy of those skills."

"Your recovery has been phenomenal, then. Seems you can't do anything but superlatively."

His heart boomed. He'd become addicted to her praise, when he'd never before cared what anyone thought about him.

Overwhelmed with gratitude that she had forgiven him to the point that she acknowledged his efforts to change for the better, and praised each instance of success, he took her supple hand and raised it to his lips.

At her audible gasp, Maksim immediately broke contact, afraid she'd consider this a breach of their unspoken pact. He couldn't risk spoiling the spontaneity she'd miraculously developed with him.

Pretending an easy smile, he hoped to dissipate tension. "I'm honored by your opinion of my efforts, *moya dorogoya.*"

He couldn't stop calling her *my darling.* But she probably thought he meant the milder *my dear,* since he used it with Leonid, too. But they were both his darlings. His only loves.

Still, he kicked himself for succumbing to the need for any physical expression of his emotions when her answering smile wasn't as open as it had previously been. Injecting as much artificial ease into his own, he handed her into his Maserati, then filled her silence with his usual commentary on the areas they were passing through.

At her insistence, after he took her to the major landmarks of the city, he swung by Volkov Iron and Steel Industries headquarters and factories. It felt as if he were seeing it through her eyes, his view of it colored by her appreciation. She told him she'd never seen anything so advanced and extensive. As usual, her approval was what counted most to him.

As the sun started to decline, and while they approached the final man-made attraction he had on his list, she suddenly turned from watching the road to him.

"You haven't told her."

His mother. About the accident. It wasn't a question. He still answered. "No."

"I'm not prying," she said. "But Mikhail came up yesterday and it was clear she didn't know you were involved in the accident. I just need to know what you told her so I won't say anything wrong if the subject crops up again."

After parking the Maserati, he turned to her, needing to make one thing clear. "You can never pry. It's your right to know anything and everything about me."

She was deeply moved, and stunned emotion swept into her eyes, darkening them.

She didn't already know that she had every right to all of him? Or was it that she didn't want to have that right, since she'd already said she wouldn't take all of him?

He forced himself to smile. "But thanks for your concern. I told her the same story, just took myself out of it. She loved Mikhail as a son, and she suffered his loss almost as much as I did. I just couldn't make it even worse than it is."

"So she doesn't know about…"

It was the first time she'd alluded to his aneurysm, even though she seemed unable to bring herself to name it. That she had brought it up must mean it had been on her mind. As, of *course,* it must have been. Then she held up a hand, asking him not to answer.

But he did. "No, she doesn't know about my…condition."

Her sigh was laden with what sounded like pained relief. "I'm glad you didn't tell her. She's so happy now."

"And it's all thanks to you."

She shook her head. "It's all thanks to Leo."

"And you. I know when my mother is being her usual gracious self and when she is emotionally involved. I can tell she considers you a daughter, not only her grandson's mother."

Those incredible eyes he wanted nothing but to lose himself in gleamed with tears. "Isn't it too early for that?"

"Time has nothing to do with how you feel about someone."

Her slow nod was an admission of how time hadn't factored into what they'd felt about each other from the first moment.

Out loud she only said, "You're right. And I'm glad you think she feels like this, since I feel the same about her. It's the best thing for Leo, to have his family in such accord. I believe he senses it and is thriving on it."

"It's the best thing for you. And for her. You two deserve to have this special connection, regardless of any other consideration, and I can only see it growing deeper by the day." Her nod was ponderous this time, then conceding. To stop himself from swooping on those serious lips, he said, "Now for our last stop in my guided tour, the oldest building in Arkhangel'sk."

In minutes, they were entering the main tower of Gostiny Dvor—The Merchant Court—and Caliope was, as usual, inundating him with questions.

It delighted him how engrossed she was. She already did know a lot about his homeland, as much as could be gleaned from the internet, but she kept asking things only a native would know, to deepen and personalize her knowledge.

He kept answering as they walked through the massive and long complex of buildings. "This place was the raison d'être of Arkhangel'sk in the late seventeenth and eighteenth centuries. During that time, Arkhangel'sk handled more than half the country's exports. As we Russians like our buildings grand, the lofty status of the city back then necessitated building something imposing. It took a team of German and Dutch masons sixteen years to build it. And this turreted trading center was born to become the nexus of all trade between Europe and Russia."

As they entered another section, answering another of her questions had him elaborating on the place's history. "Yes, everything arrived or left from this network of depots. Luxurious European textiles like satin and velvet were imported, while flax, hemp, wax and timber were exported. But after Peter the Great conquered the Baltic coastline and moved the capital to St. Petersburg, most foreign trade was rerouted and the Arkhangel'sk trade center was abandoned. But by the mid-twentieth century, at the height of communist decay, many of the buildings here followed suit in deterioration and were demolished. After the fall of the Soviet empire in the latter half of the century, the crumbling place was elected to house a local-history museum, but for a long time restoration was never completed due to lack of funds."

"Until you, Arkhangel'sk's archangel, waved your magic wand—" she spread her arms in an encompassing movement "—and restored it to its former and current glory."

He blinked in astonishment. "How do you find these things out? I'm sure they're not on the internet."

She gave him a self-satisfied look. "I have my ways."

Unable to stop, he traced that mischievous dimple on her right cheek. "You have your ways…in everything."

For a long moment, he thought she'd reach up and drag him down for the kiss he knew she was burning for as much as he was.

But she turned away, pretended to look around before returning her gaze to him, with her desire under control. "So are you planning on feeding me, or are you out to make me lose the weight I've put on with Tatjana's mouthwatering feasts?"

Suppressing his own hunger, he fell into step with her as they exited the complex, grinning down at her. "I'm definitely feeding you. There can't be enough of you for me."

Before the heat that flared in her eyes reduced him to ashes, she suppressed it. "There definitely is enough of me, thanks. So take me somewhere with a weight-conscious menu."

He raised an eyebrow at her. "Seafood?"

She burst out laughing. As his other eyebrow joined in his perplexity, she spluttered, "Long story."

On their way to the restaurant, she told him of Aristedes's seafood-related teasing of her during that dinner. He laughed at her account, and they kept laughing all through their meal, about one thing or another. It was amazing how much had changed between them, yet how much remained the same.

They lingered over their meal for hours; then he took her driving outside the city until they reached the nearby Severodvinsk. On its outskirts, he parked the car in the best possible spot, then waited, a smile dancing on his lips in anticipation of Caliope's reaction.

For a while there was none. She was engrossed in discussing Leonid's birthday, expressing her delight that Maksim was flying her family and friends out for the celebration. Then she suddenly stopped and swung her gaze around to stare out of the windshield.

"The aurora!"

His lips spread as she squealed in excitement, sat up straight, eyes wide with wonder, as she, for the first time, witnessed nature's own light show and fireworks.

He watched her as she started swaying with every change in the celestial lights. The glowing curtains undulated as if raining from the heavens in emerald shimmers tinged with cascades of rubies and sapphires and laced with diamonds. They seemed to be dancing to an unheard rhythm, the same one that had caught Caliope and was moving her body with every sweeping arch, with every wave and curl of light moving across the sky, punctuated with sudden rays shooting down from space.

It was a long while before she could tear her eyes from the spectacle. "I've heard how the aurora was spectacular, seen photos and footage of it, but nothing conveyed even one iota of its reality. It's…beyond description."

He nodded, overjoyed at her enthrallment. "That it is. But it's more spectacular than usual tonight. It must have decided to put on an unprecedented show just for you."

She pulled one of those delicious comical faces.

"Yeah, sure. It's all on account of the exceptionally clear sky or stronger solar winds…or some other factor."

"Granted, that's the scientific explanation. But why now, and so suddenly? It didn't start showing off until you took notice and started watching."

"Then what are you proposing? That the wavelengths of my delight boosted the magnetic waves causing this phenomenon?"

"Thought waves are electric and magnetic. Why not?"

She pondered his question, her eyes pools reflecting the myriad emissions before she smiled and sighed. "Yeah. Why not? I am enchanted enough to cause it to show off for me."

She sank back in her seat to continue watching the magnificent display, sighed again then suddenly turned to him, face flooding with dismay. "Leo would have loved this! He would have freaked out!"

"It'll still be here for the next three months. We'll bring him another time, after making sure he sleeps during the day so he'll be awake for the show. Tonight I wanted you to relax and enjoy yourself, be yourself, not Leonid's mother."

She relaxed back in her seat, her dainty lips twisting. "You make it sound as if I have no life outside him."

"You only have work. You have no recreation, no fun."

"Look who's talking!"

"I looked, and I didn't like what I saw. Neither of us has to work that hard anymore."

"Who's working hard? I've barely worked since… Well, since you came back. And come to think of it, neither have you."

"I *have* almost ground to a halt for the past three

months," he admitted. "But I thought you were working as hard as ever to make up for the times we spent together."

"Are you for real?" She pulled another of those adorable faces. "Apart from the daylong outings and the ton of indoor activities you always plan, it's a miracle I've had time to bathe."

That image of her bathing, the very thing he'd tormented himself with this morning, hit him between the eyes—and in the loins. But the tenderness that she aroused in him was just as fierce. He wanted to give her everything and ensure her fulfillment in every way.

"You only had to tell me I was interfering with your ability to work."

"And what would you have done?" Her eyes gleamed with challenging mischief. "Don't tell me you would have come less frequently for shorter durations. I think it was beyond you to do that. I actually thought it quite a feat that you didn't set up camp in my living room to be with Leo around the clock."

"It wasn't only Leo's side I could barely leave, *moya dorogoya*." All traces of levity fled at his rasped confession. "But I would have made sure your work never suffered. Don't you know by now that I'll do anything to ensure that you have everything you need, want or aspire to in your life?"

Her eyes became black wells ringed in azure fire as she bit her lower lip, nodded. She knew he meant it.

But did she know *she* meant everything to him?

He opened his mouth to tell her that, that he loved her, worshipped the dirt beneath her feet. But the look in her eyes stopped him. She looked almost…lost. And professing his feelings to her would put her in an even more untenable position.

So he said nothing, just took her hand and leaned back in his seat, pretending to watch the magical manifestation across the sky. Soon she followed suit, and they spent another hour watching in silence until she asked him to take her home.

Maksim stood beneath the stinging, scalding jet of water, willing his senses to subside, his arousal to lessen enough so he wouldn't burst something vital. Like his aneurysm.

Not funny, Volkov. He knew physical stress had nothing to do with the possibility of that ticking bomb in his head going off. If it ever decided to go, it would, just like that. Now it was his heart that might race itself to a standstill.

Caliope had wanted him tonight. He could tell with every fiber of his being that she'd been craving him from that first night. But tonight, being alone and free from distractions, her hunger had almost killed him. Up till the moment they'd parted ways in the hallway.

If he pushed, if he went to her now, snatched her up into his arms and marched back to his suite, he knew she'd go up in flames in his arms. She'd beg him to take her, plunder her to sobbing, nerveless satiation.

But he couldn't. It wouldn't mean anything if she didn't seek him as she once had, out of her own free will and full choice. So though he craved her desperately, would do just about anything to have her, he couldn't take her power away like that.

Which meant he'd live in hell for the rest of his miserable life—one that he could only pray would be long, for Leonid's sake—and try to find a way to withstand the torture of her nearness.

It was no use now. His body remained clenched under the unremitting barrage of yearning that neither punishingly hot nor cold water had ameliorated. He rinsed the hair she'd told him she loved long, combed it back out of his eyes with his fingers, reliving the times she'd done that, until he couldn't bear the phantom sensations of her hands running through…

"Maksim."

He squeezed his eyes tighter. He kept hearing her voice calling him. As she used to—intimate, hot, hungry.

"Maksim."

There he went again. But this time, it sounded so… real.

Knowing he'd kick himself for being a wishful fool, his eyes snapped open to make certain. And through the heavy spray and the misted glass of the cubicle…there she was. *Caliope.*

As if from the depth of a dream, he pushed the door open.

And she was really there. Standing framed against the closed, ivory-painted door in a satin-and-lace nightgown and robe a darker shade of her eyes, just like he'd imagined in his fantasies.

His senses rioted so violently, he almost charged her. But he had to wait for her to tell him what she wanted.

For soul-searing moments she stared at him, her eyes briefly leaving his to skim over his body, wincing as she saw the evidence of his accident in his fading scars, then gasping at the sight of his arousal, before returning to his face.

He could barely hear her whisper over the still-pounding shower. "I couldn't wait any longer."

Then she moved, strode toward him, picking up speed with every urgent step. With the last one she threw herself against him under the gushing spray of water.

He almost lost his balance with her hurtling momentum and barely steadied them, looked down at her in pure astonishment. Was this really happening?

In answer to his silent disbelief, she climbed him, winding herself around him, twisting in his arms, forcing him to press her against the marble wall.

His hand behind her head and his arm at her back took the impact at the last second. They remained like this for endless moments, panting, their bodies and gazes fused. And he saw it all written all over her face, in the depths of her eyes: memories, longing, hunger…everything.

Then her hands were stabbing into his hair as he'd been yearning for them to minutes ago, grabbing his head by its tether and dragging his lips down to hers. She wrenched at them, and when he only surrendered to her fervor, paralyzed under the onslaught of her feel, the disbelief at her actions, she whimpered in frustration, bit his lower lip, hard.

A guttural growl rumbled from his gut as he dropped her to her feet and tore the clinging wet ensemble off her body. Then she was naked against him. She crushed her swollen, hard-tipped breasts against his chest, rubbed her firm belly feverishly against his steel erection.

Before his mind overloaded, he dropped to his knee to rid her of her last barrier, that wisp of turquoise lace. But as he started worshipping the feast of her long-craved flesh, her hands were again gripping his hair, pulling him back up to his feet. Straining against him, climbing him again, trembling all over now, she clamped her legs around his buttocks and sobbed, streams of tears flowing with the water sluicing over her face.

"I need you inside me...now, Maksim, *now*."

"Caliope, *moya serdtse*..."

He didn't recognize the voice of the beast who'd growled this to her, proclaiming her his heart. He was abruptly at the end of his tether, no more finesse, no more restraint. She'd demolished his control with her distressed demand.

Fusing their mouths together, he flexed his hips, his manhood nudging her entrance, and went blind with the sledgehammer of pleasure as her hot and molten core opened for him. Passion roared as she surrendered fully, all of her shuddering apart for his invasion, his completion.

But as he began to ease himself inside her, she bit down hard on his lip again. "I can't *bear* slow or gentle. Give me all you have, all your strength and greed. Devastate me, *finish* me."

He would have withheld his next heartbeats than deny her what she needed. Holding her gaze that shimmered with tears, he stabbed his girth inside her, hard and fierce. Her hot, honeyed flesh yielded to his invasion as he watched greedily the shocked wonder and pained pleasure slashing across her magnificent face, squeezing out of her in splintering, ravenous cries.

He bottomed out in her depths with that first ferocious plunge, dropped his forehead to hers, groaned deep and long at the severity of sensations. "Caliope, at last, *moya dusha,* at last..."

"Yes...Maksim, do it, take everything, do it all to me. I missed you so much, I've gone insane missing you...."

Unable to hold back anymore, he rammed into her, that unbearable tightness still the same sheath of madness he remembered, even after she'd given him Leonid. The impossible fit, the end of his exile, coming home inside her, sent him out of his mind. He withdrew and rammed back again and again, turning her cries to squeals, then shrieks. She thrashed against him as her slick flesh clamped around his length with a force he was only too familiar with, had craved to insanity. The herald of her orgasm. He knew what it would take now to give her an explosive release, wring her voluptuous body of every last spark of sensation and satisfaction.

He built the momentum of his thrusts until he was jackhammering inside her in frantic, forceful jabs. Her convulsions started from the farthest point he plunged, constricting her whole body around him, inside and out. Her shrieks became one continuous scream, stifling as bursts of completion raged through her.

He withstood her storm until she'd expended every shudder and tear, then he finished her as she'd always craved him to, impaling her beyond her limits, nudging the very core of her femininity, releasing his agonized ecstasy there, in one burst after another of scorching pleasure.

She sagged in his arms, nerveless, replete. He, too, could barely stand, so sank down, containing her. It felt as if she had been made to fit within him, as if he had been made to wrap around her.

His mind was a total blank as his tongue mated with hers in a languid, healing duel. He'd thought he'd starved for her taste. He'd been wrong. He'd shriveled up and expired. Drinking from its very fount was a resurrection.

A long, long time later, he relinquished her lips to

gaze down at her. Her head fell back against his shoulder, her eyes drugged with satisfaction.

Then those lips he'd kissed swollen moved, and that beloved voice poured out in a heartbreakingly tender melody.

Then he realized what she'd said.

"Will you marry me, Maksim?"

Eight

Maksim stared at Caliope's flushed face and intoxicated eyes and wondered if his mind had finally snapped.

If he'd been able to think at all about what her coming to him meant, he wouldn't have dared to hope for more than her finally accepting him as a lover again. So he couldn't be hearing what he wanted to hear. Since he hadn't wanted to hear *that*.

This meant…this was real. She meant it.

One question expanded to fill the world. But he couldn't ask it just yet. He had to take her out of here.

Coordination shot from the one-two combo of satiation and shock, he turned the water off, then scooped her up. He stepped with his armful of replete woman outside the shower, dried her then carried her to bed. She surrendered to his ministrations like a feline delighting in her owner's cosseting.

Coming down beside her on the bed, entwining their nakedness, sweeping her beloved flesh in caresses and her face in kisses, he asked the one thing left in his mind.

"Why? What changed?"

She pulled back to stare into his eyes. And the change in hers startled him. They looked somber, sorrowful.

"Don't…*bozhe moy,* please don't. I can't bear you

to feel a moment's distress. I don't need explanations. I don't need to know anything more than that you're here in my arms."

She cupped his face in her hands, her eyes beseeching. "But I need you to understand why I said no, why I held you at arm's length the past three months." She paused, inhaled a shuddering breath. "It was because of Leonidas."

Her dead brother, the one she'd named Leonid after.

Feeling her revelations would hurt her, he didn't want her to go on. But he also sensed that she needed to unburden herself. He turned his lips into the palm caressing his face and nodded, encouraging her to continue.

She did, sharing with him the intensely personal loss for the first time. "I never told you much about what happened, because we didn't delve into each other's private lives before, then because it remained too painful even when we did. Leonidas was…was the closest to me in age, and in everything. My only friend. My Mikhail." He ran soothing hands down her back, fortifying her when she faltered. She went on, her voice subdued. "He, too, was into extreme sports, though the extreme exertion variety. He was competing in a decathlon when he suffered a severe fracture in his left knee. During treatment, it was discovered the fracture had tumors behind it, in his tibia and femur around the joint—what he'd long thought was overtraining pain. After investigation, it was found to be an extremely malignant form of osteosarcoma."

His heart convulsed. He now knew where this was probably going. He hugged her closer, as if to ward off the desperation she'd felt for the sibling she'd loved most in the world.

"We told everyone his surgery was to fix his fracture. Only I knew it was a tumor-resection, limb-salvage surgery. But he was already in an advanced stage with metastasis to the lungs. We were told with aggressive treatments he had about fifty percent chance of survival. I talked him into going for it, since he was otherwise healthy and could withstand treatment, and I'd be there with him every step of the way. He agreed and I moved in with him, and we went through the cycles of treatment, which he weathered as best as could be expected."

Her eyes started to overflow with remembered despair, her whole body buzzing with the desolation of reliving the ordeal. "But a year later, another tumor was found, and this time there would have been no way to salvage his leg. And his survival rates had also plummeted. As we left the hospital, he told me he wanted to be on his own for a while, would come home later. But in two hours, I was contacted by the police. He'd just had a fatal car crash."

It was agonizing to see the shock in her eyes as if it was fresh, as if she relived the loss all over again.

"I…I thought I had more time with him. But he was suddenly gone, and everything I'd been bottling up since the discovery of his cancer and during his agonizing treatments—the pain, the fear, the constant anxiety— came crashing down on me. It was such a devastating blow, knowing it had all been for nothing. For months I didn't know that I'd ever rise from beneath the rubble. Then I met you."

When she'd detailed the emotional abuse her mother had gone through at the hands of the father she'd never seen, he'd thought this explained her no-strings-attached position on intimacy when they'd met. But this revelation gave a far deeper dimension to her mindset at the time. She'd met him in the aftermath of this life-changing loss, must have been reeling, needing closeness yet dreading it.

Remorse tore into him again, fiercer than ever before. "And I exposed you to more distress, especially when I deserted you, and then came back offering you more angst and uncertainty."

Her tears abruptly stopping, a look of urgency and conviction replaced the despondency on her beloved face. "No, Maksim. I see now that your problems did seem insurmountable to you back then, and I no longer think telling me about your past at the time would have led to us working things out. We both had to go through all this to know ourselves better, and to find out what we mean to each other, for better or for worse."

Still feeling unworthy of her love and forgiveness, after all that he'd put her through, he pulled away and sat up. "I understood why you said no to my proposal. I was too much of a risk, on every front, and you had your priorities right. But I didn't imagine you had such personal injury and dread to fortify your rejection. Now that I know, I can't understand why you've suddenly changed your mind about us."

She sat up, too, a goddess of voluptuousness, her breasts full and lush, her waist nipped, her thighs long and sleek, her hair gleaming silk around her polished shoulders. His body roared, forcing him to snatch the covers to hide his engorged erection, angry at his reaction when he should be tending to her emotional needs.

But she pressed her softness into his hardness, palm spreading over his heart, turning arousal to distress.

"There's nothing sudden about it," she murmured against his chest. "I refused you that first night because

I thought I could go back to my old life, raising Leo alone without you. But I couldn't act on my conviction and I let you in, and there's no changing that you are part of our family, part of *us,* now. *Ya lyublyu tebya... nye magoo zheet byes tebya....* I love you and I can't live without you, Maksim. So will you marry me, *moy lyubov?* You've already claimed me as yours."

Hearing her calling him her love, admitting his claim to her heart, her life, was beyond endurance.

What had he done?

He had craved her nearness and passion, but he hadn't thought she'd open herself so completely to him like this. He'd only ever wanted the best for her, and Leo.

"What if you were right to refuse me? What if the worst thing that ever happened to you is when I insinuated myself into your lives? What if something happens to me…?"

She stemmed the flow of his doubts and trepidations in a desperate kiss. "I already loved you with everything in me *before* you left. It was why your departure devastated me. And I've loved you more with each moment since your return. If anything happens to you now, whether we're married or not, it would shatter me just the same. So really, all I've been achieving by keeping you away is depriving us of all the intimacy only we can give each other, and having the pain without the pleasure."

His whole body stiffened as if under a barrage of blows. To imagine her in pain was unendurable. He'd wanted to love her, but he hadn't wanted her to suffer the agony of loving him to the same degree, to live in fear for him.

As if realizing the trajectory of his thoughts, she tugged on his hair to bring him out of his surrender to recriminations. "As you said that first night—nobody knows how long they'll live, or how long they'll have with someone. All we can do as finite humans is take whatever we can whenever we can and make the best of it. And you are the best possible *everything* that has ever happened to me. You're also the best father I've seen or imagined, surpassing even Aristedes."

The delight of her adulation, the dread of her dependence, sank into his heart with joy and terror.

But he'd created this impossible dilemma. She already loved him as much as he loved her, and he would hurt her whether he gave her the closeness and commitment she now craved or if he maintained their status quo. He'd been a fool not to realize how risky this all was, to think they could share so much without dragging her down into the well of addiction with him. He'd done this to her, and could only now give her whatever she wanted. Every single second of his life, every spark of his being.

What she already had total claim to.

Now she needed his corroboration. And for him to provide a distraction from all this overwrought emotion.

He forced a grin to his lips. "Better than the legendary Aristedes, huh? And you're not biased at all, of course."

An impish grin overlapped her urgency, transforming her face. "Not one tiny bit. He's a close second, granted, but you're the unapproachable number one." She pushed him on his back, coming to lie on top of him, pressing her hot length to his every inch. "So since it would be for better or for worse between us from now on, whether I marry you or not, 'not' is only pointless denial. So I again ask you, *moy serdtse*. Marry me."

He gazed up at her adoringly, unable to do anything anymore but risk living with constant worry and dread for the pleasure and privilege of any time they could have together.

"*Pozhaluista, moy lyubov*... Please, my love, say yes."

How could he say anything else? "Yes, *moy dusha*, yes.... I'm all yours to do with as you please."

He rose beneath her and swept her around until he was pressing down on her between her eagerly spreading legs.

Tears of happiness glittered as she arched, opening herself for his domination. "As soon as possible?"

"How about tomorrow?" He delivered the words into her lips as he thrust inside her, going home.

The shock of his combined proposition and invasion tore a cry from her depths.

With ecstasy shuddering across her face, she wrapped herself around him, taking him deeper, and moaned, "Yes."

Caliope still couldn't believe it.

She'd gone to Maksim's room last night without thinking.

She'd just been unable to stay away anymore. None of what had happened—their intimacies, her confessions, her proposal—had been in the least premeditated. Not only hadn't she thought of impassioned arguments to convince him to marry her beforehand, she hadn't even first convinced *herself*. She'd just gone to him, and had taken this life-altering step.

But then her fate had changed forever the moment she'd met his eyes across that reception hall three years ago. There'd always been no going back. The only difference now was that she was finally at peace with it, wouldn't settle for anything less.

If she couldn't be with him, she wanted nothing at all.

She passed by one of the ornate mirrors studding the walls of the mansion and met her own eyes. And winced.

Could it be more obvious that she'd barely survived a night of wild possession with that incomparable Russian wolf?

Everything about her was sore and swollen; even her hips swayed in a way that said she'd been plundered. As she'd begged him to when he'd attempted gentleness. She'd wanted him to dominate and devastate her. And how he had.

They hadn't slept at all, but who needed sleep? The rush of his lovemaking would keep her awake and going for a week straight. She felt as energized and as alert as she'd ever been. But it had only been after making love to her for the fifth time that they'd finally taken a breath not laden with delirium, and she'd started having qualms about saying yes to his proposition of an immediate wedding.

Fearing their anniversary would be supplanted by Leo's birthday, she'd proposed they keep their guests here for a few days and then have their wedding at the end of the week.

But he'd insisted that they didn't need a specific date every year to celebrate their marriage, since he'd be celebrating with her every single day. And she'd believed him.

So they were having their wedding today.

At 6:00 a.m. sharp, he'd gone to prepare everything and she'd given him carte blanche to do whatever he saw fit. She had no demands, only wanted to have the freedom of showing him that he was her everything. And to announce their bond to the world.

She'd seen tears fill his eyes before. But last night, they'd flowed. Hers had flooded in response, then deluged when he'd asked *her* to tell the world, starting with his mother.

He wanted her to be the one to give his mother what he knew would be the best gift anyone could give her, after that of Leo. A wife for her son. A daughter-in-law. A daughter, period.

And she had a six-thirty meeting with Tatjana at the chamber where they'd planned on holding Leo's birthday party, and where they'd now also have their wedding. Leo had practically been the one to pick the setting in the dance hall or "hall of mirrors". His delight in its painted ceilings and ornate, mirror-covered walls had been so explicit, he'd had them stay there at least an hour a day, as he pranced on top of tables in front of the mirrors, turned upside down to see himself from all different angles and rolled on the ground to stare at the ceiling. It was also the setting for a most important milestone. He'd taken his first steps there a couple of days after they'd arrived in Arkhangel'sk.

He'd chosen well, since it was the mansion's largest and most decorated room. But with the list of people Tatjana had invited, seemingly all the citizens of Arkhangel'sk, they'd need more than that space. Maybe even *all* of the mansion.

Her feet almost leaving the ground, she rushed through said mansion, feeling again as if she'd stepped back in time, all the time half expecting she'd meet figures from the era of the tsars.

It almost seemed an anachronism that the people she did meet, those who worked on the estate and on Tatjana's myriad community projects—all part of her continuous efforts to act as the community's uncrowned queen—were all jarringly modern.

She smiled left and right to everyone she met, almost running the last steps as she entered the dance hall.

The sight that greeted her had her heart doing its usual jig. Tatjana and Leo were perfect together. She was grateful every minute she'd agreed to come here, to give them all this rich and unique relationship. Rosa, an integral part of the family now, was also having the time of her life here, and apparently finding the love of her life, too, in Sasha, Maksim's chauffeur/bodyguard.

Could things get more perfect?

As soon as she thought that, her heart quivered with trepidation.

Could anything be this perfect…for long?

"Caliope, *moya dorogoya!*"

Tatjana's cheerfulness jerked her out of those dark thoughts, and she ran to her and to Leo.

For the next fifteen minutes, Tatjana didn't give her the chance to say much of anything as she supplied her with every minute detail of the birthday-party preparations, then solicited her opinion on changes in the color schemes, menu and seating plans.

Leo soon got bored, and Rosa took him away to what Maksim had transformed into every child's wonderland.

Then Tatjana was sweeping her along to her favorite sitting place, the grand living room. It was studded with paintings and decorations that felt like a documentary of the long history and glory of the Volkov family. Something Maksim had never mentioned.

As much as he was copious with his information about the country and the region, he'd been stingy with family details.

From what he'd told her of his father and grandfather, she understood his reluctance. She'd at first thought it wasn't a good idea to know more than she already knew. But now she felt she needed to glean as much information as possible in order to know him from every facet. She'd tried to broach the subject many times, but he'd always ingeniously escaped giving any details.

But here she was, with the one other person who could supply her with the knowledge she needed. Not that she had one single idea how to introduce the topic. If she asked outright, it would appear as if she was prying into matters Maksim hadn't seen fit to share with her. Which, of course, she was.

But what was she *thinking?* She should be telling Tatjana of the wedding, not trying to get her to spill the Volkov family secrets!

Tatjana offered her a plate of *pirozhki,* mouthwatering pastries filled with potato and cheese, with a side bowl of *smetana,* delicious sour cream that Russians used copiously.

Cali reciprocated by handing her tea, then began, "Tatjana…"

Clearly not realizing that she was cutting her off, Tatjana said, "Maksim didn't tell you much about his father, did he? Or about my marriage to him? Besides it being an abusive relationship that ended horrifically?"

Whoa. Had she been thinking of it so intensely she'd telepathically conveyed her burning curiosity to Tatjana?

She could only shake her head.

Tatjana sighed. "It pains me that he can't forgive or forget."

Cali put down the *pirozhki,* suddenly finding eating impossible. "Is it conceivable to do either when such wrongs have been dealt? I wondered how you survived when he first told me. But now that I've seen you, I know you're the strongest person I've ever known, and you can weather anything. And from the way you talk about your late husband, I can sense that *you,* at least, have forgiven him. And I wonder how you did it."

"I want to tell you how so you can understand Maksim better. But I have to tell you my life story to explain."

Cali nodded, even the slight movement difficult.

Tatjana sighed again. "I first saw Grigori when I was twenty and he was twenty-nine. I was working in one of the timber factories here when he came with his father, the city's governor, to learn the ropes of the position he would occupy, which would place him on his father's and grandfather's paths, as high-ranking Soviet officials. I was struck by him, and he was as struck by me."

She paused for a brief moment before continuing. "But all talk of equality in communism aside, a poor factory worker and a young man from what was considered the new royalty in Soviet Russia was an impossible proposition. But he moved heaven and earth, and fought his father and family long and hard to have me. Though I was at times disturbed by his intensity, I was hopelessly attracted to him. And he did seem like a fairy tale come true to the girl I was then."

She took a sip of tea, encouraged Cali to do the same. Cali gulped down a scalding mouthful, on the edge of her seat, the feeling that she'd plunged into a past life and another era intensifying.

Tatjana went on. "Then we were married. But for years, I couldn't conceive. Everyone kept pushing him to leave me, as not only was I inappropriate but barren. I think he thought it was him who was barren, and he grew progressively more morose, especially as his positions kept getting bigger and his responsibilities with them. It was five years after we got married that I became pregnant. I think he always had unreasonable doubts that Maksim was his."

Was that what had driven him to abuse his wife and son? He'd believed she'd betrayed him to conceive, then saddled him with the fruit of her infidelity to raise as his own?

"Not that his abuse started only then. It just started to become a pattern." So much for that theory. The bastard had already been an unstable monster. "But it was a terrible time all around. We were passing through the worst phases of the Cold War, and the situation of almost everyone in Russia was dismal. Having a husband who slapped me around, but otherwise gave me, and my family, everything, seemed like such a tiny quibble in comparison to those who had no homes or jobs or food. And I was inexperienced for my age, having been totally sheltered living here, so I didn't know any better."

Just like Cali's mother. It made her again realize just how much women today took for granted all the rights and powers they'd gained in the past fifty years.

"After the birth of Maksim, Grigori was promoted to become the vice governor, a position he soon realized he was totally unsuited for. But he couldn't admit that or risk dishonoring his father—and himself—forever. He knew what happened to those they considered inadequate in the hierarchy. He struggled, and it only got worse as time went by. Reports of his mistakes and investigations into his failures began to accumulate, and he began to disintegrate."

Cali had to bite her tongue. If the older woman

thought she'd make her sympathize with the weak bastard who'd scarred Maksim, and almost had made him destroy what they'd had and had now regained by a sheer miracle, she had another think coming!

Unaware of her venom, Tatjana went on. "He started to take it out on me more often, but as Maksim grew bigger and began to stand up for me and antagonize him for what he did to me, he turned his wrath on him. I believe he was more convinced every day that Maksim couldn't hate him like that if he was his. Then, in spite of all my measures, I got pregnant again. I thought of terminating the pregnancy, but ultimately didn't have the heart to and was forced to tell Grigori. His paranoia increased, but he didn't fully break down until he was fired from his position, just five months after Ana was born. We were given a month's notice to vacate this residence for his replacement. On the day we were set to leave, he went berserk, accusing me of being the reason for all his ill fortune, that I blighted him with my two bastards and… the rest you know."

Oh, she knew. And now hated Maksim's father all the more. Try as she might, she just couldn't understand how Tatjana managed to remain this adjusted, considering everything she'd endured.

Tatjana sighed. "Now comes the part about me and Maksim. We came out of the hospital to find no home and no family, as my parents had died and I had no siblings, and Grigori's family wanted nothing to do with us. He'd made a lot of enemies here and so much of his failures were snowballing." She sighed again, remembered sadness tingeing her face. "The whole place seemed to be going to hell. I worked any job I could find, and my darling Maksim was with me every step of the way, studying, working, doing everything for me that grown men couldn't. I don't think I would have survived without him.

"Then the Soviet Union collapsed and it was mayhem for a long while. I was almost afraid Maksim had turned to crime when he kept coming home covered in cuts and bruises. But he was actually defending the helpless here against the criminals who were exploiting them. And instead of working in a job in the industries here, he wanted to introduce something new to the region, so he could rule it. He chose steel. But he needed to learn the process from the ground up, so we went to Magnitogorsk, the center of steel industries in Russia. He made a living for us right away, then kept soaring higher every day. By the time he was in his mid-twenties, he'd already become a millionaire. He took us back here to set up Volkov Iron and Steel Industries and bought me this place."

Caliope had given up trying to hold back the tears. Imagining Maksim as a young boy, then teenager, then young man, as he struggled through the most unforgiving of social, political and financial circumstances, fending for his mother and all who needed his superior courage and strength and intellect, surmounting any difficulties and coming out not only on top but as such a phenomenal success, was beyond awe inspiring.

To think he was hers was still unbelievable.

But another thing was incomprehensible. "Why did you want to reclaim the place where you'd both suffered so much?"

Tatjana's eyes, which were so much like Maksim's, melted with tenderness. "Because my main memories here consisted of being with my beloved son. And my parents until they died. And after the loss and the pain began to fade away, I needed those precious memories back."

"But what about Maksim?" Cali said. "Doesn't your staying here make it hard for him to spend time with you?"

"I do know that the good memories with me don't make up for the horrible ones for him. But it's not only family nostalgia that made me wish to be back here. I have a responsibility to the people here, who stood by me at my worst times, and whom Grigori's mismanagement had harmed. I wanted to provide as many jobs and do my part in developing the community on a cultural and social level as Maksim was doing on an economic one."

This explained so much. Everything, really. She now finally and fully understood how he'd become the man she loved and respected with all her soul.

And now it was time to give Tatjana the wonderful news.

But Tatjana wasn't finished. She put her cup down and reached for both of Cali's hands, her eyes solemn. "I know Maksim always carried within him the fear that he might manifest his father's instability, but I assure you, Caliope, Maksim is nothing like his father or his menfolk. He'd been tested in the crucible of unendurable tests and had remained in control and never exhibited his father's volatility, not for a moment. In fact, he becomes more stable under pressure." Fierce maternal faith crossed Tatjana's face and her voice filled with urgency. "So you have absolutely *nothing* to fear. Maksim would rather die than raise a hand against anyone weaker, let alone those whom he loves and who depend on him."

Cali was the one who squeezed Tatjana's hands now,

soothing her agitation. "I know that, Tatjana. I'm certain of it as much as I'm certain that I'm alive."

"Then why won't you marry him?" Tatjana cried.

So that was what this was all about? Her future mother-in-law selling her on the idea of marrying her son?

Joy fizzed in her blood as her lips split in a grin that must have blinded Tatjana.

"Who said I won't? I'm marrying him…today!"

Nine

After announcing to Tatjana the wedding would be that very same day, and after the older woman had gotten over her *very* vocal shock, she hadn't even attempted to talk her into a postponement to give them time to prepare. According to Maksim's mother, this was three years overdue and they weren't putting it off one second longer. And then they still had twelve hours. *Plenty* of time in the hands of someone versed in preparing celebrations.

Of that Cali was sure. Between Maksim and his mother, who'd each separately promised her a wedding to rival those of the tsars, she knew they could make anything come true.

Not that she cared about what the wedding would be like. She only wanted her family and friends here to see her exchange vows with Maksim, even in her current jeans and ponytail if need be. All that truly mattered was becoming Caliope Volkov...

Caliope Volkov. She liked that. No. She *loved* that. And she loved that Leo would become Leonidas Maksim Volkov. His doting father had said he'd grow into a fearsome man, both lion and wolf.

Though she was considering changing Leo's name

to Leonid, as Maksim called him. To give tribute to
Leonidas yet at the same time pay proper homage to
Leo's heritage. Maksim had refused that categorically,
saying that he'd stop calling him Leonid if she thought
he preferred it, that he just found it more natural to say.
He wanted her to honor her brother and best friend, and
was honored that she'd named his son after him.

When they couldn't reach a compromise, he'd suggested they leave it up to Leo to choose when he grew
older.

Not that this was a time to think of names. Now it
was time to be swept into the whirlwind of preparations.

"So your man is so stingy, he wants to squeeze one
major and another monumental event into one?"

Cali rushed out of the bathroom at hearing the deep
teasing voice, squealing in pleasure at finding Aristedes
and Selene and their two kids standing on her suite's
doorstep.

Though she was already so tired all she wanted was
to collapse in bed and snooze for ten hours straight, she
hurtled herself at the quartet, deluging them with hugs
and kisses.

As she carried Sofia and cooed to her how her auntie
had missed her and how her cousin Leo couldn't wait
to have someone his age around, Aristedes continued
his mockery.

"I've heard of double birthdays or weddings, but a
baby birthday and the wedding of said baby's parents?
That's new."

Selene nipped his chin in tender chastisement. "You
are *not* going to start playing the nitpicking brother-in-
law."

Aristedes turned indulgent eyes to his wife. "That's my kid sister over here. You bet I'm going to watch that Russian wolf's every breath and hold him accountable for her every smile. And if I see as much as one tear…"

Selene curled her lips at him. "You mean like the rivers you made me cry once?"

He narrowed his eyes, clearly still disturbed that he'd caused her pain for any reason. "That was before we married."

Selene arched one elegant, dark eyebrow at him. "And now you're walking the line because I have not one but three hulking, overbearing Greek brothers watching your every breath and holding you accountable for my every smile."

"If you think those brothers of yours have *any*…"

"Down, Aris." Selene dragged him down for a laughing kiss. "That was just me teasing you to make you lay off Maksim." At his harrumph, which said he took severe exception to any allusions—if even in jest—that her brothers could *ever* influence his behavior, especially concerning her, she turned to wink at Cali. "He still has humorless blackouts. But I'm working on him."

"You've done a miraculous job so far." Cali giggled, fiercely happy to see how adored her eldest brother was by the woman who owned his heart. "Before you, we didn't think he had humor installed at all. We didn't think he was human!"

"Like your man, you mean?" Aristedes twisted his lips, hugging Selene more securely, his eyes darting to keep track of Alex, who'd climbed Cali's bed and was playing with the articles on her nightstand. "He was established as an arctic Russian robot of the highest order."

Selene chuckled. "Seems we'll discover that your man and mine are twins separated at birth."

Cali burst out laughing. "Just substitute Russian for Greek and anything you say about one could well be describing the other."

Aristedes pursed his lips, not quite mockingly this time. "Good news for your man is he finally did the right thing. And he wore you down in record time, too."

"You're wrong on both counts, since I was the one who asked him to marry me, and three months felt like forever."

A lethal bolt of lightning burst in Aristedes's steel eyes. "You mean you were the one trying to pin him down to a commitment all this time?"

She held up a placating hand. "First, 'down, Aris,' like Selene just said. Second, there is no pinning down involved. We both want this with every fiber of our beings. Third, he asked me to marry him the first night he came back and I turned him down, but he proceeded to dedicate his life to me and Leo anyway. Then just yesterday, I faced it that we have no life without him. But knowing he'd never ask again, so he wouldn't pressure me, I had to propose this time."

Still looking unconvinced, Aristedes growled under his breath. "This had better be the truth, Cali."

Did he suspect she had their mother's victim affliction? The very thing their sisters had, to one degree or another?

She held his eyes reassuringly. "It is. I don't have a blind-eye-turning bone in my body."

His eyes bored into hers as if to gauge the veracity of her claim. Then he inhaled. "As long as you're sure…"

"I am." She handed him Sofia, who'd nestled into her

neck and gone to sleep, and ran to fetch Alex. Once she had him carrying both of his children, she turned him around toward the door. "Now I'll borrow your wife and you go fetch me Melina, Phaidra, Thea and Kassandra, too."

"You called?"

The cheerful voice was Thea's. The next second, she had appeared in the doorway, followed by everyone Cali had just named. They were all wearing the same dress that was sculpted over Selene—an incredible sleeveless creation with an off-shoulder décolletage, nipped waist and flowing skirt in powder-blue, supple satin embroidered with gold thread. Which meant they were serving as her bridesmaids. The ever-present lump in her throat expanded.

"How's that for fast service?" Kassandra chuckled.

"You're mind readers." Cali pounced on them and dragged them in, before turning back to Aristedes. "You go see what Maksim has planned for you during the ceremony, but behave or I'll sic Selene on you." Aristedes gave a sigh of mock resignation, dropping a kiss on her cheek, then another on Selene's lips.

Before he walked away, she clung to him. "Is he here?"

His lips thinned. "Andreas? I would have skinned him alive if he didn't come."

She winced. "You have a thing for skinning alive men who don't perform to your standards, don't you?"

He exhaled. "Lucky for him, I won't have to this time. He wasn't coming when it was only Leo's birthday, but as per his words, 'not even a bastard like him would miss his kid sister's wedding.'"

Not exactly the enthusiasm she would have hoped

for from her older brother, but all that mattered was that Andreas was here. Everyone was here.

Her eyes filled, her chest tightened. As it seemed was her natural state these days.

Aristedes kissed her again. "Now hurry and be a ready bride so I can give you away. And ladies, don't get so carried away dressing her up that you lose track of time and keep us waiting too long."

"We don't *have* long," Cali wailed as she closed the door to drown out the sound of his infuriating chuckling, then turned to the grinning women. "Wait until you see what Maksim sent me for a wedding dress. I'm afraid to even…approach the thing, let alone wear it. And to think I sent away those stylists and beauticians Maksim hired to help me get ready, thinking I can manage."

Selene smiled. "Based on his similarity to Aris, I bet he has them standing by in case you change your mind."

"He did send in plan B." Melina pointed at herself.

Phaidra nodded. "Yep. He barely saluted us before almost chasing us here so we'd run to tend to your needs."

"But what were you thinking sending professionals away, you silly girl?" Thea scolded. "Since when do you know the first thing about makeup and hairdressing, when you never use any with your disgustingly perfect coloring and hair?"

Cali sighed as they approached the dressing room. "Your all-too-kind compliments aside, that's why I didn't want their services. Makeup and a hairdo would make me look different, and I don't want Maksim to find a woman he doesn't know walking down the aisle to him. Then I saw the so-called wedding dress and its accessories and almost fainted. Here…" She turned on the dressing room's lights. "You'll see what I mean."

Everyone blinked and their jaws dropped.

But it was Kassandra, of course, who recognized what that masterpiece was.

Her exclamation reverberated in the spacious room. "That's Empress Alexandra Feodorovna's dress!"

Yep. Maksim had gotten her the dress of the freaking last tsarina of Russia. She'd recognized it from her extensive research into his motherland's history.

Kassandra shook her head in disbelief. "It has to be a replica. That V-shaped satin inlay in the bodice below the embroidery was red in the original. This one's is—" she swung her dazed gaze to Cali "—the exact color of your eyes."

Cali's eyes misted again at the lengths he'd gone to at such short notice. "I thought so at first, but couldn't figure out how he could have had a replica made in under ten hours. The more plausible, if more insane, explanation is that he had the original customized to me."

"But...but—he couldn't have!" Kassandra looked faint with even imagining this. This would be tantamount to sacrilege to the designer in her. "That dress, if it's the real thing, is a...a *relic*. He couldn't have tampered with it for any reason. And how could he have gotten his hands on it at all? God, Cali, just *who* is this man you're marrying?"

"A very, *very* influential man, m'dear," Selene retorted.

But Kassandra was rushing to closely examine the dress in openmouthed shock and wonder and was joined by the others.

Selene remained beside Cali. "For your ears only, Cali, since the ladies are overwhelmed enough, I wouldn't put obtaining such an artifact past Maksim.

Literally anything is possible with our one-in-a-billion men."

Kassandra turned stricken eyes to them. "It's done ingeniously, but I can detect where the azure inlay overlies the original red. It is *the* dress."

Cali shuddered. "So I was right to fear touching it."

Thea scratched her head. "Apart from its pricelessness, how do you put it on? I don't see any zippers or buttons."

"It does seem as if there is no way to get into it," Phaidra agreed.

"Oh, of course there is." Kassandra waved their stymied perplexity away with the assurance of an expert. "And it's a good thing you declined putting on makeup, Cali. I would have had an ulcer dreading you'd smudge this one-in-history masterpiece." She picked up the extremely heavy dress reverently, her eyes eating up the details before turning to the others. "You ladies sit down over there—" she indicated the brocade couches on the other side of the room "—while I get Cali into this, and we'll get this show on the road."

Selene curtsied. "You're the boss here, Kass."

Melina bowed before Kassandra with arms stretched in mock worship. "She is the goddess, you mean. She conjured those bridesmaids' dresses in Maksim's demanded shade for all of us in under three hours!"

Imitating their sister, Thea and Phaidra bowed to Kassandra, who touched their gleaming heads in mock magnanimity, before they all burst out laughing.

Sobering a bit, Kassandra said, "Seriously, I couldn't have gotten everything done on *that* short a notice. I made the final selections, but it was Maksim's magic wand that had the dresses adjusted and flown in to your doorsteps in time."

As Cali's eyes welled and her sisters swooned over her groom's gallantry, Kassandra shooed them away again.

Clearly delighted to not have to handle Cali's wedding artifact, to sit down and watch as if they were in a fashion show, everyone hurried to comply with Kassandra's directives while Cali rushed after her to the changing room.

Ten minutes later, she stood gaping at herself. It was a good thing she'd declined a professional hairdo and makeup. With only the dress, she looked totally transformed. The white satin masterpiece molded to her like an extension of her. The bodice opened on a plunging off-the-shoulders oval décolleté, pointing into a sharp V at the nipped waist. The long sleeves opened longitudinally at the armholes and flowed down, folding back to expose her arms whenever she moved them. The skirt was bell shaped in the front with a detachable ten-foot train at the waist that folded softly at the back with pleats of tulle.

The bodice below the décolleté, with that newly installed azure-satin inlay, was embellished in prominent silver flower wreaths, and the borders of the sleeves and train, as well as the middle of the bodice and skirt, were all embroidered in complex golden garlands. A panel of gold velvet traveled down the midfront with pearl and diamond buttons, and the *kokoshnik,* the headdress that stood for a veil, was exquisite snow-white lace worked with the same designs.

Cali let out a ragged breath, still hardly believing her own eyes. "I don't think I could have gotten into this thing if you weren't here, Kass."

"I trust Maksim will know how to get you out of it?" Kassandra chuckled, then frowned in alarm. "Do you get how we put it on you to instruct him if he runs into trouble? If he gets frustrated being unable to peel it off you and damages it, I'd…"

"Yeah, have an ulcer."

"Ulcer is for makeup smudges," Kassandra scoffed. "For an actual tear? Nothing less than an aneurysm."

Cali's heart slammed painfully against her ribs.

Of all the things to mention, why would Kassandra say this specifically? Was this more than a coincidence? The fates telling her something through her unwitting friend…?

Just how ridiculous was she being? People blurted out things like this all the time. It was she who was hypersensitive to it.

Her smile wavered as she met the other woman's eyes in the mirror. "Shall we let my sisters be the ones to help with the headdress and accessories?"

"Yeah, they can help with all the indestructible articles. And let's have Phaidra twist your hair up like her own hairdo. It'll suit you and the accessories perfectly."

Even in her lingering dismay, she smiled at Kassandra's protectiveness of the dress, which only a true artist would feel toward an irreplaceable work of art.

The others' reaction to her appearance confirmed that she looked like a totally different woman. Her sisters, especially Melina, as her eldest sister, went all teary eyed at the sight of the baby of the family looking like an empress, and basically *becoming* an empress of the new world, since her groom was an emperor of industry and commerce.

As they gathered around her, Kassandra stopped them

from hugging her so *their* makeup and perfume wouldn't stain the dress. Teasing Kassandra about her new obsession, they started adorning Cali in the jewelry Kassandra insisted *had* been that particular dress's, especially the breathtakingly ornate crown of white gold, pearls and diamonds.

Then it was time. To marry Maksim.

She rushed out of the suite as fast as the dress allowed her with the rest behind her, trying to help her with her train, then giving up because she needed no help at her speed, since it flew behind her on the marble floors of the mansion.

They had to pull her back at the entrance of the dance hall so she wouldn't spill in. She forced herself to walk in as if she weren't a mass of excitement and screaming nerves.

And she found herself stepping into a place she felt she'd never seen before. It had been transformed into a scene from the most sumptuous times of imperial Russia. The paneled-in-gold walls gleamed under the combined lights of the crystal and gold-plated metal sconces hanging between them and the spotlights that were directed toward the thirty-foot painted ceiling, reflecting on the scene to drench it in a magical golden glow.

Against each side of the length of the gigantic rectangular hall, endless tables were set, leaving the rest of the elaborate hardwood floor empty, with only an aisle running down its middle. The tables were covered by an organza tablecloth with the symbol of the estate—a cross between a phoenix and an eagle with its wings spread—repeated in a pattern throughout. Tatjana had told her that the extravagant sets adorning the tables came from a service of Sevres porcelain Napoleon Bonaparte had given to Tsar Alexander. There were only about three hundred people seated there, with the rest of the guests attending the reception/birthday afterward.

Among those, she looked for one person first. Andreas.

It was actually hard to believe he'd come for her wedding, when he hadn't for Leonidas's funeral.

She didn't look long. He stood out in the bright, festive scene, emanating his own deep shadows. He wasn't sitting with the rest; he was standing almost at the entry, apart, alone. And, as always, he looked like a barely leashed predator, his black hair and eyes matching the darkness he exuded.

He met her eyes across the distance, didn't smile. Then he raised his hand and placed it flat over his heart.

Her nerves jangled. She loved Andreas but had never figured him out—or if her emotions were reciprocated, if he even felt anything for anyone. This simple gesture somehow told her everything he'd never said. He did love her—and probably loved the rest of his siblings, too, just in his own detached, unfathomable way.

Unfortunately, she couldn't stop to savor this rare moment, had to relinquish his gaze, move on.

Tatjana captured her focus next. She was at the middle of the table to the left, looking majestic in an elaborate gold-satin dress that she believed belonged to one of Russia's grand duchesses. Rosa, in something sumptuous from Tatjana's wardrobe, was standing behind her, with an enthralled Leo in a vivid blue-and-gold miniature of an adult costume, looking so absolutely adorable her heart flailed in her chest.

She kept her eyes averted from the end of the hall. She knew Maksim was there, flooding the hall with his overpowering presence, permeating her cells with his influence. She wanted to keep him for last. There would be no looking anywhere else after she laid eyes on him.

Aristedes, in his resplendent tuxedo, strode toward her, smiling into her dazed eyes as he took her arm.

As they walked down the royal-blue-satin aisle, spread on both sides with white-and-gold rose petals, he said, "Your man throws a mean party in record time. At least I hope he does, and this isn't how he intended to celebrate a one-year-old's birthday."

She wanted to explain that this was all new, but had no more breath. Only her feet remained working on autopilot. For she had finally looked down the aisle. At Maksim. It was a miracle she remained erect.

With every step closer he came into clearer focus, inducing more tremors into her limbs and heart.

He was wearing the adult-size version of Leo's costume, imperial clothes, though she failed to pinpoint its origin. His shoulders and chest looked even more imposing than usual in a midthigh coat in vivid blue, the same hue of the inlay in her dress but many shades darker. It was embroidered exquisitely with gold thread and cord in a horizontal repetitive pattern, each ending where golden buttons closed the coat down his massive chest. At his hard waist it opened down to reveal white gold-embroidered satin pants gathered into navy-and-tan leather boots.

And then she looked up at his face, and that was when she almost fell to her knees.

The mahogany hair that now rained down to his shoulders was scraped away from his leonine forehead and gathered back into a ponytail, the severe pull emphasizing his rugged bone structure, the lupine slant of his eyes and the sensual hardness of his lips.

He looked way more than heart-stopping. And he looked…hungry. She felt him devouring her from afar, felt her body readying itself for his possession, didn't know how she'd survive the time until she could have him again.

Then they reached him where he stood on the draped-in-satin, five-step platform, and Aristedes unhooked his arm from what she realized had been her spastic grip.

He held out his hand to Maksim, who gripped it in a firm handshake, then drew him into one of those sparse male hugs. Cali heard their brief exchange.

"Make her happy, Volkov," Aristedes said. *Or else* was conveyed clearly.

It was lucky she hadn't applied makeup or she would have ended up a streaked mess when she heard Maksim's answer.

"I live to make her happy, Sarantos."

The two most important men in her life parted with a final look of understanding. Then Aristedes placed her hand in Maksim's and stepped down.

Everything from the moment her groom took her hand onward went by in a dreamlike blur.

Maksim tucked her to his side as if he were afraid she'd disappear as an ornately dressed minister started reciting the marriage vows first in Russian, then in English. After she'd recited them after him in a fugue, another man stepped forward, took the minister's place and recited vows in Greek.

No longer able to manifest surprise or to deal with these spikes in emotion, she only looked up at Maksim, love and gratitude flowing from her eyes. He hugged her tighter, his eyes smoldering with passion so fierce it singed her soul.

After they'd exchanged their own vows, and he'd kissed her senseless, he held her swooning mass to his side as he gestured to someone in the distance. In moments, Rosa came rushing up the platform with Leo popping with excitement in her arms. He threw himself at both of them, but it was Maksim who had the coordination to catch him.

Holding both of them to his heart, he addressed the guests.

"Every man lives searching for a purpose in life. If he is blessed, he finds it and can dedicate his life to it. I have been blessed beyond measure. I give you my purpose, my blessings, the owners of my heart and soul and everything that I am and have. My bride, the love of my life, Caliope Sarantos Volkova, and my son and heir, Leonidas Sarantos Volkov."

Everyone stood as one, cheering and raising their glasses in a toast to the family, and Cali broke down at last, burying her face into Maksim's chest, sobbing, while Leo jumped up and down in his father's embrace and screeched in elation, as if realizing that this was a momentous moment in all their lives.

The out-of-body feeling she'd been experiencing only deepened as the celebrations continued, merging the wedding with the birthday. Maksim took her to salute their guests before heading outside the hall, where she found the rest of the mansion *was* spread with tables for the attendees, with the children converging on Leo's wonderland.

She thought she laughed with her family, chattered in Russian with Tatjana's acquaintances, joked with

Maksim's business associates who wanted to know how she'd melted that iceberg. She believed she joined in dancing the *khorovod,* the Russian circle folk dance, which her family eventually turned into the *pidikhtos,* Crete's version of the dance.

Then she was hugging and kissing endless bodies and faces, the only ones she'd remember later being her family, especially Andreas, who promised he'd come visit her…sometime.

Then she was held high in Maksim's arms, swept through the mansion to a wing she hadn't been in before. As she peeked over his shoulder, she found Kassandra and Selene running to keep up with his urgent strides. A beaming Kassandra explained with gestures that they were coming to get her out of the dress. Seemed she'd taken Maksim aside and convinced him to recruit her for the chore.

Inside a suite that Maksim had lavishly prepared for their wedding night, he reluctantly set her down on her feet, thanked Kassandra and Selene then whispered in her ear that he'd be waiting for her inside and strode away.

After a giggling Kassandra and Selene helped her out of the dress, Kassandra worshipped it back onto its hanger and Selene gave her a package that had been waiting on a coffee table. Then with one more hug, both ladies disappeared, leaving her standing in her lacy underwear and high-heeled sandals.

Cali's hands shook as she opened the package, which Maksim must have commissioned Kassandra to get for her. Inside was the most luxuriously erotic getup she'd ever seen.

Trembling all over with anticipation, she substituted

it for her underwear, a dream of brilliant pearl-white stretch lace and satin that cupped her breasts into a deep cleavage and showcased the rest of her to the best advantage.

Unable to wait to see its effect on Maksim, she teetered inside, wishing he hadn't changed into anything himself, since she'd spent the whole evening dreaming of stripping him out of that costume. Yet part of her was also wishing that he *had* already disrobed, since she couldn't wait until she had his flesh beneath her hands and lips.

She entered a bedroom that was spread in gold and azure and lit with what must be a thousand candles. Maksim was at the far end with only those white pants on. His whole body bunched at the sight of her, like a starving predator who'd just spotted the one thing that would slake his hunger.

She almost fell to her knees when he rumbled, *"Moya zhena...nakonets."*

My wife. At last.

Maksim watched the incandescent vision that was his bride. He'd spent the previous night drowning in her. Instead of sating him, it had only roused the beast he'd been keeping on a spiked leash, fueling his addiction to searing levels.

He'd felt her equal craving all through the wedding, her impatience to continue making up for fifteen months of separation and starvation. He'd intended to drag her into the depths of passion the moment she walked in, give her what she needed, invade her, finish her, perish inside her.

Then she had glided in, and he'd called her his wife…
and only when he'd said it had it fully registered.

She was his *wife*.

And what he felt now was…frightening. So much so
it brought his old fears crashing down on him, paralyzing him.

But after her own moments of paralysis, when
he didn't go to her, she started walking toward him,
looking…celestial. It almost made him regret asking her
friend to get her something made to worship her beauty.
Her friend had chosen *too* well.

Then she was against him, running feverish hands
and lips over his burning flesh, her eyes eating him up,
her body grinding against his, pulling him down to the
bed, taking him on top of her. Opening her legs for his
bulk, undulating beneath him in a frenzy, she demanded
him inside hers, riding her, pleasuring her, fulfilling her.

Her hands tangled in the string tying his hair back,
almost tore at it as she tugged at his scalp, the exquisite
pain lashing at his barely contained fervor.

Then her fingers bunched into his hair and she
brought his head down to hers, his lips fusing with the
fragrant, warm petals of her flesh to breathe a white-hot
tremolo into his depths. *"Moy muzh."*

His every nerve fired. *My husband.*

And to have her say it in Russian. That she'd learned
the language, and that well, for him…the gratitude he
felt was at times…excruciating.

Spiraling, he tried to rise off her, to ration his response. But her pleading litanies to hurry, to take her,
now, now, were like hammers smashing his control. Her
beloved body quivered beneath his, her cherished face
shuddered.

It was too much. He wanted too much. All of her. At once.

His growl sounded frightening in his ears as he sank his teeth where her neck flowed into her shoulder. She jerked and threw her head back, giving him a better bite. He took it. He was a hairbreadth from going berserk.

Then as she gazed up at him through hooded eyes, she made any attempts at curbing his passion impossible. "Show me how much you want me, Maksim." Her voice reverberated in his brain, dark and deep. Wild. "Brand me as yours, seal our lifelong pact, give me everything…take everything."

With a grunt of surrender, he freed her silky locks from the high chignon he'd longed to demolish all evening, pulled her head to the bed for his devouring. She bombarded him with a cry of capitulation and command.

He rose to free himself from the confines of his pants, to tear that tormenting figment off her, then hissed in relief when he found her wearing nothing beneath it. His fingers slid between the lips of her core before dipping inside her, finding her flowing with readiness.

Blind with the need to ride her, he locked her thighs over his back, drove her into the mattress with a bellow of conquering lust and embedded himself inside her to her womb.

They arched back. Mouths opened on soundless screams at the potency of the moment. On pleasure too much to bear. Invasion and captivation. Completion. New, searing, overpowering. Every single time.

His roar broke through his muteness as he withdrew. She clutched at him with the tightness of her hot, fluid femininity, her delirious whimpers and her nails in his buttocks demanding his return. He met her eyes, saw everything he needed to live for. He rammed back against her clinging resistance, his home inside her. The pleasure detonated again. Her cry pierced his being. He thrust hard, then harder, until her cries stifled on tortured squeals.

Then she bucked. Ground herself against him. Convulsed around him in furious, helpless rhythms, choking out his name, her eyes streaming with the force of her pleasure.

He rode her to quivering enervation. Then showed her the extent of his need, her absolute hold over him. He bellowed her name and his surrender to her as he again found the only profound release he'd only ever had with her, convulsing in waves of pure culmination, jetting his seed into her depths until he felt he'd dissolved inside her.

Even as he sank into her quivering arms, he was harder than before. Which didn't matter. He had to let her sleep.

He tried to withdraw. She only wound herself tighter around him, clung to him.

"There will be more and more, soon and always." He breathed the fire of his erotic promise into her mouth. "Rest now. You've been awake for forty-eight hours, and I've taxed you in every possible way beyond human endurance."

She breathed her pleasure inside him, thrust her hips to take him deeper inside her. "I can only sleep if you stay inside me. I can't get enough of you, *moy dorogoy muzh*."

"Neither will I of you…ever." She was driving him deeper into bondage. And he wouldn't have it any other way.

He drove back into her and she pulsed her sheath around him until he groaned. "Tormentress. Just wait until you're rested. I'll drive you to insanity and beyond."

In response to his erotic menace, she tossed her arms over her head, arched her vision of a body, thrust her breasts against his chest and purred low with aggressive surrender. Still jerking with the electrocuting release, he turned her, brought her over him, her shudders resonating with his.

"Give me your lips, *moya zhena.*"

As she gave him what he needed, her lips stilled while fused to his, exhaustion claiming her.

As she finally surrendered to slumber, totally secure and trusting in his arms, he knew.

His resurrected fears were totally unfounded. Even through the inferno of lust, tenderness and giving had permeated him. His feelings weren't forged in selfishness and dependence but fueled by the need to enrich her life, be the source of her fulfillment. His pleasure lay here, in being hers.

He took her more securely into his containment and surrendered to their union on every level. And to peace.

For the first true time in his life.

Ten

Cali stretched in the depths of utter bliss.

She wanted to never surface, to lie here on top of her Great Russian Wolf forever.

For the past four months since their wedding, she'd gone to sleep like that, after nights of escalating abandon.

But she had to wake up. She'd promised Tatjana to spend the day with her. At least she thought she had. After a night of mind-scrambling pleasure at Maksim's hands, she wasn't even sure where she was.

She actually had to open her eyes to make certain they *were* back in Russia. They'd just come back last night after a taking-care-of-business, apartment-buying stint in New York.

She'd thought this mansion had become her home, but then she'd also felt at home on their first night in their new NYC apartment. If she hadn't been certain by then, she was now. Anywhere Maksim was would always be home to her.

She propped herself up with palms flat over his chiseled chest to wallow in his splendor.

Unbelievable. That *did* just sum him up. And every moment of every day with him. She sometimes still did find herself disbelieving this was all really happening, wondered if it was possible she'd ever get used to his… *their* perfection.

But then why should she? How *could* she get used to this? Nope. It was *im*possible. There was nothing to do, and nothing she *wanted* to do, but live in a state of perpetual wonder.

Just looking at him had her heart trying to burst free of its attachments and her breath refusing to come until she drew it mingled with his beloved scent. So she did.

At the touch of her lips on his, he smiled in his sleep and rumbled, *"Lyublyu tebya."*

She caught the precious pledge in an openmouthed kiss.

He instantly stirred, dauntingly aroused, returned the kiss then took it over.

She gasped with pleasure as he swept her around, bore down on her. "Love you more, Maksim."

"There's no way you love me more, *moye serdtse.* I've waited all my life for you, knew it the moment I saw you."

She arched up, opening herself for him. "Same here."

He rose on his knees and positioned himself at her molten entrance, held her immobile by her hair for his passionate onslaught, the way she loved him to. *"Nyet,* I'm older, so I don't only love you more, I've loved you longer."

She cried out with the searing pleasure of his words and his plunge into her body. Their hunger was always too urgent at first. It took only a few gulps of each other's taste, a few unbridled thrusts to have them convulsing in each other's arms, the pleasure complete.

After the ecstasy he drove her to demolished her completely, he twisted to lie on his back and draped her over him again, a trembling blanket of sated flesh.

A sigh of contentment shuddered out of him after the burst of exertion and satisfaction.

She raised an unsteady head to savor his beauty. "You're feeling quite smug, aren't you? You think you've claimed the More and Longer Loving title for life, don't you?"

"If this ruffles your feathers too much, I can be persuaded to grant you equal billing in the 'More' category. The 'Longer' one, alas, is an unchangeable fact of time. Being the spring chick that you are, you just don't have the creds."

She drove her hands into the thick, mahogany hair that now fell past his shoulders at her demand, tugged sharply, knowing he loved it when she played rough. "Do you know what happens to condescending wolves, even the one-of-a-kind specimens?"

He stretched beneath her languidly, provocation itself. "*Da*...they get punished, with even more love and pleasure."

"Damn straight." She swooped to devour those maddeningly seductive lips, took him over this time, tormented and inflamed and owned every inch of him until she had him begging her to ride him. And she did. Hard and long, until they both almost shattered with pleasure.

Afterward, tingling with aftershocks, she let him haul her to the shower, where they spent an indeterminable time leisurely soothing and pampering each other.

They'd just exited the bathroom guffawing as he chased her to tickle her when a knock came on the door.

She bolted away from Maksim's groping hands and

started jumping into her clothes. "Leo! Hurry, put something on."

He picked up his jeans, his smile unfettered. "Our son has an impeccable sense of timing. He lets us feast on each other in peace, then comes to join in for playtime."

She prodded him along and he shoved himself with difficulty into his jeans, wincing and muttering that only *un*dressing was safe with her around.

Her wide grin of triumph elicited a growled promise of retribution as she rushed to the door.

As soon as she opened it, Leo bolted inside without even looking at her. She laughed. The wily boy was preempting her, wasn't risking her telling Rosa to take him away for now. And he was after his daddy anyway, his biggest playmate and fan.

She exchanged a few words with Rosa, setting up the day, then turned to her men, delight dancing on her lips at the sight they made together.

Leo was popping up and down with arms stretched up for his daddy to pick him up. Maksim was standing above him, looking down at him.

Her smile faltered. The sense of something wrong hit first. What it was registered seconds later.

It was the way Maksim was looking down at Leo… as…as if…

As if he didn't know him.

Even worse, it was as if Maksim wasn't even aware *what* Leo was, where or who *he* was…

A bolt of ice froze her insides wholesale. Her heart exploded from the rhythm of serenity to total chaos.

"Maksim…?"

His eyes rose to her and what she saw there almost had her heart rupturing. Horror. Helplessness.

Then he collapsed…like a demolished building. As if every muscle holding him up had snapped, every bone had liquefied.

"Maksim!"

Her scream detonated in her chest and head, its sheer force almost tearing them apart. Hurling herself across the room, she barely caught him, slowing down his plummet before he keeled over Leo, desperation infusing manic strength into her limbs.

Shuddering, she crumpled with Maksim's insupportable deadweight to the ground, barely clearing Leo, who'd frozen to the spot, eyes stricken, fright eating through his incomprehension by the second. Any moment now he'd realize this was no game. Any moment now Maksim would…would…

She screamed for Rosa, a scream that must have rocked the mansion, bringing Rosa barging into the suite in heartbeats.

She heard herself talking in someone else's voice, rapid, robotic. "Get my phone, take Leo away, keep everything from Tatjana for now, get Sasha. *Go.*"

She'd lived through a dress rehearsal of this catastrophe a thousand times in her mind. Leaving nothing up to chance, Maksim had coached her in the exact measures she'd take in case the worst happened. This constant dread had been the only thing polluting her psyche, eating away at her stamina. But the more time that had passed without even the least warning signs, the more she'd hoped it would never come to pass.

But it had. It *had.*

His aneurysm had ruptured.

Keeping her dry-as-rock eyes on Maksim's wide-open, vacant ones, she speed-dialed Maksim's emergency medical hotline. As per the plan, they assured her a helicopter would be there within minutes. The specialists he'd elected to handle his case would be waiting at the medical center of his choice.

Then she waited. Hit bottom, went insane over and over, waiting. Her heart had long been shredded, but it kept flapping inside her like a butchered bird only because Maksim's heart still beat powerfully beneath her quaking arms. The rest of him was inert. Feeling his vigor vanished, his very *self* extinguished, was beyond horrifying. Those eyes where his magnificent, beautiful soul resided had emptied of everything that made him himself. Then it got worse.

At one point, something came across them, something vast and terrible spreading its gloom, eclipsing their suns. Something like anguish. No...regret. Then his lips moved in a macabre parody of their usual purpose and grace. His voice was also warped, sending more gushes of terror exploding through her.

She thought he said, *"Izvinityeh."*
Forgive me.
Then his eyes closed.
And she screamed and screamed and screamed.

She didn't stop screaming, she thought, until the medics arrived. Once there was something to do, solid steps to be taken, a switch was thrown inside her, shutting down the hysteria of powerlessness. And the rehearsed drill took her over once again.

She talked to him all the time they installed their resuscitation measures on the short flight to the state-of-the-art medical center he'd erected in the city. She told him all the good news she could—that his vitals were strong, that he had gone into shock and his whole body was flaccid, but he wasn't exhibiting any hemiparesis, which would indicate neurological damage. She told him she was there and would *never* leave his side, that he had to fight, for Leo, for his mother. But mainly for her.

She couldn't live without him.

Then they arrived at the hospital and the perfectly oiled machine of intervention he'd put in place months ago took over. She ran beside his gurney as he was taken to the O.R., but the doctors, as per his orders, wouldn't let her scrub in or watch the surgery from the gallery.

Unable to waste time arguing, she succumbed, but wouldn't be convinced to go to the waiting area. She collapsed in front of the O.R. where the man who embodied her heart and soul would be cut open, where he would struggle to stay alive. She had to be as close as possible. He would feel her, and she would be able to transfer her very life force unto him to keep him alive, to restore him.

And she wept. And realized that she'd never truly wept before. *This* was weeping, feeling her insides tearing, her psyche shattering, her very being dissolving and seeping out of her in an outpour that could never be stemmed. Only Maksim, only an end to his danger, could stop the fatal flow.

In the unending torment of waiting, she registered somewhere in her swollen, warped awareness that Aristedes and Selene had come. Their very presence reinforced the horror of what she already knew, counting the minutes since Maksim had been taken into the O.R. He'd been in there for over twelve hours.

After failing to make her get off the ground, they'd

sat down there beside her, respecting her agony, trying to absorb it in the solidarity of their silence.

"Mrs. Volkov."

That voice. She'd know it among a million.

Maksim's neurosurgeon.

She shot up to her feet. But her legs had disappeared. With a cry of chagrin, she collapsed back down. Aristedes caught her, Selene shooting up to help him support her.

The moment she could feel her legs again, she pushed them away and staggered to Dr. Antonovich. This was hers alone to hear, to bear. Just like Maksim was hers alone.

Dr. Antonovich talked quickly as she approached him, as if afraid she'd attack him if he didn't. "Mr. Volkov made it without incident through surgery. He's in intensive care now, where he will stay for the next two weeks as we monitor him."

Alive. *He was alive.* He'd survived this catastrophe that had been casting its dreadful shadow over their lives.

But… "What—what is his condition now?"

Dr. Antonovich attempted to take her arm, to support her as she swayed. She shook her head, needing only answers, facts.

Nodding with understanding, he began quietly, "During his last checkup six months ago, the aneurysm had still been located where attempts to approach it would have caused serious brain damage or even death. But in the interim, it had expanded downward, which at once caused it to rupture, and enabled us to try a new kind of treatment through a noninvasive, endoscopic trans-nasal approach. I'm happy to report the aneurysm has been totally resected and the artery fully repaired."

She absorbed the information rabidly. But it still didn't tell her what to expect next. "What about prognosis?"

"Since his aneurysm was posttraumatic, Mr. Volkov has no underlying weakness in his vessels, and the possibility of recurrence is nil. While that is great news, it was the rupture of the original aneurysm that we had worried about. To tell you the truth, with Mr. Volkov's general condition in the months after his accident, I had little hope he'd survive a rupture. The last time he came in six months ago, he'd shown little physical progress. But the man I operated on today was the most robust person I've ever seen. If I had to hazard a guess, I'd say you're the reason behind his miraculous improvement."

Maksim had said that. That she and Leo were a magical elixir, that being with them—with *her*—had revitalized him, gave him new capacities and limitless strength. It had been why she'd let her guard down, believing nothing would happen to him.

"What does his general condition have to do with his prognosis?" she choked out.

"Everything. Apart from the neurological condition after rupture, it's what decides the prognosis. As a surgeon who deals almost exclusively in cerebral accidents, I almost never give optimistic percentages. But with Mr. Volkov in superb physical condition, if the next two weeks pass without incident, I believe he has an over ninety percent chance of making a full recovery."

She pounced on him, digging her shaking hands into his arms. "What can I do? Tell me there's something I can do."

He extricated himself gently, took her arm. "You can keep on doing exactly what got him to this state of superb health. And once he clears the sensitive postoperative period, both of you can forget about this uncertain phase of your lives."

She stopped, the tears that hadn't slowed during their conversation flowing faster. "Wh-when can I see him?"

The surgeon ventured a faint smile. "Mr. Volkov has instructions firmly in place about every possible development of his condition. You and anyone you indicate are to have full access to him, night or day, as long as there is no medical reason not to. You can even stay with him in ICU."

She grasped his arm again. "I—I can?"

The man nodded. "He funded the whole hospital, and keeps upgrading it at our request with the latest technology. The only thing he ever asked for in return was that, if he ever needed our services, we would arrange for you to stay with him while he recuperates, if that was what you wanted…."

And she broke down, the agony of loving him and fearing for him, demolishing her. "I want… God, oh, God… I want…I want nothing else in the world… *please.*"

The first three days, Cali stayed by Maksim's side around the clock, counting his breaths, hanging on to the exact shape of his heartbeats and brainwaves. There was no change whatsoever. His vitals remained strong and steady, but he didn't regain consciousness.

The only reason she didn't go berserk was that the doctors insisted he was sleeping artificially. He'd been sedated to give his brain the chance to recover during this sensitive phase, when awareness would tax it. Dr. Antonovich was being extra careful, as she'd begged him to be, even if it freaked her out of her mind to see her indomitable Maksim so inert.

It was amazing how perfect he looked. The noninvasive technique had left his hair untouched, and it appeared as if he were sleeping peacefully, whole and healthy.

On the fourth day, they let him wake up. For one hour in the morning and another in the evening.

That first time he opened his eyes, she almost died of fright. The blank look he gave her had nightmares tearing into her mind. Of amnesia…or worse.

Then his gaze filled with recognition. Before jubilation could take hold, gut-wrenching emotion surged to the surface and the tears that constantly flowed gushed. She kissed him and kissed him, telling him she loved him, loved him, loved him, that she'd always, *always* be beside him, would never, ever leave his side, and that it was only a matter of time before they had their perfect life back.

He made no response as she talked and talked until she was terrified *he* couldn't talk. At last he told her he was just tired, then listlessly turned his head away and closed his eyes. She didn't think he slept, just kept his eyes shut. Until they'd come and put him under again.

When she'd pursued Dr. Antonovich with her report of his first weird waking episode, he said it was natural for Maksim to wake up groggy and not all there. When she insisted he'd been neither, just…blunted, he'd gone on to explain the obvious, that the brain was an unpredictable organ and she'd have to play it by ear, let him go through his recovery in his own pace and not worry, and mostly not let him feel her anxiety.

Determined to take the surgeon's advice, she told herself that anything she felt was irrelevant. Hard facts said Maksim was neurologically intact. And that was far more than enough. If it took him forever to bounce back from this almost lethal ordeal, it would be a price she'd gladly pay.

And he did bounce back, faster than his surgeon's best hopes. The two weeks in ICU became only one, with everyone, starting with Tatjana and Leo, coming to visit during his waking hours at his request. He was transferred to a regular suite and the sedation was confined to the night hours; then even that was withdrawn. By the next week, the surgeon saw no reason to keep him in hospital, discharged him with a set of instructions for home care and follow-ups, but gave him a clean bill of health.

But Maksim was subdued, only exhibiting any spark around his mother and son. With them he was almost his old self. Cali kept telling herself she was imagining things, and that even if she wasn't, there was a very good reason for this.

He was depleted, out of sorts, had just survived a near-fatal medical crisis and must be shaken to the core. But he couldn't show any of this to Tatjana and Leo. He hadn't even told his mother of his condition in fear of worrying her, and would now do anything to reassure her of his return to normal. He also wouldn't risk scarring Leo's young and impressionable psyche by allowing any of his post-traumatic stress to rise to the surface around him.

But around her? He could let his true condition show

without having to bear the effort of putting on an act, and he could count on her to understand.

And she did understand. She only missed him. *Missed* him.

He was there but not there. He talked to her, especially when others were around, and she did feel his gaze on her sometimes, but the moment she turned to him, starving for connection, he looked away and sent her spiraling back into deprivation.

But she would persevere. Forever if need be. That was her pledge to him.

For better or for worse. For as long as she lived.

Three months after Maksim's discharge from the hospital, Cali's resolve was starting to waver.

Instead of things getting better, if even slightly, they only got worse.

The proof had come two weeks ago, when Dr. Antonovich had given him the green light to resume all his normal activities without reservations. It was as if he'd released him from a prison he'd been dying to break free of. He'd hopped onto a plane and gone on a business tour…alone.

He *had* called regularly during the past two weeks to reassure them, but called her own phone only when his mother didn't pick up. Even when he did, he said nothing personal, let alone intimate, just asking about Leo or asking her to put him through.

On the day he was supposed to come back, she'd run out of rationalizations. There was no escaping the one possible conclusion anymore.

He was avoiding her.

And for the first time since she'd laid eyes on him, she

dreaded seeing him, meeting his gaze. Or rather having him escape meeting hers again.

Just minutes later, he walked into the living room, where they were all gathered waiting for him. And the sight of him felt like a stab through her heart.

He'd lost weight since his crisis, understandably. But it wasn't only that his clothes hung around him that hurt. It was what felt like a statement that he'd withdrawn his emotional carte blanche from her.

He'd cut his hair.

It was now even shorter than when she'd first seen him across that reception hall—almost cropped off.

She felt catapulted back in time, only worse. Back then his eyes had smoldered with hunger; now they only filled with heaviness.

She still rushed to join in welcoming him, only to feel the white-hot skewer in her gut turning when he slipped away from her embrace, pretending to answer Leo's demand for his attention. She sat there with the talons pinning her smile up for Tatjana's and Leo's sake, sinking into her flesh and soul with every passing moment, until Leo fell asleep and Tatjana excused herself for the night. With just a curt good-night, Maksim walked out, too.

And she reached breaking point.

She had to know what was wrong or she'd lose her mind.

Forcing herself to follow him, dreading another brush-off, she approached the suite he'd moved to since he'd gotten out of hospital, with the excuse that he was suffering from bouts of insomnia at night and didn't want to disturb her.

Tiptoeing in, she found him sitting on the edge of a chair in the sitting area, his elbows resting on his knees, his cropped head held in his hands, his large palms covering his face. His shoulders, now looking diminished, were hunched over, his whole pose embodying the picture of defeat.

Her heart did its best to tear itself out of her chest.

A burst of protectiveness welled up inside her, had her running toward him, desperately needing to ward off whatever was weighing him down. His head snapped up at her approach, and for moments, she saw it. The unguarded expression of…torment.

Crying out with the pain of it, she hugged him fiercely, withdrawing only to hold his face in trembling hands, rain kisses over his face, his name a ragged litany, a prayer on her lips.

After only moments, he pulled away, his hands clamping hers, taking them away from his face. Her heart twisted in her chest at his clear and unequivocal rejection.

"I'm not ready for this."

This. Her nearness? Her emotions? What was…*this?*

She pried her hands from his warding grip, the sick electricity of misery that had become her usual state erratically zapping in her marrow. "Dr. Antonovich said you might suffer from some mood swings for a while."

He heaved up to his feet. "I'm suffering from nothing."

"This was a major trauma and surgery in your most vital organ. It's only expected you won't bounce back easily."

"He gave me a clean bill of health. There's nothing wrong with me. Just because I'm not up for sex doesn't mean I'm malfunctioning."

It felt like he'd backhanded her.

Was that how abused people felt? Would a physical blow have hurt more?

"I didn't say that," she choked. "And I'm not asking for sex or expecting it. I just want to…"

"You just want to touch me and kiss me. You want me to show you intimacy and emotion, what I showed you from the time I came back till the aneurysm ruptured." His voice hardened. "I tried to show you that I don't want any of that anymore, but you won't take a hint."

"It's all right. I understand…"

"You don't," he bit off. "You don't *want* to understand."

She swallowed back the sobs, unable to bear his harshness, which she'd never before been exposed to.

Then she remembered. "Dr. Antonovich said there was a chance of some personality changes…"

"There are no changes. This is me. The *real* me."

His growl fell on her like a wrecking ball. A lightning bolt of understanding.

"You mean it wasn't the real you before? Since your accident? Since you came back?"

He made no answer. And that was the most eloquent one.

"You mean when you left me, it was because you wanted nothing more to do with me? Then you had the accident, and thinking you'd die any moment made you vulnerable, made you need intimacy, to reaffirm your life? Or even worse, that aneurysm was pressing on your brain, causing your radical personality change. And once it was treated, you reverted to your real self, the self that didn't love me, that left me without a backward glance?"

The dismal darkness in his gaze said he hated hearing that. Because it was true. Because he felt terrible about it, but couldn't change it. He couldn't force himself to love her when he no longer felt anything.

His love for her had been injury induced. Now that he'd been fixed, he'd been cured of it.

She still had to hear him say it. "Do you want me to leave?"

His eyes were suddenly extinguished, as if everything inside him had just turned off, died. "I…think it would be best."

She'd hoped…until the words had left his mouth.

Her whole being lurched with agony so acute she caved under its onslaught; her face, her insides, all of her felt like a piece of burned paper crumbling in a careless hand.

One thing was still left unsaid. Not that it would change anything. It just had to be said.

"I'm…pregnant."

He nodded as if he, too, barely had enough life force to sustain him. "I know."

So he knew. Nobody had noticed as she'd lost so much weight. But he knew her intimately…as he no longer wanted to know her. As he seemed unable to contemplate knowing her.

"What I told you over two years ago stands."

About supporting her and his child. His *children* now.

She'd be a single parent now, not to one but two children. After she'd known what it was to share a child with him.

And she wailed, "Why did you ever come back? Why didn't you just leave me in my ignorance of what it could be like?"

He wouldn't look at her as he rasped, "I can't change the past, but this is better for the future, Caliope. I know you don't need anything, but you and…the children would still have everything that I have, and would have all my support in any way you'll allow. If you still let me be Leo's father, and the new baby's when it's born, you don't have to see me, too. In fact, I'd rather you didn't."

And the heart that had already been shattered was pulverized. "Did you *ever* love me, Maksim?"

He sat down heavily in his chair, throwing his head back, squeezing his eyes. "Don't dredge everything up, Caliope. Don't do this to yourself."

"I have to. I must make sense of this or I'll go insane."

He opened his eyes, looked at her with a world of dejection and said nothing.

No. He'd never loved her.

There was nothing more to say. To feel. To hope for. She turned and walked away.

At the door, she felt compelled to turn back.

Strange how he still looked like the man she loved. The man who'd loved her. When that man had never existed.

"Since you told me of your aneurysm, I lived in fear of losing you. Now that I have, I'm only glad I didn't lose you to death. Even though I feel like a widow."

And she said goodbye. To the man who never was. To happiness and love and everything hopeful and beautiful she'd never have again.

Back in her suite, she stepped into the shower cubicle and stood limply beneath the powerful spray as the water changed from punishingly cold to hot, shudders spreading from her depths outward.

She squeezed her eyes, needing tears to flow, to release some of the unbearable pressure. None came. She'd depleted every last one and would forever be deprived of their relief.

Waves of despair almost crushed her, shudders racking her so hard until she could no longer stand, and she sank in an uncoordinated heap to the cubicle's marble floor.

She lay there for maybe hours.

At last she exited the shower, dressed, packed her bags, gathered a bewildered Leo and Rosa and swept them back to New York.

Eighteen hours later, she entered her old building's elevator. She'd sent Leo with Rosa for the night.

She was…finished, didn't want to expose her son to more of her anguish. He'd felt it all through the flight, had fussed and wailed most of it. He must have also felt she was taking him away from his daddy.

Not that she would. Maksim would come for Leo, and she'd let him see him every day if he wanted. Despite everything, one thing was undeniable: Maksim loved his son. It had nothing to do with whatever he felt…or rather, *didn't* feel for her. That father/son bond hadn't been the aneurysm's doing, so it had survived its removal.

It was her love that had been so superficial, so artificial, it had vanished at the touch of a scalpel.

The ping of the elevator lurched through her. She stumbled out, walked with eyes pinned to the ground. She'd have to sell the apartment. Too many memories with Maksim here. She had to purge him from her life. If she hoped to survive.

Then she raised her eyes…and he was there.

He'd been sitting on the ground by her door, was now

rising to his feet. Her legs gnarled together. And he was there, stopping her from plummeting to the ground.

Her eyes devoured him for helpless moments before common sense kicked in. "Leo… He's not with me…."

"I know. I'm here to talk to you."

And she panicked, pushed frantically out of his supporting arms. "No. No, no, *no*. You can't keep reeling me in, shredding me apart, throwing me out then doing it again. I won't let you do this to me. Not again. Not ever again."

Caliope's words fell on Maksim like fists dipped in ground glass…smashing into his heart and brain.

But he had to do this. He had to make her understand.

Taking the keys from her limp hands, he opened her door, urged her inside. "I have to talk to you, Caliope. After this, you'll never have to see me again."

The defeat and despair in her eyes made him wish again that he'd died on that operating table.

"It's you who doesn't want to see me, Maksim. You've reverted to your true nature, but I'm the same person who's always loved you, who can't stop loving you. I wish there was some medical procedure that would keep me from feeling like this, but if there were, I couldn't have it, because of Leo and the baby. You said you'd rather not see me again, and you were right. I *can't* see you again. Just thinking of you makes my sanity bleed out. Just looking at you makes my blood congeal inside my arteries with grief. If you want your children to have a mother and not a wreck, you won't let me see you again."

He deserved all that and more. But he had to do this.

He caught her arm as she turned away. "I left you once without explanations. I have to explain this time."

"I don't want your explanations. I don't care *why* you're killing me. It won't change the fact that you're killing me all the same."

He groaned, "Caliope…"

She stepped away unsteadily. "Okay, that was over the top. I am too strong to shrivel up and die. I will regain my equilibrium and go on. For myself as well as for my children."

His hands fisted, cramping with the need to reach for her. "This is what I want you to do. To move on, to forget…"

"You don't get to tell me what you want anymore," she cried out, strangled, shrill. "You don't get to pretend you care about what happens to me. I don't want to move on, and I don't want to forget. If it weighs on your conscience, I can't help you there. The man I love exists here—" she thumped her chest hard with her fist, face shuddering, eyes welling "—and here." Another jarring punch against her temple, her whole frame quaking with the rising tide of misery. "*He's* in my senses and reflexes, *he's* part of my every cell. Even if you're not him anymore, you can't take *him* away from me, so the new you can feel better…"

His own torment burst out of him on a butchered groan. "I was aware all the time after I collapsed, Caliope."

That brought her tirade to an abrupt end.

He went on. "All through the trip to the hospital, up to when they forced you, per my orders, to stay out of the O.R. I saw, *felt everything*. I was *mutilated* by what it did to you when I collapsed. I've never seen anyone so…wrecked, known someone could suffer so totally, so horrifically. And I realized that I'd done that to you. I've been far more selfish than you once accused me of being, involving you in this doomed relationship, where I get to have the happiness and blessing of your love as long as I live, only to leave you with the anguish of my loss and the curse of my memory."

Tears still cascading down her cheeks, she gaped at him.

"Dr. Antonovich might say he's over ninety percent certain I'm fully recovered, but there is still a percentage I'm not. And I can't bear making you live in constant dread waiting for me to collapse again, and maybe this time not making it…or worse."

Her tears suddenly stopped. Everything about her seemed to hit pause.

Then a cracked whisper bled out of her. "You mean you did love me? And never stopped?"

There was no way he could stop the admission now. "I've loved you from the first moment I saw you. I don't think I can stop loving you, even if they remove my whole brain."

This time her voice was more audible as her eyes became fiercely probing. "And you decided it was better for me to lose you while you were still alive? That's why you pulled away after your surgery, to build up my resentment toward you, so that if you eventually died it wouldn't hurt me as much?" His nod was wary, the dreadful feeling he'd botched this whole thing creeping up his spine. "Then why did you follow me here? Wasn't my leaving what you were after?"

His breath left him in a strangled rasp. "I've been trying to make you opt for saving yourself. I wanted you to walk out angry and indignant, intending to put me behind you. But you were *demolished* instead, without any hope of getting over me. *Bozhe moy*...the last things you said, about going insane not knowing...about feeling like a widow. What you said now...about loving me no matter what..."

He felt totally lost, no longer knowing what he was here to do or how he could possibly get her to save herself.

He tried again. "I couldn't leave you without an explanation again. I couldn't bear letting you keep on thinking I didn't love you. I love you so much, love our family and our lives together, I can't breathe with it most of the time. But I *can't* expose you to heartbreak of this magnitude again."

A long, full moment dragged by, then her murmur sounded more like the Caliope he knew. "One final question. If I were the one who got injured or crippled, would you abandon me?"

"Caliope, *nyet*..."

She plowed on. "If you knew I would possibly die at any moment, would you give up one single day with me now, live whatever time I had left apart from me to save yourself the anguish you'd feel if I died while we were in utmost closeness?"

Feeling his brain simmering, his eyes filling with acid, he protested, his voice a ragged, broken moan. "I'd give my very life for any time at all with you. For a month. A day. An *hour*. And nothing would ever take me away from your side if you love me, no matter what."

"Something *is* taking you away, when I love and need you, right now. You. You're the one who keeps depriving me of you."

And he realized. He hadn't only spoiled his mission, he'd closed the trap shut behind him…and her.

"*Bozhe moy,* Caliope, dying or worse, living crippled, is far preferable to me to hurting you. But whatever I do, I'll end up hurting you, and I thought…" He exhaled roughly. "I no longer know what I thought. Everything worked out in my mind when I was trying to drive you away…then I saw and felt the reality of your pain, and knew it wouldn't just end if I made you leave…"

He stopped, stared at her helplessly, loving her so much it overpowered him, defeated him.

And she gently drew him to her, clasping him into heaven, her supple arms sheltering him, taking him away from all his fears and uncertainty. "Then just accept your fate, Maksim, being mine for the rest of our lives, however long that will be. Just be ecstatically happy and humbly thankful, like I am, for every second we have together. Stop trying to save me future pain and only hurting me now and forever. Start loving me again and let me breathe again."

And just like that, every last shackle of anxiety snapped and every insurmountable barrier of dread came crashing down.

He surged around her, crushed her in his arms. "I can never stop loving you. I *won't* stop loving you even when I stop breathing. You are my breath, in my every cell, too. My heart beats to your name, my senses clamor for your being. I am yours, and I beg you to never let me go."

Her tears flowed again, this time of joy, of healing, drenching his chest, cleansing his soul. "I've never once let you go, mister. I've been clinging to you with all I have, but you're the one who keeps leaving every time your misguided chivalry and skewed self-sacrificing tendencies act up."

"If I ever stray again, out of any new bout of stupidity, club me over the head and drag me back into your embrace."

Her lips trembled in a smile of such acute love, he dropped his head in her bosom and let his tears flow.

Her hands shook over his head, sifting through his now bristly, short hair. "Mmm… I can and will carry out the clubbing part, but you're no longer a good candidate for being dragged back where you belong. No hair."

His laugh choked in his crowded chest. "That hair is growing back, waist length if you like."

"Ooh, I like." She leaned back in the circle of his arms. "And I want, Maksim, and need…and crave. Three months without you has taken me through all the stages of starvation."

"Can I dedicate the next thirty years to rectifying my major crime of three months of tormenting you in vain?"

She clung around his neck. "Make it fifty and you're on."

Feeling he'd just closely escaped an eternal plummet into hell, he swept her to bed, where he reunited them flesh in flesh, never to be sundered again.

And this time he knew that any lingering anxiety would only serve to intensify their union, make them revel in and appreciate each second they had together even more. If this wasn't survivable, who cared? Life itself ended, but this, their love, never would.

When the storm of passion had abated after a long night of wild abandon, he rose over her, caressing her from buttock to back, marveling in her beauty, wallowing in her hold over him. "Can we go retrieve our little lion cub now?"

She arched sensuously, the very sight of contentment. "Oh, yes. He's desolate without his dada. And Maksim…"

"Da, moy dusha?"

"If our baby is a boy, I want to name him Mikhail. If it's a girl, Tatjana Anastasia."

He buried his face in her neck, groaning, "You'll really kill me with too much love."

"I want to make you live like you never did."

And he told her what he'd once thought and never put it into words to her. "You do. Without you, I existed. With you, I'm alive, alight. I don't think I'll ever find enough ways to thank you for that, to show you how much I love you."

"When you weren't showing me you love me by leaving me, you did wonders."

Feeling beyond humbled by her blessing, he cupped her precious cheek. "For showing me the good inside of me, for giving me the best of everything, for loving me even when I made it impossible, for never giving up on me until I got it right…I promise you, you've seen nothing yet."

His own personal piece of heaven shone with tears and adoration. "I'll hold you to that. And I'll hold on to you. I'm never letting you go again."

"Never again, *moya zhena, moya dusha,*" he pledged. "Never, my wife, my soul. This time, forever."

* * * * *

USA TODAY bestselling author **Heidi Betts**, an avid romance reader since junior high, knew early on that she wanted to write these wonderful stories of love and adventure. It wasn't until her freshman year of college, however, when she spent the entire night before finals reading a romance novel instead of studying, that she decided to follow her dream.

Soon after Heidi joined Romance Writers of America, her writing began to garner attention, including placing in the esteemed Golden Heart contest three years in a row. The recipient of numerous awards and stellar reviews, Heidi's books combine believable characters with compelling plotlines and are consistently described as "delightful," "sizzling" and "wonderfully witty."

For news, fun and information about upcoming books, visit Heidi online at heidibetts.com.

Books by Heidi Betts

Harlequin Desire

Bedded Then *Wed*

Blackmailed into Bed

Fortune's Forbidden Woman

Christmas in His Royal Bed

Inheriting His Secret Christmas Baby

Her Little Secret, His Hidden Heir

On the Verge of I Do

Secrets, Lies & Lullabies

Project: Runaway Heiress

Project: Runaway Bride

Visit the Author Profile page at Harlequin.com for more titles.

HER LITTLE SECRET, HIS HIDDEN HEIR

Heidi Betts

For my wonderful new Harlequin Desire editor, Charles Griemsman. It's been a delight working with and getting to know you this past year, and I'm looking forward to sharing many more "Desire-able" moments in the future.

Prologue

Vanessa Keller—soon to be simply Vanessa Mason again—sat at the foot of her hotel-room bed, staring at the small plastic wand in her hand. She blinked, feeling her heart pound, her stomach roll and her vision go fuzzy around the edges.

As bad luck went, this ranked right up there with having your plane go down on the way to your honeymoon destination or getting hit by a bus right after you'd won the million-dollar lotto.

And the irony of the situation…

A harsh laugh escaped her lungs, taking with it a puff of the stale air she'd been holding onto for the past several minutes.

She was newly divorced from a husband she'd *thought* was the man of her dreams, staying in a downtown Pittsburgh hotel because she didn't know quite what to do with her life now that the rug had been yanked out from under her. And if that wasn't enough to make her wonder where things had gone so wrong, now she was pregnant.

Pregnant. With her ex-husband's child, when she hadn't managed to conceive in the three years they'd been married, even though they'd tried…or at least hadn't worked to prevent it.

What in heaven's name was she going to do?

Pushing to her feet on less-than-steady legs, she crossed to the wide desk against the far wall and dropped into its cushioned chair. Her hands shook as she laid the small plastic stick on the flat surface and dragged the phone closer.

Taking deep, shuddering breaths, she told herself she could do this. Told herself it was the right thing to do, and however he reacted, she would handle it.

This was not a bid to get back together. Vanessa wasn't sure she would want to, even with a baby now in the picture. But he deserved to know he was going to be a father, regardless of the current state of their relationship.

With cold fingers, she dialed the familiar number, knowing his assistant would answer. She'd never cared for Trevor Storch; he was a weaselly little brownnoser, treating her more as an annoyance than as the wife of the CEO of a multimillion-dollar company and *his boss*.

After only one ring, Trevor's squeaky, singsong voice came on the line. "Keller Corporation, Marcus Keller's office. How may I help you?"

"It's Vanessa," she said without preamble—he knew full well who she was. He was probably privy to more of the details about her marriage and subsequent divorce than he deserved to be, too. "I need to talk to Marc."

"I'm sorry, Miss Mason, Mr. Keller isn't available."

His use of her maiden name—not to mention calling her *Miss*—struck Vanessa's heart like the tip of a knife. No doubt he'd done it deliberately.

"It's important," she said, not bothering to correct or argue with him. She'd done enough of that in the past, as well as overlooking his snide attitude just to keep the peace; she didn't have to do it anymore, either.

"I'm sorry," he told her again, "but Mr. Keller has instructed me to tell you that there's nothing you could possibly have to say to him that he wants to hear. Good day."

And with that, the line went dead, leaving Vanessa open-mouthed with shock. If hearing herself called "Miss Mason" rather than "Mrs. Keller" felt like a knife tip being inserted into her heart, then being told her ex-husband wouldn't even deign to speak with her any longer thrust the blade the rest of the way in to the hilt and twisted it sharply.

She'd known Marc was angry with her, knew they'd parted on less than friendly terms. But never in a million years would she have expected him to cut her off so callously.

He'd loved her once, hadn't he? She'd certainly loved him. And yet they'd come to this—virtual strangers who couldn't even speak a civil word to one another.

But that answered the question of what she was going to do. She was going to be a single mother, and without Marcus's money and support—which she wouldn't have taken, with or without the prenup—she'd better find a way to take care of herself and the baby—and she'd better do it fast.

One

One year later...

Marcus Keller flexed his fingers on the warm leather of the steering wheel, his sleek black Mercedes hugging the road as he took the narrow curves leading into Summerville faster than was probably wise.

The small Pennsylvania town was only three hours from his own home in Pittsburgh, but it might as well have been a world away. Where Pittsburgh was ninety percent concrete and city lights, Summerville was thick forests, green grass, quaint houses and a small downtown area that reminded Marcus of a modern version of Mayberry.

He slowed his speed, taking the time to examine the storefronts as he passed. A drug store, a post office, a bar and grill, a gift shop…and a bakery.

Lifting his foot from the gas, he slowed even more, studying the bright yellow awning and fancy black lettering declaring it to be The Sugar Shack…the red neon sign in the window letting customers know they were open…and the handful of people inside, enjoying freshly made baked goods.

It looked inviting, which was important in the food

service industry. He was tempted to lower his window and see if he could actually smell the delicious scents of breads and cookies and pies in the air.

But there was more to running a successful business than a cute name and an attractive front window, and if he was going to put money into The Sugar Shack, he wanted to know it was a sound investment.

At the corner, he took a left and continued down a side street, following the directions he'd been given to reach the offices of Blake and Fetzer, Financial Advisors. He'd worked with Brian Blake before, though never on an investment this far from home or this close to Blake's own offices. Still, the man had never steered him wrong, which made Marcus more willing to take time off work and make the long drive.

A few blocks down the street, he noticed a lone woman walking quickly on three-inch heels. Given the uneven pavement and pebbles littering the sidewalk, she wasn't having an easy time of it. She also seemed distracted, rooting around inside an oversize handbag rather than keeping her attention on where she was going.

A niggle of something uncomfortable skated through his belly. She reminded him somehow of his ex-wife. A bit heavier and curvier, her coppery hair cut short instead of left to flow halfway down her back, but still very similar. Especially the way she walked and dressed. This woman was wearing a white blouse and a black skirt with a short slit at the back, framing a pair of long, lovely legs. No jacket and no clunky accessories, which followed Vanessa's personal style to a T.

Shifting his gaze back to the road, he tamped down on whatever emotion had his chest going tight. Guilt? Regret? Simple sentimentality? He wasn't sure and didn't care to examine the unexpected feelings too closely.

They'd been divorced for over a year. Better to put it all behind him and move on, as he was sure Vanessa had done.

Spotting the offices of Blake and Fetzer, he pulled into the diminutive three-car lot at the back of the building, cut the engine and stepped out into the warm spring day. With any luck, this meeting and the subsequent tour of The Sugar Shack would only take a couple of hours, then he could be back on the road and headed home. Small town life might be fine for some people, but Marcus would be only too happy to get back to the hustle and bustle of the city and the life he'd made for himself there.

Vanessa stopped outside Brian Blake's office, taking a moment to straighten her blouse and skirt, run a hand through her short-cropped hair and touch up her lipstick. It had been a long time since she'd gotten this dressed up and she was sorely out of practice.

It didn't help, either, that all of the nicer clothes she'd acquired while being married to Marcus were now at least one size too small. That meant her top was a bit too snug across the chest, her skirt was a good inch shorter than she would have liked and darned if the waistband wasn't cutting off her circulation.

Thankfully, the town of Summerville didn't require her to dress up this much, even for Sunday services. Otherwise, she may have had to invest in a new wardrobe, and given what a hard time she was having just keeping her head above water and her business afloat, that was an added expense she definitely could not afford.

Deciding that her appearance was about as good as it was going to get at this late date, she took a deep breath and pushed through the door. Blake and Fetzer's lone receptionist greeted her with a wide smile, informed her that Brian and the potential investor were waiting in his office, and told her to go right in.

She took another steadying breath and before stepping inside sent a quick prayer heavenward that the wealthy entrepreneur Brian had found to hopefully invest in her fledging enterprise would find The Sugar Shack worthy of his financial backing.

The first thing she saw was Brian sitting behind his desk, smiling as he chatted with the visitor facing away from her in one of the guest chairs. The man had dark hair that barely dusted the collar of his charcoal-gray jacket and was tapping a tan, long-fingered hand on the arm of his chair, as though he was impatient to get down to business.

As soon as Brian spotted her, his smile widened and he rose to his feet. "Vanessa," he greeted her, "you're right on time. Allow me to introduce you to the man I *hope* will become an investor in your wonderful bakery. Marcus Keller, this is Vanessa Mason. Vanessa this is—"

"We've met."

Marcus's voice hit her like a sledgehammer to the solar plexus, but it was only one of a series of rapid-fire shocks to her system. Brian had spoken her ex-husband's name and her stomach had plummeted all the way to her feet. At the same time, Marcus had risen from his seat and turned to face her, and her heart had started to pound against her rib cage like a runaway freight train.

She saw him standing in front of her, black hair glinting midnight blue in the dappled sunlight streaming through the tall, multipaned windows lining one wall of the office, his green eyes gleaming with devilment. Yet his suit-and-tie image wavered and no amount of blinking brought him into focus.

"Hello, Vanessa," he murmured softly.

Brushing his jacket aside, he slipped his hands into the front pockets of his matching charcoal slacks, adopting a negligent pose. He looked so comfortable and amused, while she felt as though an army of ants was crawling beneath her skin.

How in God's name could this have happened? How could she not know that *he* was the potential investor? How could Brian not realize that Marcus was her *ex*-husband?

She wanted to kick herself for not asking more questions or insisting on being given more details about today's meeting. But then, she hadn't really cared who Brian's mystery investor was, had she? She'd cared only that he was rich and seemed willing to partner up with small business owners in the hopes of a big payoff down the road.

She'd convinced herself she was desperate and needed a quick influx of cash to keep The Sugar Shack's doors open. But she would *never* be desperate enough to take charity from the man who had broken her heart and turned his back on her when she'd needed him the most.

Not bothering to address Marcus, she turned her gaze to Brian. "I'm sorry, but this isn't going to work out," she told him, then promptly turned on her heel and marched back out of the office building.

She was down the front steps and halfway up the block before she heard the first call.

"Vanessa! Vanessa, wait!"

The three-inch pumps she'd worn because they went so well with her outfit—and because she'd wanted to make a good impression—pinched her toes as she nearly ran the length of the uneven sidewalk in the direction of The Sugar Shack. All she wanted was to get away from Marcus, away from those glittering eyes and the arrogant tilt of his chin. She didn't care that he was yelling for her, or that she could hear his footsteps keeping pace several yards behind her.

"Vanessa!"

Turning the corner only a short distance from The Sugar Shack, her steps faltered. Her heart lurched and her blood chilled.

Oh, no. She'd been so angry, so eager to get away from her ex-husband and escape back to the safety of the bakery that she'd forgotten that's where Danny was. And if there was anything she needed to protect more than her own sanity, it was her son.

Suddenly, she couldn't take another step, coming to a jerky stop only feet from the bakery door. Marcus rounded the corner a moment later, coming to an equally abrupt halt when he spotted her simply standing there like a panicked and disheveled department store mannequin.

He was slightly out of breath, and she found that more than a little satisfying. It was a nice change from his normal state of being calm, cool and always in control. And nothing less than he deserved, given what he was putting her through now.

"Finally," he muttered, sounding completely put out. "Why did you run?" He wanted to know. "We may be divorced, but that doesn't mean we can't sit and have a civil conversation."

"I have nothing to say to you," she bit out. *And there was nothing she had to say that he wanted to hear.* The cruel declaration replayed through her mind, bringing with it a fresh stab of pain and reminding her of just how important it was to keep him away from her child.

"What about this business of yours?" he asked, running a hand through his thick, dark hair before smoothing his tie and buttoning his suit jacket, once again the epitome of entrepreneurial precision. "It sounds like you could use the capital and I'm always on the lookout for a good investment."

"I don't want your money," she told him.

He inclined his head, acknowledging the sincerity of her words. "But do you need it?"

He asked the question in a low tone, with no hint of condescension and not as though he meant to dangle his wealth over her head like a plump, juicy carrot. Instead, he sounded willing to help her if she needed it.

Oh, she needed help, but not of the strings-attached variety. And not from her cold, unfeeling ex-husband.

Fighting the urge to grab whatever money he was willing to toss her way and run, she straightened her spine, squared her shoulders and reminded herself that she was doing just fine on her own. She didn't need a man—any man—to ride in and rescue her.

"The bakery is doing quite well, thank you," she replied, her voice clipped. "And even if it weren't, I wouldn't need anything from you."

Marc opened his mouth, about to reply and possibly try to change her mind, when Brian Blake rushed around the corner. He skidded to a jerky halt when he saw them, looking frazzled and alarmed. For a second, he stood there, breathing heavily, his gaze darting back and forth between the two of them. Then he shook his head and his puzzlement seemed to clear.

"Mr. Keller...Vanessa..." He took another moment to suck in much-needed oxygen, his Adam's apple riding up and down above the tight collar of his pale blue dress shirt. "This isn't at all how I'd planned for this meeting to go," he told them apologetically. "If you'll just come back to the office.... Let's sit down and see if we can't work something out."

A touch of guilt tugged at Vanessa's chest. Brian was a good guy. He didn't deserve to suffer or be put in the middle of an acrimonious situation just because she despised Marc and refused to have anything more to do with him—let alone go into business with him.

"I'm sorry, Brian," she apologized. "I appreciate everything you've done for me, but this particular partnership just isn't going to work."

For a minute, Brian looked as though he meant to argue. Noting the firm expression on her face, however, he released a sigh of resignation and nodded. "I understand."

"Actually," Marc said, "I'm still very much interested in hearing about the bakery."

Brian's eyes widened with a spark of relief, but Vanessa immediately tensed.

"No, Marcus," she told him, her firm tone brooking no arguments. Not that that had ever stopped him before.

"It sounds like it might be a sound investment, *Nessa,*" he retorted, arching a single dark brow and using his old pet name for her. No doubt to put her off balance. "I drove three hours to get here and I'd prefer not to turn right around and go back empty-handed." He paused for a beat, letting that sink in. Then he added, "At least give me a tour."

No. Oh, no. She definitely couldn't let him into the bakery. That would be even more dangerous than simply having him in town, aware that she lived here now, as well.

She opened her mouth to say so, linking her arms across her chest to let him know she had no intention of changing her mind, when Brian stopped her. Touching her shoulder, he tipped his head, signaling her to follow him a few steps away, out of earshot of Marcus.

"Miss Mason. Vanessa," he said, dropping formalities. "Think about this. Please. I know Mr. Keller is your ex-husband—although I had no idea when I set up today's meeting. I never would have asked him to come here if I had—but if he's willing to invest in The Sugar Shack, as your financial advisor, I have to recommend that you *seriously* consider his offer. You're doing all right at the moment. The bakery is holding its own. But you'll never be able to move forward with your plans to expand without added capital from an outside source, and if worse comes to worst, one bad season could cause you to lose the business entirely."

Even though Vanessa didn't want to listen, didn't want to believe Brian was right, she knew deep down that he was. The Sugar Shack might be her livelihood, but smart financial planning was his. She wouldn't have begun working with him in the first place if she didn't think he knew what he was doing.

Casting a glance over her shoulder to be sure Marc couldn't overhear their conversation, she turned back and whispered, "There's more at stake here than just the bakery, Brian." So much more. "I'll let him look around. Let the two of you talk. But no matter what kind of plan you two come up with, no matter what offer he might make, I can't promise I'll be willing to accept. I'm sorry."

He looked none too pleased with her assertion, but he nodded, accepting that she would only be pushed so far where Marcus Keller was concerned.

Returning to Marc, Brian informed him of her decision and they started forward again, toward the main entrance of the bakery. The heavenly scents of freshly baked bread, pies and other pastries filled the air the closer they got. As always, those smells caused Vanessa's stomach to rumble and her mouth to water, making her hungry for a piping-hot cinnamon roll or a plate of chocolate chip cookies. Which probably explained why she hadn't quite managed to shed all of her baby weight yet.

At the front door, she stopped abruptly, turning to face the two men. "Wait here," she told them. "I have to warn Aunt Helen that you're in town and explain what's going on. She never particularly liked you," she added, aiming her comment directly at Marc, "so don't be surprised if she refuses to come out while you're here."

He shot her a sardonic grin. "I'll be sure to keep my horns and tail hidden if I run into her."

Vanessa didn't bother responding to that. She was too afraid of what kind of retort might spill from her mouth. Instead, she spun and pushed her way into the bakery.

Keeping a smile on her face and cheerily greeting customers who were sipping cups of coffee, tea or cocoa, and enjoying some of her and her aunt's most popular baked goods, she hurried to the kitchen.

As usual, Helen was bustling around doing this and that. She might have been in her seventies, but she had the energy of a twenty-year-old. Up at the crack of dawn each morning, she always went to work immediately, gathering ingredients, mixing, rolling, cutting, scooping…and managing to keep track of whatever was in the ovens, even three or four different items all set at different temperatures for various amounts of time.

Vanessa was a fairly accomplished baker herself, but readily admitted it took some doing to keep up with her aunt. Add to that the fact that Helen helped her man the counter *and* take care of Danny, and Vanessa literally did not know what she would do without her.

The squeak of the swinging double doors cutting off the kitchen area from the front of the store alerted Helen to her arrival.

"You're back," her aunt said without bothering to look up from the sugar cookies she was dusting with brightly colored sprinkles.

"Yes, but we have a problem," Vanessa told her.

At that, Helen raised her head. "You didn't get the money?" she asked, disappointment lacing her tone.

Vanessa shook her head. "Worse. The investor Brian has me meeting with is Marc."

The container of sprinkles fell from Helen's hand, hitting the metal cookie sheet and spilling everywhere. Not a disaster, just a few cookies that would turn out sloppier than usual. And whatever didn't look appropriate for sale could always go on a plate as an after-dinner treat for themselves.

"You're kidding," her aunt breathed in a shocked voice.

Vanessa shook her head and crossed to where Helen stood rooted to the spot like a statue. "Unfortunately, I'm not. He's outside right now, waiting for a tour of the bakery, so I need you to take Danny upstairs and stay there until I give you the all clear."

Her fingers moved at the speed of light as she undid the knot at Helen's waist, slipping the flour-dusted apron over her head and tossing it aside. Her aunt immediately reached up to pat her stack of puffy, blue-washed curls.

Rushing across the room, Vanessa paused to stare down at her adorable baby boy, who was lying on his back in a small bassinet, doing his best to get his pudgy little toes into his perfect pink mouth. As soon as he saw her, he smiled wide and began to gurgle happily, sending a stab of love so deep through Vanessa's soul, it stole her breath.

Lifting him up and onto her shoulder, she wished she had the time to tickle and tease and coo with him. She loved running the bakery, and was very proud of what she and Aunt Helen had managed to build together, but Danny was her pride and joy. Her favorite moments of the day were those she got to spend alone with him, feeding him, bathing him, making him laugh.

Pressing a kiss to the side of his head, she whispered, "Later, sweetheart, I promise." Just as soon as she could get rid of Marc and Brian.

Turning to her aunt, who had come up behind them, she handed the baby off.

"Hurry," she said. "And keep him as quiet as you can. If he starts to cry, turn on the TV or the radio or something to try to cover it up. I'll get rid of them as quickly as I can."

"All right," Helen readily agreed, "but keep an eye on the ovens. The pinwheel cookies only need another five minutes. The baklava and lemon streusel cake will be a while longer. I set the timers."

Vanessa nodded her understanding, then with Helen bustling off to hide Danny in the small apartment they kept over the bakery, she pushed the now-empty bassinet across the kitchen and into a back storage room. Grabbing an extra white tablecloth with blue and yellow eyelet lace trim, she used it to cover the large piece of telling furniture.

Leaving the storage room, her gaze darted left to right and up and down, searching for any remaining signs of Danny's presence. A few stray items, she might be able to explain…

A rattle? *Oh, a customer must have left it—I'll have to put it in the Lost and Found.*

A handful of diapers? *I keep those on hand for when I watch a friend's baby.* Yes, that sounded plausible.

A half-full bottle in the fridge or a prescription of ear drops in Danny Keller's name from a recent infection? Those might be a little tougher to justify.

She used a clean towel to brush away some of the worst of the spilled sprinkles and grabbed the pinwheels from the oven to keep them from burning, but otherwise left the kitchen as it had been when she'd walked in. Then she pushed back through the double swinging doors into the front of the bakery…and ran smack into a waiting Marcus.

Two

Marc's arms came up to seize Vanessa as she flew through the double doors from the kitchen and hit him square in the chest. The impact wasn't hard enough to hurt, although it did catch him slightly off guard. Then, once he had his hands on her, her body pressed full-length along his own, he didn't want to let go.

It had been a long time since he'd held this woman. Too long, if the blood pounding in his veins and the heat suffusing his groin were any indication.

She was softer than he remembered, more well-rounded in all the right places. But she still smelled of strawberries and cream from her favorite brand of shampoo. And even though she'd cut her hair to shoulder-length, she still had the same wavy copper locks that he knew from experience would be soft as silk against his fingertips.

He nearly reached up to find out for sure, his gaze locked on her sapphire blue eyes, when she pulled away. He let her go, but immediately missed her warmth.

"I told you to wait outside," she pointed out, licking her glossed lips and running a hand down the front of her snug white blouse. The material pulled taut across her chest, framing her full breasts nicely.

He probably shouldn't be noticing that sort of thing about his ex-wife. But then, he was divorced, not dead.

In response to her chastisement, he shrugged a shoulder. Her annoyance amused him all to hell.

"You were taking too long. And besides, this is a public establishment. The sign in the window says Open. If it upsets you that much, consider me a customer." Reaching into his pocket, he retrieved his money clip and peeled off a couple of small bills. "Give me a cup of black coffee and something sweet. You choose."

Her eyes narrowed and she skewered him with a look of pure disdain. "I told you I don't want your money. Not even that," she added, her gaze flickering to the paltry amount he was holding out to her.

"Have it your way," he told her, sliding the bills back under the gold clip and the entire bundle back into his front trouser pocket. "So why don't you start the tour. Give me an idea of what you do here, how you got started and what your financials look like."

Vanessa blew out a breath, fluttering the thin fringe of her bangs and seeming to come to terms with the fact that she wasn't getting rid of him anytime soon.

"Where's Brian?" she asked, glancing past his shoulder and searching the front of the bakery for her financial advisor.

"I sent him back to his office," Marc answered. "Since he's already familiar with your business, I didn't think it was necessary for him to be here for the tour. I told him I would stop in or call after we've finished."

Tiny lines appeared above Vanessa's nose as she frowned, bringing her attention back to him, though he noticed she wouldn't quite meet his gaze.

"What's the matter?" he teased. "Afraid to be alone with me, Nessa?"

Her frown morphed into a full-fledged scowl, drawing her brows even more tightly together.

"Of course not," she snapped, crossing her arms over her chest, which only managed to lift her generous breasts and press them more snugly against the fabric of her blouse. "But don't get your hopes up, because we *aren't* going to be alone. Ever."

As hard as he tried, Marc couldn't stop an amused grin from lifting his lips. He'd forgotten just what a fiery temper his little wife had, but damned if he hadn't missed it.

If he had anything to say about it, they very well *would* be alone together at some point in the very near future, but he didn't bother saying as much since he didn't want to send her into a full-blown implosion in front of her customers.

"So where do you want to start?" she asked, apparently resigned to his presence and his insistence on getting a look at her bakery as a possible investment opportunity.

"Wherever you like," he acquiesced with a small nod.

It didn't take long for her to show him around the front of the bakery, given its size. But she explained how many customers they could serve in-shop and how much take-out business they did on a daily basis. And when he asked about the items in the display cases, she described every one.

Despite her discomfort at being around him again, he'd never seen her so passionate. While they'd been married, she'd been passionate with him, certainly. The sparks they'd created together had made Fourth of July fireworks look like the flare of a wooden matchstick in comparison.

But outside of the bedroom, she'd been much more subdued, spending her time at the country club with his mother or working on various charitable committees— also with his mother.

When they met, Vanessa had been in college, not yet decided on a major and he freely admitted that he'd been the driving force behind her *not* graduating with the rest of her class. He'd wanted her too much, been too eager to slip his ring on her finger and make her his—body and soul.

But he'd always expected her to go back to school, and would have supported her a thousand percent, whatever she wanted to do with her life. Somehow, though, she'd gotten distracted and fallen into simply being his wife. A Keller woman whose main purpose was to look good on his arm, add reverence and prestige to the family name, and help raise money for worthy causes.

He wondered now, though, if that's what *she'd* wanted. Or if she'd maybe wanted more than to be simply Mrs. Marcus Keller.

Because while he knew she was proud of the fundraising work she'd done while they were married, she'd never talked about it with this level of enthusiasm in her voice or this much animation to her beautiful features.

He also wondered how well he'd really known his own wife, considering that—with the exception of a few romantic, candlelit meals she'd prepared for him while they were dating—he hadn't even realized she liked to cook or was a world-class baker. But after sampling some of her creations, he decided that if a successful business could stand on its product alone, she may just be sitting on a gold mine.

Finishing the last bite of the banana nut muffin she'd offered, he actually licked his fingers clean, wanting to savor every crumb.

"Delicious," he told her. "So why didn't you ever bake like this while we were married?"

He didn't know if it was his tone—which he'd thought was pleasant enough; he certainly hadn't meant for it to sound accusatory—or the question itself that got her dander up, but she immediately stiffened and took a step away from him, the brief pleasure he'd noted on her face fading away.

"I don't think your mother would have appreciated me messing up her pristine kitchen or getting in Cook's way," she replied tersely. "It might have been the Keller *family* estate, but she runs the place like a monarchy."

No doubt she was right. Eleanor Keller was rather stuck in her ways. Raised in the lap of luxury and used to servants bustling around her, ready to do her bidding, she wouldn't have looked kindly upon her own daughter-in-law doing something as lowly or mundane as preparing a meal or baking desserts, regardless of how talented she might be in that respect.

"You should have done it, anyway," Marc told her.

For a minute, Vanessa didn't reply, though her mouth tightened into a flat line. Then she murmured, "Maybe I should have," before spinning on her heel and leading him away from the counter and display cases.

She pushed through a set of swinging doors painted yellow with The Sugar Shack emblazoned on them in a playful white font and led him into the kitchen. Along with a wave of heat wafting from the industrial ovens lining one wall, the smell of baking was even stronger here, making him hope Vanessa might offer to let him sample a few more items as part of his tour.

While explaining the setup of the kitchen and how she and her aunt shared both baking and front counter duties, she moved around checking timers. Slipping a thick oven mitt on one hand, she began removing cookie sheets and pie pans, setting them on a wide metal island at the center of the room.

"A lot of the recipes are from Aunt Helen's personal collection," she confided, using a nearby spatula to transfer cookies from sheet to cooling rack. "She's always loved to bake, but had never considered opening her own shop. I couldn't believe she wasn't earning a living with her talents, since everything she makes tastes like heaven. I'm pretty good in the kitchen myself—I must get it from her—" she added with a lopsided grin "—and I guess after a bit, the two of us decided to make a go of it together."

Marc rested his hands on the edge of the island, watching her work. Her movements were smooth and graceful, but also quick and efficient, as though she'd done this a million times before and could do it with her eyes closed, if necessary.

He definitely didn't want to close his eyes, though. He was enjoying the view, struck once again by how much he'd missed being near Vanessa.

The divorce had been so cut and dry, finished almost before he knew what was happening. One minute he'd been married to a beautiful woman he'd adored, thinking everything was fine. The next, she'd announced that she couldn't "live this way anymore" and wanted a divorce. Within a few short months, the papers had been signed and she'd been gone.

Looking back, he admitted that he probably should have fought harder to make their marriage work. At the very least, he should have asked why she was leaving him, what it was she needed that he wasn't giving her.

At the time, however, he'd been busy with the company and the demands of his family and let his pride take the position that he didn't want to be married to any woman who didn't want to be married to him. A part of him, he understood now, had also thought Vanessa was just being dramatic. That she was threatening him with divorce because he hadn't been as attentive to her as she might have wanted, or that once she saw that he wasn't going to put up a fight, she would change her mind and recognize how good she had it.

But that hadn't happened. She hadn't changed her mind and by the time he'd realized she wasn't going to, it had been too late.

"Blake showed me some of your financials," he said, wondering if she'd rap his knuckles with her spatula if he tried to snitch one of the mouthwatering, fresh-from-the-oven cookies. "It looks as though you're doing fairly well."

Without bothering to glance in his direction, she nodded. "We're doing okay. Could be better. We've got a lot of overhead, and the rent for this building wipes us out most months, but we're holding our own."

"Then why are you looking for an investor?"

Finishing up what she was doing, she set aside her spatula and oven mitt, and turned to face him more directly. He noticed, too, that she straightened slightly, shoulders pulling back as though she expected a confrontation.

"I have an idea for expansion," she said slowly, obviously weighing her words carefully. "It's a good idea. I think it will go over well. But it's going to require a bit of construction and more start-up cash than we've got at our disposal."

"So what's the idea?" he wanted to know.

She licked her lips and Marc watched the delicate tendons of her throat convulse as she swallowed before answering. "Mail order. I want to start with a Cookie-of-the-Month Club subscription service that could one day be turned into a catalog business for all of our products."

Judging by the quality of the items he'd tasted so far, he thought it sounded like a damn good prospect. He would certainly consider buying a year's worth of baked goods as quick and easy holiday gifts for numerous family members and business associates. And maybe even one for himself, because he would certainly enjoy a box of The Sugar Shack's cookies showing up on his doorstep once a month.

Not that he told Vanessa as much. Until he decided for sure whether or not he was going to invest in her and her aunt's little bakery, it was better to keep his thoughts to himself.

"Show me where the construction would take place," he said instead. "I take it you have some back storage area that you could convert, or are maybe thinking of renting the empty building next door?"

She nodded. "The space next door."

Double-checking the rest of the timers and contents of the ovens, she made her way out of the kitchen, trusting Marc to follow. They passed a narrow stairwell outside of the kitchen but tucked away from the front of the shop so that it was nearly invisible to anyone who didn't know it was there.

"Where does that lead?" he asked, inclining his head.

If he wasn't mistaken, he thought Vanessa's eyes went wide and some of the color drained from her face.

"Nowhere," she said quickly. Then, apparently realizing that he would know *something* was at the top of those stairs, she added, "It's just a small apartment. We use it for storage, and as a place for Aunt Helen to nap throughout the day. She wears out easily."

Marc raised a brow. Unless she'd aged exponentially in the year or two since he'd last seen Vanessa's aunt, he found that hard to believe. The woman might be pushing eighty, but there wasn't a bone in her body that could be labeled *old,* and for as long as he'd known her, she'd had the disposition of a hummingbird. But he let it go, deciding that if the building's second story didn't have anything to do with the bakery or his possible investment, then there was nothing up there he needed to know about.

Instead, he allowed her to lead him back through the front of the bakery and outside to the space for rent next door. Though it was locked and they were unable to enter, he could see clearly through the plate glass windows that it was half the size of The Sugar Shack, but completely empty, which meant that there would be very little remodeling necessary to turn it into anything Vanessa wanted. And if his vision of the mail order aspect of the business matched hers, he imagined it wouldn't take much more than a few computers, several packing stations, and a direct and open path connecting it to The Sugar Shack for easy access.

While he continued to peer inside, studying the structure of the connected, unrented area, Vanessa stepped back, standing in the middle of the sidewalk.

"What do you think?" she asked.

He turned to find the afternoon sun glinting off her hair, making it shine like a new penny. A flash of desire hit him square in the chest, nearly knocking him back a pace. His throat clogged and he felt himself growing hard despite the knowledge that he had no right to be attracted to her any longer.

But then, who was he kidding? They might not be married anymore, but he had a feeling it would take a lot more than a signed divorce decree to keep his body from responding to his ex-wife's presence. Something along the lines of slipping into a coma or having a full frontal lobotomy.

Tamping down on the urge to step forward and run his fingers through her mass of copper curls—or do something equally stupid, like kiss her until her knees went weak—he said, "I think you've done very well for yourself." Without him, he was sorry to acknowledge.

She looked only moderately surprised by the compliment. "Thank you."

"I'm going to need some time to look at the books and discuss things with Brian, but if you're not still completely set against working with me, there's a good chance I'd be interested in investing."

If he'd expected squeals of joy or for her to throw herself into his arms in a display of unabashed appreciation, he was doomed to disappointment. She nodded sagely, but otherwise didn't respond.

And he didn't have a reason to stick around any longer.

"Well," he murmured, stabbing his hands into his pockets and rocking back slightly on his heels, "I guess that about does it. Thank you for the tour—and the samples."

Damn, he felt like a teenager out on his first date, and the polite smile she offered only made matters worse.

"I'll be in touch," he told her after a moment of awkward silence.

Tucking a strand of hair behind one ear, Vanessa tipped her head, but said, "I'd prefer you have Brian call me, if you don't mind."

He did mind and a muscle in his jaw ticked as he ground his teeth together to keep from saying so. As much as it annoyed him, though, he understood her reluctance to be in contact with him again. He suspected that even if he offered to sink a boatload of money into Vanessa's enterprise, she might refuse just on principle. A ridiculous principle that would only cause her to end up shooting herself in the foot, but principle all the same.

Vanessa remained on the sidewalk outside The Sugar Shack, watching as Marc walked away, back toward the offices of Blake and Fetzer. Not until he was well out of sight, and she felt sure he wasn't going to turn around and come back, did she let herself release a pent-up breath.

Then, as soon as the pressure in her chest eased and her heart was beating normally again, she spun around and returned to the bakery, heading straight for the stairs that led to the second floor apartment. Halfway up, she heard some of her aunt's favorite 1940s big band music playing, and beneath that, the sound of Danny fussing. Taking the last several steps two at a time, she hurried in and found her aunt pacing back and forth across the floor, bouncing and hushing and doing everything she could think of to calm the red-faced child in her arms.

"Poor baby," Vanessa said, reaching for Danny.

"Oh, thank goodness." Helen sighed in relief, more than happy to hand over her squalling charge. "I was just about to give him a bottle, but I know how much you prefer to feed him yourself."

"That's all right, I've got him now," Vanessa told her, continuing to bounce Danny up and down as she moved to the ugly, beige second-hand sofa along the far wall, unbuttoning her blouse as she went. "Thank you so much."

"How did things go? Is Marcus gone now?" Her aunt wanted to know.

"Yes, he's gone."

When the words came out more mumbled than intended, she realized it was because she wasn't entirely pleased with that fact. She might have thought Marc was out of her life for good, and may have been desperate to keep him away once he'd shown up in Summerville unexpectedly, but she realized now that seeing him again hadn't been entirely unpleasant.

One glance from those moss-green eyes and her body went soft and pliant. Her blood turned the consistency of warm honey, her brain functioning about as well as too-flat meringue.

Spending a short amount of time with him while she'd shown him around the bakery had been…not horrible. If it hadn't been for the secret she was hiding just one floor above, she may even have gotten him that cup of coffee and invited him to stay a while longer.

Which was a really bad idea, so it was better that he'd taken off when he had.

She had Danny pressed to her chest, content now that his belly was being filled, when she heard footsteps coming up the stairs. Considering that everyone who knew about the second floor apartment—namely she and Aunt Helen—was already up there, she suspected she was about to get a very rude surprise.

There was no time to jump up and hide the baby, no time to yell for Aunt Helen to run interference. One minute she was glancing around for a blanket to cover her exposed chest, and the next she was frozen in place, staring with alarm at her stunned but furious ex-husband.

Three

Marc honestly didn't know whether to be stunned or furious. Perhaps a mix of both. He wondered if the *whooshing* sound in his ears and the tiny pinpricks of white marring his vision would ever go away.

It wasn't hard to figure out what was going on.

First, Vanessa had lied to him. The space above the bakery wasn't used primarily for storage and as a place for her octogenarian aunt to nap when she started to feel run-down. It was actually a fully furnished and operable apartment, complete with a table and chairs, a sofa, a television…a crib in one corner and a yellow duckie blanket covered with baby toys in the middle of the floor.

Second, Vanessa had a child. She wasn't sitting for a friend; hadn't adopted an infant after their separation just for the thrill of it or to exert her independence. Even if she hadn't been *breast-feeding* the baby in her arms when he'd walked in the room, the protective flare in her eyes and the alarm written all over her face told him everything he needed to know about her connection to the child.

Third and finally, that baby was *his*. He knew it as well as he knew his own name. Felt it, deep down in his bones. Vanessa would never have been so determined to keep him from discovering she was a mother if that weren't the case—if she didn't believe she had something momentous to hide.

Not only that, but he hadn't become the CEO of his family's very successful textile company by being stupid. He could do the math. The only way Vanessa could have such a young infant was if she'd either been pregnant before their divorce had become final or if she'd been cheating on him with another man. And despite the differences that had pushed them apart, infidelity had never been one of them—not by him and not by her.

"Want to tell me what's going on here?" he asked, slipping his hands into the front pockets of his slacks.

It was safer that way. Burying his hands—now curled into tight, angry fists—in his pockets kept him from reaching out to strangle someone. Namely her.

And though his words might have been delivered in the form of a calm, unruffled question, the sharp chill of his tone let her know it was a demand. He wasn't going anywhere until he had answers. All of them.

Out of the corner of his eye, he saw a blur of blue-topped motion as Aunt Helen bustled forward and tossed a blanket over Vanessa's half exposed chest and the baby's head. Marc didn't know which was more disappointing—losing sight of his ex-wife's creamy flesh...or of the child he hadn't known existed until thirty seconds ago.

"I'll be downstairs," Helen murmured to her niece before turning a critical glare on him as she passed. "Yell if you need me."

What Aunt Helen had to be annoyed about, Marc couldn't fathom. *He* was the victim here. The one who had never been told he was a father, who'd had his child kept from him for so long. He didn't know how old the baby was, exactly, but given the amount of time they'd been divorced and the nine months of her pregnancy, his guess would be about four to six months.

Vanessa and her wily Aunt Helen were the bad guys in this situation. Lying to him. Hiding pertinent facts from him for the past year.

After glancing over his shoulder to be sure they were finally alone, he took another menacing step forward.

"Well?" he prompted.

At first she didn't respond, buying some time by re-arranging the lightweight afghan so that it covered her exposed flesh, but not the baby's face. Then with a sigh, she raised her head and met his gaze.

"What do you want me to say?" she asked softly.

Her seeming indifference had his molars grinding together and his fingers curling even tighter, until he thought his knuckles would pop through the skin.

"An explanation might be nice." *Followed by a few hours of abject groveling,* he thought with no small amount of sarcasm, while outwardly he struggled not to let his true level of annoyance show.

"I didn't realize it at the time, but I was pregnant before the divorce became final. We weren't exactly on speaking terms then, so I couldn't find a way to tell you, and to be honest, I didn't think you'd care."

Fury bubbled inside his chest. "Not care about my own child?" he growled. "Not care that I was going to be a father?"

What kind of man did she think he was? And if she could believe he was the sort of man who wouldn't care about his own flesh and blood, why had she bothered to marry him in the first place?

"How do you know it's your baby?" she asked in a low voice.

Marc laughed. A sharp, humorless bark of sound at the sheer ridiculousness of that question.

"Nice try, Vanessa, but I know you too well for that. You wouldn't have broken your vows to have some sleazy, sordid affair. And if you'd met someone you were interested in while we were still married…"

He trailed off, a sudden thought occurring to him that hadn't before. "Is that why you asked for a divorce? Because you met someone else?"

It would be just like her. She would never have cheated on him, never been physically unfaithful. But emotional infidelity was another matter, and toward the end, he had to admit that they hadn't been as close or connected as at the beginning of their relationship.

With his brother as second-in-command, he'd taken over the Keller Corporation and started spending longer and longer hours in the office or traveling for business. Vanessa had complained about feeling lonely and being treated like an outsider in her own home—which was something he could understand, given his mother's less-than-warm nature and the fact that she'd never really cared for the woman he'd married. Hadn't she made that clear from the moment he'd first brought Vanessa home for a visit and announced their engagement?

But even though he'd *heard* Vanessa's complaints, he knew now that he hadn't *listened*. He'd shrugged off her unhappiness, thinking perhaps she was turning into a bit of a bored trophy wife. He'd let himself be consumed by work and told himself it was just a phase—that she'd get over it. He even thought he remembered suggesting she find a hobby to keep her busy in hopes that it would distract her and keep her off his back.

No wonder she'd left him, he mentally scoffed now. *He'd* have left him after being dismissed like that.

By her own husband. The man who was suppose to love, honor and cherish her more than anyone else on the planet. Boy, he'd really messed up on that one, hadn't he?

As always, hindsight was twenty-twenty…and made him want to kick his own ass.

Which meant that if Vanessa *had* met another man, Marc couldn't really blame her for leaving him in hopes of moving into a situation that made her happier than the one she'd been in with him.

The thought of another man touching her, being with her—especially with his baby growing inside her belly—made his vision go red around the edges and his mind fill with images of tearing the aforementioned male who'd dared to touch his woman limb from limb. But he couldn't *blame* her, not when so much of what had gone wrong between them was his own fault.

"Is it?" he asked again, suddenly needing to know. Though he wasn't sure what difference it would make now.

"No," she answered quietly. "There was no one else. Not for me, anyway."

He raised a brow. "What does that mean? That you think *I* was being unfaithful?"

"I don't know, Marc. Were you? It would certainly explain all those extra hours you were supposedly spending at work."

"I had just taken over the company, Vanessa. A lot of things required my attention, practically around the clock."

"And I wasn't one of them, apparently," she muttered, bitterness clear in her tone.

Marc rubbed a spot between his eyes where a headache was brewing. He'd heard that level of frustration and discontent in her voice before, so many times. The same as he'd heard her complain that he wasn't spending enough time with her.

But what choice did he have? And why couldn't she have cut him some slack? The twenty-four-hour workdays hadn't lasted forever. Nowadays, if he was at the office past five, it was usually because he didn't want to go home. Why bother, when there was nothing much there for him to enjoy other than a soft bed and a giant plasma television?

"This again?" he ground out. "Do we really have to get into this *again?*"

"No," she replied quickly. "That's the nice thing about being divorced—we really don't."

"So that's why you didn't tell me you were pregnant?" he demanded. "Because I wasn't paying enough attention to you before the divorce?"

A furrow appeared in her brow. At her breast, the baby continued to suckle, though he could only hear the sounds, not see the child's mouth actually at work.

"Don't be obtuse," she snapped. "I wouldn't keep something like that from you just because I was pouting or angry with you. If you'll recall, we didn't exactly part on the best terms, and *you* were the one who refused to speak to *me.* That sort of thing makes it difficult to have a personal heart-to-heart."

"You should have tried harder."

Blue eyes flashing, she said, "I could say the same about you."

Marc sighed, rocking back on his heels. It was nice to know that even after a year apart, they could jump right back to where they'd left off.

No growth or progress whatsoever, and to make matters worse, there was a whole new wrench thrown into the works. One with his blood running through its veins. One that he should have been told about from the very beginning.

But arguing with her about it or getting red in the face with fury over having his child kept from him for so long wasn't going to get him anywhere. Not with Vanessa. She would simply argue right back at him and they would end up exactly where they were—in a stalemate.

Striving instead for calm and diplomacy, he said, "I guess that's something we're going to have to agree to disagree about." For now. "But I deserve a few answers, don't you think?"

He could see her mulling that over, trying to decide how much pride or privacy it would cost her to share the details of the last year of her life…and fess up to something he suspected even she knew had been wrong—namely keeping his child from him.

"Fine," she relented after a moment, though she sounded none too pleased with the prospect.

While he weighed his options and tried to decide where to start, she shifted the baby in her arms and quickly rearranged her clothing beneath the veil of the knitted throw to make sure she was completely covered.

The child, Marc noticed, was sound asleep. Eyes closed, tiny pink mouth slack with sleep. And suddenly he knew exactly what he needed to know most of all.

"Is it a boy or a girl?" he asked, his throat clogging

with emotion, making the words come out scratchy and thick.

"A boy. His name is Danny."

Danny. Daniel.

His son.

His chest grew tight, cutting off the oxygen to his lungs, and he was glad when Vanessa rose from the sofa, then turned to toss the afghan over the back so she wouldn't see the sudden dampness filling his eyes.

He was a father, he thought, blinking and doing his best to surreptitiously suck in sharp, quick breaths of air in an attempt to regain his equilibrium.

When he and Vanessa had first gotten married, they'd discussed having children. He'd expected it to happen before long, been ready for it. When it hadn't in the first year, or the second, the idea had drifted further and further to the back of his mind.

And that had been okay. He'd been disappointed, he supposed, but so had she. But they'd still been happy together, still optimistic about the future, and cognizant of the fact that they hadn't even begun to explore all of their options yet. If getting pregnant the fun, old-fashioned way hadn't worked out, he was sure they'd have discussed adoption or in vitro or even fostering.

But as it turned out, they hadn't needed any of that, had they? No, she'd been pregnant when they'd signed the divorce papers.

"When did you find out?" he asked, following her movements as she trailed slowly across the room. The baby—Danny, his son—was propped upright against her shoulder now and she was slowly patting his back, bouncing slightly.

"A month or so after the divorce was final."

"That's why you moved away," he said quietly. "I expected you to stick around Pittsburgh after we split. Then I heard you'd left town, but I never knew where you'd gone." Not that he'd intentionally tried to check up on her, but he'd kept his ear to the ground and—admittedly—welcomed any news he managed to pick up through the grapevine.

She shrugged one slim shoulder. "I had to do something. There was nothing left for me in Pittsburgh and I was soon going to have a child to support."

"You could have come to me," he told her, just barely able to keep the anger and disappointment from seeping into his voice. "I would have taken care of you *and* my child—and you know it."

She stared at him for a moment, but her face was passive, her eyes blank, and he couldn't read her expression.

"I didn't want you to take care of us. Not out of pity or responsibility. We were divorced. We'd already said everything we had to say and gone our separate ways. I wasn't going to put us both back in a position we didn't want to be in just because our reproductive timing was lousy."

"So you came here."

She nodded. "Aunt Helen had only been living here a couple of years herself. She moved in with her sister when Aunt Clara became ill. After she died, Helen claimed the house was too large for one person and she could use the company. Unfortunately, she's never met a problem that couldn't be solved—or at least alleviated—with food, so she baked and I ate. Then one day, I got the brilliant idea that we should open a bakery together. Her recipes are amazing, and I've always been pretty handy in the kitchen myself."

"Good for you," Marc said.

And he meant it. It hurt to realize that he'd never known she had such amazing cooking or baking abilities, or that she'd preferred to move away and live with her aunt in Mayberry R.F.D. over coming to him when she'd discovered her pregnancy.

He certainly had the means to care for her and their son. Even if reconciliation hadn't been an option, he could have set her up in a small house or apartment, somewhere he could visit easily and spend as much time with his child as possible.

He could have provided for her, provided for his child, in ways she could never dream of simply by running a single bakery—no matter how popular—in such a rural area.

But then, Vanessa knew that, didn't she? She was well aware of his and his family's financial situation. While they'd been married, if she'd asked him to buy her a private island paradise, he could have done so as easily as most people bought a pack of gum.

Which was probably why she'd chosen to move away and find a way to support herself. From the moment they'd met, his money hadn't impressed her. Oh, she'd enjoyed their two week honeymoon in the Greek isles, but she'd never wanted him to give her silly, expensive things just for the sake of it. She'd never wanted priceless jewels or a private jet, or even her own platinum card for unlimited shopping sprees.

When they'd first been married, she hadn't even wanted to move into his family home, despite the fact that his brother and his brother's family resided there and the estate was large enough to house a dozen families comfortably. Possibly without any of them coming into contact with the others for weeks at a time.

Keller Manor boasted a mansion the size of six football fields with separate *wings,* for heaven's sake, as well as three isolated cottages on its surrounding two hundred acres. But Vanessa had wanted to find an apartment of their own in town, then maybe later buy a house for just the two of them and any children that came along.

Marc wondered now if he shouldn't have gone along with her on that idea. At the time, staying at the mansion had been easy, convenient. He'd thought it would be the fastest way for Vanessa to bond with his family and start feeling like a true Keller.

Now, however… Well, considering how well that *hadn't* turned out, he was beginning to think he'd made a lot of wrong decisions while they were together.

After patting the baby on the back for a good five minutes—burping him, Marc assumed—Vanessa moved to a navy blue playpen and started to lean over, presumably to lay Danny down for the rest of his nap.

"Wait," he said, reaching out a hand and taking a step forward before halting in his tracks. What was he doing? Why had he stopped her?

Because he wasn't yet ready to lose sight of his son. Or to be distracted from the reality that he was suddenly a father. A *father.* A fact that part of him still couldn't seem to comprehend.

"Can I hold him?" he asked.

She looked down at the child sleeping in her arms, indecision clear on her face.

"If it won't wake him," he added as an afterthought.

Lifting her head, Vanessa met his gaze. It wasn't fear of waking the baby that caused her hesitation, he realized—it was her fear of having him near their son, of sharing a child who had been hers alone up until now. Not to mention a secret she'd had no intention of sharing anytime soon, but that had been unexpectedly revealed all the same.

Finally, with a sigh, she seemed to reach a decision. Or perhaps come to her senses, since they both knew there was no way he'd be kept from his child now that he was aware of Danny's existence. No way in hell.

"Of course," she said, the words sounding much more agreeable than she felt, he was sure. Meeting him halfway, she carefully transferred the child from her arms to his.

The last child Marc had held who was this size, this age, had to have been his three-year-old niece. But as adorable as his brother's children were, as much as he loved them, it didn't hold a candle to how he felt now, cradling *his own* child to his chest.

He was so tiny, so beautiful, so amazingly peaceful in sleep. Marc soaked in every minuscule feature, from the light dusting of brown hair covering Danny's head to his satin-soft cheeks, to the tiny fingers he curled and uncurled just beneath his chin.

Marc tried to imagine how Danny had looked as soon as he'd been born…his first day home from the hospital…how Vanessa had looked all rounded and glowing in pregnancy. Tried and failed, because he hadn't been there, hadn't known.

A furrow of irritation drew his brows together and he knew he couldn't leave Summerville without his son, without spending more time with him and hearing every detail of the months that he'd missed of this child's life.

Drawing his attention back to Vanessa, he said, "It

looks like we've got a bit of a problem here. I've been left out of the loop and have some catching up to do. So I'm going to give you two choices."

Before she could interrupt, he pressed on. "You and Danny can either pack a bag and come back to Pittsburgh with me, or you can give me an excuse to stick around here. But either way, I *will* be staying with my son."

Four

Vanessa wanted nothing more than to snatch Danny away from Marc and go running. Find a place to hide herself and her baby until he lost interest and went back from whence he came.

She knew her ex-husband better than that, though, didn't she? He would be more inclined to give up breathing or walking upright than he would to walk away from his child.

There was nowhere she could go, nowhere she could hide that he wouldn't find her. So she might as well save herself the time and trouble and just face the music. She'd composed the symphony, after all.

She'd also been prepared to tell him about her pregnancy as soon as she'd discovered it for herself. Just because things hadn't worked out quite the way she'd planned didn't mean she should disregard her moral values now.

But that didn't mean she was ready to pack up and follow him back to Pittsburgh like a lost puppy. She had a life here. Family, friends, a business to run.

On the other hand, the thought of Marc staying in Summerville made her heart palpitate and brought her as close to suffering a panic attack as she'd ever felt.

How could she possibly handle having him underfoot—at the bakery and maybe even living with them at Aunt Helen's house?

She was trapped between the proverbial rock and a hard place, both of which looked suspiciously like her ex-husband. Stubborn, stoic, amazingly handsome in a suit and tie.

"I can't go back to Pittsburgh," she blurted out, pretending the sight of Marc holding their infant son in his big, strong arms didn't tug at parts of her that had no business being tugged.

"Fine," he said with a nod, his face resolute and jaw firm. "Then I guess I'm relocating."

Oh, no, that was worse. Wasn't it? Rock, hard place… rock, hard place. Her chest was so tight with panic, she was beginning to see stars from lack of oxygen.

"You can't stay here forever," she told him. "What about the company? Your family?" My sanity?

"It won't be forever," he responded.

Looking more reluctant than she'd ever seen him, he handed Danny back to her, careful not to wake him. Then he reached into his jacket pocket and removed a slim black cell phone.

"But if you think that anything back home—with the company or my family—is more important than being here with my son right now, you're crazy. I can afford to take a few weeks away, I just have to make sure everyone knows where I am and can keep things running smoothly in my absence."

With that, he turned and headed for the stairs leading back down to the bakery, dialing as he went.

Rocking back and forth, Vanessa stared down at her sleeping son and felt tears prickle behind her eyes.

"Oh, baby," she whispered, pressing a kiss to his smooth forehead. "We're in so much trouble."

For Vanessa, having Marc "move" to Summerville felt very much like when she'd first met him.

She'd been putting herself through school by waiting tables at an all-night diner near the college campus. He'd been attending school on his father's dime, breezing through classes and spending his free time playing football or attending frat parties.

He'd walked into the diner late one night with a pack of his friends, all of whom could have been male models for some brand of expensive cologne or another. She'd served them pancakes and eggs, and enough soda to float the *Titanic.* And even though she'd noticed him—she'd noticed all of them; how could she not?—she hadn't thought much of it. Why should she, when he was just one of a thousand different customers she served day in and day out? Not to mention one of the many young, carefree men who breezed through school—and life, it seemed—while she worked her fingers to the bone and burned the candle at both ends just trying to *stay* in school?

But then he'd shown up again. Sat in her section again. Sometimes with friends, other times by himself.

He'd smiled at her. Left huge tips, sometimes a hundred percent in addition to his check total. And made small talk with her. It wasn't until much later that she realized she'd told him nearly her entire life story in bits and pieces over a matter of weeks.

Finally, he'd asked her out and she'd been too enamored to say no. Half in love with him already and well on her way to head over heels.

Those same sensations were swamping her now. Shock, confusion, trepidation... He was a force to be reckoned with, much like a natural disaster. He was a tornado, an earthquake, a tsunami swooping in and turning her entire life upside down.

Within the hour, he'd been in touch with everyone he'd needed to contact back in Pittsburgh. Put out the word that he would be staying in Summerville indefinitely, and that his right-hand men—and women—were in charge of Keller Corp until further notice.

As far as Vanessa knew, though, he hadn't told them why he would be away for a while. She'd overheard him on the phone with his brother, but all Marc had said was that the business he was thinking of investing in looked promising and he needed to stick around to take a closer look at the premises and financials.

Keeping the true reason to himself was probably a smart move, she admitted reluctantly. No doubt if Eleanor Keller learned that her cherished son had a child with his evil ex-wife, she would go into a tizzy of epic proportions. Her already just-sucked-on-a-lemon expression would turn even more pinched and she would immediately begin plotting ways to get both Marc and Danny back into her circle of influence.

But not Vanessa. Eleanor would be plotting ways to *keep* Vanessa from reentering her or her son's lives.

Vanessa imagined that where Marc took it as a given that he was Danny's father, Marc's mother would insist on having a paternity test conducted as soon as possible. She would pray for a result that proved Danny was another man's child, of course, leaving Marc free and clear.

Free and clear of Vanessa, and free and clear to marry

someone else. A woman Eleanor would not only approve of, but would probably handpick herself.

She didn't verbalize her inhospitable thoughts to Marc, however. He didn't know how truly horrid his mother had been to her while they'd been married and she saw no reason to enlighten him now.

"There," he said, pushing through the swinging door into the kitchen where she and Aunt Helen were keeping themselves busy. He slipped his cell phone into his pocket, then shrugged out of his suit jacket altogether.

"That should buy me a few weeks of freedom before the place starts to fall apart and they send out a search party."

Aunt Helen was up to her elbows in bread flour, but her feelings on the subject of Marc staying in town were clear in the narrow slits of her eyes and the force she was using to knead the ball of dough in front of her.

She didn't like it one little bit, but as Vanessa had told her while Marc was making phone calls, they didn't have a choice. Either Marc stuck around until he got whatever it was that he was after, or he would drag Vanessa and Danny back to Pittsburgh.

She'd considered a third option—sending Marc back to Pittsburgh on his own—but knew that if she pushed him on the issue, it would only cause trouble and hostility. If she refused to allow Marc time with his son, in one town or another, Vanessa had no doubt it would only spur her ex-husband to throw his weight and his family's millions around.

And what did that mean? A big, ugly custody battle.

She was a good mother, so she knew Marc could never take Danny away from her on that basis alone. But she didn't fool herself, either, that the system wouldn't be swayed by the amount of money and power the Kellers could bring to bear. Eleanor alone wasn't above bribery, blackmail or making up a series of stories to paint Vanessa in the most negative light possible.

No, if there was any way to avoid a custody fight or any amount of animosity with Marc whatsoever, then she had to try. It might even mean making arrangements for shared custody and traveling back and forth to Pittsburgh or having Marc travel back and forth to Summerville. But whatever it took to keep Marc happy and Danny with her, she would do.

Even if it meant letting her ex move into her life—and her business and possibly her house—for God knew how long.

Finished filling a tray with fresh squares of turtle brownies, Vanessa wiped her hands on a nearby dish towel. "What about your things?" she asked. "Don't you need to go home and collect your personal items?"

Marc shrugged, and she couldn't help but notice the shift of firm muscle beneath his white button-down shirt. She remembered only too well what lay beneath that shirt, and how much she'd once enjoyed knowing it belonged to her and her alone.

"I'm having some clothes and such shipped. Anything else I need, I'm sure I can purchase here."

He hung his jacket on a hook near the door, where she and Helen kept their aprons when not in use, then crossed to the bassinet she'd dragged back out of the storeroom once Marc had figured out what was going on. Danny was sleeping inside, stretched out on his little belly, arms and legs all akimbo.

"The only question now," Marc said, gazing down at his son, then reaching out to stroke a single finger over Danny's soft cheek, "is where I'll be staying while I'm in town."

Vanessa opened her mouth, not even sure what she was about to say, only to be interrupted by Helen.

"Well, you're not staying in my house," her aunt announced in no uncertain terms. Her tight, blue-washed curls bobbed as she used the heels of her hands to beat the ball of bread dough into submission.

Though her aunt's clear dislike of Marc brought an immediate stab of guilt and the sudden urge to apologize, Vanessa was unaccountably grateful that Helen had the nerve to blurt out what she'd been unable to find the courage to tell him herself.

"Thank you so much for the kind invitation," Marc said, lips twisted with amusement, "but I really couldn't impose."

How typical of him to take Helen's rudeness in stride. That sort of thing never had fazed him, mainly because Marc knew who he was, where he came from and what he could do.

Plus, Aunt Helen hadn't always hated him. She didn't hate him now, actually, she was just annoyed with him and took his treatment of Vanessa personally.

Which was at least partly Vanessa's fault. She'd shown up on her aunt's doorstep hurt, angry, broken and carrying her ex-husband's child.

After spilling out the story of her rocky marriage, subsequent divorce, unexpected pregnancy and desperate need for a place to stay—with Marc filling the role of bad guy-slash-mean old ogre under the bridge at every turn—her aunt's opinion of him had dropped like a stone. Ever since then, Aunt Helen's only objective was to *not* see her niece hurt again.

Vanessa was still fighting the urge to make excuses for Helen when Marc said, "I thought maybe you could recommend a nice local hotel."

Vanessa and Helen exchanged a look.

"Guess that would be the Harbor Inn just a couple streets over," Helen told him. "It's not much, but your only other option is Daisy's Motel out on Route 12."

"Harbor Inn," Marc murmured, brows drawing together. "I didn't realize there was a waterway around here large enough to necessitate a harbor."

Vanessa and Helen exchanged another look, along with mutual ironic smiles.

"There isn't," Vanessa told him. "It's one of those small town oddities that no one can really explain. There's no harbor nearby. Not even a creek or stream worth mentioning. But the Harbor Inn is one of Summerville's oldest hotels, and it's decorated top to bottom with lighthouses, seagulls, fishing nets, starfish…"

She shook her head, hoping Marc wouldn't think too badly of the town or its residents. Even though some parts were a little backward at times, this was her home now and she found herself feeling quite protective toward it.

"If nothing else, it's an amusing place to stay," she added by way of explanation.

He looked less than convinced, but didn't say anything. Instead, he moved away from the bassinet and started to unbutton his cuffs, rolling the sleeves of his shirt up to his elbows.

"As long as it has a bed and a bathroom, I'm sure it will be fine. I'll be spending most of my time here with you, anyway."

Vanessa's eyes widened at that. "You will?"

One corner of his mouth quirked. "Of course. This is where my son is. Besides, if your goal is to expand the bakery and possibly branch out into mail-order sales, we've got a lot to discuss, and possibly a lot to do."

"Wait a minute." She let the spatula in her hand drop to the countertop, feeling her breath catch. "I didn't agree to let you have anything to do with The Sugar Shack."

He flashed her a charming, confident grin. "That's why we have so much to discuss. Now," he said, flattening his palms on the edge of the counter, "are you going to show me to this Harbor-less Inn, or would you prefer to simply give me directions so you and your aunt can both stay here and talk about me after I leave?"

Oh, she wanted to stay behind and talk about him. The problem was, he knew it. And now that he'd tossed down the gauntlet by effectively *telling* her he knew that's exactly what would happen the minute he left the room, she had no choice but to go with him.

Which was exactly why he'd done it.

Reaching behind her back, she untied the strings of her apron and pulled it off over her head.

"I'll take you," she said, then turned to her aunt. "Will you be okay on your own while we're gone?"

The question was just a formality; there were plenty of times when Vanessa left Helen in charge of the bakery while she ran errands or took Danny to the pediatrician. Still, her aunt shot her such a contemptible look that Vanessa nearly chuckled.

"All right. I'll be back in a bit."

She headed for the door, saying to Marc as she passed, "I just need to grab my purse."

He followed her out, waiting at the bottom of the

stairs while she ran up to collect her purse and sunglasses.

"What about the baby?" he asked as soon as she returned. "He'll be fine."

"Are you sure your aunt can take care of him *and* the bakery at the same time?" he pressed as they moved past the storefront's display cases and small round tables toward the door.

Vanessa smiled and waved at familiar customers as she passed. Once outside, she slipped on her sunglasses before turning to face him.

"Don't let Helen hear you asking something like that. She's liable to hurl a cookie sheet at your head."

He didn't laugh. In fact, he didn't look amused at all. Instead, he looked legitimately concerned.

"Relax, Marc. Aunt Helen is extremely competent. She runs the bakery by herself all the time."

"But—"

"*And* watches Danny at the same time. We both do. Truthfully, she's been a godsend," Vanessa admitted. "I don't know what I'd do without her."

Or what she would have *done* without her, when she'd found herself jobless, husbandless and pregnant all in the space of a few short months.

"So are we taking your car or mine?" she asked in an attempt to draw Marc's focus away from worrying about Danny.

"Mine," he said.

Vanessa kept pace with him as he turned on his heel and started down the sidewalk in the direction of Blake and Fetzer where he'd left his Mercedes. She was still dressed in the skirt and blouse she'd worn for her disastrous meeting earlier that morning. She wished now that she'd taken the time to change into something more comfortable. She especially wished she'd exchanged her heels for a pair of flats.

Marc, however, looked as suave and at ease as ever in his tailored suit pants and polished dress shoes. His jacket was slung over one shoulder, his other hand tucked casually into his slacks.

When they reached his car, he held the door while she climbed in the front passenger side, then rounded the back and slid in behind the wheel. He slipped the key in the ignition, then sat back in his seat, turning to face her.

"Will you do something for me before we head for the hotel?" he asked.

A shiver of trepidation skated beneath her skin and she immediately tensed. Hadn't she already done enough? Wasn't she already *doing* enough simply by accepting Marc's presence in town when what she really wanted to do was snatch up her child and head for the hills?

She also couldn't help remembering the many times they'd been alone in a car together in the past. Their first dates, where they'd steamed up the windows with their passion. After they were married, when a simple trip to the grocery store or out to dinner would include soft, intentional touches and comfortable intimacy.

She was sure he remembered, too, which only added to the tightening of her stomach and nervous clench of her hands on the strap of her purse where it rested on her lap.

"What?" she managed to say, holding her breath for the answer.

"Show me around town. Give me the ten-dollar tour. I

don't know how long I'll be here, but you can't be dropping everything every time I need directions."

Vanessa blinked and released her breath. Okay, that wasn't nearly as traumatizing as she'd expected. It was actually rather thoughtful of him.

Since her mouth had gone dry, for a second she could only lick her lips and bob her head in agreement. With an approving nod, he started the car and began to pull out of the lot.

"Which way?" he asked.

It took her a moment to think of where to start, and what she should show him, but Summerville was so small that she finally decided it wouldn't hurt to show him pretty much everything.

"Take a left," she told him. "We'll do Main Street, then I'll take you around the outskirts. We should end up at the Harbor Inn without too much backtracking."

A lot of the local businesses he could make out for himself. The diner, the drugstore, the flower shop, the post office. A little farther from the center of town were a couple of fast-food restaurants, gas stations and a Laundromat. In between the smattering of buildings were handfuls of houses, farms and wooded parcels.

She told him a bit of what she knew about her neighbors, both the owners of neighboring businesses and some of the residents of Summerville.

Like Polly—who ran Polly's Posies—and went around town every morning to deliver a single fresh flower to each store on Main Street free of charge. The vase she'd provided Vanessa was front and center on the counter, right next to the cash register, and even though she never knew what kind of flower Polly would choose to hand out on any given day, she had to admit the tiny dot of color really did add a touch of hominess to every single business in town.

Or Sharon—the pharmacist at Main Street Drugs—who had given Vanessa such wonderful prenatal advice and even set her up with her current pediatrician.

She had such close relationships with so many people in town. Something she'd never had while living in Pittsburgh with Marc. In the city, whether visiting the grocery store, pharmacy or dry cleaner's, she'd been lucky to make eye contact with the person behind the counter, much less make small talk.

Here, there was no such thing as a quick trip to the store. Every errand involved stopping numerous times to say hello and catch up with friendly acquaintances. And while she'd never missed that sort of thing before, she knew she would definitely miss it now if she woke up one day and realized it was no longer a part of her life.

"That's about it," she told him twenty minutes later, after pointing him in the general direction of the hotel where he would be staying. "There isn't much more to see, unless you're interested in a tour of the dairy industry from the inside out."

A small smile curved his lips. "I'll pass, thanks. But I think you missed something."

She frowned, wondering what he could possibly mean. She hadn't shown him the nearest volunteer fire department or water treatment plant, but those were several miles outside of town, and she didn't think he really cared about that sort of thing, anyway.

"You didn't show me where *you* live," he supplied in a low voice.

"Do you really need to know?" she asked, ignoring

the spike of heat that suffused her from head to toe at the knowing glance he sent her.

"Of course. How else will I know where to pick you up for dinner?"

Five

As much as Vanessa would have liked to argue with Marc about his heavy-handedness, in the end, she didn't bother. He had a nasty habit of getting his way in almost every situation, anyway, so what was the point?

She'd also reluctantly decided that, for as long as Marc was determined to stay in her and Danny's lives, it was probably better to simply make nice with him. There was no sense antagonizing him or fighting him at every turn when he potentially held so much of her future in his hands.

At the moment, the only thing he seemed to want was time with and information about his son. He wasn't trying to take Danny away from her or making threats about trying to take him later, even though they both knew he was probably within his rights to do so.

The threatening part, not the actual taking. But if she were in his shoes, anger and a sense of betrayal alone would have had her yelling all manner of hostile, menacing things.

So this afternoon when Marc asked her to show him where she lived with Aunt Helen, she took him to the small, two-story house on Evergreen Lane. It wasn't much compared to the sprawling estate where he'd grown up with servants and tennis courts and a half mile, tree-lined drive just to reach the front gate, but in the last year, it had become home to her.

Helen had given up her guest room to Vanessa and helped turn her sewing room into a nursery for Danny. She'd volunteered her kitchen to thousands of hours of trial and error with her family recipes before they'd felt brave enough to move forward with the idea of actually opening a bakery of their very own.

In return, Vanessa helped with the general upkeep of the house, had planted rows of brand-new pink and red begonias in the flower beds lining the front porch and walk, and had even taught Helen enough about computers to have her emailing with friends from grade school she'd never thought to be in contact with again.

Though Vanessa still believed there was no way she could ever truly repay her aunt's kindness in her time of need, Helen insisted she enjoyed the company and was happy to have so much youth and activity in the house again. Which, in Vanessa's book, made the tiny white house on less than an acre of mottled green and yellow grass more of a home than Keller Manor, with all its bells and whistles, could ever be.

Taking a deep breath, she checked herself over in the bathroom mirror one last time—though she wasn't sure why she bothered. Yes, it had been a while since she'd had a reason to get so dressed up, let alone get so dressed up twice in one day.

But even though jeans and tennies were more her style these days, Marc had seen her in everything from ratty shorts and T-shirts to full-length ball gowns and priceless jewels. Besides, she wasn't attempting to impress him this evening, was she? No, she was pacifying him.

After showing him to the Harbor Inn and then letting him drop her off at The Sugar Shack once again, Vanessa had finished off her day at the bakery, closed up shop, and headed home with Danny and her aunt. While Helen had fixed dinner for herself and kept Danny entertained, Vanessa had run upstairs to change clothes and retouch her makeup.

She wasn't fixing herself up for Marc, she told her reflection. She wasn't. It was simply that she was taking advantage of a dinner invitation that included the chance to look like a woman for a change instead of a frazzled working mother struggling to be a successful entrepreneur.

That's the only reason she was wearing her favorite strapless red dress, strappy red heels and dangling imitation ruby earrings. It was over-the-top for even the priciest restaurant in Summerville, but she didn't care. She might never get the opportunity to wear this outfit again…or to remind Marc of just what he'd given up when he let her go.

The doorbell rang before she was ready for it and her heart lurched in her chest. She quickly swiped on another layer of lipstick, then made sure she had everything she needed in the tiny red clutch she'd dug out of the back of her closet.

Halfway down the stairs, she heard voices and knew Aunt Helen had answered the door in her absence. She didn't know whether to be grateful or nervous about that; it depended, she supposed, on Aunt Helen's current disposition.

At the bottom of the landing, she found Aunt Helen

standing inside the open door, one hand on the knob. No shotgun or frying pan in sight, which was a good sign.

Marc stood on the other side of the door, still on the porch. He was dressed in the same charcoal suit as earlier, forest-green tie arrow straight and jacket buttoned back in place. His hands were linked behind his back and he was smiling down at Aunt Helen with all the charm of a used car salesman. When he spotted her, Marc transferred that dimpled grin to her.

"Hi," he said. "You look great."

Vanessa resisted the urge to smooth a hand down the front of her dress or recheck the knot of her upswept hair. "Thank you."

"I was just telling your aunt what a lovely home she has. At least from the outside," he added with a wink, likely because Aunt Helen had obviously failed to invite him inside.

"Would you like to come in?" Vanessa asked, ignoring her aunt's sidelong scowl.

"Yes, thank you." Marc ignored the scowl, too, brushing past Aunt Helen and into the entranceway.

He gave the house a cursory once-over and Vanessa wondered if he was comparing it to his own lavish residence, possibly finding it lacking as an appropriate place for his child to be raised. But when he turned back, his expression held no censure, only mild curiosity.

"Where's Danny?" he asked.

"The kitchen," Helen supplied, closing the front door, then moving past them in that direction. "I was just giving him his dinner."

Marc shot Vanessa a glance before waving her ahead of him as they followed Helen through the living area to the back of the house. "I thought you were still breast-feeding."

She flushed, feeling heat climb over her cheeks toward her hairline. "I am, but not exclusively. He also gets juice, cereal and a selection of baby food."

"Good," he murmured with a short nod, watching as Aunt Helen rounded the kitchen table and took a seat. "The longer a child breast-feeds, the better. It increases immunity, builds the child's sense of security and helps with mother/child bonding."

"And how do you know that?" she asked, genuinely surprised. Danny was strapped into his Winnie the Pooh swing, face and bib spattered with a mixture of strained peas, strained carrots and applesauce. He looked like a Jackson Pollock painting as he kicked his feet and slapped his hands against the plastic sides of the seat that held him.

Without waiting for an invitation, Marc sat down opposite Aunt Helen, leaning in to rub Danny's head. The baby giggled and Marc grinned in return.

"Contrary to popular belief," he murmured, not bothering to turn in her direction, "I didn't become CEO of Keller Corp by nepotism alone. I actually happen to be quite resourceful when I need to be."

"Let me guess—you dug out your laptop and hit the internet."

"I'm not telling," he answered, tossing her a teasing half smile. Then to Aunt Helen, he said, "May I?" indicating the array of baby food jars spread out in front of her.

The older woman gave him a look that clearly said she didn't think he was capable, but she waved him on all the same. "Be my guest."

He picked up the miniature plastic spoon with a cartoon character on the handle and began feeding Danny in tiny bites, waiting long enough in between them for the baby to gum and smack and swallow.

Vanessa stood back, watching…and wishing. Wishing she hadn't agreed to go out to dinner with Marc this evening, after all. Wishing she hadn't invited him in and that he hadn't wanted to see Danny before they left. Wishing this whole scene wasn't so domestic, so bittersweet, so much of a reminder of what could have been.

Marc looked entirely too comfortable feeding his son, even dressed as he was in a full business suit. He was also oddly good at it, which she wouldn't have expected from a man who hadn't spent much time around babies before.

When Danny began to fuss and wouldn't take another bite, Marc set aside the jars and spoon, and brushed his hands together.

"I'd like to pick him up for a minute," he said, splitting his gaze between his expensive suit and his infant son, who was doing his best imitation of a compost pile, "but…"

"Definitely not," Vanessa agreed, grabbing a damp cloth to wipe the worst of the excess food from Danny's mouth and chin. "Let Aunt Helen get him cleaned up and maybe you can hold him when we get back, if he's still awake."

Marc didn't look completely pleased with that idea, but since the alternative was ruining a suit that probably cost more than most people's monthly mortgage payment, he wisely refrained from reaching out and getting covered by Gerber's finest.

"Shouldn't we go?" she prompted as he pushed to his

feet and Aunt Helen rounded the table to scoop Danny from the swing.

Still looking reluctant to leave, Marc nodded and followed her back through the house to the front door. Outside, he led her to his car, which was parked at the curb, and helped her inside.

"What do you do when he's a mess like that?" Marc asked once he'd climbed in beside her.

She twisted in her seat to face him, noticing the frown pulling at the corners of his mouth. "What do you mean?"

"How do you not pick up your own child?"

Vanessa blinked, wondering if she'd heard him correctly. Oh, she heard the words clearly enough, but was that a hint of guilt stealing through his tone? *Guilt* from a man she hadn't thought understood the concept? Who'd let her walk away without a fight, with barely an explanation?

"Marc." Shaking her head, she ducked her chin to keep him from seeing the amusement tugging at her lips. "I know this is all new to you. I know finding out about Danny was quite a shock, but you have nothing to feel guilty about. He's a baby. As long as all of his needs are met, he doesn't care who's feeding him, who's holding him, who's changing his diaper."

If anything, Marc's frown deepened. "That isn't true. Infants know the difference between their parents and simply a babysitter, between their mother and their father."

"All right," she acquiesced, "but rest assured that there are plenty of times I don't pick him up right after he's eaten because I don't want him to get food on my clothes. Or worse yet, yurk on me."

"Yurk?"

"It's what Aunt Helen and I call a 'yucky burp,'" she explained, wrinkling her nose in distaste. "Believe me, once you've had soured milk or formula spit up all over you, you learn fast not to wear nice clothes around a baby and to keep a towel handy."

Without a thought of what she was doing, she reached across the console and patted his thigh. "If you're going to be in town for a while to spend time with him, get yourself some nice, cheap jeans and T-shirts, and expect them to get dirty on a regular basis. But don't worry about tonight. I didn't hold him this morning, either, because I was dressed up for my meeting with you. That's one of the great things about having Aunt Helen around. I can't do everything all by myself and she helps to pick up the slack."

Meeting her gaze, Marc wrapped his fingers around hers, holding her hand in place, even when she tried to pull it away. "I should be the one helping you with Danny, not your aunt. But don't worry, we're going to talk about that over dinner. Among other things."

Despite the threat of The Big Talk and being pinned to her chair like a bug under Marc's intense scrutiny and personal version of the Spanish Inquisition, dinner was actually quite enjoyable. He took her to the hotel's dining room, which was actually one of the more moderately upscale restaurants in town and attempted to ply her with wine and crab cakes. Of course, since she was breast-feeding, the wine was a no-no, but the crab cakes were delicious. Maybe because he let her eat them in peace.

As soon as the waitress topped off their coffees and they'd made their dessert selections, however, she knew the stay of execution was over. Marc cupped his hands around the ceramic mug and leaned forward in his seat, causing her to tense slightly in her own.

"What was the pregnancy like?" he asked, getting straight to the point, as usual.

Vanessa blew out a small breath, relieved that he was at least starting out with an easy question instead of immediately launching into demands and ugly accusations.

"It was pretty typical, I think," she told him. "Bearing in mind I'd never been pregnant before and didn't really know what to expect. But there were no complications and even the morning sickness wasn't too bad. It didn't always limit itself to mornings, which made getting the bakery open and working twelve-hour days a bit of an adventure," she added with a chuckle, "but it wasn't as terrible as I'd expected."

From there he wanted to know every detail of Danny's birth. Date, time, length, weight, how long her labor had lasted—all facts that she'd taken for granted. In his shoes, though, she could imagine how desperate she would be to learn and memorize every one of them.

"I should have been there," he said softly, staring down at the table. Then he lifted his gaze to hers. "I *deserved* to be there. For all of it."

Her heart lurched and she braced herself for the onslaught, for every bit of anger and resentment she knew he had to be feeling…and that she probably deserved. But instead of lashing out, his voice remained level.

"As much as it bothers me, there's no going back, we can only move forward. So here's the deal, Vanessa."

His green eyes bore into her, the same look she suspected he gave rival business associates during mergers and tricky acquisitions.

"Now that I know about Danny, I want in on everything. I'll stick around here for a while, until you get used to that idea. Until I get the hang of being a father and he starts to recognize me that way. But after that, I'm going to want to take him home."

At that, at the mention of his home, not hers, Vanessa went still, her shoulders stiffening and her fingers tightening on the handle of her coffee cup.

"That's not a threat," he added quickly, obviously noticing how tense her body had gone. "I'm not saying I want to take him back to Pittsburgh forever. I honestly don't know yet how we're going to work out the logistics of that, but we can discuss it later. I'm only talking about a visit so I can introduce him to my family, let my mother know she has another grandchild."

Oh, Eleanor would love that, Vanessa thought with derision. She'd be thrilled with another grandchild, especially another *male* grandchild to carry on the Keller name. But that grandchild's mother was another story— and Marc's mother would only truly be happy with Vanessa out of the picture.

"And what if I don't agree? To any of it."

One dark brow winged upward. "*Then* I'll be forced to threaten, I suppose. But is that really the direction you want to go? I've been pretty amicable about this entire situation so far, even though I think we both know I have more than enough reason to be furious over it."

Taking a sip of his coffee, he tipped his head to the side, looking much calmer than she felt.

"If you want me to be furious and toss around ugly threats you know I can follow through on, that's fine, just say the word. But if you'd rather act like two mature adults determined to create the best environment possible for their child, then I suggest you go along with my plans."

"Do I have a choice?" she grumbled, understanding better than ever the adage about being stuck between a rock and a hard place.

Marc's smile was equal parts cocky and confident. "You had the choice of whether or not to tell me you were pregnant in the first place, and you decided not to, so… not really. The ball is in my court now."

Six

The ball was most definitely in Marc's court—along with everything else. But then, she'd known that the minute he'd walked up the stairs to the bakery's second-floor apartment and discovered he had a son, hadn't she? Her only option now was to play nice and hope he would continue to do the same.

Marc's hand was on her elbow as they left the restaurant, guiding her along the carpeted passage toward the lobby. Old fishing nets and decorative life preservers lined the walls and she suddenly realized how odd the decor must seem to outsiders.

Those who were familiar with Summerville never gave it a second thought, but anyone coming into town for the first time must wonder at the hotel's name and decor without a significant body of water nearby to back them up. Especially since the hotel's dining room didn't even particularly specialize in seafood dishes.

"Come upstairs with me," he murmured suddenly just above her ear.

Tearing her gaze from a large plastic swordfish caught in one of the nets, she flashed Marc a startled, disbelieving look, only to have him chuckle at her reaction.

"That isn't a proposition," he assured her, then waggled his eyebrows in an exaggerated attempt at flirtation. "Although I wouldn't be opposed to a bit of after-dinner seduction."

At the lobby, he steered her to the left, away from the hotel's main entrance and in the direction of the wide, *Gone with the Wind*-esque stairwell that led to the guest rooms.

"I have something to show you," he continued as they slowly climbed the stairs, her heels digging into the thick carpeting, faded in places from years of wear.

"Now that sounds like a proposition. Or maybe a bad pickup line," she told him.

He slanted her a grin, digging into his pocket for the key to his room. Not a key card, but an honest to goodness key, complete with a giant plastic fob in the shape of a lighthouse.

"You know me better than that. I didn't need cheesy pickup lines with you the first time around, I don't need them now."

No, he hadn't. He'd been much too charming and suave to hit on her the way ninety percent of guys did back then. Which was only one of the things that had made him more appealing, made him stand out from the pack.

When they reached his door, he unlocked it, then stepped back to let her pass into the room ahead of him. She'd visited the Harbor Inn before, of course, but had never actually been in one of the guest rooms, so for a second she stood just inside the door, taking in her surroundings.

Even if the large brass plaque on the front of the building hadn't identified the hotel as a historical landmark, she would have known it was old simply from the interior. The elaborately carved woodworking, the barely preserved wallpaper and the antique fixtures all would have tipped her off. Certain things had been updated, of course, to keep the hotel functional and modern enough that guests would be comfortable, but a lot had been left or restored to maintain as much of the original furnishings and adornments as possible.

Marc's room was blissfully lacking in the oceanside motif. Instead, the walls boasted tiny pink roses on yellowing wallpaper, and both the single window and four-poster bed were covered in white eyelet lace. Very old-fashioned and grandmotherly.

It was almost funny to see tall, dark, modern businessman Marc standing in the middle of all the extremely formal, nineteenth century finery. He looked completely out of place, like a zebra in the dolphin enclosure at the zoo.

But *looking* out of place and *being* out of place were two different things, and Marc didn't seem to feel the least bit out of place. Closing the door behind them, he shrugged out of his charcoal suit jacket and tossed it over the back of a burgundy brocade wing chair on his way to the brass-plated desk against the far wall.

While he lifted the lid of his laptop and hit the button to boot up the computer, Vanessa stood back and enjoyed the view. Shallow of her, she was sure. Not to mention inconsistent, considering how vehemently she protested—to herself and anyone else who would listen—that the divorce had been a blessing and she was over him. Completely and totally over him.

Being his *ex*-wife didn't keep her from being a living, breathing, red-blooded woman, however. And every one of the red-blooded cells in her body appreciated the sight of a healthy, well-built man like Marc walking away.

His broad shoulders and wide back stretched the material of his expensive white dress shirt as he moved. Dark gray slacks that probably cost more than she made at the bakery in a week hugged his hips, and more importantly, his butt. A very nice, well-rounded butt that didn't seem to have changed much since they'd been together.

Lifting a hand to her face, she covered her eyes and silently chastised herself for being so weak-willed. What was wrong with her? Was she crazy? Or catching a bug? Or were her hormones still dreadfully out of whack because of the pregnancy?

Spreading her fingers a few brief centimeters, she peeked through and knew exactly what her problem was.

Number one—she knew what lay beneath all that cotton and wool. She knew the strength of his muscles, the texture of his skin. She knew how he moved and how he smelled and how he felt pressed up against her.

Number two—her hormones probably *were* out of whack—and not just the pregnancy variety. The regular ones seemed to be turned all upside down, as well.

Which was no surprise. She'd always been a total pushover where Marc was concerned. One smoldering look and her bones had turned to jelly. One brush of his knuckles across her cheek or light touch of his lips on hers and she'd been putty in his hands.

Given how long it had been since they'd been together—how long it had been since she'd been anything more than a human incubator and a first-time mommy— it was no wonder, really, that her mind was wandering down all sorts of deliciously naughty garden paths.

And no doubt if Marc knew, or even suspected, he

would take full advantage of her vulnerability and inner turmoil, so it would be wise of her not to do or say anything to give him the wrong idea. Or any ideas at all, for that matter.

Through her fingers, Vanessa watched him undo the top couple of buttons of his shirt and loosen his collar. Such a familiar habit. She remembered him doing the same thing almost every night when he got home from work. He would usually spend a couple of hours in his home office, but taking off his jacket and tie, loosening his collar and rolling up his sleeves were the first steps toward relaxing for the evening.

She lowered her hands from her face just before he picked up the laptop and turned back around. Crossing the room, he lowered himself to the edge of the bed, set the laptop beside him, and then patted the pristine white coverlet.

"Come sit down for a minute," he said, "I want to show you something."

Vanessa raised a brow. "That sounds like another bad pickup line," she told him.

Marc chuckled. "Since when did you become so cynical? Now, come here so I can show you some of these plans I worked up for The Sugar Shack."

That got her attention, allaying some of her suspicions and fears—and giving rise to new ones. Moving to the bed, she sat down, tucking the skirt of her dress beneath her to keep from flashing too much leg.

He clicked a couple of buttons, then turned the screen so she could see it more easily. "You said you want to expand into the store space next door, right? Use it for a possible mail-order division of the business."

"Mmm-hmm."

"Well, this is a quick prospectus I worked up before dinner for what I think it would cost to renovate the space, what your expenses and overhead would be, et cetera. Of course, there are a lot of aspects to the bakery business I'm sure I'm not familiar with, so it will need to be adjusted. But this gives us a rough estimate and an idea of where to start."

He got up for a second and stretched to reach the bureau, grabbing a large yellow legal pad before returning to the bed, sending the mattress bouncing slightly.

"And this is a rudimentary sketch of a possible layout for the expansion. Counters and shelving and such."

She pulled her attention away from the document on the computer screen to the tablet he was holding out to her. She studied the drawing for a minute, picturing everything exactly as it would look next door to The Sugar Shack.

It was good. Encouraging, even. And the idea that something so simple might one day soon be a reality caused her heart to leap in her chest.

There was only one problem.

Lifting her head, she met Marc's gaze. "Why did you do all this?" she asked, passing the legal pad back to him.

"Nothing is written in stone," he murmured, setting aside the tablet and turning the laptop back toward him. "And it won't be cheap, believe me. But the expansion is a good idea. I think it's a smart move and has the potential to really pay off in the long run. Especially if you do well enough to start that Cookie-of-the-Month Club thing you mentioned."

Her heart jumped again, making her palms damp and her throat tight. It was so nice to hear someone sharing her enthusiasm about branching out with the bakery and actually supporting her ideas.

But in this case, there were strings attached. So many strings.

"That doesn't answer my question," she said softly. And then she asked again, even though a part of her was afraid of his response. "Why did *you* do all this?"

He sat back, clicking the lid of the laptop closed and moving the computer to the nightstand, along with the legal pad.

"You need a partner to pull this off, Vanessa. You know that, or you wouldn't have gone to Blake and Fetzer for help."

Her pulse slowed and the temperature in the room fell ten degrees. Or maybe it was only her own internal temperature that dropped like a stone.

"I told you, Marc, I won't take your money."

Shoulders going back, his spine straightened almost imperceptibly, and his jaw went square and tight. A clear indication he was about to get stubborn and lay down the Law According to Marc Keller.

Mouth a thin, flat line, he said, "And I told you, Vanessa, that I'm not going anywhere. Not for a while, anyway."

A beat passed while the tension seemed to leak from his stiff form and jump across the bed into her. The last thing she needed was a reminder of Marc's refusal to leave town now that he knew about Danny, and all the fears and concerns his presence brought to the surface.

"So as long as I'm sticking around," he continued, "we might as well use the time wisely. Why not get started on the expansion and put you one step closer to your goal?"

Oh, he was smooth and made so much sense. She'd always hated that, because it put him entirely too close to being right.

Of course, he usually *was* right, at least where business issues were concerned, which was even more annoying. Especially since he knew it and often came across as just this side of smug in that awareness.

"I don't want your help, Marc."

Rising from the bed, she linked her arms around her middle and paced across the room. When she hit the closed door, she turned and paced back, keeping her gaze locked on the worn and faded carpeting beneath her feet.

"I don't want to be tied to you, to owe you for anything."

"Well, it's a little late for that, don't you think?"

She stopped, lifted her head to meet his eye. One dark brow was raised, his lips curled in a wry half smile.

"We have a child together. I'd say that ties us together more strongly than any business plan or partnership ever could."

She blinked. Dammit. There it was again. He was right and being smug about it.

For better or worse, they *were* tied to each other now until the end of time through their son. Birthdays, school events, extracurricular activities, chicken pox, measles, puberty, girlfriends, his first tattoo or piercing...

She shuddered. Oh, God, please no piercings or tattoos. That might actually be the one parental matter she'd happily delegate to Marc for a good old-fashioned father-to-son heart-to-heart.

But given how ugly and heartbreaking—at least on her part—their separation had been, it was no wonder she wasn't looking forward to sharing any of that with him. And no wonder she'd tried to keep Danny a secret to begin with. It might not have been the right thing to do, but it sure made life a lot less complicated.

"That's different," she said quietly.

He inclined his head, though whether in agreement or simply acquiescence, she wasn't sure.

"However you feel about that," he said slowly, "it doesn't change the facts. I'm going to be in Summerville, getting to know my son and make up for lost time, for several weeks, at least. You might as well take advantage of that—and of my willingness to invest money into your bakery."

Pushing up from the bed, he came to stand in front of her, cupping his hands over her shoulders. His slightly callused palms felt rough against her bare skin, his warmth seeping into her pores.

"Think about it, Nessa," he murmured barely above a whisper. His eyes, as green and lush as summer moss, bored into hers. "Use your head here instead of sticking to stubborn pride. The smart and savvy businesswoman in you knows I'm right, knows this is an opportunity you'd be crazy to pass up. Even if it is coming from your despicable ex-husband."

He said the last with a quick wink and a self-deprecating quirk of his full, sexy lips.

It was that wink and the fact that he knew how badly she *didn't* want him around but apparently wasn't holding it against her that made her stop and think, just as he'd suggested.

Think through his offer logically and reasonably, and with the level-headed, straightforward intelligence that had convinced her to take the risky financial plunge of opening The Sugar Shack with Aunt Helen in the first place. Weigh her options. Weigh her desire to expand the bakery and accept a much-needed infusion of cash and support against her desire to keep Danny to herself, keep miles upon miles of distance between her and Marc—both figuratively and literally—and maintain complete control over her business rather than sharing it with a third party who may or may not be as genuinely committed to its growth and success as she and her aunt were. Or worse yet, had the power to crush her and her business at the slightest provocation.

And there would be provocation, wouldn't there? There already was, in that she'd kept first her pregnancy and then Danny's existence from him to begin with.

For all she knew, he could be hiding his true feelings from her, being kind and considerate and generous in an effort to lull her into a false sense of security. Then the minute she agreed to take his money, to let him partner with her in the bakery and to be a part of Danny's life, he would spring the trap, taking *everything* from her.

Her business, her security, her *son*.

Did she really believe that, though? Despite the bitterness involved on both sides of their divorce, he had never been deliberately cruel. He hadn't tried to hurt her, hadn't used his powerful influence or family fortune to leave her destitute.

Thanks to the prenuptial agreement his family—or more to the point, his mother—had insisted on before their wedding, Vanessa had left the marriage with not much more than she'd walked into it with, but she was well aware that it could have been worse.

She had friends who had gone through much nastier divorces. She'd heard the horror stories where women who had been married to extremely wealthy men were put through the wringer and kicked onto the street with barely the clothes on their backs, sometimes with their children in tow.

Marc had never been that type of man. He'd always had a very low-key personality, opting for silent fury over angry blow-ups.

Even during their marriage, he might not have been as attentive as she would have liked or taken her complaints about his family or his distance seriously, but he had never resorted to petty arguments or name-calling. A couple of times, she'd even wished for something like that, if only as proof that he still cared enough to fight. With her or for her; back then, either would have translated as caring *at all*.

But his response to marital conflict had always been to lock his jaw, slip into stony silence and go back to the office to work even longer hours that pushed them even farther apart.

Marc was also one of the most honest men she'd ever met. It would be just like him to compartmentalize their current relationship.

Anything involving Danny would remain strictly personal, and he would deal with her on a personal, father-to-mother level. Anything involving her bakery would remain strictly a business venture and he would treat it as such.

If he pulled out of The Sugar Shack, it would be only his money and professional ties that went with him, not his love for Danny or determination to be in his son's life. And on the other side of the coin, if they were at odds about something that concerned Danny, he would never pull his financial backing of the bakery just to make her life miserable.

Unfortunately, she'd never been quite as good at keeping her work and her personal life separated. She loved The Sugar Shack. It was a part of her, built of blood, sweat, tears and most of all, heart. If it failed, if something happened to it or she had to close the doors, a very big part of her would die with it.

But even more important than that, and definitely what owned a much bigger portion of her heart and soul, was Danny. She would light a match and torch The Sugar Shack down to the ground if it meant keeping her child happy and safe.

And for better or worse, Marc was Danny's father, a part of him. He was also probably the only investor she would ever find who was actually willing and able to give the bakery an influx of much-needed cash, and who apparently thought her ideas for expansion held actual merit.

Anyone else would have already jumped at the offer. But there was so much at stake for her—and for Danny and Aunt Helen.

She'd been silent for so long, she was surprised Marc didn't check her for a pulse. She also suspected she would have the mother of all headaches soon just from the strain of thinking so hard. It was as though a Ping-Pong championship tournament was taking place inside her brain.

But in the end, she didn't follow her head or even her heart. She followed her gut.

"All right," she told him, the words nearly torn from a throat gone tight with the strain of her internal struggle. "But I don't want your charity. If we're going to do this, then I want it to be completely official and aboveboard. We'll have Brian draw up investment papers, or make it a legal loan that I *will* pay back, or however these things are normally done."

Marc smiled gently, the sort of smile a parent offers a recalcitrant child, almost as though he was getting ready to humor her.

"Fine. I'll call Brian in the morning and get the ball rolling." She nodded slowly, still reluctant, still unsure. Gut or no gut, agreeing to let Marc become a partner in her and her aunt's business still made her hugely uncomfortable, and there was no guarantee that it wasn't a monumental mistake.

"So that's the business end of things. We'll iron out the details tomorrow," he said. Then he ran his hands down the bare flesh of her arms from her shoulders to her elbows and lowered his voice to a near whisper. "Now on to something a bit more personal."

Her first thought was that he wanted to discuss Danny again, and her heart dropped all the way to her stomach, only to jump back up and lodge in her throat. Her chest grew tight as she held her breath and waited—for the bomb to drop, for him to demand full custody or announce that he was taking their son back to Pittsburgh with him.

Instead, he tugged her close, lowered his head and kissed her.

Seven

For a moment, Vanessa stood completely frozen, eyes wide, shock holding her immobile. But then his heat, his passion, seeped into her, and she began to lean against him, his eyes sliding closed on a silent sigh.

Marc's hands slipped from her elbows to her waist, pulling her even more tightly to him and holding her there with his arms crossed like iron bands at her back. His lips were warm and firm and masterful, plundering even as he attempted to coax and seduce.

He tasted like coffee and cream, and felt like heaven. Just as she remembered.

Kissing Marc had always been pure pleasure, like a cool glass of water on a hot summer day or sinking into a relaxing bubble bath after a long, exhausting day at work.

Hand drifting up to cup her cheek, Marc pulled away just enough to let her catch her breath and meet his gaze. His eyes were dark with a desire that Vanessa knew must be reflected in her own. Whether she wanted it or not, whether she liked it or not, there was no denying the heat that flared between them. Even now, after a year of separation, after the end of their marriage.

"I've been wanting to do that all evening," Marc murmured, his thumb slowly stroking just beneath her lower lip.

She wished she could deny feeling the same way, but had to admit that the thought of kissing him again had crossed her mind a few times since their unexpected reunion, as well. Especially during dinner, while they'd stared at one another across the candlelit table.

But kissing him wasn't a good idea. Being alone with him in his hotel room for much longer wasn't a good idea.

She should leave. Put a hand to his chest, push him away and get out while she could still make her legs move.

His other hand came up to frame her face, his fingers running through the hair at her temple.

Move, legs, move.

But her legs didn't move. It was as though her entire body had turned to stone, every muscle statue-still.

"This is a bad idea," she told him, putting her thoughts into words and forcing them past stiff, dry lips. "I should go."

A hint of a grin played at the corners of his lips. "Or you could stay," he whispered, "and we can see about turning a bad idea into a good one."

Inside, she was shaking her head. *No, no, no.* Sticking around was only going to turn the bad that had already happened into much, much worse.

No, she needed to leave. And she would, just as soon as she could get her body to obey the commands of her brain.

But the connection between the two had obviously been blocked or severed or scrambled in some way. Because she didn't move. She didn't step back, or push him away, or voice further arguments against making any more monumental mistakes.

She simply stood there and watched his mouth descend once again. Stood there and let his lips cover hers, let his fingers dig into her hair and cradle her scalp. Let his tongue tease and taunt until she had no choice but to open her mouth and invite him inside.

Oh, this is a bad idea, she thought, as her own arms came up to wind around his neck, her fingers toying with the hair at his nape. *A very, very bad...*

His tongue twined with hers and she groaned, any semblance of rational thought flying right out the window. Good or bad, she was in it now, with very little might left to fight. She wasn't even sure she wanted to anymore.

Though they were already touching, he tugged her even closer, so that her breasts flattened against his chest and the evidence of his arousal pressed between her legs.

Being a woman kept her arousal from being as obvious, but it was there, without a doubt. Besides the fact that her heart was pounding and her temperature was slowly reaching the boiling point, inside the cups of her bra her nipples were turning into tight, sensitive pearls. Lower, her knees were weak and her panties were growing damp.

It wouldn't take much more of Marc's intense ministrations for him to know just how aroused she was, too. Already, his hands were wandering down her sides and over her hips, his fingers slowly rucking up the skirt of her dress until he could touch her stockinged thighs.

Her own fingers went to the buttons at the front of his shirt, slipping one after another through their holes. When she reached the bottom, she switched to unbuckling his belt and loosening the top button of his dress slacks, then tugging the shirt's tail free. Once both sides fell open, she slipped her hands under the expensive material and put her palms flat against the warm, smooth skin of his chest and stomach.

He groaned. She moaned. The sounds met and mingled, sending shivers from their locked lips all the way down her spine.

As though he felt them, too, Marc's hand went to the small of her back and followed the line of her vertebrae up, up, up. He kneaded her neck a short second before catching the clasp of her dress's zipper and tugging it down in one long *ziiiiiiiiip* of sensation.

Curling her nails into his chest, she slumped into him as wave after wave of longing rolled through her. It was almost too much to bear, melting her bones and stealing the breath from her lungs. If he hadn't been holding her, she was sure she would have collapsed to the ground in a pile of skin and rumpled red fabric.

He released her mouth, allowing her to suck in some much-needed oxygen while he tugged at her dress, letting the flowy fabric pool at her feet. Hooking his thumbs into the waist of her pantyhose, he started to skim them down her legs, following them until he knelt in front of her on one knee.

With a hand at her ankle, he said, "Lift."

She did, and he slipped both her matching red heel and the stockings off her foot.

"Lift," he said again, repeating the motion on her other ankle, leaving her standing in the middle of the room in nothing but her bra and panties.

Thank goodness she'd taken as much care choosing those as she had her dress and shoes. She'd had absolutely no notion and no intention of letting him get so much of a glimpse of her underthings, but now she was infinitely relieved that she'd made a point of wearing a brand-new matching set. A strapless red demi-bra with scalloped lace edging and lacey, boy-cut panties that covered more than enough in the front, but left half moons of bare flesh visible from the back.

From his position on the floor, Marc must have noticed the peekaboo style of the underwear, because he lifted his head and shot her a grin that could only be described as wolfish.

"Lovely," he murmured, his hands cupping the backs of her calves, then her knees, then her thighs until her thighs quivered and she wasn't sure she could remain upright much longer.

Her tongue darted out, licking dry lips. "Mothers always tell their children to wear nice underwear, just in case," she managed in a shaky voice. "Now I know why."

Marc chuckled. A low, sexy sound that beat at her insides like tiny orange flames.

"These are better than nice," he told her, cupping her bottom and pressing a kiss to the bare skin of her belly, just below her navel. "But I'm pretty sure this isn't the kind of 'just in case' they're talking about."

A noise rolled up her throat that was meant to be a laugh. It came out more of a strangled hiss.

"But you like them, right? Better than plain white cotton?"

Kissing a line up the center of her torso, he climbed slowly to his feet. "Better than white cotton," he agreed. Then when he got to her mouth, he added, "But I don't really care, since you won't be wearing them much longer."

Reaching around her back, he unhooked her bra in one quick, deft movement. Only the last-minute crossing of her arms kept the garment from falling away completely.

"Now take them off. Both of them."

The gruff order sent her stomach flip-flopping and brought goose bumps to every inch of her exposed flesh. Which, considering her state of undress, was a considerable amount.

Despite the desire coursing through her veins, however, she suddenly felt awkward and exposed. She'd come this far, even knowing it was a colossal mistake.

It wasn't wise to be alone in the same room with Marc fully clothed, let alone do what they were doing. But being with him again brought back so many incredible memories and sensory perceptions that she'd thought she would never experience again. So she'd thrown up a thick, tall wall in her brain to keep right from wrong apart. And another between her brain and her heart to keep them from playing tug-of-war while she was enjoying Marc's kisses and touch. Now here she stood, half-naked, her ex-husband telling her to drop the two tiny bits of lace and fabric that kept her from being totally naked, and her nerves were calling foul.

For a brief moment, she considered jumping back into her dress and running for the hills. But that nice, thick wall was still firmly in place, leaving just enough want to overshadow future regrets.

What she needed, she realized, was a more level playing field.

Arms still crossed over her breasts to hold her bra in place, she stepped back. Just one small step away from him.

"Not yet," she told him, the words coming out more confidently than she felt.

He arched one dark brow and the message in his eyes clearly telegraphed that if she tried to cut and run, he would chase after her.

But she had no intention of running, only of evening things out a bit so that she wasn't the only one suffering a chill from the hotel's drafty old windows.

"You're overdressed," she pointed out. "So you first."

His right brow rose to meet the left and a muscle began to twitch along his jaw. Lifting his arms to waist height, he unbuttoned one cuff, then the other. With a roll of his broad shoulders, he shrugged out of the shirt completely, letting the pristine white material float to the floor behind him.

Vanessa swallowed. Making him strip down to next to nothing had seemed like a good idea at the time, but now that his chest was bare, she wasn't so sure. The very sight of that flat stomach and those tight pectorals had her mouth going desert dry and her heartbeat fluttering in her throat like the wings of a butterfly.

Without giving her time to regroup or even brace herself for more, he moved his hands to the front of his slacks and slowly lowered the zipper. Kicking off his shoes, he let the pants drop and stepped away from the entire pile—away from the clothes and one step closer to her.

"Better?" he asked, barely a foot of space separating them while the corners of his mouth curved in predatory amusement.

Not better. Definitely not better. If possible, it was worse. Because now, in addition to feeling anxious and exposed, she was also feeling extremely overwhelmed.

How could she have forgotten what this man looked like naked? Or nearly naked, at any rate.

There were male models out there being used for Calvin Klein and Abercrombie & Fitch ad campaigns who couldn't hold a candle to a fully dressed Marc. Undressed, in only his underwear, he blew them out of the water.

Out of his underwear...well, out of his underwear, he could blow water out of the water. No one would ever ask him to be a spokesperson for designer clothing or cologne, though, because putting him on billboards would cause women everywhere to swoon on the spot. They would cause traffic accidents and hit their heads on the pavement, and those were just lawsuits waiting to happen.

When they'd been married, Marc's good looks had amused her. The fact that he turned heads and invited so much female attention hadn't bothered her in the least, because she knew that at the end of the day, he was all hers. Other women could look, but she was the only one who got to touch.

They'd been divorced for over a year, though. How many other women had gotten to touch him in that time? How many heads had he turned who'd also managed to turn his?

As though sensing the direction of her thoughts, he lifted a hand to stroke her cheek. "Cold feet?" he asked quietly.

She shook her head in denial, but inside she was thinking, *Cold everything.*

She'd left him, been the one to initiate the divorce in the first place, but even so, she didn't want to think about him being with other women. It left her more than cold; it left her shaken.

Closing the space between them, he carefully pried her arms away from her breasts, but used his own chest to hold the bra in place. He ran his hands down the insides of her arms, then linked their fingers together. Just the way he used to, the way that used to make her feel so close to him, so cherished.

Pressing his lips to hers, he whispered, "Let me warm you up." Then he kissed her and started backing her slowly toward the bed.

The backs of her thighs hit the edge of the mattress and she toppled over, but Marc followed her down, so smoothly, it felt almost choreographed. The movement finally dislodged her bra and he grabbed it by one of the cups, tossing it aside.

His chest pressed her breasts flat and abraded the tight peaks of her nipples. She moaned, wrapping her arms around his shoulders while he kissed all but about three functioning brain cells straight out of her head.

Shifting his hands to her hips, he hooked his thumbs into the waist of her panties and dragged them down. He lifted her just enough to slip them off, then quickly shed his own.

They were both blessedly naked, pressed together like layers of cellophane. Insecurities threatened to surface again, reminding her that it had been months upon months since they'd been together…that she'd gone through a pregnancy and childbirth since then…that she'd spent her first trimester in a deep depression over the breakup of her marriage and the prospect of being a single mother—and therefore had spent a good deal of time in bed with cartons of ice cream and cookie dough that never quite made it into the oven.

In addition to baby weight, she'd put on pity-party weight, and though she'd been much more disciplined since she'd stopped feeling sorry for herself, she still hadn't managed to shed all of those extra pounds. Her hips were wider than before, her stomach far from flat, her thighs a bit more well-rounded.

The only upside to her new, more curvaceous figure was her bosom. Whether it was due to the pre-baby caloric binges or the post-baby breast-feeding, the increased bra size was kind of nice. And being bigger up top helped to keep the rest of her body in proper proportion.

But whether her recent physical changes were good or bad, Marc didn't seem to mind either way. In fact, he didn't even seem to notice. Or if he did, he was enjoying them enough that he didn't feel the need to comment.

Knowing that allowed Vanessa to relax and stop obsessing. Marc's hands on her body, his mouth trailing along her jaw, her throat, her shoulder, her collarbone, were too potent to ignore for long, anyway. As was the need to touch him in return.

She stroked his back, toyed with the hair at the nape of his neck. Nibbled his ear and rubbed her cheek against the slight stubble that was growing in and would need to be shaved clean again in the morning.

His erection was pressed between them, rubbing in tantalizing places and she arched slightly to feel even more of that rigid length against her belly and lower. With a low growl, Marc sank his teeth into the muscle that ran from the side of her throat to her shoulder. She sucked in a sharp breath, groaning at the light stab of pleasure-pain and digging her nails into the flesh of his back to repay the favor.

He chuckled against her skin and she felt the vibrations clear down to her bones.

"Stop teasing," she ordered more than a little breathlessly just above his ear.

"You started it," he retorted, words muffled as he spoke into her skin. He trailed wet, openmouthed kisses across her chest, over the mound of one breast, tighter and tighter around her nipple.

"Besides, I'm not finished yet," he added a moment before taking that nipple into his mouth and suckling gently.

Oh, mercy. Vanessa's upper body shot off the mattress, pleasure streaking through her like lightning. She couldn't even cry out, the oxygen was knocked so thoroughly from her lungs.

She clung to his shoulders, panting and writhing as he didn't just tease, but tortured. He licked and nipped and sucked at one breast before moving to the other and driving her crazy all over again.

When he finished, he lifted his head and smiled down at her. A wicked, devilish smile.

He started to lean down and she was afraid of what he might do. She wasn't sure she could take much more, whether he decided to continue his cruel ministrations to her breasts or to move lower.

Oh, no, he couldn't go lower. Another time, maybe. Another time, she was sure she would be delighted, and more than willing to reciprocate.

But tonight, it would be too much. She couldn't bear it.

So before he got any bright ideas, she linked her legs

around his hips and reached between them to take him in a firm, but careful grasp. He let out a hiss of breath, lips pulling back from his teeth and his eyes falling closed.

"Enough," she told him.

His lashes fluttered and he gazed down at her. "Do you want me to stop?" he murmured.

The bastard. He knew she didn't want him to stop, he was just teasing her—*torturing* her—again.

Giving him a little taste of his own medicine, she tightened her fingers around his arousal, causing him to gasp and flex his hips.

"Not stop-stop," she clarified, as though there were really any doubt, "just wrap up the opening act and get to the big bang already."

He arched a brow, his lips splitting into a wide grin. "The 'big bang,' huh?"

She felt her cheeks heat at her choice of words. Then again, she was lying naked beneath her ex-husband, all but done with the dirty deed, as it were. Was there really any reason to be embarrassed about *anything* at this point?

Taking a deep breath and pulling her chin up a notch, she said, "You heard me."

"Well," he replied slowly, that same predatory gleam in his eyes, that same sly smile, curving his mouth, "I'll see what I can do to deliver."

It was her turn to arch a brow and adopt an overconfident expression. "You do that."

His grin widened a second before he swooped in to place a rough, hard kiss on her lips. Then he reached down to cover her hand with his. Slowly, he pried her fingers away from that most sensitive of body parts and raised her arm over her head, pinning it to the mattress.

Shifting, he settled more fully between her legs, the tip of his erection nudging her opening. And then he slid home, slowly, carefully, his mouth still covering hers, absorbing the heartfelt moans his agonizing entry dragged from her throat.

She clutched at his hands, both of them, where they held her own flat to the mattress. And he squeezed back, groaning against her lips as his hips began to move.

Inch by inch, he filled her up, stretching muscles and tissue that had been too long unused. It didn't hurt, though. On the contrary, it felt amazingly, wonderfully perfect.

Like so many times in the past, she marveled at how well they fit together, how every part of her body seemed to be molded, sculpted, designed for every part of his body. Even with the physical changes she'd gone through over the past year, that hadn't altered.

Levering himself up on his elbows, he released her mouth, giving her the chance to bite her bottom lip and tilt her head back in growing ecstasy. He did the same, nostrils flaring as he pulled out, then drove back in, slowly at first and then faster and faster.

She lifted her own hips, meeting him thrust for thrust, letting the motion, the flesh-on-flesh sensations wash over her in ever-increasing waves. Her lungs burned, struggling for air while the rest of her body struggled for completion. Every part of her tingled, tightening in longing, in expectation.

She wanted—no, *needed*—what only Marc could give her. And while slow and steady might be good for some things, like marathons and piano lessons, that's not what she was interested in right now. She wanted hard and fast and now, now, now!

"Marc, please," she begged, wrapping her arms more securely around his neck before leaning up to nip his earlobe. Then she sank her teeth even harder into his shoulder.

His entire body shuddered from head to toe above her, his hands grasping her waist and digging in. He pounded into her with even more force, making her cry out, making himself cry out.

Pressure built until she wanted to scream and then suddenly the dam burst. Pleasure spilled over her in a splash of heat and colorful sparks, like fireworks going off overhead.

She called his name and clung to him for dear life, absorbing the delicious impact of his final thrusts, and finally his full weight as he collapsed atop her with a long, low groan of satisfied completion.

Eight

"This was probably a bad idea," Vanessa murmured.

Marc had wondered how long it would take her to start in on her list of regrets.

They were lying side by side, flat on their backs on the lumpy, queen-size hotel room mattress. Vanessa had the sheets pulled up to her armpits, held in place over her ample breasts by both hands. He was a bit more relaxed, stretched out and letting the sheet fall where it would, low on his abdomen and across his hips.

But while he was obviously taking their minor indiscretion in stride, he couldn't disagree with her on the "bad idea" part. He wasn't sorry, since making love with Vanessa wasn't something he could ever regret or apologize for, but she was right that it hadn't been the smartest decision of his life.

He wasn't even sure what had possessed him to kiss her in the first place.

Maybe because he'd been thinking about it all night, his eyes straying over and over again to her mouth and the luscious cleavage visible above the bodice of her siren-red sex goddess dress.

Maybe because he hadn't been able to get her out of his head since the moment he'd seen her again after such a long absence…and after pretty much determining that he would never see her again at all.

Or maybe because she was simply irresistible. For him, she always had been.

It almost didn't surprise him that they'd made a child together at the very moment that their marriage had been falling apart around them. Despite their differences and the problems that had plagued them there at the end, physical compatibility had never even made it onto the list. No matter how bad a day either of them might be having, no matter how big a fight they might have had, it never seemed to take them long to come back together and set the sheets on fire.

It was a relief to know that hadn't changed. They were no longer married, she'd hidden his son from him and neither of them had a very clear vision of what the future held, but at least he knew the passion was still there. More than passion—lust and longing and desire thick enough to land a 747 on.

His leg brushed against hers beneath the covers and a jolt of that passion times ten shot through him. She jerked away from him, letting him know in no uncertain terms that his current state of semi-arousal would definitely be going to waste.

"You're right," he said, agreeing with her earlier statement. "Probably wasn't the wisest thing to do. At least not under the current circumstances."

"There's the understatement of the century," she grumbled, rolling to the side of the bed and carefully sliding her bare legs out from under the top sheet.

She sat there for a minute, not moving, and Marc took the opportunity to admire the short fall of her copper hair around her shoulders, the supple line of her spine, and the gentle curves of her torso from the back. She'd put on a bit of weight with the pregnancy, but it didn't take away from her attractiveness one damn bit.

If anything, it made her even more beautiful, filling her out with sensual, womanly curves in all the right places. He had certainly enjoyed exploring those curves with his hands and lips, feeling them so soft and gentle against his much harder naked length.

One corner of his mouth lifted in amusement, not only from the delectable view, but from the snarky tone of her voice. She'd always had such a way with words, and a way of delivering them that often delighted him.

It had annoyed the hell out of her when she'd been in a snit, telling him off, and would catch him grinning. Not because he wasn't listening or taking her seriously, but because he'd always loved watching her and listening to her—even when she was chewing him out.

The way she moved, pacing back and forth and waving her arms. The way her breasts rose and fell in agitation, following the cadence of her rant. What could he say…it turned him on. And nine times out of ten, their arguments had led to phenomenal make-up sex, so there was really no downside to riling her up a little more by letting her think he was laughing off her anger or upset.

In hindsight, he could see how that might have led to some of the problems that had prompted them to split. He'd never meant to deride her feelings or opinions on anything, he'd simply believed their relationship was secure enough that any differences or misunderstandings they had would blow over just as they had in the past.

How wrong he'd been. And he hadn't seen it coming until it was too late. Too damn late.

"It can't happen again," she said, still facing the other direction.

For a moment, he remained trapped in his head and thought she was talking about their divorce. That definitely couldn't happen again, and if he had it to do over, it might not have happened in the first place.

Then he realized she meant the sex. Tonight's unplanned, unexpected, but definitely not unsatisfying, indiscretion.

"Marc," she said when he didn't respond. Twisting slightly, she tilted her head until she could see him from the corner of her eye, then repeated more firmly, "This can't happen again."

Rolling to his side, he propped himself up on one elbow, letting silence fill the room while he studied her. After a minute or two, he murmured, "What do you want me to say, Vanessa? That I'm sorry we made love? That I don't hope we get the chance to do it again…frequently and with great enthusiasm?" He shrugged the shoulder that wasn't holding him up. "Sorry, but I'm not going to do that."

"What is wrong with you?" she charged, all but leaping from the bed, dragging the sheet along with her. It caught on the corners of the mattress, of course, but not before sliding from his hips and leaving him in the buff down to his ankles.

She turned, yanking at the cheap, industrial grade white cotton until it came free, pointedly ignoring his total nudity. With a huff, she yanked the quilted coverlet from the foot of the bed and tossed it over him, head and all. He chuckled, lowering it just in time to watch her wrap the sheet like a toga around her own naked form.

"We're divorced, Marcus," she pointed out, as though

he weren't painfully aware of their current marital status. Or lack thereof.

She stormed around the room gathering her clothing, piece by discarded piece. "Divorced couples aren't supposed to sleep together."

"Maybe not, but we both know it happens all the time." He waved a hand to encompass the rumpled bed and their current states of postcoital undress.

"Well, it shouldn't," she argued back, doing her best to hold up the sheet while she struggled into her underwear. "Besides, you hate me."

A beat passed while the air in the room sizzled with growing tension. "Says who?"

At the softly spoken question, Vanessa jerked to a halt and lifted her head to meet his gaze. The lower half of the sheet, which had been hiked up around her thighs while she fought with her panties, fell to the ground.

"Don't you?" she asked just as softly. "I mean, you do. I know you do. Or at least, you should. I didn't tell you I was pregnant. I didn't tell you about Danny."

His brows crossed and his mouth dipped down in a scowl at the reminder. He'd been working hard to forget that part of his reason for being in town. Or more to the point, had been willing to suspend his anger and feelings of betrayal long enough to partake of Vanessa's lovely body and enjoy the tactile sensations of having her in his arms and bed again after so long.

He took in her still half-naked form, wrapped like a Greek goddess in pristine white cotton. Sure, all of the reasons he *should* hate her were still there. And no doubt they had many issues to work out. But for some reason, at that moment, he just couldn't get his temper to flare.

"Here's a bit of advice," he told her, cocking a brow

and trying not to let his frown slip up into a grin. "When someone has temporarily forgotten that they have a reason to be mad at you, it's probably better not to remind them."

"But you should be mad at me," she said quietly, holding his gaze for a long, drawn out second before turning her back to him and continuing to dress.

Marc watched as she struggled with her bra, then let the sheet fall as she hooked the bit of lingerie behind her back. He watched the light play on the pale canvas of her skin and the smooth lines of her body as she moved.

Interesting, he thought, fighting the urge to drag her back to bed. She seemed to *want* him to be angry with her.

On the one hand, at least he knew she hadn't slept with him in an effort to cloud his mind and seduce him into forgetting that she tried to keep his son from him. On the other, she'd have been wise to do almost anything to stay on his good side at this point. To avoid acrimony, a possible custody battle or to keep him from simply picking up and taking Danny home with him, leaving her few options to get him back.

Granted, before today, he hadn't spoken with Vanessa in over a year, and the fact that she'd left him meant he probably hadn't understood her all that well to begin with. But the only explanation he could think of for why she'd remind him of what stood between them was that she *needed* something between them. A wall. A barrier.

If he hated her, he might not want to be with her again. If he hated her, he might get fed up and storm home to Pittsburgh—preferably without Danny.

Oh, they'd work out some sort of custody agreement. On that, he would insist. And he was sure Vanessa wouldn't argue too strongly against it, not now. Agreeing to let him see Danny on a regular basis or even let him take their son back to Pittsburgh for the occasional extended visit would be the lesser of two evils for her now.

But he'd been in big business long enough to know that when someone gave up something too easily, it was usually because they were trying to get or retain something even more important to them. His best guess was that Vanessa was trying to retain distance.

She'd wasted no time moving to Summerville the minute their divorce was final, and as far as he could tell, she'd been perfectly happy settling in with her aunt and making her mark on the small town through The Sugar Shack.

If Fate hadn't somehow intervened to bring him here himself, he never would have known where she'd relocated to or that she had a child. *His* child.

Oh, yes, she'd wanted distance then, and she wanted it now. And if she pissed him off—or kept him pissed off—then he'd be less likely to stick around for any length of time, wouldn't he?

Which only made him want to stick around more. He was contrary like that sometimes, a fact Vanessa was well aware of. She should have known that if he caught on to her little plan, he'd make a point of doing pretty much the exact opposite of what she wanted, just to vex her.

Of course, there was a good chance she didn't even realize she had a little plan. That she was running heavily on instinct, her current thoughts and actions more subconscious than anything else.

But it still intrigued him, and if he hadn't wanted to stick around before just to be close to the child he hadn't known existed, he certainly did now. He was even look-ing forward to it, considering the entertaining side ben-efits he'd recently discovered could be added to his stay.

Tossing back the covers, he moved to the edge of the bed and sat up. "Well, I'm sorry to disappoint you, but I don't hate you."

He pushed to his feet and walked toward her stark naked. Where she'd fought so hard to protect her mod-esty and stay covered, he didn't bother and wasn't the least bit self-conscious about his nudity.

When she saw him coming, she took a jerky step back, away from him, but he wasn't really after her. Bending at the waist, he scooped up the tangled ball of his pants and underwear.

"I'm not happy about what you did," he clarified, climbing into his clothes with slow, deliberate move-ments, "and I can't say that I don't harbor a bit of anger and resentment over it. Or that there won't be moments when that anger and resentment flare hotter than any-thing else."

He leaned down for his wrinkled shirt and shrugged it on, but didn't bother buttoning it, leaving his chest bare down the middle. "But we've covered that ground already. Keeping Danny from me—or the pregnancy to begin with—was wrong. That's time and an experience I can't get back. Now that I know I have a son, however, things are going to change. I *am* going to be involved in his life—and therefore in yours."

She was standing only about three feet from him, clutching that red dress to her breasts to cover as much of her front as she could. It was silly and useless, a bit like locking the barn door after the bull had already escaped, but Marc found her false sense of modesty oddly endearing.

"You should probably come to terms with that," he told her matter-of-factly. "The sooner, the better."

She simply stood there, staring at him. Her eyes sparkled like polished sapphires, but whether with fear or rage or mere confusion, he couldn't quite tell.

While he had her off balance—which was a nice switch, frankly, since she'd pretty much had him off balance from the moment he'd driven into town—he tossed another can of gasoline on the bonfire that just seemed to continue blazing between them.

"Here's something else you should probably take into consideration," he said quietly, widening his stance and crossing his arms determinedly in front of him.

Vanessa didn't reply. Instead, she cocked her head, the tendons at the sides of her throat convulsing as she swallowed, waiting nervously for him to elaborate.

"We didn't use a condom, which means that you may even now be pregnant with our second child."

Nine

Oh, God.

Marc's words slammed into Vanessa's chest like a bullet, knocking the air from her lungs and making her literally stagger on her feet.

What had she been thinking? Bad enough she'd fallen into bed with her ex-husband faster than a star falls from the sky, but she'd completely forgotten about protection of any kind. It had never occurred to her to insist he use a condom, and since she was a new mother, still breast-feeding and with absolutely zero romantic prospects on the horizon, it hadn't been necessary for her to be on birth control.

She tried to do the math in her head, to figure out when her last period had been and when she was due again, but panic kept her thoughts in a tailspin.

And what about the breast-feeding? Wasn't it supposed to be harder to get pregnant while still nursing?

Dear God, please let that be true, because she couldn't even fathom the idea that she might actually be pregnant *again,* unexpectedly, unplanned and by her *former* husband. It was almost too horrifying to contemplate.

"I'm not," she said, as though saying it firmly and decisively enough would make it true.

Marc raised a dark, sardonic brow. "How can you be so sure?"

"I'm just not," she insisted, tearing frantically at her dress until she got her feet inside and could yank it up. Never mind that it was open all the way to her bottom in the back because she couldn't raise the zipper without help. She would walk home with it hanging loose, if she had to, rather than ask him for one iota of assistance.

"And what were you thinking?" she charged, stamping a foot as she slipped it into a strappy red heel. "How could you do that—let *me* do that—without taking precautions?" She cast him an angry, accusatory glare. "I've never known you to be so irresponsible."

He shrugged, looking exponentially more casual and unconcerned than she was feeling at that particular moment. "What can I say? I was swept away by your beauty and passion, and the exhilaration of being with you again after such a long absence."

Pausing in the act of shoving on her other shoe, she tilted her head in his direction and gave a loud, unladylike snort. *"Please,"* she scoffed.

"Is that so hard to believe?" he asked, still wearing the blank mask that gave her no clue of his true emotions.

Was he upset that they'd forgotten to use protection? Happy? Angry? Excited? Confused? Nauseous?

Because she was nauseous. And upset and angry and confused. There was no happiness or excitement anywhere on her radar.

If it turned out she really was pregnant…oh, God, please don't let her be pregnant again—not by Marc, and not so soon after Danny's birth…she would of course love the baby. Unconditionally and without question. But the difference between loving an existing child and loving the notion of carrying an as-yet imaginary one—especially under these circumstances—was like the difference between black and white, hot and cold, thirsty and drowning.

She loved Danny with all her heart and soul. She wouldn't trade him for anything, or even go back and undo the events that had led to his birth.

But she sure as *hell* wouldn't choose to be pregnant again. Not so soon after having one child, not without benefit of marriage, and not with a man she'd so recently divorced.

She was already linked too closely to Marc, thanks to his discovery of Danny's existence. But the thought of being even more closely connected to him through a second child would be a nightmare come to life.

He was almost foaming-at-the-mouth rabid about staying close to her now that he knew about Danny. Having him know from the very beginning that he was going to be a father a second time would turn him into near-stalker material. She would never get rid of him, not even for short amounts of time while he commuted back and forth between Pittsburgh and Summerville.

Oh, no, knowing Marc, he would do something ridiculous like move to Summerville himself, or insist they get remarried and then drag her back to the city where she would be trapped and miserable all over again.

No, no, no, no, no. Vanessa's head was shaking like a tambourine as she ran her gaze around the room, looking for anything she might have forgotten. Her purse, her watch, an earring…

"I think you underestimate your appeal," Marc remarked, apparently missing the nuclear meltdown taking place inside her.

Small red clutch in hand, she shot him another withering glare before spinning on her heel and marching toward the hotel room door.

"Vanessa."

Her free hand was out, reaching for the knob, but his sharp voice stopped her in her tracks. She didn't turn to look at him, but remained still, waiting for him to continue.

"I'll see you at the bakery first thing tomorrow, eight o'clock sharp. Be sure Danny is with you."

A shudder rolled through her, and she wasn't sure if it was aversion to having to deal with him again in the morning or relief that that was his only parting remark.

With a jerky nod, she pulled the door open and started to step into the hall.

"And I'll want to know as soon as you do," he went on, stopping her a second time.

Her heart lurched in her chest. "Know what?" she asked, forcing the words past her tight, dry throat.

"Whether or not we'll be presenting our son with a little brother or sister nine months from now."

Marc wasn't at The Sugar Shack when she and Aunt Helen arrived with Danny in tow at five o'clock the next morning. Vanessa wasn't surprised, since he'd said he would meet her there at eight, and frankly, she could use the short reprieve.

It might only be three hours, but it was three hours without having to see or deal with Marc. And after last night, she needed them. Desperately.

While she and Aunt Helen bustled around readying the bakery for the breakfast opening, she tried her best to put him and the myriad of issues between them out of her mind. Not for the first time…not even for the five hundred and first time…she wondered how she'd managed to get herself into such an incredible mess.

It felt as though her life had turned into some kind of daytime soap opera, and the worst part was that she knew those things were never-ending. They just went on forever, with more and more dramatic cliff-hangers cropping up to throw the main characters into a tizzy.

Well, she didn't need any more tizzies. And she sure as heck didn't need any more drama. If she could have, she'd have canceled her own personal variation of *As the World Spins Out of Control*.

Unfortunately, those few hours of blessed freedom sped by much too quickly. Before she knew it, Summerville's early risers were filing in for a morning coffee and croissant on their way to work, or to sit and enjoy a more leisurely sticky bun with a cup of hot tea. Even before the clock struck eight o'clock, her eyes were practically glued to the front door, waiting for Marc to arrive.

But the clock did strike eight and he didn't appear. Then it struck ten after, twenty after, quarter to nine, and he was still nowhere in sight.

She should have been relieved, but instead, Vanessa found herself beginning to worry. It wasn't like Marc to be late for anything, especially after making such a production of warning her of where he would be when—and where he fully expected her to be to meet him.

She rang up an order for four coffees and a box of mixed Danish pastries with one eye on the time, trying to decide if she should bask in her apparent—and most likely fleeting—freedom, or call the Harbor Inn to check on him.

By nine-thirty, she'd not only decided to call the hotel,

but if he wasn't there, intended to drive over herself to search his room, and call the police, if necessary. But before she could untie her apron and ask Aunt Helen to cover the front counter for her, the bell above the door rang and Marc strolled in, a charming smile on his face.

As hard as she tried not to notice, he looked magnificent. In place of his usual suit and tie, he wore tan slacks and a light blue chambray shirt. The shirt's collar was open, cuffs rolled up to midforearm.

Anyone else might see Marc and think he was just a run-of-the-mill guy, out and about on a beautiful summer day. But Vanessa knew better. If one looked closer, one would notice the solid gold Rolex, the seven-hundred-dollar Ferragamo loafers and the air of absolute power and confidence that surrounded him.

This was Marc's casual appearance, but as wise men knew, appearances could be extremely deceptive.

He walked through the maze of small round tables as though he owned the place, his smile turning more and more predatory the closer he came to the tall glass display case that separated them.

"Good morning," he greeted, sounding much too chipper for her peace of mind.

"Morning," she returned with much less enthusiasm. "You're late. I thought you said you'd be here at eight."

One solid shoulder rose and fell in a casual shrug. "I had some errands to run."

She raised a brow, but didn't ask because she wasn't sure she wanted to know.

"Do you have a minute?" he asked.

She glanced around, judging the number of customers at the tables and the few people who were milling in front of the display case, trying to decide which sweet was most worth ruining their diets.

With a quick nod, she moved toward the kitchen and dipped her head through the swinging double doors. "Aunt Helen, could you work the register for a second? I need to speak with Marc."

Aunt Helen finished what she was doing and came out, wiping her hands on the front of her apron while Vanessa removed hers and hung it on a small hook on the far wall. Her aunt cast Marc a cautious, almost disparaging glance, but held her tongue, thank goodness.

Vanessa hadn't told Aunt Helen what happened with Marc the night before. She'd given a brief recap of dinner, acting as though all they'd discussed was the bakery and a potential business agreement, and that everything had remained very professional. But she hadn't mentioned word one about following him up to his hotel room or letting things get out of control. And she certainly hadn't shared the fact that her hormones had so overwhelmed her common sense that she'd allowed Marc to make love to her without any form of doctor-recommended birth control.

Knowing the whole story would only have increased Aunt Helen's animosity toward Marc. There was a time, not so long ago, when Vanessa welcomed her aunt's protectiveness and having someone to talk to about everything she'd been through both before and during the divorce.

But things had changed now. Not necessarily for the better, but in ways she couldn't avoid. Marc knew about Danny, was determined to be a part of his son's life, and that meant he was going to be a part of hers. For better or worse, she had to find a way to make peace with her ex-husband, if only to keep the next eighteen years of her life from being a living hell.

In order to do that, and also keep the peace with her aunt, she had to avoid bad-mouthing Marc. She probably shouldn't have done so in the first place, but she'd been so hurt, so miserable, that she'd had to talk to *someone,* and Aunt Helen's had been the perfect shoulder to cry on.

Marc came up behind her, laying a hand gently on her elbow. As soon as she was sure Helen was settled behind the counter, she let him lead her across the bakery and through the shared entrance that led to the empty space next door.

She thought they were simply going to use the area to talk privately, and her stomach was nearly in knots wondering what sort of shoe or bomb or anvil he would drop on her this time. But rather than stopping in the center of the empty space, he kept walking, pulling her with him to the front of the building and the glass door that opened out onto the sidewalk.

"Do you have a key for this?" he asked, pointing to the door's lock.

"Yes. The landlord knows I'm interested in renting the space and occasionally lets me use it for small bits of storage. Plus, I can let other potential renters in if he isn't available."

"Good," he replied, his warm hand still cupping her elbow more intimately than she would have liked. "I'm going to need it."

She blinked. "Why?"

"To let those guys in," he answered, cocking his head in the direction of the glass and the street beyond. "Unless you want them traipsing through your bakery and dragging all their dirty, heavy equipment with them."

Following his gaze, she blinked again, only then noticing that the sidewalk outside the empty storefront was littered with men in jeans and work shirts unloading toolboxes, sawhorses, lumber and various cutting implements from the row of pickup trucks parked at the curb.

"Who are they?" she asked in dismay.

"Your construction crew."

She met Marc's gaze and must have looked as confused as she felt because he quickly elaborated.

"They're here to clean the place up and start putting in your shelving and countertops."

"What? Why?"

Her ex-husband's expression went from being amused at her utter shock to exasperated at her apparent denseness. "It's all part of the expansion plan, remember? We've got to get this section of the building renovated for The Sugar Shack's mail-order distribution and that Cookie of the Month thing you have in mind."

Her gaze swung from Marc to the workers outside, to Marc, to the workers… She now knew exactly how wild animals felt when caught in the middle of the highway by bright, oncoming headlights.

"I don't understand," she said with a slow shake of her head. "I didn't hire them. They can't start working here because I haven't rented the space yet. I don't have the money."

Marc gave a perturbed sigh. "Why do you think I'm here, Vanessa? Aside from wanting to spend time with Danny. Don't you remember what we discussed last night?"

She remembered last night. Vividly. And she remembered his parting shot that he hadn't used a condom, she hadn't been on the pill and she might very well be pregnant with his child. Again. The rest was a bit more of a blur, especially at this particular moment.

One of the workers came to the door. Marc made a motion with his hand, indicating that he needed a minute or two more, and the man nodded, returning to his truck.

"Look, it's taken care of, okay?" Marc told her. "I talked to the building's owner about the modifications we want to make. The space will be rented in your name, and part of the agreement will include permission to make any changes we see fit to better our business. Brian is putting together the paperwork and will deliver the contracts today. I'll have him get me a copy of the key from the landlord, but for now I need the one you have."

"But…" She was starting to sound like a broken record. "If Brian hasn't talked to Mr. Parsons yet, how do you know he'll agree to let us—*me*—rent this space?"

His mossy green eyes sparkled with self-assurance. "Vanessa," he said slowly, as though speaking to a small child or particularly slow adult. "It's taken care of. The building is for rent, I told Brian to rent it. What more do you need to know?"

She was finally catching on. Or rather, finally fully absorbing the situation and Marc's deep-rooted resolve to stay in town.

"Let me guess. 'Money is no object,'" she mimicked, adopting a low, masculine voice that was clearly supposed to be his. "You told Brian what you wanted—with no limit on how much you were willing to spend—and are leaving him to do whatever he has to for you to get your own way."

Releasing her elbow, he propped his hands on his hips, letting out a frustrated breath. "What's wrong with that?" he wanted to know.

She wished she could say nothing. She wished she didn't mind that he was using his wealth and prestige to assist her in her business and help to make the bakery an even bigger success.

There had even been a time when that sort of power and cocky confidence would have impressed her. Now, though, it only made her nervous.

"I don't want to be indebted to you, Marc," she told him softly, honestly. "I don't want to owe you anything, or know that The Sugar Shack has only expanded, is only successful, because you rode into town and saved the day with the Keller family fortune."

"Why does it matter where the capital comes from, Vanessa? The important thing is that you're getting your additional space and branching out into mail order."

Shaking her head, she crossed her arms beneath her breasts and took a step back. "You don't understand. It *does* matter, because if you come in waving your checkbook around and running roughshod over me and everyone else in this town, then it's not *my* business anymore. It's just another insignificant acquisition for Keller Corp's multimillion-dollar holdings."

Widening his stance, he copied her defensive position of arms over chest. "Don't give me that. You asked Brian Blake to look for an investor you could work with. Preferably a silent one who would be willing to flush copious amounts of money into the bakery, but not have much say on how it was run or what you did with the cash. For the most part, that's exactly what I'm doing. So your problem isn't that I'm 'waving my checkbook around,' as you so eloquently put it. Your problem is that it's *my* checkbook."

"*Of course* that's my problem," she snapped, his earlier frustrations rubbing off on her. "We've been down this road before, Marc. The money, the influence, expecting everyone and everything to fall into line simply because your name is Keller."

Uncrossing her arms, she raised her hands to cover her face for a minute, trying to collect her thoughts and her temper. Once she lowered them, her tone was more subdued.

"Don't get me wrong, I liked it for a while. I enjoyed the lifestyle being your wife afforded me. The parties, the wardrobe, never having to worry about making ends meet."

Oh, yes. After a lifetime of struggling, of working her fingers to the bone just to get by, marrying into money had been a welcome reprieve.

"But you have no idea what it was like to be your wife and live under that roof without truly being a Keller."

His eyes narrowed, their green depths filling with genuine confusion. "What are you talking about? Of course, you were a true Keller. You were my wife."

"That's sure not how it felt," she admitted softly, remembering all the times his mother had made a point of reminding her that she was a Keller by marriage only, making her feel as though she had no business even crossing the threshold of Keller Manor without a mop and feather duster in her hands.

"I'm sorry." His arms slid from his chest and he started to reach for her, then seemed to think better of it and dropped his hands to his sides. "I never meant to make you feel like an outsider."

Guilt stabbed through her at the hurt look on his face. She opened her mouth to tell him that he hadn't been nearly as big an offender as his mother, but a sharp rap on the glass cut her off, startling them both.

The same worker as before, apparently the man in charge of the rest of the crew, made an impatient face and tapped his watch. Time, as they said, was money, and he obviously wasn't making any standing around on the sidewalk. Of course, Vanessa was sure Marc was paying them well, and most likely by the hour, regardless of whether they were actively working or not.

Marc lifted a hand, giving him the *just a second* gesture before turning back to her. "I'm going to need that key before these guys decide to sledgehammer their way in here."

She licked her lips and swallowed, reluctant to do his bidding. She and Marc had been on the verge of an honest-to-goodness adult conversation. One where she'd finally almost worked up the courage to tell him the truth behind why she'd gotten fed up and left in the first place. She'd tried so many times in the past to let him know how she was being treated, how much she felt like an outcast in what was supposed to be her own home, but she'd never quite been brave enough to blurt it out.

Part of her had believed that if he loved her enough, if he understood her as much as a husband was supposed to understand his wife, then he would know what she was trying to say all the times she'd hinted at her growing unhappiness. Now, she realized that nobody should be expected to be a mind reader, especially someone of the male persuasion.

If only she had been wise enough and gutsy enough to simply tell him what was going on. Things might have turned out so differently.

But that was water under the bridge and any chance

they might have had of wiping the slate clean this morning had disappeared with the carpenter's untimely interruption.

Licking her lips again, she inclined her head. "I'll get the key," she said, turning on her heel and hurrying away.

Ten

"**I** swear, that racket is enough to make me want to jump into this oven myself."

Vanessa raised her head from the perfect circles of pastry dough she was currently topping with raisin filling to watch Aunt Helen slide a tray of baklava into one of the industrial ovens and slam the door with a clang that only punctuated the loud, staccato sounds of construction coming from the other side of the bakery walls.

It hadn't been easy to put up with both the noise and the added traffic of having so many workers around. She'd made dozens of apologies to customers, as well as creating *Please excuse our dust* and *Apologies for the excessive noise* signs. Thankfully, no real dust or debris had made it into the actual bakery side of the building, but having the crew around all day every day didn't make it easy for folks to come in and enjoy a *quiet* cup of tea and scones.

"They'll be finished soon," she told her aunt, repeating the line the construction foreman had been giving her for the past week. She was familiar enough with this type of thing to know that "soon" was an extremely relative term, but given the fact that they really were making amazing progress, she thought the job would likely be done in just another week or two.

"And you have to admit, it's been nice of Marc to do all of this for us."

Aunt Helen gave a derisive snort. "Don't fool yourself, dear. He isn't doing it to be nice. He's doing it for himself, and to keep you under his thumb, and you know it."

Vanessa didn't respond, mostly because her aunt was right. Without a doubt, Marc wouldn't still be in town if there wasn't something in it for him.

He wanted to be close to Danny and indeed spent almost every evening at Aunt Helen's house with them. They ate dinner together. He helped feed Danny, gave him baths and put him to bed. At his insistence, she'd shown him how to change a diaper, and amazingly, he now did that almost as often as she did. They played on blankets on the floor, and took walks, and went to the park, even though Danny was too young to truly enjoy it.

It all felt so normal, and Vanessa had to admit…nice.

But just as Aunt Helen had reminded her, she couldn't forget for a minute that there were strings attached to everything Marc did. He wanted to know his son, which was understandable and seemed innocent enough on the surface.

Beyond that, though, she knew the entire situation was steeped in ulterior motives. Or at least the potential for ulterior motives.

Right now, Marc was using the remodeling and bakery expansion as an excuse to be close to his son, and something to occupy his time while Danny took frequent naps. But what would happen later?

What would happen once he decided he'd gotten to

know Danny as well as he could here in Summerville and wanted to take him back to Pittsburgh to assume his rightful place on one of the silver-lined branches of the Keller family tree?

What would happen when the novelty of helping her create a mail-order business for The Sugar Shack wore off and small town living began to bore him?

And why did she bother wondering about such silly questions, when she already knew the answers?

The past couple of weeks, Marc had reminded her more of the man she'd fallen in love with and married than ever before. He'd been kind and generous, sweet and funny. He held doors for her, offered to help her clear the table after meals and put their son down for naps.

And he touched her. Nothing overt or overly sexual that a casual observer might notice, even considering how they'd spent his first night in town. Just a light brush of his fingers now and then—down her arm, over the back of her hand, along her cheek as he tucked a strand of hair behind her ear.

She tried not to read too much into the familiar gestures, but that didn't keep her pulse from thrumming or her heart from hammering inside her chest. Aunt Helen had complained more than once that the house or bakery was too cold, but turning up the air conditioning was the only way Vanessa could think of to combat the erratic spikes in her body temperature that Marc's constant presence and attentions created.

Speak of the devil.

No sooner had the memory played through her head than Marc pushed open the swinging kitchen doors, and she nearly bobbled the spoon she was using to dollop raisin filling onto the tray.

There went her temperature again, causing her skin to flush and perspiration to break out along her brow and between her breasts. At least this time, she could blame it on the ovens and all the hard work she was putting in trying to fill an order for six dozen raisin-filled cookies by three o'clock.

"When you get a minute," he said, "you should come over and see what you think. The crew is almost finished, and they want to know if there's anything else you'd like done before they go."

"Oh." That brought Vanessa's head up.

She'd been over to the other side of the shop a couple of times during the construction, but hadn't wanted to get in anyone's way. Plus, Marc had been so on top of things that her presence and input hadn't really seemed necessary.

But now that the renovations were nearly complete, she was suddenly excited to see how it looked. To start picturing herself there, boxing up her fresh-baked delights, overseeing the extra employees they would likely have to hire. Or would *get* to hire, if the mail-order idea was as successful as she hoped.

Sparing a glance at Aunt Helen, she dropped her spoon back in the bowl of lumpy, dark brown cookie filling, and began wiping her hands clean on a nearby towel.

"Do you mind?" she asked her aunt.

"Of course not. You go, dear," Aunt Helen told her, bustling over to take over with the cookies. "I'll just finish with these, and after you get back, maybe I'll take a peek at the new space myself."

Vanessa smiled and gave her aunt a peck on the cheek, then pulled off her apron and followed Marc. The occasional bit of sanding or hammering met her ears even before they reached the entryway between the two storefronts, but it had been going on for so long that it was nothing more than background noise now, and none of her regular customers seemed to notice or was bothered by it anymore.

Marc opened the door to the other side of the bakery and pushed back the sheet of thick plastic that had been hung as an extra precaution against sawdust and paint fumes. Holding it aside, he let her duck in ahead of him.

An awed sigh escaped her lips as she straightened and took in her nearly finished surroundings. The room was beautiful. More than she ever could have imagined, even after being in on the initial stages of planning.

Shelves and countertops of various sizes and heights lined the walls, creating more work space than she ever could have hoped for. The floor and ceiling had both been redone, and everything had been painted to match The Sugar Shack so that it was obviously an extension of the bakery itself.

"Oh!" Vanessa cried, putting her fingers to her lips.

"Does it meet with your approval?" Marc asked, amusement evident in his tone.

She was sure he could tell by her shaking hands and watery eyes just how pleased she was, but still she managed a breathless whisper, "It's wonderful."

Spinning around, she slowly took it all in again, and then again, her amazement growing with each turn. She didn't stop to think about how it had come about, the strings that were attached, or how costly the bill might be when it finally came due. All she knew was that this portion of the building was hers now, her chance to grow and expand the business of her heart.

With a tiny squeal of glee, she threw her arms around

Marc's neck and squeezed him tight. Almost immediately, he circled her waist, hugging her back.

"Thank you," she whispered near his ear. "It's perfect."

When she pulled away, an odd expression crossed his face, but before she could question it, the foreman appeared at her left shoulder. She was coming to think of him as the King of Rude and Untimely Interruptions.

"I take it she likes her new work area," he said with a smile, addressing Marc.

Considering that her arms were still linked around her ex-husband's neck, that wasn't a difficult observation to make. Feeling suddenly self-conscious, Vanessa cleared her throat and stepped back, putting a more respectable amount of distance between them.

"She does seem to like it," Marc replied.

"It's more than I ever could have hoped for," she told the two men. "Even after seeing the blueprints and design specs." She shook her head, sliding her hands into the pockets at the front of her white capris to keep from fidgeting. "I never imagined it would look this good."

"Glad you're happy. If there's anything else you need, or any changes you want done, let me know. We'll be here until about four putting on the finishing touches."

She couldn't imagine anything she would want changed, but while the two men talked business, she wandered around the drastically altered space. Admiring, touching, mentally filling the shelves and working behind the counters. She loved the sculpted molding and detail that precisely matched that of the bakery and marked it as hers.

Hers!

Well, hers and Aunt Helen's. And Marc's or the

bank's, since she was sure there was going to be a hefty price to pay to someone at some point.

But even though she'd resisted being tied to her ex-husband in such a way, she couldn't deny that he had given her something no one else could—or would—have, and so quickly. She never would have been able to get things done in such short order with another investor or a loan directly from the bank.

Footsteps sounded behind her on the hardwood floor and she turned to see Marc coming toward her once again.

"They'll be cleaned up and out of here in a few more hours. And the computer equipment will be delivered tomorrow, so you can start setting up then, if you like."

Vanessa clasped her hands together, just barely resisting the urge to rub them together like some sort of devilish cartoon character. She was so excited, she almost couldn't contain herself.

They would need a website…and someone to design and maintain it, since she knew next to nothing about that sort of thing. They would also need packaging, and to set up an account with a reliable shipping company, and specialty shipping labels, and possibly even a catalog.

Goodness, there was so much to do. More, possibly, than she'd realistically considered.

Alarm began to claw at her insides and her chest became suddenly too tight to breathe. Oh, God, she couldn't do this. It was too much. She was only one person, for heaven's sake, and even if she counted on Aunt Helen's help, that made them only two people, one of whom had reached retirement age twenty years ago.

Which basically put her back to being only one person, who *could not* handle this type of workload alone.

"I know you have a lot to do," Marc said, cutting into her panicked thoughts and allowing a small bit of oxygen to enter her lungs again, "but before you get too wrapped up in all of that, there's something I've been meaning to discuss with you."

She took a deep breath and forced herself to relax. One day at a time, one step at a time. She'd come this far, she could make it the rest of the way…even if it took her months to accomplish what a rich and powerful Keller heir could do practically overnight.

"All right."

"There's some company business that I need to return home to deal with."

"Oh." Her eyes widened in surprise.

She'd gotten so used to Marc being around that the idea of him leaving caught her unaware. Ironic, given how badly she'd wanted him to go back to Pittsburgh when he'd first arrived. Now, though, it was hard to picture the bakery or her day-to-day life without him in it.

Shaking off that rather revealing but unwelcome train of thought, she nodded her acceptance. "Okay, that's fine. I understand you have important work back in the city, and you've certainly done more than enough while you've been here."

She stopped herself just short of thanking him, but only because she was afraid that would fall too close to… well, thanking him, when he wasn't really doing her any favors. Oh, he'd been wonderfully helpful, but not out of the goodness of his heart. Better to take what he'd so generously offered and get him out of town before he started calling in vouchers and demanding repayment in ways she was unwilling or unable to fulfill.

A slow smile started to spread across his features and her pulse jumped. That wasn't a happy smile, it was an I-know-something-you-don't-know, cat-who-swallowed-the-canary smile.

"What?" she asked, drawing back slightly in wariness.

"You think I'm going to just pick up and leave, don't you?"

She had. Or perhaps she'd simply been hoping.

"It's all right, I understand," she said again. Sweeping an arm out to encompass their surroundings, she added, "This is all amazing, a wonderful start. Aunt Helen and I can certainly take over from here."

That smile stretched further, flashing bright white teeth, and a feeling of dread washed over her.

"I'm sure you and Aunt Helen will do a great job in getting the ball rolling. But that will have to wait until after we get back."

Vanessa blinked, replaying his words in her head. The feeling of dread started to dissipate, which was good... except that it seemed to be transforming into more of an all-over numbness that kept her brain from functioning properly.

She cleared her throat. "We?"

Marc inclined his head. "I want you and Danny to return to Pittsburgh with me so I can introduce my family to my son."

Eleven

"No."

Spinning on her heel, Vanessa stalked away, leaving Marc in the rippling wake of that cold, perfunctory response. Granted, he hadn't expected her to jump with joy at the prospect of going back with him, but he'd thought she would at least be reasonable about it.

With a sigh of resignation, he followed her through the plastic-draped doorway and into the bakery side of the building. She was already out of sight, likely in the kitchen, which meant she'd been moving at a pretty good clip.

He lifted a hand to push through the swinging door only to have it push back toward him, nearly cracking him in the face. Aunt Helen's blue eyes widened in startlement when she saw him, but she didn't say a word, simply tipped up her chin and pranced off for the front counter.

No love lost there, he thought, stepping into the kitchen and finding Vanessa exactly where he expected—standing at one of the large central islands, seemingly busy and focused on more food preparation. Even if she hadn't just walked away from him in a huff, he'd have known she was agitated by her jerky movements and the ramrod stiffness of her spine.

"Vanessa," he began, letting the door swing closed behind him.

"No."

She spat the word, then punctuated it with the slam of her rolling pin on the countertop. Cookie trays, cooling racks and miscellaneous utensils clattered against the stainless steel surface.

"No, Marc. No," she repeated with equal fervor, turning on him, her white-knuckled fingers still clinging to one of the rolling pin handles. "I am not going back there with you. I am not walking into that museum you call a home and dealing with your mother, who will look down her aristocratic nose at me just like she always has. And how much more judgmental and condescending do you think she'll be when you tell her I had a child out of wedlock? The fact that Danny is yours will be irrelevant. She'll criticize me for not telling you the minute I found out I was pregnant. She'll accuse me of going through with the divorce even though I knew I was carrying your baby, depriving you of time with your child and her of time with her grandchild. Of depriving *the world* of knowing about the existence of another great and wonderful Keller descendant."

Since that was pretty much exactly what he'd accused her of when *he'd* first learned of Danny's existence, he wasn't quite sure how to respond. Especially knowing how haughty his mother could be at times.

Vanessa let out a breath, seeming to lose a bit of her steam. In a lower, more subdued tone, she said, "Either that, or she'll deny Danny altogether. Declare he's not really a Keller, because of course she's always accused me of being a tramp, anyway. Or decide not to claim him as a Keller heir because we weren't married at the time of his birth."

She shook her head. "I won't do it, Marc. I won't go through that again and I sure as hell won't put my son through it."

Jaw clenching, he bit out, "He's my son, too, Vanessa."

"Yes," she acquiesced with a short nod of her head, "which is why you should want to protect him, too. From everything, and everyone."

Releasing the rolling pin, she put one hand flat to the island, the other on her hip and squared off, a mother bear ready and willing to protect her young, no matter what. "Danny is innocent. I won't let anyone make him feel less than perfect, less than wonderful. Ever. Not even his own grandmother."

Marc put his hands to his hips and cocked his head. "I had no idea you hated her so much," he murmured quietly.

"She was horrible to me," Vanessa retorted, rolling her eyes. "She made my life miserable while we were married."

For a minute, he didn't say anything, trying to gauge the truth of her words.

Had his mother really been that awful to her, or was Vanessa exaggerating? He knew women didn't always get along with their husbands' families and that mother-in-law/daughter-in-law relationships could often be acrimonious.

Heaven knew his mother wasn't exactly the warmest person in the whole world, even with her own children, but had she really been so cruel to Vanessa when he hadn't been around?

"I'm sorry you feel that way," he said carefully, "but I have to go back. Not for long—a few days, maybe a week. And I'd like to take Danny with me."

At that, Vanessa opened her mouth and he knew another argument was coming.

"You can't really stop me from taking him along," he told her flatly. "He's my son and you've kept him from me—and from my family—all this time. I think I deserve to take him home with me for a while."

Cocking his head, he fixed her with an intense, no-nonsense stare. "And we both know I don't need your permission."

"Are you threatening to take him from me?" she asked in a low voice.

"Do I need to?" he responded just as softly.

Though her mouth flattened in obvious anger, he could see the pulse beating frantically at her throat and her blue eyes glittering with emotion.

"It's just for a few days," he assured her again, feeling the odd need to wipe the fear and brimming tears from those eyes. "A week at the most. And you're more than welcome to come along, keep an eye on both of us. Why do you think I invited you in the first place?"

She licked her lips, swallowing hard. "You're going to make me do this, aren't you?" she asked in a wavering but resolved voice.

"I'm going to do this, with or without you. What part you play in the situation and how close an eye you keep on Danny is entirely up to you."

She gave him a look that clearly said she didn't think the choice he was giving her was any choice at all, but damned if he'd back down or go home, even for a short stay, without his son. He'd only just discovered he was a father; he wasn't going to walk away that easily.

Nor was he willing to let Danny out of his sight for that long. It might only be a handful of days by the calendar, but he'd gotten so used to seeing his son each and every day, to spending true quality time with him, that even twenty-four hours would feel like a lifetime at this point.

The same could be said of being away from Vanessa, he supposed, but then, his attraction to her had never been in question.

No, his thoughts now had to be for his son. And though he would never intentionally cause his ex-wife this much anxiety or upset, he couldn't honestly be sure that she wouldn't pick up Danny and run with him the minute he drove out of town.

It would mean leaving her aunt and bakery and the life she'd built here in Summerville, but she'd kept Danny's existence from him once. What was to say she wouldn't try to *steal* the baby from him this time around?

There was also the small issue of her current physical condition. Like it or not, there *was* a chance she was pregnant again, and until he knew for sure one way or the other, he didn't intend to let her get away or keep another of his children a secret from him for a year or more.

Which meant that if he couldn't stay in Summerville and keep an eye on her and Danny every minute, then he would have to take Danny with him back to Pittsburgh. Vanessa could go along or not, but the one thing he could count on was that if Danny was with him, she wouldn't be hieing off to parts unknown.

Mouth set in a mulish slant, she mumbled, "This is extortion, you know."

He raised a brow and resisted the urge to chuckle. "I'd hardly call it that."

"What would you call it, then?"

"Fatherhood," he replied. "I'm simply exerting my parental rights. You remember what those are, don't you? They're what you denied me for the past year while you kept Danny to yourself."

He hadn't meant to let his bitterness over the past slip out, but he could tell by her expression that she'd heard it loud and clear.

"I'm not letting you take Danny anywhere without me," she said stubbornly.

Her implication being that if he insisted on taking Danny home to visit his family, she would be going along, however reluctantly.

"If you can be ready by tomorrow, we'll leave around noon."

"I'm not sure I can be ready quite that early."

Marc tipped his head and gave a short nod. "Fine, make it one o'clock, then."

The last thing Vanessa wanted to do was leave Summerville and the nice, tidy life she'd built for herself to return to the lion's den that was Keller Manor. It might have been only temporary—very temporary, if Marc's promise held true—but whether it was five days or only one, every minute was bound to feel like an eternity.

Which was why she didn't rush when it came to packing for herself and Danny. She took her time discussing her absence with Aunt Helen and setting up a couple of extra employees to cover for her, wanting to make sure

The Sugar Shack really would run smoothly while she was away.

Then she actually solicited Marc's help in gathering everything they would need to take Danny on even a short trip. She was pretty sure he had no idea just how involved traveling with a baby could be.

While she decided about which of her own items and outfits to pack, she put him in charge of gathering up Danny's clothes and toys. Making sure they had enough diapers and wipes, bottles and formula. Blankets, booties, hats, infant sunscreen and more.

Vanessa kept thinking up new things to add to the list, hiding her amusement when Marc would begin to grumble and reminding him that returning to Pittsburgh was his idea. They could skip all of the fuss and muss, if he'd only agree to let her—and Danny—stay in Summerville.

Each time the topic came up, however, any mention of canceling the trip or of his going without them simply caused his jaw to go taut, and he would silently return to collecting Danny's things or securing the safety seat in the back of his Mercedes.

By one the next day—because try as she might, she hadn't been able to postpone any longer—they were standing on the curb, ready to leave. Danny was in his car seat, kicking his legs and gumming his very own set of brightly colored plastic keys, while Marc waited near the front passenger door. A few feet farther along the sidewalk, Vanessa and Aunt Helen stood hand in hand.

"You're sure you want to do this?" her aunt asked in a hushed voice.

Oh, she was very sure she *didn't*. But she couldn't say that. Partly because she'd grudgingly agreed to go and partly because she didn't want Aunt Helen to worry about her.

"I'm sure," she lied, even though her fingers were chilled inside her aunt's solid grip. "It will be fine. Marc just wants to introduce Danny to his family and take care of some business with the company. We'll be back by the end of the week."

Aunt Helen raised a brow. "I hope so. Don't let them drag you down again, darling," she added softly. "You know what it did to you last time, living under that roof. Don't let it happen again."

A lump formed in Vanessa's throat, so large, she could barely swallow. Pulling her aunt close, she hugged her tightly and waited until she thought she could speak.

"I won't," she promised, blinking back tears.

When she could finally bring herself to pull away from her aunt's embrace, she turned toward Marc and the waiting car. Though she knew he was eager to get on the road, his expression gave away nothing of his inner thoughts or feelings.

"Ready to go?" he asked in an even tone.

Since her throat was still tight with emotion, she could only nod before climbing into the front seat. Once her legs were tucked safely inside, he closed the door for her and she reached for the safety belt while he moved around to the driver's side.

Flipping down the visor, she used the tiny rectangular mirror to make sure Danny was still okay, doing her best to ignore Marc's sudden, overpowering presence as he slipped behind the wheel.

How could she have forgotten how small cars were? Even given the roominess of his sleek, black Mercedes with its supple, tan leather interior, it suddenly felt as though all of the oxygen had been sucked out of the air, making it hard for her to draw a breath.

After fastening his own seat belt, Marc turned the key in the ignition and the engine purred to life. Rather than pull right out, though, as she'd expected, they simply sat there for a moment. So long, in fact, that she turned her head to look at him.

"Is something wrong?" she asked, thinking that perhaps they'd forgotten something. Although how that could even be possible, she didn't know. They'd packed just about everything *but* the kitchen sink, as the over-stuffed trunk and half-stuffed backseat could attest.

"I know you don't want to do this," he said, his moss-green eyes glittering into hers. "But it's going to be all right."

She held his gaze for a moment, feeling that lump in her throat—which had finally started to recede—swell up again. Then she nodded before turning her attention back to the view straight in front of her.

But what she was really thinking was, *Famous last words*. Because she didn't think there was any way that this little visit to Marc's family could possibly be anything less than a complete disaster.

Twelve

Unfortunately, the drive to Pittsburgh flew by much more quickly than Vanessa would have liked. Before she knew it, they were pulling up the long, oak-lined drive to Keller Manor.

Every inch of blacktop that passed beneath the Mercedes's tires made her heart beat faster and her stomach sink lower until she started to worry she might actually be sick.

Don't be sick, don't be sick, don't be sick, she told herself, taking deep, even breaths and praying the mantra would work.

Marc pulled to a stop beneath the wide porte cochere and within moments a young man was opening her door, offering a hand to help her out, then rushing to open the rear door so she could see to Danny. Marc had obviously called ahead to let the family know he— or perhaps they—would be coming.

She'd never seen this particular young man before, but then, Eleanor Keller tended to go through household staff faster than allergy sufferers went through facial tissues. Marc's mother also liked to have someone on hand to do her every bidding at the snap of her fingers. She employed gardeners, chefs, maids, a butler, an on-site mechanic and at least one personal assistant.

How many of them Vanessa would come in contact with during her stay was left to be seen, but one thing she did know was that she would treat them a heck of a lot better than Eleanor did. She would treat them like actual human beings rather than servants or robots programmed to be seen, but not heard, and to do exactly as they were told—nothing more and nothing less.

Coming around to her side of the Mercedes, Marc popped the trunk, then tossed his keys to the kid in the short red jacket that marked him as a Keller Manor employee. It even had a gold crest of sorts embroidered over the left breast pocket.

"We aren't traveling light," Marc told him, one corner of his mouth twisting upward. "But it all goes in my suite."

Vanessa opened her mouth to correct him. Marc had brought a single overnight case with him, while all the rest of the belongings filling the car were hers or Danny's. And they definitely did not belong in Marc's rooms.

But he apparently knew what she was about to say, because he pressed his index finger to her mouth, effectively cutting off her disagreement.

"They go in my rooms," he said again, so that only she could hear. "You and Danny will be staying there with me while we're here. No arguments."

Marc might be high-handed and controlling, but just because he said "no arguments" didn't mean she wasn't going to give him one. She opened her mouth again to do just that, but he covered her lips with a quick, hard kiss.

"No arguments," he repeated a shade more sternly.

"It will be better for everyone involved. Trust me on this, okay?"

She so didn't want to. There was something deeply ingrained in her since their divorce that made her not want to trust him or listen to him or even believe a word he said.

But the fact was, she did trust him. Sharing a suite with him would be awkward and uncomfortable, but considering where this particular suite of rooms was located—inside the dreaded Keller mansion—it might actually be safer than staying in a room of her own. In addition to being quite spacious, Marc's suite also happened to be the one they'd lived in together while they were married, so at least she would be in a familiar setting.

"Fine," she muttered, slightly distracted by the lingering remnants of his kiss. He tasted of mint, and she could have sworn it was of the mentholated variety, because her lips were still tingling from the contact, however brief.

"Good," he replied, looking much too pleased with himself for her peace of mind. Then he scooped Danny out of her arms, tucking him against his own chest. "Now let's go inside and introduce our son to the rest of his family."

At that, Vanessa's stomach started to pitch and roll again, but Marc reached for her hand and the warmth of his fingers clasping hers was as calming as a glass of merlot. Well, almost. She was still jittery and her breathing was shallow as they stepped through the wide, white double front doors.

Built of redbrick and tall, Grecian columns, the entire mansion looked like a throwback to *Gone with the*

Wind's Tara—pre-Civil War destruction, of course. Secretly, however, Vanessa had always thought Marc's mother was trying to compete with a much larger residence, like the White House. And was winning.

Just inside the main entrance, the foyer sparkled like the lobby of a grand hotel. The parquet floor had been waxed to a high gloss. The chandelier hanging overhead glittered with polish and a thousand bits of glass shaped like teardrops reflecting the light of another thousand brightly lit bulbs.

In the center of the floor, an enormous display of freshly cut flowers rested on a sizcable marble table. And behind that, a wide, curved staircase was only one of the many ways to get to the second floor and opposite wings of the house.

It all looked exactly as it had the day Vanessa had left. Even the bouquet, which was large enough to bring Seabiscuit to his knees, was the same. Oh, they were different flowers, she was sure; Eleanor had new ones delivered every morning for the entire house. But they were the same *type* of flowers, the same colors, the very same arrangement.

She'd been gone a year. A year in which just about everything in her life had changed substantially. But if not even the flowers in the Keller's foyer had changed, she had little hope that anything—or anyone—else under the mansion's million-dollar roof had.

They didn't have coats, so the butler who had opened the door for them moved on down the long hallway to one side of the stairwell—likely to alert his mistress to their arrival. Seconds later, he returned to help the young man who was unloading the car carry their things to Marc's suite.

A moment after they disappeared upstairs, Eleanor emerged from her favorite parlor.

"Marcus, darling," she greeted Marc—and only Marc.

At the sound of her ex-mother-in-law's voice, Vanessa's heart lurched and she murmured a quick prayer asking for the strength and patience to get through this agonizing visit with the Wicked Witch of Western Pennsylvania.

The witch in question was dressed in a beige skirt and jacket over a pristine white blouse, all of which likely cost more than The Sugar Shack's monthly profits. Her hair was a perfect brownish-blond bob and her diamond jewelry—earrings, necklace, lapel pin and one ring— all matched and were no doubt very, very real. Eleanor Keller would never stoop to wearing cubic zirconia or costume jewelry, not even on an ordinary, uneventful weekday.

"Mother," Marc returned, leaning in to peck each of the older woman's cheeks. Bouncing Danny slightly in his arms, he added, "Meet your newest grandchild, Daniel Marcus."

Eleanor's pinched mouth twisted into what Vanessa suspected was meant to be a smile. "Lovely," she intoned, not even bothering to reach out and touch the baby. She simply perused him from head to toe.

Vanessa stiffened, offended on her child's behalf. But then Eleanor's attention shifted to her and she knew she would soon be offended on her very own behalf.

"I don't know what you were thinking," Marc's mother chastised, "keeping my son's child from him all this time. You should have said something the moment you discovered you were pregnant. You had no right to keep a Keller heir to yourself."

And it begins, Vanessa thought, with no sense of surprise whatsoever. She also wasn't offended, though she knew she had every right. Probably because Eleanor's reaction to her reappearance was exactly what she'd expected.

"Mother," Marc snapped in a tone Vanessa had rarely, if ever, heard from him.

Vanessa turned her head to study him, stunned by the look of anger on his face.

"We discussed this when I called," he continued. "The circumstances surrounding Danny's birth are between Vanessa and myself. I won't have you insulting her while we're here. Is that understood?"

Vanessa watched with wide eyes while Eleanor's lips flattened into a thin, unhappy line.

"Very well," she replied. "Dinner will be served at six o'clock. I'll leave you both to get settled. And please remember that we *dress* for meals in this house."

After flicking a disdainful glance over Vanessa's modest outfit of magenta slacks and sleeveless polka-dot blouse, Marc's mother turned on her heel and clicked her way back across the parquet floor.

Releasing a pent-up breath, Vanessa muttered, "That went well."

She meant it to be sarcastic, but Marc simply smiled.

"I told you so." Hiking a drowsy Danny higher on his shoulder, he said, "Let's go upstairs and unpack. I think Danny could use a bit of a nap, too."

Reaching out, she brushed a hand over her son's brown, baby-soft hair. "He shouldn't be tired, he slept in the car."

Marc flashed her a grin. "It didn't take."

She chuckled, because she couldn't seem to help herself. This was the Marc she remembered from when they'd first started dating, first been married. Funny, kind, thoughtful…and so handsome, he took her breath away.

Warmth suffused her as he took her hand and started toward the wide stairwell. It spread from her fingertips to every other part of her body, making her tingle, and bringing up all sorts of wonderful memories.

How could being this close to Marc again feel so good, so right, when being in this house again felt so very wrong?

Marc watched Vanessa move around his suite, getting ready for dinner. Danny was sleeping in the sitting room, in a crib that had been set up at his request before their arrival.

But it was his ex-wife's presence that had his gut clenching and his mind spinning. She looked right here. It *felt* right to have her here again.

He wasn't sure he meant *here* as in his family's home, though. It wasn't about having her back at the Keller Manor, or even in his private suite under his family's roof.

It was about having her with him, in his bedroom, no matter where that room happened to be located.

He'd missed that. Missed seeing her things spread out on top of the bureau and cluttering the bathroom vanity. Having her clothes hanging with his in the closet, the scent of her perfume lightly permeating his work shirts and the sheets on the bed.

He'd missed simply watching her, like this, as she moved around the room getting dressed, fixing her hair, doing her makeup or choosing which pieces of jewelry to wear.

Granted, she didn't have as many of those things with her this time as she had when they'd been man and wife, but that didn't keep her from falling into the same old habits or her movements from being achingly familiar. She was even wearing her favorite perfume—probably because she'd left a bottle on the dresser when she'd moved out and he hadn't been able to bring himself to get rid of it.

Now, he was glad. He'd given it to her for their anniversary, after all. So very long ago, it seemed. But the fact that she was wearing it again, that she was here with him, and apparently still trusted him... It made him wonder if maybe they could work out their differences and give each other another chance.

"How do I look?" she asked suddenly, breaking into his thoughts.

"Beautiful," he replied, without having to think about it, without even having to look. Though he did—long and hard. Looking at her was always a pleasure.

She was wearing a simple yellow sundress and sandals, with her hair pulled back above her ears so that her natural copper curls were even more prominent. His blood stirred in his veins, arousal pouring through him, and he licked his lips, wishing he could lick *her*—like a sweet, lemon-flavored popsicle.

Her eyes turned smoky and she offered him a small, sultry smile before brushing her hands down the sides of her skirt.

"Are you sure? You know what your mother is like and I didn't really pack anything dressy. I should have remembered her rule about formal dinners."

She paused to take a breath, then blew it out and wiped her hands on her skirt again in that same nervous gesture. "Of course, I don't have very many formal clothes anymore, so I couldn't have packed them even if I'd wanted to. I thought maybe some of my old clothes would still be here, but..."

She trailed off, her gaze skittering away from his, and Marc felt a stab of guilt somewhere around his solar plexus.

"I'm sorry. Mother had them thrown out after you left. I didn't expect you to be back, so I didn't think to keep any of them."

The truth was, they'd been too painful a reminder of her. Of her desertion, of the divorce papers he'd signed willingly more out of anger than any real desire to be single again and of the happier times they'd had together before things had somehow gone terribly wrong.

He shouldn't have let his mother dispose of them, he realized that now. It had been his place to deal with them, and he probably should have tracked Vanessa down to see if she wanted any of the items shipped to her before having them carted away. But at the time, he'd just wanted them gone and had been almost relieved when his mother had declared it was time to rid the house of any reminders of his ex-wife's abandonment.

The only thing that had been left behind was that crystal decanter of perfume.

"You look beautiful," he repeated, striding across the thickly carpeted floor to grasp her shoulders. "And we're not here to impress anyone. Not even Mother," he added with a grin.

When her mouth twitched with the beginnings of a smile and at least some of the anxiety seemed to drain away from her features, he leaned in and kissed her. He kept it light, even though that was far from what he really wanted.

Just the firm press of lips to lips instead of a ravaging of tongues. Just the brush of his fingertips over the warm skin of her bare shoulders instead of his hands delving inside her bodice and beneath the hem of her skirt.

He lingered for a few precious, breathless moments, then released her, stepping back before the full proof of his desire for her became obvious. Her freshly applied lipstick was smudged and he reached out to brush a spot with the edge of his thumb.

"Maybe we should skip dinner and go straight to dessert," he suggested in a low, graveled voice.

"I don't think your mother would like that very much."

He was pleased to hear the same huskiness in her voice as in his own. It meant he wasn't alone in the passion causing his pulse to hammer and hum.

"I don't think I give a good damn," he muttered with no small amount of feeling behind the words.

"As bad an idea as that probably is, I sincerely wish we could. Anything would be better than having to face your mother again."

The corner of Marc's mouth quirked down in a frown. Was she implying that staying in the room to make love with him would be only slightly less miserable than an evening spent in his family's company? He wasn't sure he liked being considered the lesser of two evils.

Before he had a chance to reply, however, a tapping sounded on the suite's outer door.

"That will be the nanny," he said, just managing to mask a sigh of disappointment.

"You hired a nanny?" Vanessa asked, sounding both surprised and disapproving.

"Not really," he replied. "One of Mother's maids is going to sit with him for a couple of hours. That's all right, isn't it?"

Her brows crossed. "I don't know. Is she good with infants?"

"I don't know," he said, repeating her phrase. "Let's go meet her and give her the third degree."

Wrapping his hand around her elbow, he pulled her with him toward the bedroom door.

"I don't want to give her the third degree," Vanessa murmured softly as they crossed the sitting room where Danny was sleeping. "I just want to know that she's qualified to sit with my child."

"We'll be right downstairs, so you can come up and check on her any time you like," he assured her, keeping his voice equally low. "Tonight can be her test run. If you like her and she does a good job, she can stay with Danny whenever you need her while you're here. If not, we'll hire a real nanny. One you feel a hundred percent confident in."

"You're placating me, aren't you?" she asked, an edge of annoyance entering her tone.

With his hand on the knob of the sitting room door, he turned to her and smiled. "Absolutely. While you're here, whatever you need, whatever you want, I intend to see that you get it."

Her eyes widened and he knew she was about to argue. So he bent down and captured her mouth, kissing her into warm and pliant submission.

When he pulled away, his own body was buzzing with

warmth, but he was far from pliant. Quite stiff and un-yielding would have been more accurate.

"Indulge me," he said, brushing a stray copper curl behind her ear while the taste of her lingered on his lips and prodded him to kiss her again. "Please."

Thirteen

As always, dinner with Marc's family was exhausting. Delicious, but exhausting.

Marc's mother was her usual haughty self, and though Vanessa had always liked Marc's brother Adam and Adam's wife, Clarissa, they were cut from the same basic cloth as Eleanor. Born with silver spoons in their mouths, they'd never known a moment of true want or need. And being raised as they had been, they were extremely refined, never a hair out of place, never a wrong word spoken.

The only reason Vanessa felt kindly toward them at all was that, despite their upbringings, Adam and Clarissa weren't quite as cold and judgmental as her ex-mother-in-law. From the moment she'd married Marc, they'd treated her like a true member of the family and had seemed genuinely sorry when she and Marc had split up.

Even tonight, knowing the circumstances surrounding Vanessa's return to Keller Manor and Eleanor's obvious disdain for her, Marc's brother and sister-in-law had treated her exactly the same as they had in the past. No sidelong glances or sharply pointed questions meant to put her on the spot or make her feel insecure, just friendly smiles and harmless banter.

That alone had helped to assuage some of Vanessa's raw and rampaging nerves when she'd first walked into the opulent dining room. Of course, Eleanor had already been seated at the head of the table like a queen holding court—and her expression alone had made Vanessa feel like a bug under a microscope.

To Vanessa's relief, her former mother-in-law had played fair through the soup and salad courses, keeping conversation light and impersonal. There were a couple of sticky moments while they enjoyed their entrees, but by the time dessert was being served, Eleanor dropped her semi-polite facade and began taking potshots at Vanessa as often as she thought she could get away with it. Some of them were direct, others more passive-aggressively delivered.

But this time, Marc actually stuck up for her—something he'd never done before, not with his mother. Possibly because in the past, Eleanor's attacks had been much more subtle, and often reserved for moments when the two of them were alone so that no one else would witness her true hatred for her son's wife.

Marc had grown up under Eleanor's frosty disposition, so he was used to her testy personality and jagged barbs. Even though her mother-in-law's malicious treatment had cut her to the quick, Vanessa truly believed that much of what Marc witnessed had gone straight over his head. He was like someone raised in the city, who wouldn't be bothered by the sounds of round-the-clock street traffic the way someone would who'd been raised in the quietness of the country.

But tonight, Marc hadn't let his mother's not-so-subtle assaults slide by. He'd caught and responded to every one, always in Vanessa's defense. And once dessert was finished, when Eleanor seemed to be working herself toward a full-blown attack, he'd announced that it had been a long day, wished his family good-night, and taken Vanessa's hand to lead her out of the dining room.

She was almost giddy with relief and unaccustomed empowerment…and was still clutching his hand like a life preserver as they jogged upstairs side by side. She felt like she had when they'd first been dating, before the realities of being Mrs. Marcus Keller had settled around her and robbed her of her happiness.

Reaching the door to his suite, they were both smiling, and she was slightly out of breath. He put a finger to his lips, signaling for her to be quiet before he opened the door.

The fact that he had to remind her to be silent made her realize how close to giggling she was. *Giggling.* Like a twelve-year-old.

Biting back the strangled sound, she kept hold of Marc's hand and followed him into the darkened sitting room. The maid-slash-nanny they'd left with Danny was sitting across the room from the crib, reading a magazine beneath the muted yellow glare of a single low-lit lamp. When she saw them, she closed the magazine and quickly rose to her feet.

"How was he?" Marc whispered.

"Just fine," the young woman answered with a small smile. "He slept the entire time."

Good news for a babysitter. Not such good news for parents who were looking forward to a full night's sleep.

"That means he'll be up in the middle of the night," Vanessa whispered to no one in particular. And then to Marc, she said, "Prepare yourself for finally experiencing the true rigors of fatherhood."

He flashed her a grin, his green eyes sparking with a blaze of heat that had nothing to do with parental exhilaration. "I'm looking forward to it."

After slipping the young maid a couple of folded-up bills that Vanessa was sure Eleanor would disapprove of, he saw her out, then joined Vanessa at the side of Danny's crib. His hand came up to rest on the small of her back, and she had to swallow a lump of emotion at the picture they must have made. Mother and father standing at the edge of their infant son's crib, watching him sleep.

This was what she'd always imagined motherhood and family would be like. It's what she'd wanted when she'd married Marc and they'd first started trying to get pregnant.

Funny how life never quite turned out the way you planned.

But this was nice, too. Maybe not ideal, maybe not the epitome of her adolescent dreams, but it still warmed her and made her heart swell inside her chest.

"I hope he's not coming down with something," she murmured, putting the back of her hand to Danny's tiny forehead. He didn't feel feverish, but one could never tell. "He doesn't usually sleep this long."

"He's had a busy day," Marc offered just as softly. "You'd be tired, too, if this were your first big trip since being born."

She chuckled, then had to cover her mouth to keep from waking the baby. With a grin of his own, Marc grabbed her arm and tugged her toward the bedroom door.

Once they were safely inside, he twirled her around and pushed her up against the hard, flat panel, covering her mouth with his own. His arms on either side of her head boxed her in, his body pressing her flat and sending a flare of heat everywhere he touched.

For long minutes, he kissed her, their breaths mingling, his tongue thrusting, parrying, drawing her into his passionate duel. She lost her breath, her vision, her sanity, her entire world shrinking to the single pinprick of reality that was Marc's solid embrace.

When he lightened his hold enough to let her gasp for air, she blinked like a newborn foal and let her head fall back against the door while he continued to nibble at her loose, tingling lips.

"This isn't what I had in mind when you said we'd be sharing your rooms," she managed—barely—after filling her lungs with a gasp of much-needed oxygen.

"Funny. It's exactly what I pictured." He murmured the words against her skin, moving to suckle the lobe of her ear around her small hoop earring.

Somehow she didn't doubt that. But letting his mother think they were sharing a room and *actually* sharing a room—a bed—were two completely different things.

"I was going to sleep on the chaise in the other room. Or slip into one of the guest rooms when nobody was looking. This…"

She moaned as his tongue darted out to lick a line of electricity from her collarbone to the hollow behind her ear. The sensation shot through her like a shock wave, turning her knees to jelly.

"Not smart. Not smart at all," she wheezed, unsure of whether the words were actually coming out of her mouth or simply echoing through her rapidly liquefying brain.

Shifting to wrap his arms around her and lift her against his body—one hand at her back, the other cradling her bottom—he turned and strode directly to the bed.

"I think it's positively brilliant," he replied, and then dropped her to the mattress like a sack of potatoes.

She certainly didn't *feel* like a sack of potatoes, though. Not when he followed her down, covering her from chest to ankle with his hot, heavy bulk.

This time, when he kissed her, she didn't think to protest where all of this might be leading. Maybe because she *knew* where it was leading. They both did.

Or maybe because his mouth on hers, his hands on her body, drove every other rational thought straight out of her head.

With deft fingers, he untied the knot of her dress's bodice behind her neck, lowering the gauzy yellow material to reveal her braless breasts. He cupped them together, kneading, brushing the tight nipples with his thumbs until she moaned and wiggled beneath him.

He returned her moan with one of his own, then let his hands slide around her waist to the rear zipper. She rose slightly and waited for the gentle *snick-snick-snick-snick* to stop, for him to tug the full skirt past her hips and thighs. Lifting himself up, he pulled the dress completely off, then divested her of her strappy sandals, as well.

She lay there in only a pair of thin, silken panties. They weren't the sexiest thing she'd ever worn, but she thanked heaven she was past the "granny panty" phase of pregnancy and new motherhood.

Judging by Marc's expression, he approved. For long minutes, he stayed propped on one strong arm staring down at her with eyes that had gone dark and primal.

A shiver stole over her at that look, at the way it made her feel.

Not helpless or vulnerable by any means. Instead, she felt powerful. That she could incite that level of heat and lust in him continued to amaze her.

It had been that way in the beginning, and for most of their marriage, but she wouldn't have expected such intense desire to still be there after all they'd been through. That it was felt a bit like a miracle, even though she had no idea how the passion they shared in the bedroom could possibly translate to their future everyday lives.

His fingers delving beneath the elastic waist of her underwear dragged her up from the quagmire of her inner thoughts, and she was more than willing to grab hold of the life rope he offered.

She let him snake the panties down her legs, laying her bare, and then wrapped her arms around his neck to pull him down for a deep, soulful kiss. With a groan, Marc ground the bulge of his still-trapped erection against her hip.

Shifting beneath him, she welcomed him into the cradle of her thighs, crossing her legs behind his waist. He groaned again—or maybe it was a growl—and pressed even closer.

There was something between them, Marc thought. Something compelling and meaningful and not to be taken for granted. And he realized suddenly that that's exactly what he'd done—he'd taken his relationship with Vanessa for granted.

He'd married her, and brought her home, and simply assumed she would always be there. How could she not be happy in a house roughly the size of Buckingham Palace on an estate that boasted a tennis court, movie theater, two swimming pools—one indoors, one out—a riding stable, gardens, walking paths, a pond…everything anyone could ever want. Add to that the fact that he had more money than Midas and Croesus combined and he'd thought there was nothing he couldn't offer her, no reason any woman would ever walk away from him.

He'd never been one to delve too deeply into his or anyone else's feelings, but these past few weeks had him thinking differently. Feeling things he'd never felt before and wondering things he'd never thought to wonder about.

Maybe money wasn't everything. Maybe situating Vanessa in his family's mansion and giving her *carte blanche* with his primary bank account hadn't been enough for her.

But wasn't that a good thing? Didn't it mean that she hadn't loved him for his money alone? For what he had or what he could give her?

He wasn't sure what to think of that, since he was rich and intended to stay that way.

What he did know was that some sort of bond obviously still existed between them.

It wasn't just the sex—although that alone was outstanding enough to give him pause. But whatever it was, still buzzing and humming whenever they were together, it warranted a few hours of serious consideration.

Was there a chance they could reconcile? Try again, start over, build something better and stronger than they'd had before?

But even if they could, should they?

It was too much to contemplate rationally at the moment, given that his mind was currently preoccupied with more immediate and infinitely more enjoyable pursuits. But he did need to think about it. Decide if what he thought he was feeling was real.

Because what he thought he was feeling was love. Love. Longing. Devotion. And a desire to once again make things with Vanessa permanent.

He groaned as her tongue swirled inside his mouth and her ankles tightened at the small of his back. The heat of her naked body burned through his clothes and suddenly he wanted them gone.

With her still clinging to him like plastic wrap, he reached between them to tug at the buttons of his shirt, his belt, the front of his slacks. She shifted when necessary, giving him the space to shrug out of his clothes with jerky movements, but never actually letting go.

Once he was as naked as she, he edged her higher on the bed, careful not to bump her into the headboard while he held her to him with one arm and rearranged the overstuffed pillows with the other. He propped a couple under her rear, lifting her so that she looked down on him and the short strands of her copper hair fell around his face, as well as her own.

Grasping her chin, he held her in place while he nibbled her lips, tracing patterns over her waist and back with his fingertips. Her skin was like the smooth perfection of an alabaster statue, all elegant dips and curves. Only where statues were cold and lifeless, Vanessa was anything but. She was passionate and beautiful, and the only woman he'd ever made love to here, in this bed.

Before their marriage, he hadn't bothered to bring women home with him, at least not in order to sleep with them. It had been easier and less complicated to limit any intimacies to their apartments or the occasional hotel room. Even with those he'd dated seriously.

After the divorce…well, the truth was that he hadn't been with another woman since Vanessa left. He'd thrown himself into his work and the company. Frankly, no one else had even remotely caught his interest in the past year. He wondered now if anyone else ever would.

Crossing his arms behind her back, he grasped her to him, flattening her full, round breasts to his chest. She ran her hands through his hair, raking her nails over his scalp and the nape of his neck, something he'd always loved. It sent shivers of arousal down his spine and blood pulsing even more heavily between his legs.

Feeling the twitch of his erection, Vanessa shifted on his lap, arranging herself at a better angle to hover just above him. She wrapped her slim fingers around his hard length and stroked him lightly for a moment before guiding him ever so slowly into her damp, welcoming warmth.

Marc hissed a breath through clenched teeth, reciting stock values in his head to keep the evening from being over much too soon. The feel of her surrounding him, of being buried inside her, was one of the most astonishing sensations he'd ever experienced. No matter how many times it happened, each was nearly a religious experience. Amazing and life-altering. Impossibly better than the time before, and certain never to be as mind-blowing again.

She fit him like a glove, snug and hot, clutching at him in a way that nearly sent the top of his head spinning off. Hands on her bare buttocks, he tugged her closer— not that there was more than the thinnest sliver of space between them to begin with. But if he could have absorbed her into him, he would have.

Her breath whooshed out as she hit his chest with

a *thump,* but he didn't give her a chance to refill her lungs with fresh air. Instead, he took her mouth while he lifted her up…and down. Up…and down. Short, jerky movements at first that grew faster and more frantic as their passions built and their mingled breathing became ragged.

Marc's heart pounded beneath his rib cage, every cell in his body tightening, straining, striving for release. He fought it, wanting the feelings to last. Wanting this time with Vanessa to last.

But holding back his orgasm was like trying to hold back a monsoon. His only hope was to hang on long enough and make sure she was with him when it happened.

Reaching between them, he trailed the flat of his hand over her abdomen and slipped two fingers into her folds in search of the secret bundle of nerves that would send her over the edge. She gasped as soon as he touched her there and he felt her inner muscles clench around him.

He cursed under his breath, working to school his breathing and praying for just a little more staying power. Just a little more.

Using the pads of those two fingers, he circled the swollen bud first one direction and then the other. Vanessa gave a long, plaintive moan, her spine bowing as she arched above him.

"That's it, baby," he panted, cocking his hips to meet her every downward thrust. "Let yourself go. Come with me."

Her body was growing taut, her movements and breathing becoming more and more frenetic as her climax approached. Marc continued to tease, continued to drive her higher and higher. Pinching, flicking, letting his nails rake across her most sensitive spot while he rocked her from below.

And then she was over, crying out as wave after wave of pleasure rippled through her, causing her to shudder from head to toe.

Marc wasn't far behind. As soon as he felt the start of her climax, he released the stranglehold on his own self-control, and followed her into bliss.

Fourteen

Vanessa awoke to early morning sunlight streaming through the half-drawn draperies and across the bed. A wide smile split her face as she stretched like a cat, feeling better than she had in a very long time.

Tilting her head, she checked the clock, then sat up quickly. Ten o'clock! How could she possibly have slept so long?

Granted, she'd had a rather rigorous evening. She and Marc had made love three times during the long night, and Danny had had them both out of bed a couple of times in between. But she still should have been up long before now, especially since Danny *had* to be awake and fussing.

Rolling to the edge of the mattress, she started to sit up only to have her hand bump something near the head of the bed. It crinkled slightly, and when she looked, she found a slip of paper lying half under Marc's pillow.

Had to go to the office, it said in her ex-husband's tall, distinctive scrawl. *Danny is with Marguerite. Home for dinner.* And it was signed, *Love, M.*

Short and to the point, which was typical of Marc. But using the L-word in a frivolous manner was not. Did he mean it? Or had it simply slipped out by habit, given their return to familiar marital intimacies?

Vanessa's heart pinched inside her chest. She wasn't sure how to feel about either possibility, so she decided not to think about it too much. At least not at the moment.

Slipping out of bed, she quickly dressed in a pair of linen slacks and a light pumpkin orange top, then made her way out of the suite and downstairs, peeking her head in several doorways as she went in hopes of finding Danny.

She found them in the library. A large blanket was spread out on the floor with Danny in the center. Toys were spread all around, and the same young maid from last evening sat at one corner, making faces and playing with the laughing child. She was definitely working overtime, Vanessa thought, making a mental note to ask Marc if she was being properly compensated.

"Ms. Keller," the woman murmured as soon as she spotted Vanessa. Pushing to her feet, she clasped her hands nervously behind her back.

"It's Mason, actually," Vanessa replied automatically. Moving toward the blanket, she knelt beside Danny and scooped him up, cradling him against her chest.

He giggled, kicked his little legs and grabbed for her hair. She chuckled in return, kissing one of his warm, chubby cheeks.

"Thank you for watching him again," she said, climbing back to her feet and taking a seat on one of the nearby sofas.

"My pleasure, ma'am. Mr. Keller said it was all right to give him a bottle and some baby cereal, so he's been fed and burped. Changed, too."

Vanessa nodded, sending the young woman a gentle smile. Her first inclination was to dismiss the maid and take over Danny's care herself. She wasn't used to having staff on hand and underfoot anymore to see to her every need or whim. And she *was* used to taking care of things—especially her son—almost single-handedly.

But the maid looked so eager to please and Vanessa knew from personal experience how demanding Eleanor could be. She was hard enough on her children and their spouses, but with her employees, she was downright tyrannical.

Standing, she gave Danny another kiss, this one in the center of his forehead, then returned him to the blanket.

"Would you mind watching him for a while longer?" she asked as she straightened. "I'd like to get some breakfast."

The young maid looked both pleased and unaccountably relieved. She quickly moved back to the blanket and took up her post at Danny's side.

"Of course, ma'am. Take your time."

"Thank you."

As familiar as Vanessa was with Keller Manor, she was anything but comfortable inside its gates and walls. It was too big and lifeless for her tastes, reminding her of some cold, cavernous mausoleum. At times, she could swear her footsteps and voice actually echoed as if she was inside a giant catacomb.

Although she knew she could go straight to the dining room, and a servant would be there to take her order in under a minute, she instead made her way to the kitchen at the rear of the house. The kitchen staff was busy bustling around, cleaning up from the rest of the family's morning meal and preparing for the afternoon one.

"Ms. Keller," one of them chirped when she saw her.

Vanessa smiled, not bothering to correct the use of her married name. If she did that every time one of the staff reverted to the family surname, she would get nothing else done.

"Hello, Glenna. It's nice to see you again."

The older woman's smile was warm and genuine, not the usual lift of dutiful lips. "You, too, ma'am."

"How many times have I told you to call me Vanessa?" she scolded with a friendly wink.

The woman nodded, but old habits died hard, and Vanessa knew every one of the Keller staff would rather be chastised by her for *not* calling her by her first name than to accidentally slip and call Eleanor by hers.

"I missed breakfast. Do you think I could get a slice of toast and some juice?" she asked. She knew better than to try to fix something on her own. She'd done that before, when she and Marc had first been married, and learned very quickly that the kitchen staff could be more than a little territorial.

"Of course, ma'am."

Glenna bustled off to fix a tray while Vanessa climbed onto a stool right there at the center island. She could have gone off to the dining room to wait, but the room was so large and empty, whereas the kitchen felt homier and buzzed with energy. She could also do without bumping into Eleanor, which was more likely elsewhere in the house.

After taking her time with *two* slices of toast and a scrambled egg because Glenna insisted she could use the protein, Vanessa strolled back to the library. Marguerite was still there, and Danny was still playing and cooing, enjoying himself just as much as when she'd left.

She laughed herself, just looking at him. There were few things in the world as delightful as a baby's heartfelt giggle, and she never grew tired of hearing her own child expressing his happiness over some silly thing like a shaken rattle or a game of peekaboo.

Joining them on the blanket, she spent the next twenty or thirty minutes entertaining Danny and chatting with Marguerite, who turned out to be a college student trying to earn extra money for tuition over her summer break. Vanessa could certainly relate, since that's exactly what she'd been doing when she'd met Marc for the first time.

"Well, isn't this a sweet little tableau."

Eleanor's crisp tone and deceptively reproving words cut Marguerite off midsentence and sent a flush of guilt toward the young maid's hairline. She immediately jumped up, fidgeting nervously.

"You may go," Eleanor told her without preamble.

Marguerite gave a quick nod, mumbled, "Yes, ma'am," and hurried out of the room.

Vanessa was just as uncomfortable with her ex-mother-in-law's sudden appearance, but refused to let it show. She certainly wasn't going to rush to her feet like some loyal subject in front of her reigning queen.

Remaining where she was, she continued playing with Danny, fighting the morbid impulse to glance in the older woman's direction.

"You didn't have to scare her off, Eleanor," she said flatly, finally looking up at her. "She's a nice girl. We were having an interesting conversation."

If possible, Eleanor's features turned even more pinched and disapproving. "I've told you before that it's unseemly to make friends with the help."

Vanessa chuckled at that, a short burst of unexpected

sound that caused the older woman's brows to pucker. "I'm afraid I don't adhere to your antiquated rules, especially since I used to *be* the help, remember?"

"Oh, I remember," Eleanor replied coolly.

Of course, she did. Wasn't that her number one complaint about Vanessa ending up married to her son? That a high and mighty Keller heir might stoop so low as to tie himself to a common, no-name waitress?

"Do you really think this is going to work out?" Eleanor continued snidely. "That you can hide my son's child from him for nearly a year, then simply bat your eyes and waltz back into the lap of luxury, trapping Marcus all over again?"

Keeping one hand on Danny's belly and rubbing him gently through the soft cotton of his teddy bear onesie tucked into a tiny pair of denim shorts, Vanessa finally turned her head to meet her ex-mother-in-law's stern, steel-gray gaze. "Contrary to your single-minded beliefs, I don't particularly consider Keller Manor the lap of luxury. You may have everything money can buy, but this house definitely isn't a home. There's no warmth here and very little love."

She paused for a moment to lift Danny against her chest before climbing to her feet. Turning, she faced Eleanor head-on. "And I'm not trying to *trap* Marc. I never was. I just wanted to love him and be happy. But you couldn't let that happen, could you?"

Shifting Danny higher on her hip, she hugged him close and continued with so much of what she'd been wanting to say for years. "God forbid Marc falls in love with a woman from the wrong side of the tracks, with red blood instead of blue running through her veins. God forbid he be happy and make his own decisions and get out from under your oppressive, all-powerful thumb."

The words poured out of her like a rainstorm, but even though a sliver of fear remained at the very pit of her belly, she also felt relieved…and stronger than she would have expected.

Why hadn't she found the courage to tell Eleanor off long before now? She might have saved her marriage. Saved herself countless tears. Saved them all months and months of misery.

Eleanor, of course, didn't take Vanessa's first act of independence at all well. Her cheeks turned an unseemly shade of pink while her eyes narrowed and her jaw locked like a piranha's.

"How dare you?" she seethed, her face turning even more mottled.

But her anger didn't faze Vanessa. Not anymore.

"I should have dared a long time ago. I should have stood up to you and refused to let you intimidate me just because you come from old money and are used to looking down your nose at people. And I should have told Marc how you were treating me from the very beginning instead of trying to keep the peace and avoid tarnishing his opinion of you."

She shook her head, sad but determined. "I was young and stupid then, but I've grown up a lot in the past year. And I have a child of my own now…one I don't intend to let you push around, or let witness you pushing *me* around. I'm sorry, Eleanor, but if you want to be in your grandson's life, you're going to have to start treating me with a little respect."

Vanessa could tell from the pinch of her ex-mother-in-law's lips that she was about as far from that happening as from flapping her arms and flying to the moon.

"Get. Out."

Eleanor spat the words like a fire-breathing dragon, as though they were two completely different sentences. Fury shook her from head to toe, and if she'd had any medical issues, Vanessa would have worried she was on the verge of suffering a heart attack or stroke.

"Get out of my house," she repeated, turning to point one long, diamond-adorned finger toward the door.

Not that Vanessa had to be told twice.

"Gladly," she said, bending at the waist to gather Danny's blanket and toys one-handedly.

With her shoulders back and her head held high, she strode past Eleanor and up the long stairwell to Marc's suite to pack her things.

Marc pulled his Mercedes in front of the house and cut the engine. Normally he would drive around to the garage, but he was only going to be a few minutes. He'd forgotten some files on the desk in his suite, and was hoping he had time to grab them, get back to the office, deal with the rest of the issues filling his long to-do list and get home again in time for dinner.

Normally, he would simply skip dinner with the family and remain at the office as long as it took to get the job done. But for some reason, his workaholic temperament seemed to have abandoned him. He barely wanted to spend the rest of the day at the office, let alone his evening, as well. Instead, he wanted to be here, at home, with Vanessa and Danny.

His mouth curved in a smile just thinking about them, and he glanced at his watch, debating how much time he could afford to spend with them before turning around and heading back into the city.

There was a taxi parked ahead of him in the driveway and he lifted a hand to the cabbie as he rounded his Mercedes, wondering what it was doing there. Perhaps his mother had visitors, though it was odd for any of her acquaintances not to have their own very expensive, chauffeured vehicles.

Bounding up the front steps, he pushed open the door and came to a screeching halt at the pile of luggage and baby items in the center of the foyer floor.

"What the hell is going on?" he muttered more to himself than anyone else.

Hearing a noise at the top of the stairs, he lifted his head to find Vanessa descending with Danny in her arms, two of his mother's staff trailing behind, arms loaded with even more of his ex-wife's and son's belongings.

"Thank you so much for all your help," Vanessa was saying. "I really appreciate it."

"What's going on?" he asked, more loudly this time.

Vanessa's head jerked up at his sharp tone or his sudden, unexpected appearance, or both.

"Marc," she breathed. "I wasn't expecting you back so soon."

"Obviously."

His brows drew down in an angry, suspicious frown as she stopped at the bottom of the steps. The two maids dipped their heads and mumbled about taking her things out to the waiting cab, then disappeared as quickly as they could.

"Sneaking off again?" he accused, not caring that his voice was cold with disappointment and betrayal.

She was leaving him again, was all he could think. He'd asked her to spend just a few days with his family—a week at the most—and she hadn't made it even two days.

They'd made love last night, more than once. Slept wrapped in each others' arms. He'd thought—stupidly, it turned out—that they had turned a corner and might actually be able to make their relationship work.

But while he'd been falling in love with her all over again, and thinking about reconciliation, she'd been planning a timely escape. Exactly the same as before.

Exactly. Because the last time she'd left him, she'd been pregnant with his child…and there was a good chance the same was true now.

"No," Vanessa said, nervously licking her lips. "I mean, yes, I'm leaving, but no, I'm not trying to sneak off. I left you a note upstairs…on the back of the one you left for me this morning."

Well, that was different, at least, he thought with a heavy dose of sarcasm.

"And a note makes up for taking off in the middle of the day while I'm at the office?" he shot back. "With my son?"

"Of course not," she returned, looking strangely not guilty. "Although when you read the note, you'll see that I explained I'm not really taking off. I'm simply leaving the estate for a hotel downtown. I was going to stay there until I had the chance to talk to you."

He cocked his head, wondering what she could be up to. But then curiosity won out and he heard himself ask, "About what?"

She swallowed hard, her blue eyes going dark and oddly blank. "Your mother asked me to leave."

His own eyes went wide in surprise. "Why?" Why would his mother ask his wife—his ex-wife, he corrected himself silently—to leave?

"For the same reason she drove me away last time—because she hates me. Or at the very least disapproves of me greatly. As far as she's concerned, I'm not good enough for you and I never will be." A small smile touched her lips as she added, "Of course, this time she was much more forthright about wanting me gone, probably because I told her off."

"You told my mother off," he murmured, trying to process what he was hearing, but growing more confused by the minute. "Why would you do that?"

The amusement that had begun to touch Vanessa's features vanished, turning her face hard and defensive.

"Because I refuse to let her push me around any longer. I refuse to let her make me feel inferior just because *she* will always think of me as a lowly waitress, unworthy of her son's misguided affections."

Marc shook his head and started forward. "This is just a misunderstanding. Mother can be distant, I know, but she's thrilled about Danny and I'm sure she's pleased to have you back at the house, as well."

He reached out to grasp her shoulders, but she took a quick, single step back.

"No. It's not a misunderstanding, Marc," she told him, her tone implacable. "I know you love your mother and I would never ask you to change that. I would never intentionally try to drive a wedge between you and your family. But as much as I love you, I can't be here anymore."

Marc's chest tightened at her words. She loved him… or claimed to, at any rate yet she was preparing to walk away and leave him. Again.

"You love me," he scoffed, tossing the declaration back in her face. "Right. You love me, but you're leaving. Again. And what about Danny? What about the child you might be carrying now? My child. Are you going to run off and hide another pregnancy from me? Keep another baby from its father?"

She blanched at that, and God help him, he was glad. He knew he was being cruel, saying things to intentionally hurt her. But damn it, he was hurting, too. He was being betrayed a second time by the only woman he'd ever loved and who'd claimed—more than once—to love him in return.

"That's not fair, Marc," she said in a small voice, tightening her grip on Danny.

"The truth hurts, doesn't it, Vanessa? Signed divorce papers or no signed divorce papers, you knew you were pregnant when you left town the last time and you didn't even bother to tell me."

Because Danny was starting to fuss at her hip, she lowered her voice, but her temper came through loud and clear.

"Don't you dare lay that entirely at my feet. I kept Danny a secret, yes, but only after you refused to speak to me. I tried to tell you I was pregnant, but you couldn't be bothered to listen."

Marc's gaze narrowed. What game was she playing at now? he wondered. If what she said was true, it was news to him—and he sincerely believed he would remember his ex-wife telling him she was carrying his child.

"What are you talking about?" he asked carefully.

"I called you. As soon as I realized I was pregnant, I called you at the office, but you said—and I quote, because I will never forget the words as long as I live—

there's nothing you could possibly have to say to me that I want to hear. End quote."

Well, now he knew something fishy was going on. Because he'd never uttered those words, not where Vanessa was concerned.

"I never said that," he murmured quietly.

"Yes," Vanessa retorted with conviction, "you did. Or at least that's the message Trevor said he was ordered to give me on your behalf."

"Trevor." It was a statement, not a question.

"Yes."

For a second, Marc wasn't certain if the thin sheen of crimson falling over his eyes was imaginary or if he was literally seeing red. He did know, however, that his blood pressure was rising like a geyser about to erupt and his hands were fisting with the urge to punch something. Or someone.

Reaching into his jacket pocket, he pulled out his cell phone and punched the button for his assistant's line at Keller Corp. Trevor Storch picked up on the first ring.

"Yes, sir," the overeager young man answered, well aware of who was calling thanks to Caller I.D.

"I'm out at the house. I want you here in under fifteen minutes."

"Yes, sir," Trevor responded dutifully and Marc could almost see him jumping up and rounding his desk before he'd even returned the telephone to its cradle.

Meeting Vanessa's wary blue gaze, he snapped his own phone closed. "He'll be here soon and then we'll get to the bottom of this mess once and for all."

Fifteen

The seconds dragged on like hours, the minutes like years. Vanessa stood at the bottom of the stairs while the stony silence in the foyer grew heavier and more suffocating.

Danny wasn't getting any lighter, either. Shifting him to her other hip, she started to lower herself into a sitting position on one of the wide, carpeted steps, but Marc moved forward to stop her.

"Let me take him," he said brusquely, holding out his arms.

For a moment, she hesitated, the panicked thought that if she let Marc take the baby, she might never get him back racing through her mind. But if she tried to hold on to him now, then her avowals that she wouldn't try to keep Marc from seeing their son would be a lie, wouldn't they?

Hoping Marc hadn't noticed her uncertainty, she handed Danny over, rolling her shoulders and stretching her arms to work out the kinks.

"He's getting big, isn't he?" Marc said, a small smile curving his lips. The first he'd offered since spotting her luggage in the middle of the entryway.

"Yes, he is."

She was about to suggest they move into one of the nearby parlors to await Trevor's arrival, but just then a squeal of brakes came from the front drive and a minute later the door swung open.

Trevor Storch was tall, thin and more gangly than athletic. He stood just inside the foyer, brown hair mussed, shoulders sloped and breathing hard, as though he'd run most of the way from Keller Corp's main office building instead of driving.

Before he could say anything or begin bowing, as was his usual custom, Marc handed Danny back to her and turned on his assistant, any sign of kindness or amusement wiped from his face. Watching him close in on the younger man, even Vanessa had the urge to shy away and cover the baby's face to protect him from the steam that was almost literally pouring from Marc's ears.

Raising a hand practically in Trevor's face, Marc said in a low voice, "I'm going to ask you some questions and I want honest answers. God help you if you lie to me, do you understand?"

Any hint of eager anticipation drained from Storch's face, along with every bit of his skin's natural color. No doubt he'd thought he was being summoned to Keller Manor to run some extra-special errand or to receive a much-deserved—in his mind, at least—promotion.

"Y-yes, sir," he stammered, struggling to regain his composure.

"Did Vanessa call the office last year, just after we were divorced, and ask to speak with me?"

Trevor's eyes darted past Marc's shoulder to where she was standing, rocking slightly with the baby, who was currently content with attempting to fit his entire fist into his wide-open mouth.

"Yes or no, Trevor?" Marc demanded sharply.

"Y-yes, sir," he said, returning his attention to his very unhappy employer. "I believe she might have."

"And did you or did you not tell her that there was nothing she had to say to me that I wished to hear?"

At that, Trevor Storch's eyes went as wide as golf balls and his jaw dropped like a boulder. "I…I…"

He closed his mouth, licked his lips nervously. Then he seemed to deflate, his shoulders sinking even lower beneath his black shirt and beige sweater-vest than before.

"Yes, sir," he replied obediently, "I did."

Even from her vantage point near the stairwell, she saw Marc's brows dart upward in astonishment. Until that moment, she knew he hadn't believed her. He'd thought she was lying, or at the very least had suspected she was reinventing history to suit her purposes.

"Why?" he asked, shock and confusion evident in his tone.

"I…I…" Trevor's mouth open and closed like a guppy's and the color returned to his face in two rosy spots of nervous embarrassment.

"Because I told him to."

Eleanor's voice, deep and stern and coming out of nowhere, made Vanessa jump. Danny jerked in her arms at the sudden movement and began to fuss. She bounced up and down and pressed a kiss to the top of his head to shush him, but the greater part of her attention was on her ex-mother-in-law and the bomb she had just dropped into the middle of the cavernous foyer.

"Mother," Marc murmured, turning in her direction. "What are you talking about?"

Eleanor stepped from the doorway of the very same

parlor Vanessa had almost suggested they move to before Trevor's arrival, the heels of her powder blue pumps clicking regally on the thick parquet tiles.

"After your separation, I instructed Mr. Storch to field any calls that came into the office from Ms. Mason and to inform her that you didn't wish to speak to her again, for any reason."

Marc swung his disbelieving gaze from his mother to Trevor and back again. Vanessa's own heart was pounding in her chest, emotion clogging her throat until it threatened to cut off her supply of oxygen.

All this time, she'd been so angry at Marc. So hurt that he could cut her off the way he had, that he could be so cruel and uncaring with a woman he'd once claimed to love...and who was unexpectedly carrying his child.

She knew, too, that Marc had probably been equally as angry and hurt at what he perceived to be her actions after they split, if he'd been expecting her to stay in at least moderate contact, only to have all of her calls impeded by his personal assistant.

Now she realized they had both been deceived.

"But...why?" Marc asked.

Eleanor's lips thinned. "She's trash, Marcus. Bad enough that you married her and brought her home in the first place. Having her continue to contact you and hang around after you finally wised up enough to divorce her would have been beyond unacceptable. As though I would ever stand by and allow her to work her wiles and trick you into taking her back."

"So you ordered *my* assistant to block *my wife's* attempts to contact me." It was a statement, not a question.

Eleanor had known Marc all his life, while Vanessa had known him for only a handful of years. Yet his mother seemed ignorant of the resentment building in the heat of his green eyes and the clenching of his fists at his sides.

"Of course," Eleanor responded haughtily, tipping her nose another few centimeters into the air. "I would do anything to protect the Keller name from gold diggers like her."

"Her name," Marc intoned from between gritted teeth, "is Vanessa."

Before his mother could respond to that bit of information, he crossed to Vanessa and plucked Danny right out of her arms. While she floundered, unsure of what to think or do, he grabbed her elbow, ran his hand the rest of the way down her arm and threaded his fingers with hers. He marched them past the pile of her packed belongings nearly to the door, stopping a mere foot from Trevor's trembling form.

"You're fired," he told the young man in a brook-no-arguments tone. "Return to the office, clear out your desk and leave. You're welcome to work for my mother, if she'll have you, since the two of you certainly deserve each other, but I don't want to see you anywhere near Keller Corp ever again. Is that understood?"

Vanessa could have sworn she saw tears fill Trevor's eyes just before he ducked his head to stare at the tops of his shoes. "Yes, sir," he said in a watery voice.

"And you," Marc continued, turning this time to glare at his mother. "I always thought Vanessa was exaggerating when she told me how badly you were behaving toward her behind my back, because I didn't want to believe my own mother would treat the woman I loved as anything other than a true member of this family. But she was right all along, wasn't she?"

Marc paused for a moment, but Vanessa didn't think it was to allow Eleanor to respond. "You won't see us again. Not here. I'll send for my belongings and anything Vanessa might have left behind. But the company is mine. Mine and Adam's. You're off the Board of Directors as of now and your name will be removed from anything related to the corporation."

Eleanor's nostrils flared as she sucked in a breath, and Vanessa saw the first shadow of fear cross her severe features.

"You can't do that," she rasped.

Marc's gaze narrowed, his expression every bit as unyielding as his mother's at that moment. "Watch me."

With that, he yanked open the front door and stalked through, tugging Vanessa along behind him. The two servants who had been helping her carry her things to the waiting taxi were standing beside the bright yellow car, doing their best to remain inconspicuous and out of what she was sure they assumed would be the line of fire.

"Put all of Vanessa's things in my car," he told them, transferring Danny back to her. The poor baby was probably beginning to feel like a racquetball, though from his happy gurgles, he seemed to think being passed from one parent to the other and back again was some sort of game.

Then Marc crossed to the cab and leaned in the open window to speak in low tones to the man behind the wheel. After Marc slipped him a few folded-up bills, the driver nodded, and Marc returned to her side.

"What are we doing?" she asked, still unable to believe all that had just happened.

Lifting a hand to cup her face, he said, "We're leaving.

We'll stay at a hotel until I can get things straightened out at the office, then we'll head back to Summerville."

"But…"

"No buts." He shook his head, his gaze immediately softening to a lovely emerald green. "I'm so sorry, Vanessa. I didn't see it. I didn't believe you because I didn't want to admit my family was anything but perfect, that one of them would treat my wife with anything but love and respect."

His thumb rubbed slowly back and forth across her cheek, and she felt herself melting.

"If I had known, if I had truly understood what you were going through, I would have stopped it. I never would have let things between us turn out the way they did."

Her throat was so tight, she couldn't speak, but she believed him. After what he'd just done, how he'd stood up to his mother and walked away from his family home *for her,* how could she not?

"I love you, Vanessa. I've always loved you and I'm so sorry for all the time I've wasted being a blind, stupid fool."

She sniffed as happy tears filled her eyes and balanced precariously on the tips of her lashes.

He leaned in, pressing his brow to hers, and said barely above a whisper, "If I could go back and do things differently, I would never let you go."

A near-sob rolled up from her chest, causing those tears to spill over and roll down her cheeks.

"I love you, too," she told him. "And I never wanted to leave, I just couldn't live that way anymore."

"I know that," he said with more understanding than she'd heard from him in longer than she could remember.

"And I didn't plan to keep Danny a secret from you. I really did try to tell you, but after Trevor refused to let me speak to you, I was so angry and hurt, thinking the directive came from you…" She trailed off, barely certain anymore of how she'd felt or what had led her to make the decisions she had.

"I know," Marc murmured, one corner of his mouth lifting in a kind, loving half smile. He looked at their son with a father's love and pride burning in his eyes before brushing a hand over the baby's downy-soft head.

"We both made mistakes and let small issues become big ones. But we won't let that happen again, will we?"

She shook her head, doing her best to blink back fresh tears.

Framing her face with his big, strong hands, he brushed his lips lightly across hers. "I really do love you, Nessa. Forever."

"I love you, too," she tried to say, but his mouth was already covering hers, kissing her deeply, with all the passion that had bloomed between them since the first moment they'd met.

Epilogue

Two years later...

Marc strolled down the sidewalk of Summerville's Main Street, nodding and waving a greeting to friends as he passed. And he was whistling, for heaven's sake. He never used to whistle, but lately, he'd caught himself doing it more and more often.

Which just went to prove that small town life wasn't quite as dull or restrictive as he'd once believed. In fact, he kind of liked it.

Of course, he didn't think his current happiness had as much to do with where he was living as it did with *how* he was living...and with whom.

Hiking Danny higher on his hip, he continued to whistle—the theme from *Thomas the Tank Engine,* no less—and grinned at his son's hearty chuckle. He was wearing a pair of denim trousers with an official Sugar Shack infant tee and tiny yellow sneakers.

The Sugar Shack merchandise had been Marc's idea and had been an immediate success. In addition to baked goods, they now sold T-shirts, sweatshirts, baby clothes, coffee and travel mugs, and even key chains. In his opinion, it was the best advertising Vanessa could get other than plain old word of mouth.

The sneakers were because Danny was walking now…well, toddling, was more like it…and because he was starting to want to dress more like his daddy. Marc's heart gave a lurch at the thought and he squeezed his son even tighter against his side.

"We're going to see Mommy," he told the little boy, then added, "Maybe she'll give you a cookie."

"Cookie!" Danny yelled at the top of his lungs, lifting his arms and clapping over his head.

Marc laughed, wondering how much trouble he would get in when Vanessa found out he was plying their son with promises of sugar first thing in the morning. But then, she ran a bakery, so she shouldn't be surprised. "Cookie" had been Danny's first word…followed by "mama," "dada" and "cake." He was working on "baklava," but at the moment it came out more like "bababa."

Reaching The Sugar Shack's wide glass storefront, he pulled open the door to the distribution side of the business. An elderly woman was just shuffling out, so he held it for her and wished her a good day before slipping inside.

Vanessa was behind the counter, but as soon as she saw them, she smiled and started around. Her copper curls—longer now than when Danny had been an infant—were pulled back in a loose ponytail, and a pristine white Sugar Shack apron covered the front of her short-sleeve blouse and shorts.

"Cookie!" Danny cried, wiggling to be put down.

Vanessa arched a brow. "His idea, I'm sure," she murmured half under her breath.

"Of course," Marc replied. "But then, what can you

expect when his mother owns the best bakery in the state? You're lucky he isn't asking for pastries morning, noon and night."

"He is, but that doesn't mean he'll get them," she answered primly.

Leaning in, she bussed Danny on the cheek, running her fingers through his toffee-brown hair, which was rather in need of a trim. They'd been talking lately about having it cut and Marc was inordinately excited about taking his son for his first visit to the barber shop. An honest-to-goodness barber shop!

When she lifted up on tiptoe to kiss him, too, he slipped his free arm around her back and pulled her in for something much longer and deeper. Trapped between them, Danny giggled when they stayed locked at the lips a bit too long and started slapping their cheeks with his small hands.

They pulled apart, and Vanessa chuckled, her face flushing a becoming shade of pink. Marc, however, was far from embarrassed; he was busy calculating how many hours were left before she closed up shop and he could convince her to go to bed early.

Too damn many, that was for sure.

"I have a surprise for you," he told her as she moved back behind the counter.

He watched her loosen the ties of her apron and slip it over her head, then dig inside a small plastic container that she kept filled with cookies just for Danny. Their son's love of sweets had prompted her to experiment with a few recipes for healthier cookies and desserts. Ones with less fat and sugar, and substitutions such as applesauce and raisin paste for the oils.

Coming around again, she handed Danny the cookie,

and Marc set him on one of the high countertops to eat it, remaining close enough to keep him from toppling off.

Without the apron, Vanessa's four months of pregnancy were much more noticeable. And just like every time he saw that tiny baby bump, Marc's chest constricted with love and pride and the overwhelming relief of knowing that—even though they'd cut it damn close—he hadn't let her get away.

As much as they'd suspected it for a while, she hadn't been pregnant when they'd walked away from his family's home. Instead, they'd had some time to settle in Summerville and adjust to once again being together. Not that there had been a lot of adjustment needed, at least not on his part.

They'd bought a large, very nice house on the outskirts of town. One that had been built years before by a wealthy businessman who'd decided to move closer to the city after he and his wife divorced.

It was smaller than Marc was used to, but exceptionally large and impressive for the area. It also had plenty of room for their growing family, and came with enough acreage to afford complete privacy, as well as room for Danny and his future siblings to play.

They had also gotten remarried. At the courthouse this time, with a minimum of fuss and muss. Only Helen had been in attendance as their witness, as well as Vanessa's matron-of-honor and Danny's stand-in-nanny. He actually thought she might be coming around to liking him, but he knew he would have to prove himself all over again to be worthy of her niece's affections before he could truly win back the woman's favor.

After everything they'd been through, it had been easy to agree that another big wedding wasn't necessary. They just wanted to be together again, undoing the divorce that they both wished had never taken place in the first place.

Then they'd discussed having another child. One he would know about and be involved with from the very beginning.

"So," Vanessa prompted. "What's my surprise?" She tilted her head and shot him an impish grin, one he couldn't resist kissing off her lips.

Breaking away much sooner than he would have liked, he reached into the back pocket of his khaki chinos and pulled out a folded-over, full-color catalog. He let it fall open and held it up for her to see.

"Oh, my God!" She gave a squeal of pleasure and grabbed it up, studying the front and back covers first, then flipping through each individual page. "I can't believe it's finally ready. It's wonderful!"

It was The Sugar Shack's very first mail-order catalog, but Marc sincerely hoped it wouldn't be the last. Since leaving Pittsburgh, he'd thrown himself wholeheartedly into helping Vanessa build her business. He still drove into the city occasionally to take care of Keller Corp affairs, but was content to allow his brother to deal with the daily running of that company and the family's other major holdings.

In addition to designing the catalog, he'd set up a website for the bakery and was looking into rental spaces in other surrounding towns with an eye toward opening more Sugar Shack bakeries in multiple locations.

"I have more good news," he said while she continued to admire the pages of the catalog.

"What?" she asked, lifting her head and looking positively giddy.

He smiled in return, because he couldn't seem to help himself. "Adam and I finalized an agreement this morning to open a Sugar Shack bakery in the lobby of the Keller Corp building."

Marc expected her to shriek with joy and throw her arms around her neck, but instead she grew quiet and simply studied him.

"What's the matter?" he asked, cocking his head in confusion. "I thought you would be happy about this."

She nodded. "I am. Everything you've done has been wonderful—more than Aunt Helen and I ever could have imagined."

"But...?"

Her mouth twisted, her eyes growing concerned. "But I worry about what your mother will think of you and Adam working together to put *my* business in the lobby of your family's company headquarters. And if we really do move back to the city one of these days the way we've discussed..."

She trailed off and he could see every one of her doubts playing across her face.

"She already knows," he told her.

Her mouth went slack with shock.

"According to Adam, she's asked about us several times, and he's been updating her. I don't want to get your hopes up—" he grinned as she rolled her eyes at the possibility "—but he seems to think she might be coming around."

Vanessa gave a disbelieving snort and he chuckled. "All right. So she'll never be the cookie-baking, story-telling sort of mother or grandmother we might wish she were, but I think walking away and cutting her out of our lives for a while showed her that I'm serious in my devotion to you. You're my wife and I won't allow anyone or anything to ever hurt you or come between us again. Not even the woman who gave birth to me."

Stepping forward, she rested her hands and then her head on his chest. "Are you sorry?" she murmured against his shirt.

Framing her face with his hands, he tipped her chin up and met her storm blue gaze. "Not even a little bit. I don't ever want you to think that, okay? You and Danny—" he tipped his head toward their crumb-covered son "—and this tiny tyke here—" he pressed a hand flat to her growing belly "—are all that matter to me. I haven't closed the door on rebuilding a relationship with my mother, but I wouldn't trade my life now with the three of you for anything in the world. Do you understand?"

It took her a second, but she nodded slowly, and he stared into her eyes until he was sure she believed him.

"Good. Then I'll get our little Cookie Monster cleaned up while you go show your aunt the new catalog. Hopefully it will put her in a good enough mood that we can ask her to watch Danny for a while this afternoon."

"Why?" Vanessa asked.

His mouth spread in a wolfish grin and he leaned in to brush his lips across hers. "Because I'm in the mood for something sweet."

Cocking her head to the side, she narrowed her eyes, giving him a sultry, seductive look. "Well, this *is* a bakery. Sweets are what we're all about."

He gave a low growl at her wicked flirtation and nearly told her how lucky she was that Danny was with them and the bakery was fronted by floor-to-ceiling plate glass windows. Otherwise, he would be lifting her onto one of the countertops and divesting her of her clothes already.

"What I want isn't on the menu."

"So you have a special order?" she asked, batting those lashes until he felt his insides start to boil.

He nodded, mouth gone too dry to respond.

"Lucky for you, and thanks to my very business-savvy husband, we're set up to take special orders now. You may have to pay extra for shipping and handling, though."

Lips twitching, he said in a low voice, "That shouldn't be a problem. In case you haven't heard, I'm rich."

She smiled softly and reached up to wrap her arms around his neck. "So am I," she whispered.

And neither of them were talking about their bank accounts.

* * * * *

We hope you enjoyed reading this
special collection from Harlequin® books.

If you liked reading these stories, then you
will love **Harlequin® Desire** books.

You want to leave behind the everyday.
Harlequin Desire stories feature sexy,
romantic heroes who have it all: wealth, status,
incredible good looks…everything but the
right woman. Add some secrets, maybe a
scandal, and start turning pages!

Enjoy six *new* stories from
Harlequin Desire every month.

Available wherever books and
ebooks are sold.

#2377 WHAT THE PRINCE WANTS
Billionaires and Babies • by Jules Bennett
Needing time to heal, a widowed prince goes incognito. He hires a
live-in nanny for his infant daughter but soon finds he wants the woman
for *himself*. Is he willing to cross the line from professional to personal?

#2378 CARRYING A KING'S CHILD
Dynasties: The Montoros • by Katherine Garbera
Torn between running his family's billion-dollar shipping business
and assuming his ancestral throne, Rafe Montoro needs to let off
some steam. But his night with a bartending beauty could change
everything—because now there's a baby on the way...

#2379 PURSUED BY THE RICH RANCHER
Diamonds in the Rough • by Catherine Mann
Driven by his grandmother's dying wish, a Texas rancher must choose
between his legacy and the sexy single mother who unknowingly holds
the fate of his heart—and his inheritance—in her hands.

#2380 THE SHEIKH'S SECRET HEIR
by Kristi Gold
Billionaire Tarek Azzmar knows a secret that will destroy the royal family
who shunned him. But the tables turn when he learns his lover is near
and dear to the royal family *and* she's pregnant with his child.

#2381 THE WIFE HE COULDN'T FORGET
by Yvonne Lindsay
Olivia Jackson steals a second chance with her estranged husband
when he loses his memories of the past two years. But when he finally
remembers *everything*, will their reconciliation stand the ultimate test?

#2382 SEDUCED BY THE CEO
Chicago Sons • by Barbara Dunlop
When businessman Riley Ellis learns that his rival's wife has a secret
twin sister, he seduces the beauty as leverage and then hires her to
keep her close. But now he's trapped by his own lies...and his desires...

HDCNM0515

*Will Rafe Montoro have to choose between the throne
and newfound fatherhood?*

Read on for a sneak preview of
CARRYING A KING'S CHILD,
a DYNASTIES: THE MONTOROS novel
by USA TODAY bestselling author
Katherine Garbera.

Pregnant!

He knew Emily wouldn't be standing in his penthouse apartment telling him this if he wasn't the father. His first reaction was joy.

A child.

It wasn't something he'd ever thought he wanted, but the idea that Emily was carrying his baby seemed right to him.

Maybe that was just because it gave him something other than his royal duties to think about. He'd been dreading his trip to Alma. He was flattered that the country that had once driven his family out had come back to them, asked them—him, as it turned out—to be the next king. But he had grown up here in Miami. He didn't want to be a stuffy royal.

He didn't want European paparazzi following him around and trying to catch him doing anything that would bring shame to his family. Including having a child out of wedlock.

"Rafe, did you hear what I said?"

"Yeah, I did. Are you sure?" he asked at last.

She gave him a fiery look from those aqua-blue eyes of hers. He'd seen the passionate side of her nature, and he guessed he was about to witness her temper. Hurricane Em was about to unleash all of her fury on him, and he didn't blame her one bit.

He held his hand up. "Slow down, Red. I didn't mean are you sure it's mine. I meant…are you sure you're pregnant?"

"Damned straight. And I wouldn't be here if I wasn't sure it was yours. Listen, I don't want anything from you. I know you can't turn your back on your family and marry me, and frankly, we only had one weekend together, so I'd have to say no to a proposal anyway. But…I don't want this kid to grow up without knowing you."

"Me neither."

She glanced up, surprised.

He'd sort of surprised himself. But it didn't seem right for a kid of his to grow up without him. He wanted that. He wanted a chance to impart the Montoro legacy…not the one newly sprung on him involving a throne, but the one he'd carved for himself in business. "Don't look shocked."

"You've kind of got a lot going on right now. And having a kid with me isn't going to go over well."

"Tough," he said. "I still make my own decisions."

Available June 2015 wherever
Harlequin® Desire books and ebooks are sold.

www.Harlequin.com

Love the Harlequin book
you just read?

Your opinion matters.

Review this book on your favorite
book site, review site, blog or your own
social media properties and share
your opinion with other readers!

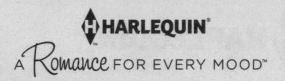